My Unborn Child

by

Orest Stocco

Savant Books
Honolulu, HI, USA
2010

Published in the USA by Savant Books and Publications
2630 Kapiolani Blvd #1601
Honolulu, HI 96826
http://www.savantbooksandpublications.com

Printed in the USA

Edited by Doris Chu
Cover Photographs by Orest Stocco
Cover Design by Daniel S. Janik

10 digit ISBN: 0-9841175-9-8
13-digit ISBN: 978-0-9841175-9-8

Dedication

For Penny Lynn Cates
With karma-free love

Contents

"Live life fully and honestly."
The Wheel of Life: A Memoir of Living and Dying
Elisabeth Kubler-Ross, M.D.

*Vanity of vanities, saith the Preacher, vanity of vanities;
all is vanity. What profit hath a man of all his labour
which he taketh under the sun? One generation passeth
away, and another generation cometh: but the earth
abideth forever. The sun also ariseth, and the sun goeth
down, and hasteth to his place where he arose. The
wind goeth toward the south, and turneth about unto
the north; it whirleth about continually, and the wind
returneth again according to his circuits. All the rivers
run into the sea; yet the sea is not full; unto the place
from whence the rivers came, thither they return
again"* (Ecclesiastes 1: 2-7).

Preface

There are two sides to the abortion issue: the pro-life side and the pro-choice side. *My Unborn Child* is the story of a third side.

Cassie O'Shaunnesy is a registered nurse with three young children. She was raised a strict Roman Catholic. Devoted to her profession, neither her career nor her faith could satisfy her longing to be more. She explores different branches of nursing, studies for a Master's degree, and becomes a spiritual seeker. This puts a strain on her marriage.

Her husband Kevin moves out of the house. To save her marriage, Cassie seduces him over wine, music, and his favorite dinner and gets pregnant; but her plan backfires. He does not want another child. She panics and has an abortion to salvage her marriage. Kevin wants a divorce. Cassie is so bereft she tries to take her own life.

Saddled with remorse, guilt, and shame Cassie has an experience with the Soul of her aborted daughter. This pulls her out of depression and changes her life forever. *My Unborn Child* tells the story of Cassie's crisis of faith and journey to wholeness.

The three sides of the abortion issue are the religious, secular, and spiritual. The religious side is based upon faith, the secular upon science, and the spiritual side upon personal experience. The religious side contends that the immortal self is created at the moment of human conception. It deems the fetus to be a little person, and it would be an act of murder to terminate the life of the fetus. Science can't determine when a fetus becomes a little person, so terminating the life of the fetus would be a matter of personal conscience. And the spiritual side posits that Soul, the pre-existent self, animates the child with self-consciousness when it takes its first breath of life, and it would not be murder to terminate the life of the fetus.

Cassie O'Shaunnesy's story is the story of this third side. It opens the window on Soul, the spiritual side of life that has mystified man since the dawn of time. *My Unborn Child* is the story of her remarkable experience.

Chapter 1

Father McDuffy's Challenge

When I first read it in the Wyedale *Gazette* I had to laugh. I was furious, but I had to laugh all the same. *"Small-town mentality,"* I snickered, shaking my head in disbelief. "How in God's name can anyone prove what he's asking, scientist or no? We haven't come this far yet; and we will never come this far, because what he's asking can't be proven. It's arrogant," I spit out, angry now. "But that's Christianity for you, isn't it? It'll never change. Not in a million years. It has too much to lose. *By God, I should answer this!"*

Memories of all my guilt and fear came rushing to my mind. I took a breath to compose myself. "I should, shouldn't I?" I challenged myself.

I folded the paper and put it away in my kitchen drawer. I don't know why I stuffed the paper in there. I never saved the *Gazette* unless there was a picture of my children or one of my patients in it. I must have put it away knowing that I would have to take up Father McDuffy's challenge, because something about it struck at the very core of my being.

"But that's his prerogative," I shrugged, with an ironic smile. "After all, it's the Christian thing to forgive, isn't it?"

It still bothered me though. I couldn't put my finger on it, but this whole anti-abortion movement oozed with that sticky spiritual goo that I had come to hate so much in Christianity. It had been almost six years since my abortion, but Father McDuffy's challenge brought it all back again, and try as I may I could not get it out of my mind.

Oh well, it's his life and his karma, I thought to myself at work the next day, trying to laugh the whole movement off. But it didn't help. I still felt like rubbing the ad in the priest's arrogant face. "What right did he have to mock women like that? What right?" I asked myself. *"Damn!"* I exclaimed, under my breath.

My mother never forgave me. She was ten times more stubborn than I was. At least I admitted my mistakes. "I'd rather burn in hell than give in to the likes of you," she used to say to my father. And she never did give in either. My mother would go to her grave before she admitted she could be wrong about abortion. But I couldn't help myself; I had to do what I did. "A fetus is not a person, Mother," I tried to reason with her when I dropped by her house to talk with her that day. "It's a biological organism. Why can't you see that?"

"That's nonsense, that's why!" my mother fired back, her green eyes on fire. "And you better ask Almighty God to forgive you, Cassie O'Shaunnesy!"

"I don't need God's forgiveness," I responded, trying to stay calm. "I have nothing to be forgiven for. I didn't do anything wrong. It's my body, and I have the right to my own body. What right does Christianity have to my body?"

"Every right!" my mother shouted at me, with all the authority of her blind faith. "It's God's law! Thou shalt not kill! Your child had as much right to live as you do, Cassie! That was my grandchild whose life you took, so let's call it for what it was. You murdered my innocent grandchild and you better ask God to forgive you before it's too late! You could get run over by a truck tomorrow and go straight to hell if you don't confess your sin..."

"Mother!" I exclaimed. "Must you?"

"Yes," she calmly replied, deliberately goading me. "I'm still your mother. And I'll tell you another thing, Cassie O'Shaunnesy. It was a sorry day in heaven when you gave up your religion for this new age malarkey. Come back to the Church, child. Get on your knees and pray for his forgiveness right now. God is merciful. He sacrificed his only begotten Son on the cross to save us from ourselves. It's not too late. I'm begging you, come back to the Sacred Heart of Jesus. That's where you'll find your salvation. Not in this new age malarkey. I'm pleading with you as the mother who gave birth to you, give up this new religion or you'll end up just like that kooky Shirley MacLaine. Her and her past lives! She's even got herself a spirit guide now. Some drunken Irish spirit, if you can believe that! She's nuttier than a fruitcake, that one! But she sure knows how to rake in the money, doesn't she? Can you imagine hard-working honest people paying three hundred dollars a plate to hear that crazy malarkey? `You are God,' she says. `You can make your own reality.' *Reality, alright!* Get out before it's too late, Cassie. Jesus is your savior, not Shirley MacLaine!"

"Oh, Mother," I sighed. "What's the point of talking to you?"

I tried to reason with her, but she wouldn't listen. It was too much for her simple faith. I didn't want to tell her, but I was compelled. I couldn't help myself. I desperately wanted my mother's blessing, so I brought up the subject of my new religion shortly after I began studying the private discourses of the Atma teaching.

I sat in the same hard-back wooden chair with the red cushion tied to the spindles that I always sat in before I married Kevin and left our boarding house that my mother still ran as much for the company of strangers, who quickly became her friends, as for the income. She made tea. The sun shone through the top panes of the kitchen window into my face, making me feel like I was in the spotlight, as I always seemed to be since I had my abortion and left the Church. It had taken me all week to muster my courage to tell my mother about Atma-Gare, and I was so nervous my legs were trembling.

"Mother, I have something to tell you," I said, swallowing hard. I had to tell her. Just like I had to confess every one of my sins to Uncle Clancy every Saturday afternoon when I was a child, I had to tell my mother about my new religion. I knew I would live to regret it, but I couldn't help myself. I thought of my father who always argued in vain with my mother, and I should have known better; but I wanted my mother to accept me for who I was and not who she wanted me to be. I opened my mouth and it all came pouring out. I knew Atma-Gare wouldn't make any sense to her, but I had to tell her anyway: "Mother, there's no such thing as mortal sin and venial sin in the new religion of

Atma-Gare. There's only freedom and responsibility," I began, and opened a door to a whole new world that would terrify her Christian Soul. "That's the goal of the spiritual life of Atma-Gare. Sin does not exist for me anymore. Only choices and experience. I don't like some of the choices that Christianity made for me, but I didn't know any better, did I? That's why I left my faith. I had no choice. I don't believe in Christianity anymore; I believe in reincarnation. I don't believe in eternal damnation anymore; I believe in karma and eternal salvation. I don't believe Jesus came into the world to save us from sin and damnation; he came to teach us the spiritual life of the Way. We can only save ourselves, but we have to find the Wayshower first. He's here today. He's the spiritual leader of Atma-Gare, and he lives in the states. This is the new religion of the Light and Sound of God. The Atma is the way, the truth, and the life, not Jesus Christ. The Atma is Holy Spirit, which is both the Light and Sound of God. The Light and Sound are the two sides of Holy Spirit. St. John called Holy Spirit the Word. The Word is the Way, Mother. Father was right. Christianity died a long time ago. But he was just as wrong as you are. God exists, but it's not Jesus Christ. Jesus was a spiritual teacher. He was not the only begotten Son of God. But we can't know that unless we find the Living Atma Master who will connect us with the Holy Current of Atma. Jesus called the Holy Current of Atma the water of everlasting life. This is why we come into the world, Mother. We come to drink in the Holy Spirit of Atma and perfect ourselves through karma and reincarnation. We live many lifetimes, not just one life like Christianity believes. But we can't break the endless cycle of life and death until we find the Living Atma Master.The world has always had a Living Atma Master, but we have to find him first. Well, I found him. And you can't imagine how grateful I am. Do you understand what I'm telling you, Mother?"

My mother stared at me like I had gone raving mad.
"Are you alright, Mother?" I asked.
"You've finally done it this time, haven't you?"
"What have I done?"
"I knew it," she calmly replied.
I waited for her to pounce. I didn't have to wait long.

4

"I knew you would go batty just like your father!" she screamed at me. "It wasn't enough for you to have an abortion and divorce your husband and shame our family, you had to get brainwashed with all this Shirley MacLaine malarkey! May God have mercy on your Soul! I did everything I could for you, Cassie! I even begged our Holy Mother to intercede for you, but the Devil got to you just like he got to your heathen father!"

"Mother, don't start. Father has nothing to do with what I believe. It's my life, and I have the right to choose my own path. Shirley MacLaine has nothing to do with what I believe in either. I have nothing to do with psychic paths. I read her books because she's a feminist, that's all. I respect her for that. She's doing the world a great service by getting people to realize their own potential, but I don't follow her teaching. I'm a student of Atma-Gare, the new religion of the Light and Sound of God. I follow the Satma, the Living Atma Master. He's my spiritual teacher, Mother, not Shirley MacLaine..."

"Well, it sure doesn't look like that to me!" my mother screamed at me, her wild green eyes glaring at me like I had grown horns.

I had to stand up to my mother. I had to defend my new life. I knew that if I backed down now I would never have the courage to stand up to her again. I silently called upon my new Spiritual Master. *"Please, Satma, help me..."*

"Maybe that's what it looks like to you," I replied, with a sudden rush of self-confidence, "but I'm not into channeling, astral projection, or spirit guides. I told you, I'm a student of the new religion of Atma-Gare. The only thing Shirley MacLaine and I have in common is that we both believe in karma and reincarnation, that's all. I have the Living Atma Master to guide me. He's the Light Giver of the world, Mother. As far as I know, Shirley MacLaine hasn't found the Living Atma Master yet, so please don't equate me with her teaching. It's not the same path. And please don't bring Father into this either. He left the Church for his own reasons and I left for mine, so let's just drop the whole subject, okay?"

"I knew it!" my mother screamed again, pulling at her thick red hair as she always did whenever she lost control of her emotions.

"Knew what?" I foolishly asked.

"The Devil's wormed his way into your brain," she replied, her eyes glaring at me with that righteous Catholic conviction that finally drove my father away. I hated that look in her eyes. It reduced me to a helpless little girl. "I knew that sooner or later the Devil would get you too!" she spit out at me. "You're your father's daughter, alright! The Devil's got you so mixed up you can't tell good from evil anymore! Can't you see that you've lost your senses? You don't believe in sin anymore and you want your freedom. That's the Devil talking! He got to you just like he got to your heathen father! Why do you think your father left me, Cassie? Why?"

"I'm beginning to understand why," I replied.

Mother was not amused. "I'll tell you why! Your father wanted his freedom from the Church to piss away our rent money, that's why! As God is my witness we pay for every sin that we commit, and your father's paying for what he did to me! *May he rot in hell!*"

"And you call yourself a Christian?" I said, defending my father.

"I am a Christian!" she spit at me. I felt her anger like a sharp dagger. "I've sacrificed my whole life for our Lord Jesus, so don't you dare presume that I'm not a Christian! Don't you dare! It's not my place to dole out forgiveness for the likes of your heathen father! He abandoned me with two mouths to feed and a stack of bills that would choke a plough horse! God has to forgive him for his blasphemy to our Lord Jesus just like God has to forgive you for murdering your child! I can't forgive you either, Cassie. I'm not a priest. My brother's the priest in this family. So don't point your finger at me, miss high and mighty! I worked my fingers to the bone to put you kids through school, and this is the thanks I get? Your brother doesn't talk to me like this. He respects his mother. He goes to Mass every Sunday with his family. He's a good father and a good provider. Why can't you be more like your brother? Why, Cassie? Why do you have to be like your heathen father? From the day he spit on the holy crucifix your father lost himself to the Devil, and you've become just like him! You've lost your way, Cassie..."

If I had heard it once, I heard it a thousand times. I looked like my mother, but I was my father's daughter, and she never made me feel any less guilty than she did my father. I tried to compose myself by doing a silent HU and calling upon the Inner Master. *"Satma, please help me,"* I pleaded.

"I'm sorry if I offended you, Mother," I replied, feeling my Spiritual Master's calming presence. "I know you worked hard for Michael and me, and I'm grateful for all the sacrifices that you made for us; but just because I don't share your faith anymore doesn't mean I don't love you. I love you Mother, but I have to be true to myself too. I have to listen to my own heart, don't I? You of all people should know that. My whole world got shattered when Kevin left me."

"You drove him away!" Mother shouted at me.

"For God's sake, enough already. I grew apart from my husband, that's all. Kevin didn't want another child. I tried to force him to save our marriage. That's why I got pregnant. But it was too late. My marriage cost me more than you can imagine, so I won't stand for you accusing me of killing my own child. I went through that madness once, and I refuse to let you put me through that again. I'd rather take my own life than kill my own child. And I tried to, Mother. Oh, yes, I tried to take my own life. I couldn't live with my guilt. So I would appreciate a little sympathy from you, if you don't mind. You're not the only person in this world who has suffered, you know. I suffered too. And so did father..."

"That's why we came into this world," my mother responded in her poor Christian martyr's voice, which I hated even more than her wild banshee voice. "That's why God sent his only begotten Son to die on the cross for us. Jesus came into the world to suffer for our sins, and now you tell me you don't believe in sin. That's the Devil talking, Cassie. Satan has wormed his way into your brain and he's eating away at you just like he did your heathen father. You better see someone. You need professional help too."

"I need professional help? Look who's calling the kettle black!"

"You need help, child," she repeated in her poor martyr's voice which made me want to scream. "The world's going to hell in a hand-basket, and you don't believe in sin? You think you can do anything you want and come back and live your life over again as if nothing happened? What kind of religion is that? *I'll tell you what kind of religion that is!"* she shouted in her banshee voice. "It's Sodom and

Gomorrah all over again! As far as I'm concerned you're no different than Shirley MacLaine! You both want your cake and eat it too! Well let me tell you something, missy new age smarty-pants. We pay for our sins in the hereafter. That's why Jesus died on the cross for us! He died to save us from our sins! So you better get on your knees and beg God for forgiveness before it's too late! Get on your knees, Cassie O'Shaunnesy, and pray for redemption! I'll pray with you. O merciful God which art in heaven, I beseech you…"

I left my mother kneeling on the polished, checked, white and black linoleum floor beside her chair, with her mother of pearl rosary beads in her hands praying for me. I wanted to tell her that she was interfering in my consciousness with her prayers, but that would only have added fuel to her fire. "I'm not coming back to the Church, Mother," I said instead. "And I'm not a heathen either," I quickly added, and walked out of her house.

I did not see my mother again for three months, but nothing had changed. She still equated everything I believed in with Shirley MacLaine. My mother had a fixation with Shirley MacLaine that kept her from seeing me for myself, but I couldn't blame her.

No one understood me. It was as though I had outgrown the whole world. For the first time in my life I had found something that made sense of life, and I could not share it with anyone, not even my father whom I loved more than anyone.

I wanted to change my life. I wanted to become more than what my world would let me be. That's why I left my religion. I was bound and gagged by my Roman Catholic faith, but my new religion let me soar without restrictions.

My new religion did not bind me with the chains of sin and guilt. It spelled out the spiritual laws of life for me. It made me aware of karma. It taught me how to be accountable for my own choices. I had to save myself. That was my responsibility, not Jesus Christ's.

My new religion did not judge me. I was in charge of my own life, and I was free to do with it as I pleased. Which was all I ever wanted. Sadly however, I had to say goodbye to my native Vancouver and move my family to Georgian Bay, Ontario where my heart told me that I could become the person I longed to be. But now I was faced with a new dilemma.

Father McDuffy struck a raw nerve with his reward in the local paper, and for the first time since I left my beautiful Vancouver I felt threatened. He challenged everything that I had come to believe in, and I could not put it out of my mind.

He knew that no one could prove "in the cold light of pure science" that a fetus is not a little person, so he could afford to be smug and offer a reward to the first scientist of any discipline who could prove in the prior existence of Soul, but his Roman Catholic conceit struck me like a steel knife in my heart because I *knew* that he was wrong!

I took the paper out of the drawer when I got home from the hospital, and as I peeled the potatoes and carrots and put on the breaded pork cutlets and prepared the mixed salad for dinner, I stared at the open page of the *Gazette* to confirm my mounting anger.

$5,000.00 REWARD
A reward of FIVE THOUSAND CANADIAN DOLLARS
will be paid by the undersigned to the FIRST scientist of
any discipline who can prove in the cold light of pure science
that a little person begins to be a person at some moment
other than the time of his or her conception in the womb.
Father Terrence McDuffy
Catholic Church of the Immaculate Conception
Wyedale, Ontario

Once again Christianity struck a blow to my very being, and I knew on some level that my mind refused to accept that I was being called upon to respond to the priest's challenge, but the last thing I wanted was to tell the world about the miracle of my unborn child.

Science could not prove what he was asking, but every word of Father McDuffy's challenge violated the sanctity of my precious miracle, and as I read the ad over and over again I sensed the ominous presence of the paternal God of Christianity casting its pall upon my new life in Georgian Bay, and my body began to tremble with old fears.

I tried to compose myself. Memories of my struggle to free myself from my Christian faith surfaced and tears came gushing from my eyes. I made no effort to stop them. I thought of my father and the last words that he said to me before he took his life.

I looked into my father's sad eyes and held back my tears. I had no idea how he would be when I visited him that day in St. Paul's Hospital when my shift ended. I didn't know if he was there or not, but I listened with all my heart.

I wanted to understand him. I wanted to know what had driven him to such despair. I wanted him to tell me so I could avoid his illness in my life, which my mother feared I had. Everyone said I was like my father, but I had taken a different path in my life. My father was a disillusioned atheist who disdained Christianity. I could not see myself in him. I wasn't bi-polar. I wasn't depressive. I wasn't delusional. I wasn't misanthropic. I loved people. I loved life. That's why I became a nurse. I wanted to serve life and be all that I could be. That's all I ever wanted. And that's all my father ever wanted of me.

"Worship God and you worship an idea, Patty," he said, calling me by my pet name, on my last visit before he took his life. I had to have him admitted to the psychiatric ward of St. Paul's Hospital where I was nursing, and he was sitting by the window with a dog-eared copy of James Joyce's *Finnegan's Wake* on his lap. My father taught English Literature at Simon Fraser University before he became afflicted with such debilitating bouts of depression that it drove him to drink and suicidal despair. It jeopardized his career and ruined his life. "Fear God, and you fear an idea," he continued, with a cold sneer on his sallow face.

I stared into my father's eyes, but said nothing. My heart was pounding.

"That's all there is to God," he concluded, and fell silent.

"What do you mean?" I asked, praying to God that he had not slipped away into one of his semi-catatonic states.

"God is nothing but a capricious idea that plays havoc with the lives of fools," he replied, with that telltale look of madness in his eyes.

I did not reply, but I felt tears welling.

"Your Catholic religion knows this better than anyone, love," he continued. "The God of Christianity is one of the most debilitating ideas ever to come out of the feeble mind of man. It has made a fool of man for centuries. One generation of fools passeth away, and another generation of fools cometh, but the sea of fools is never full. Unto the place from whence these fools come, thither they return again..."

"That's not fair, Father," I said, grabbing his hand to hold and hopefully pull him back. He patted mine with his free hand and stared hard into my eyes.

"Listen," he said to me, with a stern look on his haggard, whiskered face. "It's not my place to tell you what to believe, love; but if you have a need for God in your life, by all the stars in the universe don't limit your belief to the God of Christianity. Jesus Christ is no more God than Judas was his traitor! Vanity of vanities, all is vanity..."

"Oh God," I sighed to myself.

"I left the Church because I could not stomach the hypocrisy of your mother's religion. Her and her perverted, sanctimonious brother..."

"Father, please," I pleaded, fearing him slipping away.

"I don't believe in God, Patty," he continued, turning his head to stare blankly at the mountains that loomed over Vancouver. "But that doesn't mean you shouldn't believe in God. I couldn't find God, but that doesn't mean God doesn't exist. God doesn't exist for me. That's all that means. I don't believe in God because I can't trust my own mind. It's deceived me once too often. Maybe you will have better luck finding God than I did, Patty. I can't penetrate that mystery. It's beyond me. But I guarantee you, you will not find God in Christianity..."

"Why, Father?" I asked, listening with all my heart for a clue to his despair.

"Christianity was a damn good idea in the beginning, love," my father continued, and turned to look at me. He had the clearest blue eyes I had ever seen in my life, and in that one fleeting moment I knew that he was as sane as he could ever be, "but along the way Christianity became perverted by its own insatiable lust for power. Look for God if you must, Patty; but don't let your mother's religion hold you back. Christianity died on the cross with that fear-mongering rabble-rouser. What the world has come to believe of Jesus Christ's message of salvation is nothing more than a fairytale spun by a sexually frustrated band of idiots full of sound and fury signifying nothing!"

"Father…"

"Out, out, o damned spot! The times are out of joint, o cursed spite, that ever I was born to set them right…"

He was gone. I could tell by his eyes. They were not my father's clear blue eyes anymore. They were the eyes of a caged Soul. I got up and stared at my father as he ranted on about the absurdity of life, quoting from one or another of the many writers that he had studied in his own disappointing search for God. I couldn't listen. It was too painful. He could go on for hours. I sniffled as tears streamed down my cheeks.

"There is only one true philosophical question…"

"Good-bye, Father," I said, and kissed him on the cheek.

He didn't hear me. Nor would he ever hear me again. Late that night he took his own brilliant, tortured life.

Chapter 2
The Dream That Changed My Life

I met the spiritual leader of my new religion in a dream eight years before I found Atma-Gare. The Satma, who is the Inner Master, let me have this dream to prepare me for meeting him out here in the physical world. But not until I saw the Living Atma Master in person did I realize the significance of the dream that changed my life.

I was in a hospital in my dream. Being a registered nurse, this didn't surprise me. I was attending to a terminally ill patient. One morning when I entered his room Fred asked me who the man was who had visited him during the night. "What man?" I asked.

"That man," he said, pointing to the corner of the room.

I saw no one. I asked Fred if the man was still standing there.

"Yes," he replied.

"What's he doing?" I asked, thinking he was hallucinating.

"Nothing," Fred said. "He's just smiling."

"Oh. Well, let's take your tray and get you cleaned up, okay?"

"You can't see him, can you?"

I didn't know what to say, so I just smiled.

"Well, he's still there, and I can see him," Fred said.

"What does this man look like, Fred?" I asked.

"He's wearing a blue suit. He's average height. He's got a high forehead, and he's a little on the thin side. He's still smiling."

"Oh," I said.

"You think I'm pulling your leg, don't you?"

"Yes, I think you are Fred," I said, and picked up the tray. I turned to leave. As I turned I saw a man standing in the corner of the room. He had on a light blue suit, had a receding hairline, and his whole countenance shone with an unbelievable warm glow of love.

Startled, I just stared at him. He looked into my eyes and gave me the most beautiful, loving smile I ever saw. I felt so much love in his eyes that to this day I can still feel the warmth of his love. "Who are you?" I asked, and just as he was about to speak I woke up from my first dream encounter with the Satma, the Living Atma Master.

Eight years later I walked into a patient's room in St. Paul's Hospital in Vancouver. It was occupied by an elderly man dying of cancer who looked very much like the patient of my dream and whose name was also Fred, and the events unfolded exactly as they did in my dream except for one thing: when I asked the man who he was he replied in a clear, distinct voice, "There's an introductory talk on Atma-Gare Saturday night. I will be there," and then he vanished into thin air.

I could not believe my eyes. I turned to Fred and asked if he could still see the man standing in the corner of the room. "No. He's gone now," said Fred.

"Where did he go?" I asked.

"I don't know."

"Was he a relative?"

"I don't think so."

"What did he want?"

"I don't know," Fred said.

That night Fred died. We didn't expect him to go so soon. I never told anyone about this experience. The next day I was in the cafeteria when I overheard two nurses talking. "Why don't you come to the introductory talk Saturday night," said the young, blond nurse. You'll find out what Atma-Gare is all about." *I couldn't believe my ears!*

"I'll think about it," said the other nurse.

"Excuse me," I said, looking at the young, blond nurse. "I couldn't help overhearing. Where is this talk taking place?"

"Are you interested in Atma-Gare?" she asked, excitedly.

"I think so," I stammered.

"Oh, good!" said the young nurse, with a sparkle in her eyes that forced me to smile. "Would you like to find out more about Atma-Gare?"

"Yes," I replied. I had goose bumps.

"We're having an introductory talk this Saturday at the Collingwood Branch of the public library on Kingsway. You're welcome to come."

Shaken by the coincidence, I said, "I think I would love to come."

"Oh, good!" she said again all excited, and she wrote out the time and address on a napkin and handed it to me. "I'll see you there," she added, with a generous smile.

My heart raced madly with the excitement of meeting the man who had vanished before my very eyes. The introductory talk was only four days away, but I could hardly wait.

By the time Saturday came around I was not sure if what I had experienced had actually happened, and the only proof I would have would be to see the man at this introductory talk. But he wasn't there. Not in person, that is. *He was there on video!*

I could not believe my eyes. It was the same slender man with a blue suit and beautiful, loving smile! He was introduced as the Satma, the Living Atma Master and spiritual leader of Atma-Gare, the new religion of the Light and Sound of God!

"The Living Atma Master is the Wayshower and Light Giver of the world," added the effervescent, young nurse whose name was Beverly Thompson.

His name was Herman Knecht, and we listened to the talk that he had given at the Atma-Gare Worldwide Seminar in St. Louis, which was titled "Soul's Journey Home to God," and then the floor was open to questions that were answered by Beverly and a gentle, gray-haired man whose name was Michael Haydon.

"Quite often the Satma will appear to people before they find Atma-Gare," said Michael Haydon. "He may come to them in their dreams, or they may just meet him and not know who he is until sometime later. It could be months, even years before one makes the connection; but he will know. You never forget the face of the Satma."

I could not believe what I was hearing!

Michael must have sensed my startled expression by the look he gave me. He didn't say anything. He just smiled, but his smile gave me the courage to speak. I shared my dream with the Satma eight years earlier, and then seeing him in the hospital room earlier in the week. Everyone listened with rapt attention. *I could hardly believe the story myself!*

"What a beautiful experience," Michael said.

"I'll say!" Beverly added, with a burst of excitement.

"You believe me, then?" I said, still shaken by my experience.

"Of course we believe you," said Michael. "Why wouldn't we?"

Six months later, after I devoured all the Atma books that I had purchased at the introductory talk on Atma-Gare, my favorite being *Seeker By The Lake* by Paul Mathew, the modern day founder of this ancient spiritual path, I formally became a member of Atma-Gare and began receiving the private discourses of the secret teaching, which were for Atma chelas only.

I did a spiritual exercise called the HU chant, which Atmans call Soul's Love Song to God, every morning for twenty minutes before beginning my day, and I kept a detailed dream journal as suggested by the Living Atma Master. Also, I began writing a monthly Atma initiate's report that I mailed to the Living Atma Master's office in Minneapolis.

"Dear Satma," I began my first initiate's report. *"I know that Atma-Gare is the spiritual path I have been looking for my whole life, and I cannot thank you enough for telling me about the introductory talk. I feel like I have come home after a very long journey. I am writing you this report because I need your help. I don't know how to say this other than to just say it. I aborted my fourth child. I still have so much guilt and shame for taking the life of my unborn child that I can hardly live with myself. Can you help me, please?"*

I had tried thousands of times to let go of my guilt, but I could not. In spite of the fact that I believed in a woman's right to her own body and that I felt justified aborting my child to save my marriage, I felt so ashamed of myself that nothing I did could remove my guilt.

From the moment I dropped my first initiate's report in the mail,

I began to feel different. I didn't make the connection for several weeks, but the more I studied the private Atma discourses and did my daily HU chant, the less hold my Christian beliefs had upon me, and I began to have a feeling that we all live more than one lifetime and that I had not really murdered my unborn child. I couldn't understand it, but I had the strangest feeling that my unborn child was still alive somewhere in the world. I don't know why I felt this way, but I did.

I had to thank the Love Song to God for this wonderful feeling. I did not believe it was possible that a simple HU chant could have such a profound effect upon my emotions, so I asked Michael Haydon, who was a Higher Initiate and ASA (Atma Spiritual Aid), to explain it to me. I invited him to lunch after my first Atma Worship Service, which he officiated in the same room in the public library where I attended the introductory talk on Atma-Gare.

"The HU chant is not like prayer, Cassie," he said, resting his fork on his plate and giving me his full attention. "It's the lost Sound of God and true spiriutal path back home to the Higher Worlds of God. As you sing this sacred name of God, it raises your vibrations and lets God into your life. As simple as it may sound, the HU chant is the key to a full, spiritually satisfying life. It has the power to heal, make you laugh, and bring tears of joy to your eyes. The HU is our personal connection with God."

"You make it sound like the perfect panacea," I responded, with a chilling touch of my father's cold cynicism.

Michael laughed. *"Indeed, it is!"*

"You're serious, aren't you?" I said.

"I couldn't be more serious, Cassie," he replied, with a sparkle in his eyes that reflected a hidden wisdom. "But as they say, the proof of the pudding is in the eating. You have to walk the path to experience the path. That's what the spiritual life of Atma is all about. Personal experience is our bedrock of truth, Cassie. Hearsay doesn't cut it in Atma-Gare. This ancient spiritual teaching is an individual path to truth. The more you live the spiritual life of Atma, the more the Atma will reveal the mysteries of life to you. It's that simple."

"The Atma is Holy Spirit, isn't it?"

"Yes. The Atma is the Voice of God."

"Can I ask you a personal question?"

"By all means."

"Can the HU heal a broken heart?"

"Yes," Michael simply said.

"How about guilt? Can the HU take away guilt?"

"Guilt for what? One's sins? We don't believe in sin in Atma-Gare. We believe only in experience. But we're not fools either. There are karmic consequences for breaking the Spiritual Laws of life. If our guilt comes from breaking the Spiritual Laws of life, we will have to deal with this guilt by resolving the karma that we created for breaking them. The HU can help us do that. The HU burns away karma. That's another benefit of the Love Song to God. So, yes, to answer your question, the HU chant does take away guilt. It washes Soul pure with the reconciling love of God."

"Thank you, Michael," I said, with a grateful smile.

I would never have absolved myself of the guilt of my abortion had I not been convinced of the power of HU. Not only did I feel less guilty with each HU that I sang, but I also began to experience the inner worlds of God in my dreams!

These worlds exist beyond the material physical world. They are the astral, causal, mental, and spiritual worlds. St. Paul mentions these inner worlds when he said he knew a man who was caught up in the third heaven; but of all the teachings that I had studied, none could show me how to get to the Higher Worlds of God. Try as I may though, I could not convince my mother of the teaching that was doing so much to heal me.

"I love Jesus, Mother," I foolishly tried to explain to her again after our long silence when she came to my house early one Sunday morning to take me to the second Mass at Uncle Clancy's church, "but Jesus is not my savior anymore. I no longer believe what the Church teaches about suffering for our sins. We shouldn't have to suffer if we don't have to. We can avoid the karma that causes suffering, but we have to know what karma is. Karma is spiritual accountability. Christianity doesn't teach karma. Christianity teaches sin, and sin is what the Church says it is. And that's not right."

"So now you know better than the Church?" my mother shot

back.

I stared at my mother sitting on the sofa dressed in her Sunday-best, two piece outfit, white hat and matching shoes and Sunday purse, and I felt like I was being scolded again like I was every time I was late getting ready for Mass. "If that's what it sounds like to you, I'm sorry," I replied, fighting back my emotions. "All I'm saying is that I don't believe sin is what the Church tells us it is. That's all I'm saying, Mother."

"You're going daft, girl," my mother replied, with that horrified look on her flushed face that told me her blood pressure had just shot up. "Our Lord Jesus Christ came into the world to save us from our sins. He sacrificed his life to show us the way into the kingdom of heaven. He didn't die in vain, Cassie. Jesus died for us. He died for you and me. He died to wash away our sins, and now you tell me that sin doesn't exist? That's the Devil talking, and you better go to confession before he steals your Soul completely..."

"This is pointless," I interrupted, wondering why I even bothered. "You won't give me a chance, will you? You have one way of looking at the world, and that's the only way there is for you. There are many other ways to look at the world, and I've found a way that makes me happy. Atma-Gare doesn't make me feel guilty like Christianity did. I'm sorry to tell you this, Mother, but I'm beginning to think you like to suffer."

"Suffering is good for the Soul, Cassie," my mother replied in her poor martyr's voice that pushed all of my buttons.

"It may be, but it's not always necessary. That's all I'm trying to say. Christianity is not the only religion in the world, you know."

"But Jesus is the only savior!" she finally exploded, jumping to her feet. "Jesus is the Son of God who died for our sins! There may be many religions in the world, but we have the one true religion! And we have the Pope! So it doesn't matter what anyone tries to tell me, I know what I know! I will go to my grave with Jesus in my heart! He's my Lord and savior, and I pray to him every day to take me into his kingdom when my time comes..."

As I listened to my mother I thought of a patient I had when I nursed at the River Bend Psychiatric Hospital after I left the Operating

Room at St. Paul's. Peter Hansen cried incessantly, but no one knew why. For months I tried to find Peter out. I approached him slowly, and gradually he began to warm up to me. One day he surprised me and said, "You're very kind to me. Why are you so kind to me?"

"And why shouldn't I be, Peter?" I asked.

"Are you a Christian?" he asked.

"Yes," I said. I was still a Catholic then.

"Do you love Jesus?" he asked.

"Yes, I do," I replied.

"Me too. Jesus died for me, you know."

"He did?" I asked, suspicious by his change of voice.

"Yes," Peter said, and smiled. It was the first time I had seen him smile, but his smile made me uneasy.

"Did Jesus die just for you, Peter?" I asked.

"What?" Peter said, still smiling.

I repeated my question. "Did Jesus die just for you?"

"Yes," he said, and his smile disappeared.

"Do you believe that, Peter?" I asked.

"Yes," he said.

"Who told you that Jesus died just for you?"

"My mother," he said. His odd smile made me nervous now. I stepped back. I was new to psychiatric nursing. Peter was diagnosed with catatonic schizophrenia and not to be trusted.

"She did?" I said. "I think your mother meant that Jesus died for the sins of the whole world, not just for you, Peter."

"JESUS DIED FOR ME!" he screamed at me.

Startled, I jumped back. I stared at Peter, waiting for whatever he might do to me. He didn't move. He started crying again.

I had to ask him. "Why did Jesus die for you, Peter?"

"Because I..."

"Why do you cry all the time, Peter?"

"Because I love Jesus," he replied.

"I love Jesus too, Peter. But I don't cry all the time."

"Jesus did not die for you. He died for me," Peter responded, and tears began to stream down his cheeks.

I didn't know what to say, so I waited nervously.

"Jesus was whipped and scorned for me. He wore a crown of thorns for me. He was nailed to the cross for me. He bled and suffered and died on the cross for me."

I stared in disbelief as the tears streamed down his face. What could he have done to take Jesus Christ's death so personally? I had to find out. "Why did Jesus die for you, Peter?" I asked again.

"Because I..."

Peter broke down and cried inconsolably. When I left psychiatric nursing and went into palliative care, he was still crying. I never did find out why he cried for Jesus, but it did not surprise me to learn that he withdrew so deeply into himself that he couldn't be reached. I shed a tear for Peter, the same kind of tear that I now shed for my mother.

She was no less trapped by her faith than Peter was by his neurotic fixation on Jesus. But rather than admit it, my mother tried to trap everyone else. Her mind was shut so tight that she had to scream to be heard. I tried to explain Atma-Gare to her again, but she would not hear of it. Atma-Gare was the Devil's work and a cult, and this got my Irish up.

"It's not a cult, Mother!" I screamed in my own demented banshee voice as I sprang to my feet and stared at my mother eye to eye. "For your information, Christ's teaching came from the same source that all spiritual teachings come from! All religions come from Holy Spirit! Just because we call Holy Spirit the Atma doesn't make Atma-Gare a cult! The Atma is the Way, not Jesus Christ! Just because Jesus said he was the way does not make him the only way to salvation, you know! He's not the only way! Why in God's name can't you see that?"

"Because Jesus is the only begotten Son of God, that's why!" she shouted back with that look I was familiar with whenever her faith was threatened. My father used to bring this frightened look to her eyes with just a few words. "Read the Gospels, Cassie," she implored me in her passive-aggressive voice. "Jesus was the good shepherd who came into the world to save us. That's why the Roman Catholic religion is the one true religion of God. Read the Holy Word of God and get out of this cult before it's too late. Come back to the Church. Go upstairs and change and come to Mass with me before you lose your Soul..."

I wanted to scream with all my might, but I sat down instead and took a deep breath to compose myself. I called upon the Inner Master for help. I did not want to lose it with my mother. I always did, but I did not want to now. She would reduce me to a little girl if I did. I closed my eyes. *"Satma,"* I pleaded, *"please help me to stay calm…"*

To my surprise, I felt myself slowly bathed in a flood of warm love and all of my fear vanished. I looked up at my mother with an equanimity I had never experienced before in my life. "I don't want to come back to the Church, Mother," I said, hearing my own voice which was unbelievably calm and confident. "I've outgrown my Christian faith. I don't know how to tell you this, but I don't want my life to be a lie anymore. That's what it felt like when I was a Catholic. My life was a lie, Mother. I tried many times to reaffirm my faith, but I could not. I felt so trapped by my faith that I couldn't breathe. My abortion brought my life to a head. I had to leave the Church. I had no choice. I could not suffer the guilt and shame any longer. I had to leave for my own sanity."

"Did you confess your sin?" my mother asked, with deliberate calmness.

"Abortion is not a sin," I replied, with equal calmness.

"Says who, your cult teacher?" she pounced.

"Says I," I replied. "And everyone else who believes in reincarnation. That's the problem with this whole abortion issue, Mother. The media always plays up the Christian side, but there are other sides to this issue, you know. Blind faith is not enough anymore. Not for me, anyway. That's why I joined Atma-Gare. It's an individual path built upon personal experience, not blind faith. I'm sorry if I've disappointed you, but I can't come back. I've outgrown my Christian faith. I've moved on to a spiritual path that speaks to my heart. Christianity has nothing to say to me anymore. Nothing at all, Mother."

My mother stared at me. She did not reply for the longest time. It was not like her. Her piercing green eyes felt like two drills boring into my Soul, but they could no longer penetrate me. I was protected.

I remained so calm that my mother was forced to speak. "Now you're talking just like that nutty Shirley MacLaine," she softly said, and I waited for the pounce. *"Wake up, Cassie!"* she screamed at me. "This new age religion is nothing but a money-grabbing scam! That's all these cults are! Beware of false prophets! They're wolves in sheep's clothing! If you don't watch it you're going to get gobbled up by this cult teacher of yours! He's a wolf in sheep's clothing! *Mark my words!"*

"He's not a cult teacher," I replied, in a calm, quiet voice. "He's the Wayshower and Light Giver of the world. Now will you please leave? You're going to be late for Mass."

Talking to my mother was like talking to a wall. But I couldn't help myself. Her approval meant everything to me. She never gave it to me though. I knew it was insane, but I had to have her blessing for leaving the Church.

I wanted Kevin's blessing too. I had a deep need that could not be satisfied. That's why we grew apart. I took from our marriage to satisfy my need, but I got so involved in my search for myself that I drove Kevin into the arms of another woman.

I should have seen it coming. But I was too involved in myself to notice how much we had grown apart. I loved Kevin, but I took our marriage for granted. As I worked on my Master's degree and hopped from one branch of nursing to another—from general nursing to Emergency, then to the Operating Room, psychiatric nursing, to geriatrics, and palliative care—Kevin was always there to support me. But when I began talking about past lives, Edgar Cayce, karma, and near death experiences Kevin began to drift away from me. My mother saw it coming, but I wouldn't listen to her.

"I love Kevin, Mother," I told her when she tried to warn me as we were doing the dishes when we had her over for our monthly family dinner. "I would do anything for him. You know that, don't you?"

"Then why don't you pay more attention to him?" she said, as she dried the casserole dish. Mother never let me use the dishwasher when she came to our house for dinner. She didn't believe in them. But the kitchen had to be spotless before she left. "You're always on the go, Cassie. It's always one thing or another with you. Some day your husband's going to surprise you. Mark my words."

She was right. Kevin could not put up with my consuming desire to satisfy my need for wholeness. Kevin had needs too. He needed to be loved, and I wasn't there for him. I gave him what was left over after my work, my children, my studies, and my search for myself, and that wasn't enough; so he found the love he needed in the arms of another woman.

His affair with his secretary hurt me so deeply that I conspired to get him back. I knew he still loved me, and I pleaded with him to talk with me. He had moved out of the house and was staying with his parents to think things through, but he agreed to come home to discuss our problems over dinner. I chose the day and made his favorite meal, prime rib roast with Yorkshire pudding and fresh peach cobbler. Mother had the children. I deliberately did not bring up the subject of reconciling. I just wanted Kevin to let his hair down and be himself, and with the flickering candlelight, two bottles of his favourite red wine, and soft music I seduced my estranged husband and we made love the way we used to make love when we first married; three times. And as I hoped, I got pregnant.

But it backfired on me. I called him at work and asked him to come to the house. I had something very important to tell him in person. The children weren't home yet.

"I'm sorry, Cassie," he said with tears in his eyes and a lump in his throat when I gave him the good news. "I can't take it anymore. I just can't, Cassie. I want a divorce."

"I tell you I'm pregnant and you tell me you want a divorce?" I stammered. *"I don't believe you, Kevin!"*

"I can't help it, Cassie. I just can't take it anymore," he cried, with a tortured look on his blood-drained face. My news shocked him, and he just stared at me in stunned horror.

"Take what, Kevin? What can't you take anymore?"

"God knows I still love you, Cassie. Oh God, I do." He broke down. He put his head in his hands and rested his elbows on his knees. It was painful enough to ask me for a divorce, but what made it unbearable for him was that I didn't know why he wanted out. This completely devastated him, and he sobbed uncontrollably.

"Why, Kevin?" I pleaded. *"Why?"*

"I just can't take it anymore," he replied, his whole body quivering with inconsolable emotion. "I can't take it anymore."

"Take what, Kevin? *Tell me, for God's sake!*"

"Another child," he replied, to my absolute horror. "I can't, Cassie. I just can't take another child. Oh God, I'm sorry. I have to go. Please forgive me, Cassie. I can't stay the night. I can't. Please forgive me..."

I put my arms around him to stop him from walking out the door. I held him desperately in my arms. He struggled to get free. "Don't leave me, Kevin. Please don't leave me. I beg you, don' t leave me. If you don't want another baby, I'll have an abortion. Please don't leave me. Kevin. Please. *I beg you, don't leave me.*"

Too frightened to speak, Kevin tore himself free and fled from me. Desperate, I had an abortion to save my marriage, but I knew in my heart that it was too late.

Kevin moved out of his parent's home and into the apartment with his secretary Belinda Holloway, and I was left to deal with the guilt and shame of my abortion alone; but once I worked my way through the unbearable pain and guilt I never again looked at my Christian faith with the same blind, unquestioning eyes.

My Unborn Child

Chapter 3

The Goodbye Dinner

It would take time to heal from Kevin's loss. I did not realize how much a part of me he had become until he left, but by then it was too late. I tried not to be bitter, but it took everything that I had to keep anger at bay, and I thank the Satma for that.

I blamed myself. That's what kept me from turning on Kevin. I could not blame him for going to the arms of another woman. I wanted to blame him, but the more I reflected on our marriage over the next few years the more I blamed myself for driving him away.

We settled our divorce like old friends who had a falling out, and came to a happy arrangement for shared custody and child support. Kevin turned the house over to me, but I was responsible for the remaining mortgage. I couldn't stay in Vancouver, though. I had to leave. I had to have a fresh start far away from home.

I invited Kevin out for dinner to tell him my news. We met at *Geno's,* our favorite Italian restaurant in Burnaby where we always shared our good news. Kevin knew Geno Savanti from his father's Honda dealership. Geno traded in his vehicle every two or three years and they became golfing buddies. Kevin introduced Geno to golf, which opened up a whole new world for Geno who had spent most of his life in his restaurant kitchen.

"Hi, Kevin," I said, as he walked up to our quiet, candle-lit corner table that Geno's wonderful wife Maria had reserved for us.

I didn't think it was possible, but for some reason he looked even better than the day I married him. Handsome and fit as always, his eyes reflected the loving father that he had become to our three beautiful children and the aggressive years of growth in his father's successful Honda dealership; but it was his boyish smile that I loved most about him. Winsome, and always so inviting that it brought a tear to my eye.

"How are you, love?" he asked, as he sat down.

"I'm fine, thank you. You look fantastic, Kevin!"

"So do you," he said, his smiling eyes taking me all in.

"Thank you. You do know I want you back, don't you?"

"Cassie..."

"Oh, Kevin, I'm only teasing. I'm happy for you. I really am."

"Thank you. Where are the kids, at home?"

"Yes. I ordered Boston Pizza for them. That should keep them happy."

"Good. How are they doing, Cassie?" Kevin asked, solicitously.

"They're fine," I said, sensing the change in his voice.

"Really?"

"Yes, really."

"Well, I guess it's not like I'm in Japan or anything," Kevin said, shrugging off his sudden rush of emotion. "I see them almost as much as you do. I'm just concerned, that's all. Are you sure they're okay?" he repeated, getting emotional again. "We've got to watch them, you know. They can play us like violins, Cassie."

I smiled, sensing that he knew why I had asked him out for dinner. Patrick must have told him. "Actually, that's what I wanted to talk about," I said, nervously.

"What? Something's wrong, isn't there? Problems at school?" Kevin said, not letting on that he knew. "What have they done now?"

"No. It's not about them," I said, with my heart in my throat. "Well, it is and it isn't. Kevin, I really don't know how to tell you this, but I've decided to move to Ontario. I need a fresh start. You have a new life going for you here, and I'm very happy for you. I need a new life too. I talked it over with the children, and they agreed on condition that they can spend the summers with you. I have to leave Vancouver, Kevin. I have to."

Kevin fell silent. He wasn't surprised by my news, but I could see his mind processing every possible option. His face betrayed his every emotion, from panic to anger to regret, and finally a reluctant smile of acceptance, and he just looked at me.

After what seemed like forever, he reached over and put his hand on mine and held it. I felt his warmth. "Then it's true. Patrick told me. Are you absolutely sure about this, Cassie?" Patrick was close to his father.

"Yes," I said.

"Why Ontario? It's so far away," he said, fighting back his emotions.

"I've got a job waiting for me there," I replied, trying my hardest to hold my emotions back. "I need a fresh start, Kevin. I honestly do. I've found what I've been looking for my whole life, and all I want to do now is live my life on my own terms."

"You always have, Cassie," he said.

"I have, haven't I?" I confessed, with a sudden rush of fresh guilt. "Well, at least I'm aware of it now," I said, and laughed nervously.

"Yes. That was the crux of it, wasn't it?"

"I couldn't help myself, Kevin. I had to find myself."

"And have you found yourself now?" he asked.

"Yes, I think so. Atma-Gare is filling the void in my life beautifully. I could not have asked for a more satisfying spiritual path."

"I'm happy for you, Cassie. I really am. I've been expecting this for the last month now, so I'm not surprised. To be honest with you, a big part of me wanted to fight you on this, but the more I thought about it the less fight I had in me. I don't want to hurt our children, Cassie. I've seen this happen too many times, and I don't want to be one of those ex-husbands. You have a right to your own life just as much as I have to mine, and I have to accept that. I know that your abortion put you through hell, and I have to respect you for trying to save our marriage; but I think our marriage had run it's course and we were destined to go our separate ways. I don't have to tell you how much I'm going to miss the children, but I can't stand in your way.

We've managed to stay friends, and I won't do anything to hurt our children. They'll never want for anything, Cassie; I promise. Dad bought into a new venture in Victoria last summer, and we're doing much better than we dreamed; and we're almost ready to start developing that piece of commercial real estate that dad's been sitting on for years. We're going to put in a strip mall. It's coming together very nicely; so don't worry about the children. You're not in this alone, Cassie. They're my children too, and I want to be a part of their life no matter where they are. I trust you. You're a great mother, Cassie; and we both want what's best for them. Besides, I can fly to Ontario any time they need me. I'll be there for them. I always have been. I promise. Whatever they need, you just call me. Okay?"

Kevin brought tears to my eyes. I had asked the Satma for Kevin to understand why I had to leave as I drove to *Geno's,* but Kevin took me by surprise. Sitting at the same private table with the checkered tablecloth where we had celebrated more than once over Geno's family house wine and gnocchi with garlic and herb sauce, freshly baked crusty buns, and tossed salad with Geno's own vinaigrette that he made with the balsamic vinegar that his brother shipped over to him with the *Savanti* house wine from the family vineyard in Tuscany, it felt like the years we were apart had collapsed into a single day.

"God, I do miss you," I said, with tears trickling down my cheeks. "Thank you, Kevin; thank you so much for being so understanding. I will always love you for this. You know that I have to do it, don't you? I have to cut all my ties, Kevin. I have to get a life of my own far away from here. You can appreciate why I have to do this, can't you?"

"I think so," he said, his voice choking with emotion.

"I should have paid more attention to you, Kevin. I knew that from the day I met you. You needed to be loved. That's all you ever wanted from me, wasn't it? Then the children came along and I couldn't give you all the love you needed. And then I got swept away with my own selfish needs and I had little left to give you. Honest to God, Kevin, I hope Belinda can love you the way I should have loved you."

"No one can love me the way you did, Cassie," Kevin jumped in and instinctively reached over for my hand like he always did whenever we bared our hearts to each other. "You were my first true love. Cassie, and I will love you till the day I die..."

I broke into a flood of tears and my body quaked with uncontrollable emotion as the reality of my move hit home. Kevin squeezed my hand with both of his and waited patiently for me to calm myself. I sniffled two or three times, and said, "I'm fine now, Kevin."

"Are you sure?" he asked, his eyes moist with his own tears of regret.

"Yes," I said, and we sipped our wine in silence with concerned glances from an elderly couple closest to our table, and Maria who kept a vigilant eye on us.

Half way through our main course of Geno's Italian Lamb Chops, I became so overwhelmed again that I had to let all of my feelings out, just as the Satma asked me to do in my contemplation before leaving the house. *"Thank him for everything,"* the Satma said to me in my mind when I asked him what I should say.

"Everything?" I repeated, not quite sure of myself.

"Yes. Thank him for everything," the Satma repeated, out loud.

"Thank you for your love, Kevin," I said, through fresh new tears of gratitude. "Thank you for our beautiful children. Thank you for being such a good father. Thank you for all the wonderful years that we had together. I will cherish them forever. Thank you for being my husband, my lover, and my best friend. I will always love you, Kevin. And I hope when the time comes I will find another man as good as you. We were really good together, weren't we?"

"The best," Kevin said, with tears trickling down his cheeks.

This was the final cut. The break that would launch me into my own life, and Kevin felt it as deeply as I did. I saw the regret in his eyes and I welled up with emotion.

"You left a big hole in my life, Kevin," I said, wiping my sniffling nose again with the tissue I had brought with me. "But I'll fill it somehow. Not right away, but I'll fill it. I just can't date anyone yet. I have to be a whole person before I can start seeing other men."

"What do you mean?" he asked, with that surprised look of innocent wonder that I used to see in his boyish eyes when we first started dating.

"I have to be a whole person to attract a whole person," I explained, and tried to muster a confident smile. "I refuse to date until I'm ready. I'm not whole enough yet, Kevin. I'll only attract a man with a hole in his life now, and two holes don't make for a whole relationship."

Kevin laughed. "It's good to have you back, Cassie..."

"Yes, it is, isn't it? That was my problem, Kevin. I didn't know I had gone away. I just got up and left whenever my heart told me to go."

"But you were so practical, Cassie," Kevin said, leaning into the table to get close to me as he always did whenever he craved more intimacy. "That's what confused me. I couldn't understand your need to find yourself. I always thought you were the most sensible person I ever met. Straight, no-nonsense Cassie. Then you began to disappear on me. Every day, a little bit of you left. Then one day you weren't there at all. That scared me, Cassie. You have no idea how scared I was to realize that you weren't there anymore. You went through all the motions, but you weren't there. I tried to bring you back, but I couldn't reach you. You heard me, but you didn't hear me. Even when we made love, you weren't really there. You were somewhere else. It was like you were another person. I couldn't take it anymore, Cassie. Like your father used to say, I was dying on the vine. I have to know one thing, Cassie. I have to know before you move to Ontario. Why? What was it you were missing in your life? We had everything; a perfect family; a beautiful house in Kitsalano; great careers, and no money or health problems. Where did you go? I have to know, Cassie. I have to know for my own peace of mind."

I took a sip of *Savanti,* and then another. Kevin's every word touched my heart. I could not disappoint him. He had to know so he could heal too.

Silently, I did a short HU. I called upon the Inner Master. *"Please, Satma, let me say the right thing. I want so much to leave on the best of terms."* I looked into Kevin's needy eyes, smiled, and spoke from the depths of my heart.

"Death, Kevin," I said, feeling absolutely confident that whatever

I was going to say would be right. "You know that Doctor Elisabeth Kubler-Ross had an enormous influence on my life. She's my role model, Kevin. Her courage and compassion have inspired me from the day I read her book *On Death And Dying.* From the moment I met her when I took her Life, Death, and Transition workshop in Seattle she made such an impression on me that it gave me the courage to seek out my own destiny. She encouraged me to experience every aspect of nursing before going into palliative care, which I wanted to do immediately. She said I needed to be well rounded to deal with what I would find caring for the terminally ill. `*Life doesn't end when you die. It starts,*' she told me. Her words haunted me, Kevin. That's why I wanted to work in the O.R. after EMERGE. I woke up one morning from a dream I had working in the O.R., and I knew that's where I had to be. I wanted to be as close to life and death as I could be. I had to be right there, on the edge of life and death. I wanted to be where life and death meet in that one moment of time. It's like the birth of a child, but only in reverse. You can't imagine the wonder of these two glorious moments, Kevin. I've experienced them both, and I can't explain them. It's life, Kevin. I had to know the mystery of life. I had to find the answer. That's where it all began for me. I woke up to life in the O.R. on the day we lost our third patient in three days. I knew there had to be more to life than these two wondrous moments. What was life all about in-between these two incredible moments? Why did we come into this world? Why did I have such a strong desire to become a nurse? Why did I feel so unfulfilled? Why couldn't my life satisfy me? How can life start at the moment of death? Is death the birth of a new life? I had to know, Kevin. I couldn't help myself. The O.R., Kevin. That's where I woke up to life and where my search for myself really began. And I have Doctor Elisabeth Kubler-Ross to thank for that."

Kevin's eyes devoured me. My every word went straight to his heart, and I *knew* that he understood me for the first time in his life. He needed a few minutes to digest what I said. "And the psych hospital?" he finally asked. "What did you get from that experience?"

"I honestly don't know why I went there," I said, keeping my promise to be totally honest with him. "I felt that's where I had to be next. I must have needed that experience to prepare myself for the next stage of my life. It helped me to understand people better, but I knew when it was over. I had to leave. That's how I've always been."

"I know," Kevin replied. "And I resented it like hell too because I never had the courage to try something new. But I admired you for it, Cassie. Did it help you?"

"What? My time at River Bend?"

"Yes."

"It helped some. But I still felt empty. No, that's not true. I've never really felt empty, Kevin. I've always felt like something was missing. Like I was incomplete. That's what I was after. I wanted to give my life a meaning that went beyond my career and family. I had to have personal meaning, Kevin. That's my father's legacy. Can you appreciate that?"

"I don't know. I've never had those kinds of feelings."

"Yes, I know. That's why I could never share this part of my life with you. You never heard me when I tried to tell you. If you did hear me, you never took me seriously. I couldn't help myself, Kevin. I had to look. It was either that or end up like my father. I can't explain this need. It's a feeling or an instinct like migratory birds must have. They go where they have to go on instinct alone. I'm sure the geese don't know why they have to go south for the winter, but they go. That's how I've always felt. I had to go when I got the urge to go to give my life more meaning. That's why I went to geriatrics after I got what I needed from my psych patients at River Bend. My heart told me to go to geriatrics before I went into palliative care, so I went. And I did learn something from my psych patients that I never knew before."

"What was that?" Kevin asked, with genuine curiosity.

I stopped to reflect. I looked into Kevin's eyes, and with an ironic smile said, "More than anything else, people need to be loved. That's what my psych patients taught me. They are the least loved people in the world. They're so lonely it makes you want to cry. I've never met anyone lonelier. They're so love-starved that they create their own reality to satisfy their need to belong and be loved. That's what life between those two moments is all about, Kevin—finding love. What's that song that Nat King Cole used to sing? Nature Boy? *'And the greatest thing you can ever learn, is to love and be loved in return...* 'Oh God. I'm sorry, Kevin. I'm so sorry for leaving you the way I did. I'm so sorry for tricking you to get you back. I wanted you back, Kevin. I wanted you back so badly..."

I broke down again. The dam finally burst and all of my emotions rushed to the surface and flooded me with love and shame and guilt and joy and anger and regret, and an overwhelming feeling of empty sadness. I had to excuse myself. I went to the lady's room and cried my heart out.

The smartly dressed silver-haired lady from the nearest table with the concerned glances walked into the washroom to see if I was all right, and I assured her that everything was fine. "He's my ex-husband, and this is our farewell dinner. I'm moving to Ontario with the children, and he's just given me his blessing," I said, through sniffles. And then I heard myself say something that surprised both of us, *"Love has scoured every corner of my heart and I'm ready now for the splendor of my new life,"* and then such a powerful feeling of goodness washed over me that the blood rushed to my face and I radiated such a joyful smile that the lady felt the warmth of my love and was compelled to put her arms around me and give me the warmest, most loving hug and I felt like I was in the arms of the Satma. And then she stood back and looked into my eyes, smiled, and quietly left me to redo my makeup.

Kevin didn't say anything when I returned, but his smile warmed my heart.

"I'm sorry, Kevin. I just had to let it out. I'm okay now."

"Are you sure?" he asked.

"Yes."

"Well, now that we're being so open and honest with each other, can I ask you something very personal?" he asked, with a serious look in his eyes.

"Of course you can," I said.

"Why are you being so good about this? Why don't you scream at me like your mother would? Why don't you slap me? I'm to blame as much as you. I wasn't there for you either, Cassie. I just didn't understand you. I don't think I wanted to. I tried to reach you, but I didn't try hard enough. It's as much my fault as yours, Cassie. I'm so sorry..."

"Kevin, please don't beat yourself up over this. How could you reach me when I couldn't reach myself? I was lost there for a long time. I went away like you said, but I didn't know I had gone away. I took you for granted, Kevin. That's what broke up our marriage. I should never have taken you for granted. You were my husband, and I shouldn't have abandoned you the way I did. It was insensitive and selfish. It would have been better had I left you for another man. At least you would have understood that."

Kevin burst into laughter. *"That, I would have understood!"*

"We're not alone, Kevin. I'm sure many marriages have broken up because of these same symptoms. It's a curse to have this selfish need to find yourself. It's a curse on marriage!" I said, and broke into an ironic chuckle.

Kevin's eyes lit up when he made the connection and laughed. It was good to hear him laugh. "Then it must be a blessing when you find yourself," he said, still laughing. "So, Cassie, have you found yourself? Please say yes. I don't want to think that all of our suffering was for nothing!"

"I'm almost there," I said, with a big, loving smile.

"Tell me more about Atma-Gare, then. You're mother thinks you've really gone off the deep end this time."

"Of course she would. Mother's a closed-minded dyed-in-the-wool Roman Catholic. Everything the Church doesn't approve of is the Devil's work for her. What about your parents, Kevin? What do they think of me now?"

"Dad's always liked you, Cassie. You're the daughter he never had, and you've given him the grandchildren that'll make him happy in his old age. Why do you think he drives himself the way he does. It's all for them. He expects them to go to university here, you know."

"I know. What about your mother? What does she think of me now?"

"You've always been a bit much for mom, but she admires and respects you in her own way. I told them about your involvement in Atma-Gare. Dad said if it works for you, that's all that should matter. He's pretty open-minded. Live and let live. That's his motto."

"Your father's always been good to me, Kevin. I'm going to miss him. So will the children. But you'll have them for summer holidays and when they go to university."

"Yeah," Kevin sighed, and fell silent for a minute or two; but his eyes did not show any regret for the decision he had made to let the children go. "Now tell me about this new job in Ontario. Where in Ontario?" he asked, in a courageous voice.

"In Georgian Bay, South Central Ontario. A quaint little farming community called Wyedale, just north of Toronto. I've accepted the position of head nurse at the district hospital in Wyedale. It's a wonderful opportunity, Kevin."

"Good for you. But why so far away, Cassie?"

I smiled to myself at the extraordinary experience that led to my decision to accept the position in Wyedale, but I couldn't share it with Kevin. It would have been too much for him, so I just said, "That's where my heart wants me to go."

"And you do listen to your heart, don't you?" he said, with a wry chuckle. "I do wish the best for you, Cassie. It's going to break my heart to see the children go, and mom and dad's heart too. But like I said, I won't stand in your way. You never stood in mine. We parted friends and I want to stay friends. I hope you find what you're looking for, Cassie. I really do."

"I've already found it, Kevin. All I have to do now is live my life. My search took me far away, and now I'm back to where I started. I think there's a poem that expresses that sentiment. My father read it to me. It might be *The Wasteland*, by T. S. Eliot."

"Don't ask me. So, when do you start your new job?"

"Just as soon as school's over. I have to be there for the middle of August. It's a beautiful old hospital with a brand new wing. I'm really excited, Kevin."

"I'm excited for you. What about the house? You can get a good dollar for it now, Cassie. It's a sellers market in Vancouver."

"I know," I said, with a big grin. "My realtor said he's already got people lined up to see it. He's confident he can get five hundred and eighty-five thousand for it. Apparently Kitsalano is a real hot spot."

"It's hot all over. And in Ontario? Have you looked for a house yet?"

"You won't believe it, Kevin," I said, and laughed. "Yes, I found a house. It was pure luck. It's a beautiful Century brick home with an extended new family room. That same house here would go for three times the price it's selling for in Ontario. I got it for two hundred and eight-five thousand. I got really lucky, Kevin!"

"Good for you, Cassie. After you pay off the mortgage you should still have a pretty nice little nest egg to invest. Call dad. He'll know where to invest it for you. Now tell me the truth. How are the kids really taking this? Is Patrick okay with it?"

"Of course he's not. He's angry and hurt. He wants to stay with you, and he would have been real trouble if I hadn't promised them the summers in Vancouver and an airline ticket for the winter breaks. Besides, before we know it he'll be coming here to university. Cindy and Mark are dealing with it much better than I expected, and I'm really grateful. It's going to be hard at first, but life's all about change, isn't it? Patrick will come around eventually."

"May I take them this weekend? I'll try to calm him down."

"Would you, please?"

"Patrick can be pretty stubborn when he wants to be. I'll take him golfing this weekend and have a talk with him. But I'd like to spend as much time with the children as I can before you leave, Cassie. You don't mind if I hog my time with them, do you?"

"Kevin..."

"I know, I know. We promised. Nothing to hurt the children. Okay, I'll pick them up Saturday morning, if that's okay with you."

"I'll tell them," I said, with so much gratitude in my heart that tears came to my eyes again. We ate our raspberry cheesecake dessert in silence.

On our way out, I smiled and whispered thank you to the lady who had comforted me, and she gave me the warmest, most loving smile. "My heart goes with you," she whispered, and reached for my hand. "You're going to be okay," she added, with a tear in her eye.

I bent over and gave her a kiss on the cheek. "Thank you," I said, with tears in my eyes. "God must have sent you here tonight."

She smiled. "It was my husband's suggestion. We're celebrating our eighteenth wedding anniversary. I met him here in Vancouver when I moved from Calgary."

Her husband's face brightened, and suddenly I *knew* why she was so emotional for me. I gave her husband a big smile, and said, "You're a very fortunate man."

"You have no idea how fortunate," he said, and smiled proudly.

With a lump in my throat, I said, "I hope to find a man where I'm moving to who will love me the way you love your wife."

"You will," his wife replied, and grabbed my hand with both of hers and held it for the longest time, giving me her strength and love and courage to move away just as she had done when she left Calgary to start her new life in Vancouver.

"God sent you here tonight," I said again, with tears of love and gratitude; and as I walked to where Kevin was waiting with Geno and Maria at the cash register, I knew in my heart that I would find the man of my dreams in Georgian Bay.

We thanked Geno and Maria, and as Kevin and Geno talked I quietly explained to Maria that we were emotional because this was our farewell dinner and we were saying goodbye, and she wished me well in my new life in Ontario.

Kevin walked me to my car, kissed me on the cheek, and we went our separate ways. I was too restless to go straight home, so I drove to Stanley Park. I walked for an hour and found myself by the sea wall where I had made my decision to abort Seana, my fourth child. I started to cry all over again.

I had decided to take my child's life to save my marriage, but I lost both Seana and my wonderful husband. I wanted to scream, but I just sobbed quietly to myself as I said goodbye to my old life in my beloved native city of Vancouver.

Chapter 4

My Last Confession

Elba Martin's "death" was my first near-death experience. During open-heart surgery she left her body and went to the inner planes, but she was told to return to her body. She did not want to return, but she had no choice; her time was not up yet. She was sixty-two.

"I didn't want to leave. It's so beautiful there. I didn't want to come back to my body," she told me. I had heard of near-death experiences in the O.R., and I had read about them, but I had never met anyone who had experienced one. Elba Martin's NDE excited me very much. "What did you see there, Elba?" I asked.

"My Jim," she replied, with a radiant smile. Her cheeks were pink, and her eyes warm and kind. "He looked so wonderful. Just like he did before he got sick."

"Jim was your husband?"

"Yes."

"Why did you come back, Elba?"

"I had to, dear. I'm not finished with my life yet."

"What do you mean?" I asked.

"I'm still needed here. But I don't know what for. I saw my Jim, and he's doing real fine over there. I'm not afraid to die now. I know he's waiting for me on the other side. It's just like here, only better. Jim and I will be together again when I die. But you think I'm being silly, don't you dear?"

"Of course not, Elba," I said, patting her arm gently.

"Well, some people do. But I don't care. I know what I experienced, and I'm not afraid anymore. I saw my Jim, and he's waiting for me to finish what I have to do here. I don't know what I have to finish, but it must be something important."

Elba crossed over to the other side after seeing her only child through a major family crisis. Her daughter's husband was killed in a head-on collision on his way home from Grouse Mountain, and Elba's granddaughter was crippled for life. The grief was too much for Elba's daughter to suffer alone. That's why Elba had to return to her body.

I saw Elba shortly before she died. I left the O.R. for psychiatric nursing, but I kept in touch with all three of my patients who had near-death experiences, and each one told me how much their life had changed since their experience on the other side.

They were no longer afraid to die, and they all had a very strong desire to leave this world a better place, however small their contribution might be. Their generous spirit excited me, but my husband could not understand my fascination with near-death experiences, nor my desire to leave St. Paul's to nurse the mentally ill at River Bend Hospital in Port Coquitlan.

But I had a strong desire to care for the mentally ill. It was another step towards my goal of caring for the terminally ill. I knew in my heart that I had to experience this branch of nursing to grow in my love and compassion for humanity.

"Caring for the mentally ill will either pry open your heart or shut it tight," Doctor Elisabeth Kubler-Ross told me when I finally met her in Seattle. *"You cannot care for the dying without an open heart,"* she added, with such easy conviction in her charming Swiss-accented English that her words touched the very core of my being. *"An open heart heals the wounded Soul, and I have yet to find a single patient who has not been wounded by life."*

When I told Kevin I was going to leave St. Paul's Hospital to tend to the mentally ill at River Bend, he blew up at me. "That's stupid! Why, Cassie? Who would want to look after crazy people?"

"I do," I replied.

"Why? Tell me why?"

"I need that experience to grow, and I'm going to have it. Isn't that a good enough reason for you?" I explained.

"No, it's not," he said, shaking his head in disbelief. "I don't want you nursing crazy people. Who knows what can happen to you there."

"I've made up my mind, Kevin."

"Here we go again. *Now it's the crazies!*"

"It's my career, Kevin, isn't it?"

"And it's our marriage, isn't it?"

"Yes, it's our marriage. But I told you I'm not sacrificing my career for our marriage. You knew that going in, Kevin. As much as I like working in the O.R., I have to give my life more meaning, and my heart tells me to look after the mentally disturbed now. They're people too, Kevin."

"Oh God, here we go again. It's always something else with you, isn't it? Yoga, meditation, Zen, Edgar Cayce, the Rosicrucians? What next, Cassie? What's after the crazies?"

"Let's drop it, okay? It's not going to interfere in our family life. I'm just nursing sick people, that's all."

"Tell me what you're looking for, Cassie. Can you do that?"

"I want my life to have personal meaning. That's not so hard to understand, is it?"

Kevin threw his arms into the air. *"Personal meaning?* What about me? What about your family? Aren't we meaning enough for you?"

"That's not fair, and you know it. My family means everything to me, and that's never going to change," I tried to explain. "I have a longing inside me that nothing seems to satisfy, that's what I mean. It has nothing to do with you and the children. I love you, and I love the children, but I have a longing that I just can't seem to satisfy. I don't know where my life is headed, but I have to be ready for what I'm going to find. That's why I do what I do, Kevin. I have to listen to my own heart. Can't you see that?"

"I don't have a clue what you're talking about!" he shouted, and stormed out of the house. That night as he sat on the bed unknotting his tie he said to me, with more emotional sincerity than I had ever

known Kevin to express but which I failed to hear, "God knows, I've tried. But you keep slipping away on me, Cassie. Every day, you slip away a little more."

"I haven't slipped anywhere. I'm right here, Kevin," I responded.

"We don't even speak the same language anymore," he said, and got up to hang his tie on the rack. He brushed his teeth, put on his nightshirt, slipped into bed, then turned to his side, pretending sleep.

He was right. We no longer spoke the same language. I never realized until Elba's NDE how much I longed to know the meaning of life, and if there was one point in my search for the Wayshower that's where it began. Elba was so down-to-earth, so honest and genuine that I had to believe her, and when I looked her up a few weeks before she died she made a lasting impression on me.

She was so resolved and comfortable with herself that she radiated a sense of peace that calmed my every concern. It was like being in the presence of something holy. "I can go now," she said, as she poured our tea.

"Go? Are you talking about dying, Elba?" I asked, fearfully.

"Yes, dear. I can go now. My daughter is strong enough to look after Suzie. She needed me. That's why I had to come back. But I'm ready to go now. My Jim's waiting for me."

"You don't want to die just yet, do you Elba?" I said.

"Oh, I've lived my life, dear," she answered, with a far-away sound to her grandmotherly voice. Her eyes were far away too. "It's been a good life. Lots of hardships, mind you. But I can't complain. I have a lot to be thankful for. The good Lord's been kind to me. I don't want to die, but after I met my Jim I'm not afraid to die anymore. I see him all the time in my dreams now. He told me it won't be long now. I don't want to leave my granddaughter, but my daughter's got herself a good man now. They're doing real fine. My work here is done, dear. My Jim's waiting for me," Elba concluded, and drifted off somewhere in deep reverie.

It was Elba's near-death experience and her attitude about dying that attracted me to Doctor Raymond Moody and his study of near-death experiences, and to the remarkable doctor who also pioneered the study of death and dying and who's memorable words became my life motto: *"The only thing I know that truly heals people is unconditional love."*

I was so inspired by "the Vulture," as Doctor Kubler-Ross was so cruelly called by her cynical detractors, that I became obsessed with the idea of dying with grace and dignity, and I geared my life towards palliative care nursing.

I would learn from the dying how to live my own life so when my time came I wouldn't die alone and loveless like my father; but I could not share this with Kevin. It was enough that he teased me by calling me "Mother Teresa's little helper." What would he have called me had I told him that I wanted to learn from my patients how to die with grace and dignity, "Mother Teresa's little nut case?"

I left River Bend Hospital because it was time to move on. I had to be close to death again, and I had to learn from it. I went back to St. Paul's, to the geriatric ward for two years, and then I went into palliative care nursing. I was intensely happy at first, but I began to have a gnawing feeling that this would not last, and after only three years in palliative care I became more restless than ever; but I had nowhere to turn now.

I was alone with the shame and guilt of my abortion. My mother could not bring herself to forgive me for taking the life of her third granddaughter, nor could I forgive myself. My anguish was so unbearable that I had to do something desperate after my uncle Father Clancy pushed me over the edge into the abyss of suicidal despair, so I left the Church for good.

It broke my mother's heart. But I had no choice. I could no longer suffer the guilt of my selfish decision. It didn't matter to me if I begged for God's forgiveness, I had taken the life of my daughter Seana, and I did not deserve forgiveness from God. Nevertheless, I felt compelled to go to confession.

"Bless me, Father, for I have sinned," I began, with a big lump in my throat. "It has been a while since my last confession," I sniffled, then wiped my eyes.

"Take your time, my child," the priest said.

"Father, I have done something so terrible…Oh God, forgive me for I have sinned. I have sinned, Father. I have committed the most terrible sin in the world. God will never forgive me. Never..."

I broke down again. My confessor waited patiently. "Calm yourself, my child. Whatever sin you have committed, our Lord Jesus in his infinite mercy will forgive you. Do you repent your sin, my child?"

"I have broken my own heart, Father. I cannot forgive myself for what I have done. I cannot. Please, Father, forgive me my most grievous sin..."

My confessor waited for me to stop crying. "There is no sin so grievous that our Lord Jesus Christ cannot forgive. He died on the cross for the sins of the whole world. What have you done, my child? Tell me your sin."

"I took the life of my own child. I broke the Sixth Commandment. I murdered my unborn child. I'm so sorry, Father. Oh God, forgive me. Please, Father, forgive me for I have sinned grievously."

There. It was finally out. I had said it. I had confessed my sin. My confessor waited for me to collect myself. "Why did you take the life of your unborn child?" he very softly asked, fearing I would break into tears again.

"I wanted to save my marriage, Father."

"Did your husband not want another child?"

"No."

"You could have given your child up for adoption."

"I was desperate, Father. I panicked. My husband left me. I tricked him to get pregnant, but he didn't want another child..."

I poured my heart out to my confessor, but I wish I hadn't. That was my last confession and the reason I left the Church for good. Something happened in that confessional box that I cannot explain. My last confession robbed me of something I would never get back. When I stepped out of that dark cubicle of sin and tears I left something behind that would be lost to me forever— my will, my pride, my dignity, my self-worth, maybe my very womanhood, the most precious piece of my Soul. I don't know what I left behind, but I never felt so empty, so alone, and so utterly abandoned in my entire life, like I had betrayed myself.

I couldn't understand it. I felt the opposite of how my confession was supposed to make me feel, and when I walked up to the altar to light a candle to the Blessed Virgin Mother after my confession, I knew in my heart that would be my last walk up to the altar of my Christian God who had taken from me what I most treasured about myself.

I had no remorse for how I felt, but it took forever to see why I could not get my mother to understand why I had to leave the Church. But one evening while doing the HU chant, I got my answer. I was sitting in my reading chair in the privacy of my bedroom. The children were asleep. As I softly sang the Love Song to God I focused my attention on my spiritual eye, a spot between my eyebrows and the window onto the spiritual worlds. I saw a dot of Blue Light. It seemed to come from a distance. I was drawn to the Blue Light, and before I knew it I was standing in front of the Living Atma Master, the spiritual leader of Atma-Gare!

Sri Herman Knecht was sitting behind his desk in his office at the Temple of Atma in Chaliceton, Minnesota. He looked exactly as he does in his physical body. He was dressed in a navy blue blazer with a white shirt and striped blue tie, and his eyes just shone with love. His hair was receding, and he was wearing glasses.

"Why is it so important to have your mother understand why you left your religion?" he asked me. His voice was so calm and kind it made me feel safe.

"I want her to understand me," I replied.

"It's not her time to understand," he said.

"She has to understand!" I shouted, to my horror.

I was so embarrassed I felt like crawling into a hole, but the Satma broke into a gentle laugh. "I would like to read you something," he said, and reached over and picked up a gilded, leather-bound volume titled *Immortal Poems of the English Language* resting on the right corner of his tidy desk. He opened it to the gold-tasseled bookmarker and read a poem called *Invictus*, by William Ernest Henly:

Out of the night that covers me
Black as the Pit from pole to pole

I thank whatever gods may be
For my unconquerable soul.
In the fell clutch of circumstance
I have not winced nor cried aloud.
Under the bludgeonings of chance
My head is bloody, but unbowed.
Beyond this place of wrath and tears
Looms but the horror of the shade,
And yet the menace of the years
Finds, and shall find me, unafraid.
It matters not how straight the gate,
How charged with punishments the scroll,
I am the master of my fate:
I am the captain of my soul."

I returned to my body with the last line ringing loudly in my ears, *"I am the captain of my soul."* I opened my eyes and stared into my bedroom in absolute wonder. I could not believe what had just happened!

After ten or fifteen minutes of processing my incredible experience with the Satma, my Inner Master, I recorded it in my journal.

I was the master of my fate, but I still had to convince my mother why I left the Church. I honestly did not know why I had to convince her, I just did; but the harder I tried to get her blessing the angrier she became, so I went to see my uncle Timothy. If I could get him to understand why I left the Church, maybe my mother would give me her blessing. But it was a foolish thing to do...

"For the love of Jesus, Patty, when are you going to come back to your good senses?" he said to me, with a paternal impatience that killed all hope.

"Please, Uncle Tim, it's important to me," I pleaded.

"What? What's so important to you now?" he impatiently asked.

Uncle Timothy was my father's brother, and a Jesuit priest. He was sitting in his big black leather chair behind his ornate walnut desk working on his Sunday sermon. I dropped in to see him one Saturday morning as I often did after I did my grocery shopping.

"I have to ask you something. It's very important," I said, very nervous.

"What?" he curtly replied.

"Are you a happy priest, Uncle Tim?" I asked, but no sooner did the question come out of my mouth than I felt like a needy little girl again.

"Now what kind of fool question is that, Patty?"

"Are you?" I asked again. My voice sounded so strange to me that it felt like a little girl trying to sound like a grown-up. My legs were trembling.

"I'm as happy as the next priest," he replied, and took out his package of Export plain cigarettes from his shirt pocket. His hand was shaking as he lit his cigarette. He took several long drags of smoke and exhaled. "Now tell me what you're leading up to," he asked, through a fog of cloudy, pale blue smoke.

"Do you ever question your faith, Uncle Tim?" I asked.

My uncle stared deep and hard into my eyes and then picked up his coffee cup and drank the remainder in one gulp. I knew it wasn't coffee.

"There's not much point in that now, is there?" he said.

"Please, Uncle Tim. It's important for me to know."

He stood up and focused his deep-set, little dark eyes on me. They took on a look that I had become very familiar with at River Bend Hospital. It was fear.

He picked up his cup but forgot that it was empty. He scowled at me. "Like I said, there's not much point in that now, is there?"

"Why not," I pressed him. "If you have doubts about your faith how can you go on living it? That's all I'm trying to say. I doubted my faith, Uncle Tim. I believed my faith would see me through anything, but it didn't. It failed me. Besides, I had an experience with my unborn child that my faith cannot explain. I had no choice, Uncle Tim. I had to look for answers outside my faith. I had to, for my own peace of mind..."

"To a point, to a point," he replied gruffly. My uncle was only five feet five inches tall, and quite stodgy. He was dwarfed by his big desk and leather chair, but he seemed to be much smaller to me that day. He took a long drag on his unfiltered cigarette, exhaled another cloud of smoke and said, "Let's not waste my time. What's on your mind, child?"

I hated being called child. His condescension made me angry. "I don't believe in eternal damnation anymore," I said, sounding just like my mother when she had something to get off her chest. "I believe we come into this world as many times as necessary to learn our lessons. I no longer believe that we only live one lifetime, because that doesn't make sense to me anymore. I believe in reincarnation now, so all I want from you is to know if it's not my right to believe what I want? Is it not my right? Tell me the truth, Uncle Tim. I have to know."

"It's your father all over again," my uncle replied, with contempt in his raspy voice. "*'I am the way, the truth, and the life; no man cometh unto the Father but by me,'* said Jesus. What more proof do you want, child? God sacrificed his only begotten Son on the cross to save us from the false gods of this world. Reincarnation is a false god. This oriental teaching is a wicked god of the mind that gives false hope to people. It's the Trickster's handiwork. Now put a stop to all this foolish thinking and come back to the Church, Patty. You don't need anything else in your life when you have our Lord Jesus Christ..."

"I want to pursue this, Uncle Tim" I replied, begging like a little girl.

"What is there to pursue?" he replied. "All you need to know you can find in Holy Scripture. Don't fill your head with false hope, Patty O'Shaunnesy. It's not healthy for your mind. I tell you, it's not healthy. Look at what happened to your father, may God have mercy on his wretched Soul..."

"My father suffered from clinical depression!" I shot back, coming to my father's defense. "He was sick, Uncle Tim!"

"The Devil works in mysterious ways," replied my uncle in his imperial voice, which spoke for the Church."Your father, my too-clever-by-half little brother, was driven to the bottle by the wretched demons of his own tortured mind. We tried everything, but he wouldn't listen to us. He was too clever for his own good. That's what killed your father..."

"What? What killed him?" I asked, fighting back my anger.

"His own demons. So don't you become like your father. Don't think you know better than the Church, Patty..."

"Clinical depression killed my father, not alcohol!" I fired back, choking back my tears. "My father was a brilliant man. He hated being depressed, Uncle Tim! That's why he took his own life!"

"Believe what you want, but your father's suicide was the Devil's handiwork," my uncle replied, with the cold detachment of a brain surgeon. "Your father was clever; but he wasn't clever enough for Old Nick, was he? Watch out for these new ideas, Patty. They glitter like stars in the night sky, but where's their light in the day? Can these new ideas take you through the narrow gate? No, they cannot. Only Jesus can. Jesus Christ is the light of the world, not these false gods of the mind!"

"Are you referring to reincarnation?" I challenged my uncle.

"By God, yes!" he exclaimed, pounding his pudgy little fist on his desk. His puffy face was all red now. He picked up his cup but it was still empty. He banged it down on his desk with disgust. "Reincarnation is a false god that's been haunting us for generations! It will destroy your Soul, child! Come back to Jesus, Patty O'Shaunnesy! Jesus Christ is the light of the world! Jesus Christ will lead you out of the valley of darkness! Come back to your faith for your mother's sake! Come back before it's too late!"

"No, I won't!" I shot back in anger. *"*My father was right! Christianity is built on nothing but blind faith and fear. You're afraid of new ideas, Uncle Tim! You're so afraid that you have to hide behind your faith! You don't want to grow in truth. That's why my father left the Church. He couldn't suffer the suffocation. And that's why I left too!"

"By God, you're just like your godless father!" he shouted, pounding both of his fists on the desk. "There's no hope for you either, is there?"

"I guess not, Uncle Tim," I replied, with surprising calmness. "I can't accept life on blind faith anymore. If I'm like my father, I'm proud of it. I can't believe a loving God can be so cruel as to punish Souls in hellfire for eternity. Father was right. Fear keeps Christians locked up where..."

"Where?" my uncle exclaimed. *"Where?"*

"In your own private hell, that's where," I replied. "Fear is the stupid man's hell, Uncle Tim. That's what my father used to say, and I believe him now. I can't live in fear anymore. I'd rather believe in reincarnation and be wrong than live my life in the fear of Christianity. My father told me before he died to choose my God carefully. Well, Uncle Tim, I've chosen reincarnation over Christianity. If I'm wrong I'll have to live with it, but at least I won't have to live with the guilt of my abortion any longer. You can keep your faith, Uncle Tim. I don't need it anymore. I'm sorry for taking up your precious time."

"Old Nick's got himself another clever one!" my uncle shot back, but his words sounded so hollow that I wanted to laugh. "*'He that followeth me shall not walk in darkness,'"* sayeth the Lord, "*'but shall have the Light of life.'* Read the Holy Book, Patty O'Shaunnesy. It's all there! Save yourself while you've still got some sense in that stubborn head of yours..."

"I've read the Holy Book, but I can't make sense of it. There are too many contradictions in the Bible. I don't know what to believe in it anymore. I can't come back to the Church, Uncle Tim. I can't fight it any longer. I've made my decision, and I'll live with it."

"*'Straight is the gate and narrow is the way which leadeth unto life, and few there be that find it,'* sayeth our Lord!" my uncle responded, with fire in his blood-shot eyes.

"Yes," I said, "but he also said that anyone who drinks old wine does not want new wine because the old wine is better. Why, Uncle Tim? Why is the old wine better than new wine? Yesterday's truth is no more valid than today's truth. Truth is truth, is it not? Why is the Church so afraid of new ideas? Tell me that, Uncle Tim?"

"You're perverting the Holy Book just like your godless father! That's the Devil's handiwork! I'll pray for you, Patty O'Shaunnesy!"

"Please don't. I don't need your prayers, Uncle Tim," I answered.

"Then may God have mercy on your Soul!" he shouted at me as I walked out of his nicotine drenched office and the one true religion that had taught me from childhood to believe everything that I was told without question.

Chapter 5

My Sister-Friend

My Christian faith was my life, and although Kevin was my husband, my lover, my best friend and father of my children he was not what I lived my life for; I lived to fulfill myself. It was a selfishness that I never understood because I am by nature a giving and generous person, but I had fulfilled myself all I could in Jesus Christ; that's why it was so much harder to let go of my faith than it was my husband.

My abortion changed that. It was the turning point of my life. It put everything on the line, and my faith failed me. My abortion forced me to die to what I believed was the soul of my existence, and as unfortunate as it was Kevin was part of this cruel death. There was no instant rebirth though, and I wandered blindly in a spiritual wasteland for months. I did not know who I was, and for the longest time I feared I would end up just as lost as my father.

Like my mother, my uncle Father Timothy O'Flanagan used his faith to hide from the truth of who he was, but the veils of illusion were rent from my eyes when I aborted my daughter Seana. I had read all the Edgar Cayce literature I could get my hands on and dozens of books on reincarnation because I had a consuming interest in past lives, but like most Christians who believe they are open-minded I never took myself as seriously as I should have until my abortion forced me to question the fundamental premise of my faith.

Had I been as open-minded about reincarnation as I thought I was, I would not have suffered the guilt and shame my abortion put me through. After I worked my way through the unbearable pain, I had to decide what spiritual path I was going to live by because I needed a new faith to see myself through life. I got no support from my family during this critical period in my life, and this hurt me more than I could bear.

It was imperative that my family understood why I had to leave the Church. I had to have their blessing. When I never got it, I felt betrayed. It was like dying another death all over again. My abortion and breakup with my husband became my rite of passage from my blind Roman Catholic faith to a bold and unpredictable new way of experiencing my own vulnerable life, and I welcomed the painful change.

Like my favorite saint, I died daily during this dark night of Soul, and although I never experienced a miraculous rebirth like St. Paul did on the road to Damascus every once in a while I enjoyed a momentary rapture. One such moment came with my sister-friend.

Carol and I rekindled our high school friendship when I brought our dog Tiger to her clinic in Burnaby. Carol Hennessey was a veterinarian and a widow with two children in grade school, but still not quite ready to get involved with another man. Her husband died of a massive heart attack while playing scrub hockey with his college buddies and had been dead two years, which was when our friendship really mattered to Carol.

"What's the occasion this time?" she asked when she stepped into my foyer with a bottle of white wine from her special reserve. Carol and I made the rounds every year to our favourite BC wineries and stocked up for special occasions. I invited her for wine and cheese and sushi that Saturday evening after my abortive talk with Uncle Timothy.

The children were staying with their father in his new house for the weekend, and I wanted to let my hair down and cut loose. After I walked out of Uncle Tim's office I felt such relief that I had to share the joy of letting go of the last hold my blind Christian faith had upon my battered, exhausted Soul, and so I called my sister-friend Carol.

Uncle Tim was like a second father to me when I was growing

up. No one else in the family but my father and Uncle Tim called me Patty. I reminded them of my grandfather O'Flanagan, whom I had never known; but the closer I got to my uncle with the probing spiritual questions I felt compelled to ask him as I grew older, the less relevant he seemed to be in my life, and I saw less and less of him as I made my own way through life's corridors.

I didn't want to see my uncle for who he really was because I couldn't betray him, but watching him Saturday morning scurry behind his faith made me feel sorry for him. For years I had read Uncle Timothy's tough Irish exterior as a sign of a strong character, but when he refused to deal with the question of reincarnation by calling it a false god of the mind I saw my uncle for what he had become—a good priest, but a pitiably weak man.

My father's words rang loudly in my mind as I listened to my uncle: *"I would sooner take my own life than live the life of a lie like my Jesuit brother!"*

"Freedom!" I shouted, grabbing Carol's arm and ushering her into the living room. "Now take your sweater off and let's celebrate!"

"Freedom?" Carol asked. "Did you and Kevin settle up?"

"Yes. But that's not what I want to celebrate tonight."

"What, then?"

"Freedom from tyranny!" I hollered.

"Oh," Carol said, with a look in her eye.

"Don't look at me like that! I haven't lost it, Carol! I'm fine. I am, honestly. I'm just happy, that's all! I'm the happiest I've been in a long time, and I want to share my happiness with my sister-friend!"

"Good!" Carol exclaimed, still unsure of me. "I'm glad you're happy. You deserve to be happy. You're a good person. Good people deserve to be happy. I'm a good person too. I deserve to be just as happy as you. *So let's be happy together, sister-friend!"*

Carol caught the spirit. "Here," I said, handing her a glass of white wine which I had waiting for us on the coffee table. "Let's toast to my newfound freedom!"

"To your freedom!" Carol shouted, and took a long drink. Incidentally," she said, mocking a serious look, "Would it be too much to ask what tyranny you're referring to?"

"The lie!" I shouted, and hoisted my half-empty glass into the air.

"What lie, might I ask?" Carol queried, with a mock frown on her strikingly beautiful, fine-boned Irish face. "Your marriage? I was under the impression that you had a very good marriage. You are a good person, are you not, sister-friend?"

"Indeed, I am a good person," I replied, in that same mock ironic tone that Carol and I often imitated when the whimsical spirit of our friendship possessed us, but reality quickly overcame me. "I did have a happy marriage, didn't I? But I was too stupid to see it. Oh, Carol, what have I done? I drove Kevin away because I had to find myself. Can you believe it? I was too goddamn busy looking for myself to notice that I was driving my husband away!"

"Yeah, right into Belinda's bed," Carol sighed, and slumped her shapely body into the sofa chair with an overwehelming sense of empathic resignation.

"It could have been any woman, Carol. I blew it. That's the long and short of it. I really blew it. *But I don't want to talk about my marriage!*" I shouted. "I want to celebrate my newfound freedom from the BIG LIE!"

"Okay!" Carol exclaimed, springing to life. "Incidentally, if you will pardon my dim veterinarian wit, what big lie might ye be talking about?"

"I went to visit Uncle Timothy today."

"I should have known!" Carol exclaimed. "He wants the lost lamb to come back into the fold, doesn't he?"

"Oh, he tried, Carol! Believe me, he tried! But you know what? He doesn't intimidate me anymore. I went to him hoping he would understand why I left the Church, but he wouldn't let up. Not on your life! But when he started in on all that nonsense about false gods I knew that something was definitely off center. *I just knew it, Carol!"*

"What false gods might ye be referring to, child?" Carol asked, mocking my uncle's condescending manner.

I burst into laughter. After we had a good laugh, I refilled our glasses and held mine up again. "Here's to the false gods of the mind that have finally freed me from the tyrannical god of my blind

Christian faith!"

"*AAAAAAAAMEN!*" Carol chorused in her beautiful singing voice with her glass high in the air in celebratory closure. She had broken away from the Catholic Church when she was only fifteen, but I never judged her. Carol was an only child, and wanted desperately to have a sister, and so did I; that's why we were such close friends in school. I broke into belly laughter. It felt so good to share my experience with my sister-friend that tears came to my eyes. When I settled down, I had to tell her my experience with Uncle Timothy.

"You won't believe it, Carol. It was the strangest experience of my life. It wasn't my uncle I was talking to this morning. My uncle was just an empty little man who spoke for the hollow spirit of the Roman Catholic Church. I can't explain it, Carol. It was surreal. That's why I want to celebrate. I knew with absolute certainty when I walked out of my uncle's office that I was no longer a Christian. *I'm no longer a Roman Catholic, Carol! I know that in the marrow of my bones now!* I'm no longer a Christian of any kind. It may be okay for some people, but I just can't stomach that faith anymore. It's so narrow-minded that it stifles me just thinking about it. That's the freedom I'm celebrating!"

"*To Cassie's freedom!*" Carol hollered, hoisting her glass high into the air again. "To freedom from the tyranny of blind Christian faith!"

"You've got it! By God, you've got it!"

"*She's got it! She's got it!*" Carol shouted, picking up on the spirit of *My Fair Lady*, one of our favorite movies. "*By God, she's got it!*"

Once again, we rolled in laughter.

After we caught our breath, Carol said, "So, what took you so long?"

"Oh yeah, smarty pants! Just because you were a little atheist most of your life doesn't make you any less trapped than I was, sister-friend!"

"Ohhhh, nasty, nasty! Well, I'll have you know, Miss Happy Christian drop-out, that I graduated from that soul-crushing Nietzschean school of thought to the intoxicating bliss of simple agnosticism, and I'm happy to inform you, Cassie O'Shaunnesy, that

I've renounced all association with those godless bastards and have acquired a membership into the spiritual race of man; so my dear sister-friend, here's to the death of my own BIG LIE!"

"Quelle coincidence!" I shouted, and jumped up and pulled Carol out of the chair and gave her a big hug and held her in my arms. "Now we're sister-friends in spirit! *"Here's to sister-friends everywhere!"*

"To sister-friends in freedom!" Carol shouted.

We drank our wine and poured another and nibbled on the cheese and crackers and sushi platters that I had picked up especially for the occasion, as we always did whenever we got together to boost each other's spirit and celebrate our friendship.

"So, tell me," I said, mocking her mock seriousness again. "When exactly did you come to see the light? Perchance, on the road to Kitsalano?"

Carol smiled her million-dollar smile, showing her perfectly straight pearl white teeth, which cost her a vacation to Florida. "I don't know," she replied, speaking frankly. "It just happened a while back, maybe six, seven months ago. It's an awful burden being an atheist, Cassie. Atheists are such snobs. I don't like being a snob. You don't think I'm a snob, do you?"

"You, a snob? *Get real!"*

"You don't think so?" Carol pleaded, mockingly.

"How can you be a snob? You're my friend, aren't you?"

Carol keeled over. I watched her rollicking with laughter and my heart opened up and tears came gushing to my eyes. *How I loved her!*

Carol never judged me. Not once did she question me as I explored all those spiritual teachings, but I hurt her when I tried to take my own life. I hurt my sister-friend deeply. She cried at the thought of losing me. She was so mad at me she would not speak to me for three months. She made me realize just how selfish suicide really is.

I loved Carol. I trusted her. That's why I opened up to her about the new religon of the Light and Sound of God. I had to share my exciting new spiritual path with her, which was not founded upon blind faith but personal experience...

"It's what I've been looking for my whole life," I said to her, over a glass of iced tea in the shade of her resplendent flowering apple tree in her back yard shortly after I became a member. "It's so fantastic it would blow your mind if I told you how I found Atma-Gare."

"I'll blow your mind if you don't tell me!" Carol exclaimed.

"Of course I'll tell you," I said, and laughed; and I told her about my dream with the Satma, then seeing him eight years later in Fred's room in the hospital, and later on video at the introductory talk on Atma-Gare.

Carol didn't bat an eye. She knew I wouldn't lie to her. She believed me instantly, and rather than pass judgment on me like my family did she accepted Atma-Gare without trying to make heads or tails of it, and for that I loved my sister-friend dearly. But my Roman Catholic faith still had an insidious hold on me that I could not let go of...

"So, what else did Uncle Timothy have to say to you?" she asked, bringing me back to the present. I was welling up with tears again.

"What else is there?" I said, fighting back my tears of love. "Oh, he wanted me to pray to Jesus and save myself. I didn't have the heart to tell uncle Tim that I didn't leave Jesus when I left the Church. I left my religion, Carol, not Jesus Christ. I still love Jesus. I just don't believe in Christianity anymore, that's all. Uncle Tim may be a Jesuit priest, but he's no different than any other Christian who accepts the meaning of life on blind faith alone. I can't do that anymore. Experience has become my new faith. That's why I joined Atma-Gare. It's an individual spiritual path. We grow in spirit according to our own experiences. I couldn't share that with my uncle. He's terrified of any teaching that threatens his faith. He's reduced himself to calling them false gods. Can you believe it, Carol? A Jesuit priest? And in this day and age?"

"What false gods?" Carol asked.

"In this case, reincarnation. Uncle Tim said something this morning that sent a cold chill up my spine. 'Reincarnation is a false god that has been haunting us for generations,' he said. A red flag went up, Carol. Christianity has built a wall around itself. It refuses to let anyone out, and it scares the hell out of Christians when someone breaks out of their fortress of blind faith. Carol, my mother's convinced I'm going to pack up and pitch a tent in front of Shirley MacLaine's house!"

Carol laughed. She knew about my mother's neurotic fixation with Shirley MacLaine. "Just let her be, Cassie. You're mother is what she is. She can't help herself."

"Yes. I know," I said.

"What else did Uncle Timothy say this morning?"

"He tried to win me back to the fold by quoting Jesus and telling me to read the scriptures, but I can't buy into that lie anymore. Not after what I've been through. Life's too short to be so stupid. That's what my father used to say. Christianity's a big con, Carol. A big confidence game like my father said it was. Well, I'm finally free of that game. Uncle Tim told me to come back to my senses, but I've never been more sensible in my life!"

"Here's to GOOD SENSE!" Carol shouted.

"And FREEDOM!" I replied.

"And FRIENDSHIP!" Carol toasted.

"And to SISTER-FRIENDS!" I returned.

"I LOVE YOU, CASSIE O'SHAUNNESY!"

"AND I LOVE YOU, CAROL HENNESSEY!"

We drank two more bottles of white wine from my special reserve with the sushi and half a bottle of Baileys Irish Cream, and the next morning we both paid for our indulgence; but I never felt so wonderful in my entire life. *I was finally free to be me!*

Chapter 6
A Man Called David Oakly

We all pay a price for being true to who we are. I was called to pay it with Father McDuffy's challenge to prove that a fetus is not a little person, but I couldn't come forward with my miracle story. It was too far outside the box. No one would believe me. I never told anyone about my unborn child. I wanted to tell my mother, but I couldn't. She would have thought I had lost my mind for sure.

I tried to push Father McDuffy's challenge out of my mind, but it wouldn't go away. It was like a bad rash. I was at my wit's end, so I called my son Mark into my bedroom one evening to reaffirm the memory of my experience with Seana.

All of my children saw Seana before I aborted her body, but Mark was the most excited by the experience. He knew who she was, and he called her by name as he watched her playing with her toes on his bed. "Mom, I don't remember very well," he said, with a disappointed frown.

"You're not much help," I said, and gently slapped him on the shoulder.

"Sorry, mom. Now if you want me to teach you how to work with Sam, I'm your man," he proudly boasted.

Sam was his computer, and Mark was our family expert.

"Thank you, Mark," I said, and gave him a hug. "So, what do you think I should do about Father McDuffy's challenge?"

"Go for it! We could use some cash flow around here!"

"We can always use some cash flow, but do you think it's a good idea?"

"I don't know, Mom. Why don't you ask your new friend David?"

David Oakly was an Atman I had recently met at the Convention Center in Minneapolis and whom I had enthusiastically told my children about. He was also attending the annual Atma Springtime Seminar, and I was startled to learn that he was from Wyedale...

"You must be kidding?" I said to him.

"Can you imagine that, Wyedale of all places?" he said, with a twinkle in his bright blue eyes; and then he added, "The Golden-tongued Wisdom of Atma must be telling us something, Cassie. That's how Rumi met Shams of Tabriz."

"I beg your pardon?" I said, with some confusion.

"There are no coincidences," he replied, with a glowing smile.

From the moment we shook hands in the Book Room at the seminar, I knew that David Oakly was different from any Atman I had ever met. I felt something flow from him to me when we clasped hands, a subtle energy, a feeling of something very special.

Just short of six feet tall, he was dressed in blue denim jeans and a white polo shirt that showed off his taut, well-toned body. He had the most clear, penetrating, steel-blue eyes I had ever seen, beautiful white teeth, and longish, thick, sandy-blond hair that called to have my fingers run through it, and a flat stomach that I noticed instantly because he reminded me of my favorite actor. Robert Redford had a flat stomach in every movie that he made, and David conjured up the image of Redford's role as the indomitable, lone trapper Jeremiah Johnson.

He instantly attracted me, like iron filings to a powerful magnet; but not quite like that, though. His magnetism had the paradoxical effect of attracting me and pushing me away from him at one and the same time. It was the strangest effect that any man ever had on me, and it made me quiver with excitement.

"How come I've never seen you at any Atma functions?" I asked, staring at him in wonder. I had attended a number of Atma functions in Georgian Bay since we moved to Wyedale the previous summer, but I had not seen David once.

"I only attend Atma functions when the spirit moves me," he replied, as if they didn't matter to him. "The truth is, Cassie, I find them boring."

"Boring?" I said, with surprise. "You're not serious, are you?"

"Of course I am," he said, with such matter-of-factness that I knew he was totally sincere. "Soul's journey through life is a journey of the alone to the Alone," he declared, as though we were old friends, "but I have yet to meet one Atman who realizes this. The Atma is life, life is the Way, and the *now* is where it's at for me. Life is my *satsang,* Cassie. You're the new head nurse at the Wyedale Community Hospital, aren't you?"

Mystified by his surprising commentary, I was more startled by his knowledge of me. "Yes, I am," I said, unable to hide my astonishment. *"How did you know?"*

"Doctor Jordon's a friend of mine," he replied.

"Oh," I said, delighted because Doctor Jordon was one of my favorite people in Wyedale. "What do you do for a living, David, if you don't mind my asking?"

"I'm a building contractor. I just built a new house in Wyedale. I'll be flipping it after I get my occupancy permit, but I'm going to live in it for a year or so first."

"A building contractor?" I said, again taken by surprise. "By the way you talk I would have thought you were a writer or something."

"Does it show?" he said, and laughed. "The truth is, I enjoy writing. Especially Sufi poetry," he added, with a new glint in his alluring, but enigmatic eyes. "I'm also working on a translation of the Sufi allegory *Conference of the Birds*, by the poet Fariduddin Attar."

"Oh. And what is Sufi poetry?" I asked, now more intrigued than ever by the most fascinating Atman, let alone man, I had ever met. Not only was David Oakly fascinating, but so easy on my eyes that my heart skipped a beat the moment I saw him!

" 'Tell it unveiled, the naked truth! The declaration's better than the secret,'" he boldly announced, obviously quoting someone I was not familiar with. "That's from *The Masnavi*, by the Sufi poet Jalaluddin Rumi," he added, his eyes sparkling. "It's time to let the cat

out of the bag, as it were. Rumi did so in his own way and in his own time with his poetry, and I'm doing so in my poetry within the exciting new context of today's Atma paradigm."

Completely mystified, I replied, "You've lost me, David."

He laughed. It was a jocular, rich laugh. "Let me spell it out for you in Atma terminology. 'There are no secrets. Truth is a simple thing. It is only the way that man looks at it that makes it appear complicated,' said the great Atma Master Zak Tarzman. Western society's fascination with Rumi's poetry today reflects man's spiritual hunger for truth. The sad truth is that man cannot find truth by looking for it, but only by living his life to the fullest. It's in the living that truth reveals itself, Cassie. That's the heart of Rumi's poetry and the Atma's basic teaching, which I'm trying to convey in my own poetry. As the inscrutable Sufi folk hero Mullah Nasrudin might say: *the light shines from within; dig your own way out of the darkness!*"

David cracked a mischievous smile, and then broke into an ironic chuckle. I smiled also; and then, to David's astonishment I said, "I can relate to that."

"You can?" he said, with obvious surprise.

"Yes," I said, with a confident smile at the memory of how I had dug my own way out of the darkness of my suicidal despair.

"Fascinating! Would it be too much to ask you to elaborate?"

"We've only just met, David. Perhaps when we get to know each other a little better," I replied, resisting the strongest urge to wink at him.

For some reason, I sensed that he was available.

"Touche!" he said, and laughed. Then, with a bemused look on his strong-chinned, handsome face that signaled encouragement, he gave me his hand. "You're a real treat, Cassie O'Shaunnesy. I look forward to seeing more of you when we get back home."

"I'd love that," I said, trying to conceal my excitement.

Although I hoped to see David again at the seminar, the only time I saw him was in the Book Room. I checked the Book Room off and on throughout the seminar, but I never saw him again. I didn't expect him to return though, because he left with a stack of new Atma books and tapes under his arm. I kept a watchful eye for him Saturday evening through all the guest speakers' talks, as well as the Living Atma Master's Sunday morning talk, but I couldn't spot him anywhere. That didn't surprise me, though. There were over three thousand Atmans at the Minneapolis Convention Center.

We were a sea of seekers from all over the world who had found our ideal path in the new religion of Atma-Gare, and the love that I experienced at my first major Atma seminar was so palpable that it stayed with me for weeks after I returned to Wyedale.

The next time I saw David was not in Wyedale, though. Surprisingly enough, I met him again at an Atma Worship Service in Newmarket the third Sunday after I came home from Minneapolis. Once again, my heart skipped a beat when I saw him. Something about him excited me more than a romantic interest. He had the same effect on me that a booster cable has on a weak battery, and this both excited and mystified me. I couldn't take my eyes off him.

He walked into the public library room late. The worship service was just about to begin, but the moment he stepped into the room the atmosphere changed instantly. It seemed to be charged by his presence, and everyone just stared at him.

This was the first time that I noticed it, but whenever David walked into a room, he didn't suck the oxygen out of the room like highly charismatic people such as movie stars or politicians often do; he did just the opposite: *he charged the room with energy!*

Edgar Smallwood, a Higher Initiate, jumped out of his chair and dashed over to David and embraced him like he was a prodigal son, and then he dashed to the back of the room to get him a chair. I wanted David to sit beside me, so I got up and pulled my chair aside to make room for his chair. Edgar placed David's chair next to mine.

David looked at me, smiled, and casually said, "Fancy meeting you here, Cassie O'Shaunnesy." Then he turned and said hello to the attractive, smartly dressed blonde to his immediate left. I had met her before, at an Atma Worship Service in Barrie, and I knew she was a divorcee with two children going to university.

Anoria gave David a warm, extended hug. Obviously they knew each other, because I caught an expression on her face that sent up a red flag. There was more to her hug than met the eye, and for the first time since my divorce all of my primal mating instincts came alive. Despite how good and wonderful a person Anoria may have been, I knew we were rivals. Just then I heard the cleric say, "Are we ready for the HU now?"

"Yes," Edgar Smallwood replied, and we closed our eyes and sang the Love Song to God for three or four minutes. When the HU came to a gentle close we sat in silence for a few more minutes, and then the Atma cleric said, "May the blessings be," and we opened our eyes and soaked in the uplifting spiritual energy that we had channeled through into the library room and into the city of Newmarket and the world with our Love Song to God.

But aside from all the uplifting spiritual energy in the room from our HU chant, I still felt David's presence beside me like a high voltage electric current, and once again his magnetism had the same effect on me as it did when we met in Minneapolis!

I wanted to get closer to him. But something about him kept me from doing so. It was the strangest sensation I had ever experienced.

I also felt Anoria's presence, and my instincts told me her relationship with David was more than just friends. I was frantically scrambling for a strategy when the cleric announced, "Today's talk is called Dreams, Atma Masters, and You. I'm going to read a passage from one of the Living Atma Master's books, and then we're going to split into smaller groups and share any experiences we had with the Satma or other Atma Masters. You don't have to share if you don't want to. And in fifteen minutes we're going to reunite into one circle and talk about them."

After the reading she got up and counted the number of people in the circle and broke us up into four groups of five people. The last group had one extra person. This was our group. We were all women except for David. Someone pointed this out to him and he said, "That's fine with me. I'm more comfortable with women than I am with men."

We all laughed, but I caught the look that Anoria gave David and I knew for certain now that they were or had been involved. I felt threatened.

When David walked into the library room he was carrying a blue Hilroy spiral-bound notebook in his left hand, the smaller size of the same kind of notebook that I used for my journals, and a cup of Tim Hortons tea. With his notebook on his lap, he took a sip of tea. "Who wants to begin?" he asked, assuming group leadership.

"I'll start," said Colleen, a short, elfin-looking woman with a small hump on her right shoulder, and she shared her experience with the Atma Master Jivan Nuri, guardian of the Atma bible, the *Shariyatma* at the spiritual city of Saguna in the Hindu Kush Mountains, who often came to her in her dreams and danced with her. Colleen loved to dance with this Atma Master. It freed her from her life's concerns, and she woke up from these dreams feeling rested, blessed, and full of inspiration. Her experience opened the door for David to talk about the Sufi order of the whirling dervishes that Rumi had established.

"This Sufi sect use the whirling dance to center themselves in what some people call the stillpoint," he explained. "But it's much more than that. This whirling dance releases Soul from the consciousness of the lower self. That's the central mystery of the whirling dervishes. Has anyone here experienced the whirling dervish dance?"

No one had. David continued, "I have several tunes. It's a sacred dance. If you get an opportunity to see a group of Sufis do this dance, it's worth taking in. It will transport you. Coincidentally," he added, glancing at me with a smile that I read as an encouraging sign, "Vision TV had a documentary on the whirling dervishes on the Mind, Body, and Spirit channel this week. It was called *Rumi: Turning Ecstatic.* Did anyone see it?"

No one else had. My friend Grace who was sitting to my immediate right, said, "I saw a movie on the whirling dervishes last summer with an Atman friend. She's a Rumi lover, but I don't remember the name of the movie."

"*The Burning Within,*" David replied.

"I think that's it. You saw it too?" Grace said.

"Yes. Vision TV also put that out. Back to the topic. Does anyone else have an experience with the Satma or an Atma Master they would like to share? If not, I have one I'd be happy to share with you."

"*I have one!*" Grace said excitedly.

"Oh, good," Colleen said.

"I don't know what made me think of this experience. I haven't thought of it for years," Grace began, her voice a little nervous. "This happened before I came into Atma-Gare. It was with Paul Mathew. I was going to have my fortune read by a psychic."

"What year was this?" Anoria interrupted.

"1970," Grace replied.

"When did Paul Mathew die?" Anoria asked.

Paul Mathew, the modern day founder of the ancient spiritual path of Atma, was the Satma, the Living Atma Master before he died of a heart attack in 1971. By a strange coincidence I had just read that information in the Atma-Gare dictionary, *The Celestial Sea of Words,* an hour before I went to the worship service that morning, so I very happily shared that information with my group even though I did it just to respond to Anoria.

"I never thought of that," Grace said excitedly.

Grace was excited because it meant that Paul Mathew had not yet died when she had her experience with him at her psychic reading. He was Soul traveling, and she saw him in his Atma Sarup, or Soul body.

"What happened, Grace?" I asked, as the thought of telling my own story with the Satma suddenly possessed me.

"The psychic couldn't read me," she explained. "I asked her why not, and she said there was a short man standing behind me who wouldn't let her read my fortune. I turned to look and I saw Paul Mathew!"

I smiled at Grace's experience with the Satma, the Living Atma Master of the time. My experience was with Paul's successor, Sri Herman Knecht, and I felt encouraged to share my own experience with the Satma. Actually I felt compelled to tell my story, because I wanted to add it to the growing cannon of Atma miracles. The thought even crossed my mind to send it to *The Atma-Gare Journal*. But I had to share it with other Atmans first to see how it would be received. I didn't want to come across as someone strange.

I nervously told my story. I didn't know what to expect, but I had no need to be nervous. David turned to me and softly said, as though sharing a secret with me, "There are those who seek the Atma, and there are those whom the Atma seeks out. You needed the eight years between your dream with the Satma and finding him in person. You needed that time to grow in spiritual consciousness enough to be pulled into the gravitational field of the Atma teachings. That's how the Divine Plan of God works."

After careful thought, I said, "Are you suggesting that it's only a matter of time before one finds the Atma teachings?"

"Exactly. Life is the real teacher. Experience makes Soul ready for the most direct path home to God, so if we don't get it right in this lifetime we just keep coming back until we do. Does anyone else have an experience they would like to share?"

No one spoke. David then offered his experience. I was on the edge of my chair because I knew it would bear his unique stamp.

"This just happened last month," he began. "I was nudged to visit an Atman friend in a community north of here, up in the Muskokas. I called her up and invited her out to lunch. She likes Chinese, so we went for the afternoon buffet. The waitress brought over three glasses of water. This intrigued me. I asked her why, and she said she thought there were three people at our table. Over lunch, my friend wanted to know about the Atma initiations. She had been a Fourth Initiate for nine years and was getting discouraged because it was taking so long to get her Fifth Initiation. Every initiation in Atma is important, but the Fifth Initiation takes the Atman out of the lower worlds and places Soul into the Soul Plane. This is where the individual Soul realizes the Atmashar state of consciousness, or what we know as spiritual self-realization consciousness. This is why the Fifth Initiation is so important, and it does take some Atmans much longer than others to get their Fifth Initiation. I explained to my friend why this was so, but I can't explain this now. The Atma gave me this information for her ears only. My friend had to hear this information to break the hold her mind had on her. When we finished lunch the waitress brought our bill and three fortune cookies. Again, I asked the waitress why three fortune cookies. Startled, she replied, `I don't know why, but I see three people sitting here.' She didn't actually see the Satma. She sensed his presence. We opened our fortune cookies. Then I asked my friend to open the third cookie, and it said, `*Good news will be coming to you soon.'* Two weeks later she got her pink slip in the mail for her Fifth Initiation."

"Wow! I can feel the energy of that whole experience," Anoria said, and then for some strange reason she got up and shifted her chair away from David and sat down again, but with the oddest expression on her face.

Why she shifted her chair away from David's, I didn't know. Was it his energy, or was she signaling me? She was just about to say something else when Charlene, who was the officiating cleric, called our attention. She asked us to put our chairs back into one big circle so we could share our personal experiences with the whole group.

We put our chairs back, but something very odd happened with David's chair that excited me at first but has bothered me ever since. This was my first definite waking dream experience, and proof that what I sensed about David Oakly was irrefutably true.

A waking dream is an anomalous experience that stands out of the ordinary events of life. It's the Atma, or Holy Spirit's way of telling us something that we need to know, and the image of David's solitary chair in our circle has burned itself into my mind!

When everyone stood up to place their chair back into one big circle, David went to the washroom. When he returned his chair was right where he left it. We had all moved our chairs back into one big circle, but there was a gap between David's chair and ours.

David picked up his notebook and teacup from his chair seat where he had placed them and sat down. He placed his cup on the floor, crossed his legs, and began writing in his notebook. Everyone stared at him.

After a few silent moments of intense scrutiny, he looked up from his notebook, glanced at everyone, and broke into laughter. "This is a waking dream. I'm in the circle, but I'm not in the circle. *Someone's telling you that I'm a lone wolf Atman!"*

Everyone erupted into laughter. David made no effort to move his chair. He kept it exactly where he had left it before he had gone to the washroom.

I knew that this anomaly spoke to what I felt about David from the moment I met him in Minneapolis, and why I had associated the image of the lone trapper Jeremiah Johnson with him. David was both a member and not a member of the Atma community. Like he said, he was in the circle but not of the circle. He sat alone. *This was his mystique, and the challenge of my life!*

I got up and self-consciously moved my chair a few inches closer to David's chair, but as I sat down I knew I had not moved close enough. I was still more one with the group circle than I was myself, and I knew in my heart that the only way to close that gap between David and me was to be more true to myself!

Nervously, I invited David for lunch after the service. Something about David Oakly so attracted me that I just had to find out what his secret was. To my joy, he accepted and suggested we go to Boston Pizza for a leisurely lunch, and the first thing I asked him over our Tuscan pizza and garden salad was, "What brought you to Atma-Gare, David?"

"The same thing that brought you," he replied.

"You know why I came to Atma-Gare. I told my story at the service. Why did you come to Atma-Gare?" I repeated, with a nervous feeling that I was prying.

He laughed, as though to himself. "Alright, I'll tell you," he said, to my relief. "I studied a number of teachings before I came into Atma-Gare, but it was Sufism that opened the door for me. After years of practicing the teaching with my Sufi Master, I was ready for the secret teachings of Atma. Fortunately for the world, the Atma teachings are no longer secret. This makes Atma-Gare the most fascinating spiritual teaching in the world today. Sadly, few people realize it."

"Why is that?" I asked, curious to hear his explanation.

"As I told you in Minneapolis, it depends upon one's level of consciousness what one's relationship with truth will be," he replied, which for some reason made me feel stupid for asking. That's when I learned to stay alert with David. "The more one experiences life, the more intimate his relationship with truth will be," he continued, in a lower voice; "and then one day he will become one with the Atma. Not everyone is ready for Atma-Gare. When life makes one ready, he will find his way to the Light Giver of the world. It's inevitable."

I paused before speaking. I didn't want to make a fool of myself.

But neither did I want David to think that I didn't have a mind of my own. "I'm beginning to realize this," I said, not quite satisfied by his answer. I was thinking of my family in particular.

I knew my mother wasn't ready for Atma-Gare, and neither were my uncle Tim and uncle Clancy. What exactly made one ready for Atma-Gare? And why Atma-Gare, anyway? This puzzled me, so I asked David to explain this mystery.

He picked up another piece of pizza, bit off the point and chewed it slowly, swallowed, and then he took a drink of his iced lemon water.

"That's a big mystery," he finally said, and took another sip of water. "We don't have a clear enough context to appreciate the purpose of life. If we did, we wouldn't be puzzled by these questions. The root of this mystery lies in the mistaken belief that intelligence and consciousness are one and the same thing. The mind and Soul are not the same. The mind is to Soul what a car is to the driver. Man believes that because he has the power to think he should be able to solve the riddle of life, but he's fooling himself. Yesterday I was listening to the radio while I worked, and the host of the show made a comment that makes my point. Bill Richardson was interviewing Mary Botsworth Frazer, who had written a book on her relationship with her brother called *Requiem for my Brother.* The theme was about death and dying. Being a skeptic, Richardson made a comment that makes my point. He said something to this effect. `Of all the billions of clever people in the world who have died, surely one of them would have figured out a way to send a message back to us from the other side to let us know they're still alive.' He was unsure of life after death. Like most people, Bill Richardson has confused intelligence with consciousness. It's not intelligence that will solve the mystery of life, but consciousness. This is the context man needs to see the big picture of Soul's purpose in life. Despite the context that Atma-Gare provides however, which is the best context that I have found in all the spiritual teachings that I've studied, it doesn't spell out clearly enough what the big picture of life really is, and this bothers me."

David stopped talking and waited for me to respond. Again, I thought carefully before speaking. "I understand what you're saying, but I'm not sure you answered my question," I said, feeling very bold.

"Why Atma-Gare? What makes Atma-Gare the spiritual path that life makes one ready for? That's a big presumption, don't you think?"

He gave me a big smile, which I took to mean that he liked that I had spoken my own mind. "Because of the Satma, the Living Atma Master," he answered, still smiling with satisfaction. "I met a Christian lady who was exploring Atma-Gare at an Atma book discussion class a couple of months ago," he explained, to make his point. "She was under the impression that Jesus and the Satma were spiritual equals. I explained to her that the Christ Consciousness and Satma Consciousness are not the same. Christ Consciousness is Cosmic Consciousness. It's the consciousness of the awakened intellectual senses on the Mental Plane, and the first phase of spiritual self-realization consciousness that takes place on the Soul Plane. The Satma Consciousness is the highest form of spiritual consciousness that man can realize, which takes place in the High Worlds of God and which Jesus did not realize. But I only confused the lady. She wasn't ready for that information. One has to grow in spiritual consciousness to be ready for the Atma secret teachings, because they're too powerful for the average person. So why Atma-Gare? Because Atma-Gare is the final gateway out of these lower worlds of material consciousness, that's why. Atma-Gare is the path that best serves Soul to complete its destiny through life, which is to grow in spiritual self-realization consciousness enough to realize our own Divine nature."

"Is this why it's so difficult to get through to some people?" I asked, so captivated by his explanation that for some strange reason I no longer felt I had to impress him. I could just be myself in all my vulnerability, which put me so much at ease that I began to enjoy his company in an entirely new way.

"Exactly," he quickly replied. "And with some people it's completely hopeless. To be perfectly honest with you, Cassie, I couldn't be bothered with most people anymore. I prefer to just live and let live now."

"Then please explain to me," I said, now very comfortable with the man I wanted to spend the rest of my life with, "what you mean by saying that Atma-Gare does not spell out the big picture. I've read all the Atma books, and I think the *Shariyatma* spells out the big picture so well that it can answer anyone's questions about life."

"Maybe," he replied, again with that look of approval on his face. My curiosity had excited his interest in more ways than one, sending a shiver up my spine. "Even so, listening to Atmans talk about their life in Atma," he explained, his eyes still smiling at me, "I get the impression that they haven't grasped the fundamental purpose of the Divine Plan of God yet. That's what bothers me, Cassie. Because if they did they wouldn't be nourishing this conceit of spiritual elitism that I sense worming its way into the Atma community."

Smiling to myself, I waited before responding. I had also sensed this elitism, both in Vancouver and in Ontario. More so in the Toronto Atma community than in our small group of Atmans in Georgian Bay. My friend Grace called it "Toronto vanity."

"You're not afraid to speak your mind, are you?" I said, with a grin. "I admire that in a person," I continued, eager to tell him a little more about myself. "My role model Doctor Elisabeth Kubler-Ross gave me the courage to stand up for myself also. *Even if the whole world is going one way and you feel you have to go another, then go your own way. If you don't, you will live to regret it,*' she told me in response to the first letter I wrote her. You remind me very much of her. I have more admiration for her than any other person I have met in my life, because she had the courage to forge her own path through life. I can only hope that I live up to my potential. But I don't know if I can," I quickly added, as Father McDuffy's ad in the *Gazette* flashed menacingly across my mind. My face flushed red with a sudden rush of humiliation.

David sensed my anxiety. "We're all put to the test in life, Cassie," he said, speaking softly. "The bigger the Soul, the bigger the challenge. But no test is too big for us. Life doesn't work that way. We're given challenges to test our character. If we pass, we move on to higher levels of consciousness. That's the mystery of spiritual growth. Whenever you're faced with a new test, ask yourself this question: am I ready to take on more responsibility? Why? Because with more consciousness comes more responsibility. That's the Atma life in a nutshell," he concluded, and finished the rest of his salad.

I was at a loss. Whether it was his soft voice that had affected me the way it did, what he had just revealed to me, or both, David had quelled my fear and I no longer felt threatened by Father McDuffy's intimidating challenge. I had to invite him home for dinner. *I had to share my experience with my unborn child with him!*

Once again to my nervous delight he accepted, and without hestitation. The following Saturday evening he appeared at my front door with a bottle of chilled, white Zinfandel wine. Unlike me, he looked relaxed and very comfortable with himself.

Dressed in casual light-tan pants and shorted sleeve. soft yellow shirt, he handed me the bottle and said, "I sensed we were having fish for dinner."

"Pacific salmon," I said, smiling at the coincidence. "I wanted to give you a little taste of British Columbia. Now, if I may, I'd like to introduce you to my three wonderful children," I said, much more nervously than I expected. "Come in here, will you, please," I said, beckoning my children from the family room.

Patrick sauntered over first, proudly sporting his Vancouver Canucks jersey. "This is Patrick, my oldest. He's fifteen, and the man of the house," I said, patting him on the shoulder. "He's a hockey player, David. He plays defense, and he loves to scrap. He looks out for his brother and sister, don't you, Patty?"

Blushing, Patrick gave David his hand to shake. "Hi," he said.

"Yes, I can see you playing defense," David said, feeling Patrick's firm handshake which his father had taught him. "And I'd bet my bottom dollar that no one messes with you, eh, Patrick?" David added with a smile.

My son's face lit up, and I knew instantly that he would like David.

Mark stepped in closer. He was wearing one of his Star Trek T-shirts. "And Mark here is my second oldest. He's thirteen and our resident computer genius. He loves to write stories and I know he's headed for Hollywood. He wants to be a computer animator."

"Hi," Mark said, shaking David's hand. "You like Star Trek, David?"

"Totally," David said, to my son's surprise. "Computer animator, eh? Like the Harry Potter series and Lord of the Rings?"

"Yeah! That's what I want to do. Did you see those movies?"

"Every one. I've read all of J. K. Rowling's books, but I love Tolkien more. I think they're really cool writers, don't you?"

"No way! You read Lord of the Rings? That's my favorite book!"

"Cool!" Cindy burst out, wanting to be included.

I laughed. "Cindy is eleven. She's my youngest and most precious..."

"Mom!" she exclaimed.

"What? Aren't you my most precious?"

"Yeah, but you don't have to tell the whole world!"

"Hi, Cindy," David said, with the warmest smile.

"We call her Puppy Face," Patrick volunteered.

"Puppy Face? How did you get that name, Cindy?"

"My dad gave it to me."

"Why?" David asked.

I laughed. "Her freckles and cute little nose," I said.

"Yeah. Dad said I look like a little puppy face," Cindy said.

"And do you mind being called Puppy Face?"

"I don't mind. I kinda like it," Cindy said, with a proud smile.

"Yeah, pet names are cool, aren't they?" David said.

"Do you have a pet name?" Cindy asked.

"I used to. One of my teachers gave it to me. He called me Little Rumi."

"Little Rumi? What's that mean?" Cindy asked.

"Rumi is my favorite poet, and I love to write poetry like Rumi; so my teacher called me Little Rumi. How about you guys, do you have nicknames?"

"Yeah, we all do," Patrick said. "Mine's Irish."

"Irish?" David said.

I laughed. "His father calls him Irish. Patrick's got a bit of a temper, don't you?"

"Yeah. So what?" Patrick said, defensively.

"Don't get touchy now. We all like your nickname, don't we?"

"Yeah," Mark said. "No one picks on me at school anymore. One troglodyte used to pick on me when we started school here till my brother talked to him."

"Yeah, right! Like I really talked to him," Patrick said. "He was a bully. I hate bullies. What would you have done, David? I mean, look at my brother. He's a nerd."

Mark was just the opposite of Patrick, who had the body of a young athlete and that Irish look in his eyes that one didn't mess with. Mark was short, skinny, and wore thick glasses. David laughed. "I'm sorry, Mark; but you do have the look troglodytes would pick on. You're fortunate to have a big brother to watch out for you."

"I know! That's why I made my brother the hero in my story. I call him Shadow."

"Shadow? That's an intriguing name for a hero."

"Yeah. No one knows who the Shadow is. He appears out of nowhere and goes back to nowhere. Just like the Atma Masters..."

"That's enough Google," Patrick said, slapping his brother on the arm.

"Alright, boys, let's not go there. Why don't you hang out in the family room and I'll call you when dinner's ready. Okay?" I said, and grabbed David by the arm and led him into the kitchen. Then I took out two wine glasses.

I handed David the bottle of white wine that I had chilling in the fridge, and then I got the corkscrew out of the drawer. "Which do you prefer?"

"Your choice," he replied.

"Let's open yours," I said, with a smile.

David opened the bottle, filled the glasses half full, handed me mine, and then held his glass up and said, "Cheers, Cassie."

"Cheers, David," I said, and took a sip. Then, mustering my courage, I said, "So, David; what do you think of the O'Shaunnesy family?"

He smiled. "Irish, Puppy Face, and Google? Is that because Mark googles the net a lot, or because of his thick glasses?"

"Both," I said, and laughed. "They're individuals, all three of them."

"That's a good thing. All the same, you must have your hands full. Have they adjusted to life in Georgian Bay yet? I'm sure they miss their father and Vancouver."

"They do, but they're going to live with their father for the summer. We have shared custody. I have them for the school year, and he has them for the summer. And they all have a Web Cam, so they get to see their father anytime they want. The Atma's been good to us, David. It was meant for us to be here. I'm sure the Atma planned it this way."

David laughed. "You won't believe this, Cassie; but I built the addition on your house for Mrs. Howe three summers ago."

The coincidence made my heart stop. *"You did?"*

"Yes," David said, with another burst of laughter.

"Wow!" I exclaimed, and put my glass down. "You'll never guess how I came by this house. What an incredible coincidence! Let me tell you the story, David. But give me a moment first..."

"By all means," he said, his eyes sharing my excitment.

"The day I came for my job interview I had lunch in one of the local restaurants and I overheard a woman telling the waitress that it was too much for her to take care of her mother in her own house, so she was going to put her mother's house up for sale as soon she got her settled into the nursing home. Long story short, I ended up buying this house because it was perfect for us. I thought it was the Atma's way of helping me start our new life here in Georgian Bay, but now you tell me that you added on the family room here! *Is the Atma telling us something, or what?"*

"Maybe," he said, with the sweetest smile.

I broke into a nervous giggle. "My mentor and role model told me that my life was already planned out for me! I'm convinced of this now!"

"Who, Elisabeth Kubler-Ross?"

"Yes," I said, trying my hardest to repress my excitement.

"If you don't mind my asking, what's the one quality about your role model that you most admire? I'd love to know," David asked, changing the tone of the conversation.

I had to pause. I reflected on her books, especially her memoir *The Wheel of Life,* her precious three letters, and her words of wisdom that she shared with me when I visited her in Arizona just before she died. Tears came to my eyes at the memory of her frail body and indomitable spirit. "Love," I said. "'*I came into this world to learn how to love,*' Doctor Kubler-Ross told me. That's what I admire most about her, David. She knew how to love."

A deep, reverential silence filled my kitchen. I did not want to share the feeling with David. I didn't want to shock him. But I didn't have to. He sensed it also.

"She's here, isn't she?" he said.

Tears of love came to my eyes. "Yes, I think so."

"You're very fortunate to be so close with your role model," he said.

We chatted some more, but the atmosphere was different. I took the salad out of the fridge and asked David to toss it with the lemon vinaigrette that I had also prepared, and then I took the casserole with my baked salmon out of the oven and brought it to the table. David brought the salad over, and I pulled out the chair at the end of the table for him and then I went back into the kitchen to fetch the vegetables and the remainder of the wine.

I called the children for dinner, and as much as I wanted to respect the reverential silence that had befallen us in the kitchen, it wasn't possible; my children had to have their way with us, which both embarrassed and excited me.

They liked David, and all the fear I had of them standing in the way of my relationship with David vanished when he said to them, "Do you guys know how lucky you are to have a mother like you have? I would've given anything to have a mother like her."

"Yeah," Mark said. "That's why we call her Super Mom."

"Until she gets her Irish up," Patrick said. "If you think I have a temper, you don't want to mess with Mom. Just a friendly warning, David."

We all laughed, and in my heart I was elated with joy. This was the first time I had been with a man since my divorce, and the children didn't feel threatened.

"Hey, David," Patrick said; "you like hockey?"

"Sorry, Patrick. I've never played, and I don't follow the NHL."

"*No way!* How about golf. You must golf, don't you?"

"Nope. I have no time for golf. Summer's my busy time of year."

"What do you do for sports, then?" Patrick asked, with some disappointment.

"Tennis when I can, but my passion's running. I'm a distance runner, Patrick. My goal is to run a marathon in each province. I've got five more to go. This summer I'm going to run the Manitoba Marathon," he said, and sipped the rest of his wine.

"You're a marathon runner?" I said, with new astonishment.

"You sound surprised," he said.

"I am. That's quite an accomplishment."

"Not really. It's more of a discipline than anything else."

Patrick was all ears. "What do you mean by that?"

"How can I explain this to you, Patrick?" David said, in a personal tone of voice that sounded like it was meant for Patrick's ears only, and then he paused to reflect. "The best explanation I can give you is to tell you what long distance running does for me physically, emotionally, mentally, and spiritually. Physically, running keeps me in shape. Not only do I get a great cardio workout, but it also revs up my metabolism and keeps my weight under control. I love to cook, Patrick. It's another hobby of mine. I'm exploring Mediterranean cuisine with a cooking club that I belong to in Mississauga, so you could say I run to enjoy food. Emotionally, running's a great way to relieve stress. I never miss my daily run. And mentally, running clears my head. Have you ever heard of what the Buddhists call the monkey mind?"

"No," Patrick said, his eyes as wide as saucers now, as were mine.

"The monkey mind is the busy mind. It's the worrywart mind. You know, like when you can't stop thinking of something? The monkey mind never stops chattering. It keeps us so busy worrying and wondering and fussing about every little thing that it keeps us from doing the really important things in life, like paying attention to our job or homework. The monkey mind likes to distract us when we're studying for exams, and it keeps us from paying attention to the teacher, and it even likes to keep us from just relaxing. It's really hard to just relax when your monkey mind is chattering away with all kinds of things to worry about. So I go for a daily run to clear my head and discipline my monkey mind. And for my spiritual body, I run to work out my really deep problems and resolve my conflicted emotional self. But that's a little more involved, though..."

"In what way?" Patrick jumped in, to my delight.

"Do you really want to know?" David asked.

"I wouldn't have asked if I didn't," Patrick said, with a little puff of his chest.

"Well, how can I explain this?" David said, very thoughtfully. "It's really deep, Patrick. It goes to the very core of who you are as a person."

"Really? How?" Patrick, who spoke for all of us, asked.

"Who are you, Patrick?" David asked.

"Patrick O'Shaunnesy," he replied, his chest puffing a little more.

"That's your personality," David said. "Inside Patrick O'Shaunnesy there's another you. This other you is the real you. Some people call the real you Soul, but no matter what we call the real you it's always struggling to come out, just like a butterfly wants to come out of its cocoon. The real you is the butterfly, and your personality is your cocoon; but it all depends on the kind of personality that you make whether the real you comes out or not. Well, Patrick, running, is like playing hockey, or playing golf, or tennis, swimming, cycling, or whatever other disciplined sport helps to let the real you come out and become a part of your personality. That's what running does for me. It makes me more me. In other words, running makes my personality more real, and anything that makes one's personality more real is a spiritual experience. Don't you feel good when you play hockey, Patrick?"

"Yeah, I do. And when I golf too."

"And why do you feel good when you play hockey or golf?"

"I don't know. I just do," Patrick said.

"Do you like playing hockey and golf?"

"I love golf too, but I love playing hockey more. Why?"

"When you do what you love to do, you feel good," David said, and then turned to me and smiled. "I like this kid, Cassie. He's my kind of guy!"

"Yeah, how come? Because I love to play hockey?" Patrick

asked.

"Yes, because you love to play hockey. I love anyone who loves what they do, Patrick," David said, which gave my other two children a chance to speak up...

"I love to write stories!" Mark said excitedly.

"I love figure skating!" Cindy exclaimed.

"Wonderful!" David responded, with equal emotion. "That's the best way to become the real you— *by doing what you love to do!*"

I could not believe my ears. David had just given my children the most insightful spiritual lesson that I had ever experienced, and I stared at him in awe. He looked at me and winked, and I got so flustered that I had to get up and go to the kitchen.

After we all had a piece of the Black Forest Cake that Cindy and I picked up at the Wyedale Bakery, and French Vanilla ice cream for dessert that my children bargained with me into getting for inviting David to dinner, Patrick went to watch his NHL game on TV. The Vancouver Canucks were playing, and Patrick was just as passionate about his hometown team as his father. Mark went to his computer to work on his new story, and Cindy went to her room to Web Cam her best friend. David and I went into the living room where I finally opened up to him as I was hoping to do. "Did you happen to read the *Gazette* last week?" I asked.

"Are you referring to the Catholic priest's reward offer?"

"Yes," I said. "That's what I'd like to talk to you about. What do you think, David? Do you think a fetus is a little person?"

David picked up his cup of tea and took a sip, and then another.

"Do you like it? It's Jasmine Green Tea," I said. He requested green tea, and that was the only kind I had in my pantry.

"Yes, very much," he said, and took another drink and placed his cup down on the coffee table. "Is a fetus a little person? That's the big question, isn't it? Father McDuffy is positive that no one can prove it's not a little person. That's why he can afford to be so arrogant. The truth is, Cassie, this whole abortion issue will never be resolved as long as there's one Christian left in this world. It's *ipso facto* impossible."

I knew what he meant, but I had to ask. "Why is that?"

"As I said, it's not possible for one to be a Christian and also believe in the pre-existence of the individual self. This has always been the dilemma about abortion. For Christians, the immortal self of man is created at the moment of human conception; ergo, Father McDuffy's absurd challenge."

"Then you believe that a fetus is not a little person?"

"Not until the fetus is animated by the pre-existent spiritual self does it become a little person," he replied, in an impersonal tone of voice.

I don't know why, but my body began to tremble nervously. "David," I said, with a self-conscious tremor in my voice. "I believe I have the proof that Father McDuffy is asking for, but I'm not sure what I should do."

Silence...

In the silence, David gave me the most penetrating look I had ever experienced. I could feel his gaze plumbing the depths of my Soul, and he had the most serious look on his face. I felt like something was about to happen.

He pursed his lips, and said, "You've heard the Call, haven't you?"

I got goose bumps. "What Call?"

"The Call of Soul," he replied.

"I don't know what you mean," I said, feeling his powerful energy like a high voltage current shooting through my body. I put my hand to my chest to calm myself.

Without cracking a smile, he gave me a look that sent shivers up my spine. "You're on your own, kid," he said. "I can give you moral support, but you have to face this test alone. Like I told you in Minneapolis, life is a journey of the alone to the Alone..."

I knew he was right. But all the same, I had to tell him my experience with my unborn child. *I could no longer bear that burden alone!*

Chapter 7

When Two Souls Connect

I excused myself and went into the kitchen to put the kettle on. We still had tea in the pot, but it was tepid and I needed time alone.

As the kettle boiled, panic set in. Was I doing the right thing? Did my unborn child come to me to save me from myself or for a much greater purpose, which Father McDuffy's challenge was calling forth? I didn't know.

I returned to the living room with a fresh pot of tea and sat down. I was very nervous. As I poured the tea David opened up the conversation with a curious question, "Have you ever heard of James Randi?"

"No, I don't think so. Who is he?"

"He's a professional magician. Actually, he's become famous for debunking psychics, mediums, spiritual healers, and so on. Sadly, Randi has convinced himself that this life is all we have, and he's offering a million dollars to anyone who can prove scientifically that man has an immortal Soul. McDuffy's challenge has as much chance of being proven as Randi's, and they both know it. This whole thing is silly, Cassie. You can't prove a spiritual fact with today's empirical science. Perhaps one day, but not now. There is only self-initiation into the mysteries of life, and when it comes to the big secrets we're definitely on our own."

"I believe you," I said, understanding the reason for his question now. I began to think David could read my mind. "All the same," I said, summoning my courage, "do you have proof that a fetus is a biological organism and not a little person? If you do, I'd love to know."

"It follows logically," he said, and took a drink of tea. "If Soul, our immortal spiritual self and true identity pre-exists our mortal human life, then a fetus has to be a biological organism and not a little person. But the bottom line is this, Cassie: at what point does the pre-existent spiritual self enter the fetus? Before birth? After birth? When? Prove this and you will resolve this whole abortion issue which has reared its ugly head again."

"You're avoiding my question," I said, with a nervous smile. "Do you have any proof that a fetus is not a little person?"

"Which would you prefer? Anecdotal, or dialectical?"

"I'd like to hear both," I said, intrigued by his answer.

"What proof do you have? Anecdotal?" he asked instead.

"If by anecdotal you mean a personal experience, yes," I said, feeling my stomach tense up. "But as much as I want to share my experience with the world, I don't know if I can. It's such a personal experience it may not mean anything to anyone but me."

David sat back on the sofa chair and stared at me. The look on his face told me what I did not want to hear. "This is the Call, isn't it?"

"I don't know," I said, but I couldn't lie to him. "Yes. I honestly feel I've been called to the challenge. I *know* I have. I don't know what to do, David. I have to think of my children. And my career. I can't afford to be labeled a nut case, as my ex would say. "

David's eyes told me that he understood. Speaking softly, to avoid upsetting me, he said, "Cassie, you have your mentor and I have mine. I prefer to tell the naked truth because I abhor secrecy. I believe hiding the truth has always done more damage to society than good. But how will one's truth be received? That's the dilemma, isn't it? I'll tell you what I've learned over the years. To receive more truth we have to share the truth we have. Like this teacup here. To receive more tea, I have to empty my cup. This is what Paul Mathew meant in his forward to *Letters to Linda* when he said that the channels get plugged up if we don't share the truth we receive from the Atma."

"May I?" I interrupted. "I'd like to look that up, if you don't mind?"

"Of course not," David said. "Volume One."

I went over to my bookshelf with all my Atma books beside the piano and found Paul's *Letter's to Linda*, Volume One. I read the forward and found the passage he was referring to. I returned to the sofa and read it out loud: *"'One learns in the spiritual works that he cannot gain the divine knowledge and hold it. It must be given out or it will clog the spiritual channels and the recipient will suffer from many problems which will eventually emerge outwardly.'"*

"That's it," he said.

"Is this your inspiration for telling the naked truth?" I asked.

"Unveiled," he emphasized. "Anyone can tell the truth veiled, Cassie. There's a world of difference in how we tell the truth. If you notice, the Living Atma Master doesn't veil the truth. He tells it as it is. Though Rumi said it well, all of my inspiration comes from the Satma, or the Atma if you will."

I liked David Oakly. He commanded my respect. All evening long he never once made me feel uneasy. I made myself feel uneasy because I had a romantic interest in him; but something about him transcended my romantic interest, and this only added to his mystique.

I never felt more naked in my entire life than I did with David, but I felt no shame in my nakedness. "I guess I have to wrestle with my conscience again, don't I?" I said, and forced myself to smile. "But I have to weigh all of my options. I have to think of my children."

"Fair enough. But the greater the truth, the greater the burden. This is why you feel compelled to share your experience, isn't it?"

"My God," I said, flabbergasted by his understanding of my dilemma. "That's my problem exactly! I can't carry this truth any longer. It's becoming much too heavy for me. Why did Father McDuffy have to put that ad in the paper, anyway? *Why?"*

"Who knows what prompted him? Maybe he wants the pro-choice camp to put up or shut up; or he may just be a little pawn in the great game of life. Personally, I think he's just an arrogant little pawn," David said, and laughed.

I laughed also. "I've never met anyone like you in my life, David," I confessed, feeling no embarrassment for revealing my emotions. "How come you're still single? Are you divorced?"

"Yes. I have one child. Samantha will be twelve on the twenty-third of next month," he answered, with love in his eyes for his daughter.

"How long have you been divorced?"

"A few years now."

"And your ex? Is she still around here?"

"She lives in the city."

"Toronto?"

"Yes. She's with another woman."

"I beg your pardon?"

"She left me for another woman," he repeated.

I didn't know what to say. "I'm sorry to hear that. I hope she found what she was looking for."

"I doubt it," he said, with a wry smile. "Julie still doesn't know what she wants. She thinks she's found it in lesbian sex, but sexual love by whatever name will only satisfy one's lower nature, never one's inner self. To satisfy the inner self's longing for wholeness one has to master their desires. What about you, Cassie? How long have you been divorced?"

"It's coming on five years now," I said, happy to be opening the door to our personal life. *"Annnnnnd?"* I said, to draw him out.

"Annnnnnd, no," he said, and laughed. "There's no one special in my life at the moment. You?"

"Maybe," I foolishly said, and blushed like a schoolgirl.

With a big smile, David said, "Are you up to a little romance, Cassie?"

"Yes!" I blurted out, and instantly broke into nervous laughter.

I hoped my laughter would mask my feelings for him, but I knew it hadn't. My face flushed ten different shades of red, but the door had been opened and I was dancing inside with so much joy I felt like a whirling dervish!

"Do you enjoy hiking?" he asked.

My heart skipped another beat. He was asking me on a date. I hadn't hiked since the year before my abortion, but I didn't want to tell him that. I couldn't lie to him either. I didn't want our relationship to

88

begin on a lie. For a split second I panicked. I didn't know how to respond. Then I remembered the words I have taped to the inside of my front door: BE TRUE TO LIFE AND LIFE WILL BE TRUE TO YOU. Those words were the post-script to the last letter my mentor wrote to me. I made them my personal credo.

"To be honest, David, I haven't done enough hiking to know. But I'm sure I can learn to love it," I replied, with my fingers crossed.

"You will," he said. "So why don't we plan a weekend together? Alone or with the children. We have some incredible hiking trails in Algonquin Provincial Park."

"I'd love that," I said, with a grin from ear to ear.

"Now, back to the issue. What about this dilemma of yours?"

I could not believe how the most important thing in my life could vanish from my mind so quickly, and I broke into laughter.

"What?" he asked.

I shook my head. "More tea? Or would you like something stronger?"

"I'm fine, thank you. Ever since I got my Fifth Initiation I have a low tolerance for alcohol. That's how the Atma works, Cassie. The pull is not as strong as it is when one's center of gravity is in the lower worlds."

I suspected he was a Higher Initiate, but I was glad he confirmed it. I didn't quite understand what he meant, though. "By pull, do you mean desire for pleasure?"

"Not necessarily. Life affords us all kinds of pleasure, but the lower self has an appetite for indulging in the five passions of the mind. We're all driven by desire. That's a fact of life. If there's one thing that I got from my years of Sufism, it's my understanding of the dual nature of the self. Would you like me to expound upon this? It would give me the context I need to respond to your question."

"By all means," I said.

"You've read most of the Atma books, haven't you?"

"I've read them all, David."

"Then you're familiar with the concept of the lower and higher self," he said, beginning his explanation. "Unfortunately, this aspect of the Atma teaching isn't given the attention I feel it deserves. The evolution of our spiritual self takes Soul through various stages of individuation. Along the way, Soul realizes its human self-consciousness. This is our lower self. The lower self evolves by satisfying the biological needs of its physical body. We have to have food to survive and sex to procreate. Sex is a natural biological urge, and woe to those who abandon to sex or deny it altogether. It takes the wisdom of a Sufi to control ones desire for sex. The lower self has needs and desires that give birth to the five passions of the mind. These passions are anger, greed, lust, vanity, and attachment. The pull that I'm referring to is the pull of the lower self to satisfy its primordial needs and desires. This is how the spiritual self grows. We gain experience by satisfying all of our needs and desires. This is how we collect the karmic energies of life that make us who we are. If you ever get a chance, read *The Drowned Book* by Rumi's father. He mastered the art of collecting the energies of life. The danger of this school of Sufi thought however lies in getting trapped by one's desires. One has to train long and hard before one can live life like Rumi's father. The mystery of the Fifth Initiation in Atma is that it lifts our spiritual self to the Soul Plane where it is no longer subject to the same pull of these primordial needs and desires of our lower self. This does not mean we enjoy life any less. On the contrary, we still have needs and desires; but we just don't have the same pull to abandon to them like we did before the Fifth Initiation. Our needs and desires become more refined as we ascend the spiritual ladder of life. In effect, we can live our life with the passion of Rumi's father if we want to because we have shifted our center of gravity from our lower to higher self. That's the secret of the Fifth Initiation in Atma. Does this answer your question?"

"I'm only a Second Initiate," I replied, overwhelmed by his explanation. "But if I understand you correctly, you're saying that you don't enjoy life any less; you just don't abandon to the pleasures of life anymore. Am I right?"

"Almost. It's not that I don't abandon to the pleasures of life, the pull to abandon is not as strong now," he replied.

"What do you mean by that exactly?" I asked, totally captivated by his wisdom and interest in me personally. I had to cross my fingers for good luck.

He reflected for a moment. "Imagine an apple falling off a tree. It falls to the ground because of the law of gravity. Now imagine the lower self being just like an apple. It is pulled by the gravitational forces of the lower worlds to remain in the lower worlds. This is why it's so easy to abandon to one's appetites. We are forever being pulled by the forces of the lower world to satisfy our appetites. These lower worlds, as you know, are the physical, astral, causal, mental, and subconscious planes. But when Soul, our spiritual self, is initiated into the Soul Plane of Consciousness, which is the first of the Spiritual Worlds of God, the pull is upward, not downward. This is what makes the Fifth Initiation so important. It changes the dynamics of spiritual growth. From the Fifth Initiation on, life no longer has the same kind of hold on Soul. But as I said, this does not mean we love life any less. In fact, we may love life much more. But it's not a love that possesses us like before. Our love for life still possesses us, but we possess our love for life. That's the critical difference. In the true sense of Christ's saying, we are in the world but not of the world. This is the paradox of the true man of God."

"Wow! So that's your secret!" I exclaimed to myself.

David saw the expression on my face. "Was that too much for you?"

"It explains a lot of things for me," I said, trying to sound calm.

"Good. Now, let's talk about your dilemma."

"Are you up to it?" I asked.

"That's why I'm here, isn't it?" he said, with a big smile.

"Among other things," I said, with a nervous laugh.

With a hint of that sweet smile that sent shivers up my spine, he said, "There's a time and place for everything, Cassie. Tonight we're going to talk about your dilemma. McDuffy got under your skin, didn't he?"

"Very much so," I said, suddenly feeling very serious. "I don't quite know how to say this, but it feels like Father McDuffy has put my whole life on the line again. My mentor wrote in her memoir that she was destined to speak for the dying. I won't presume to put myself on the same level as Doctor Elisabeth Kubler-Ross, but if I'm going to be true to my role model I have to tell you that I honestly feel like I'm being called to speak for every woman's right to her own body. I've given this a lot of thought since my abortion, David, and I think the Atma let me have the miracle with my unborn child for two reasons: first, to save me from myself because I had fallen into a state of suicidal depression; and second, to tell the story of my unborn child for the sake of women everywhere. But I don't know if I can."

"I can appreciate your dilemma," he said, in his soft voice that made me feel safe and secure. "What would your mentor do, Cassie? Try to imagine Doctor Kubler-Ross in the same situation. What do you think she would do?"

"I don't have to put her in my shoes. She was faced with many experiences where she had to expose herself to the world. Her pioneering work on near-death experience placed her in a situation similar to mine. She wrote in her memoir that a tiny 'two pound nothing' spent most of her life battling the 'Goliath-sized forces of ignorance and fear.' She was born last in a set of triplets. Her doctor called her a two pound nothing. She had to prove herself her whole life. Well, she did. That's why she's my role model. So I know what she would do, David. I'm just not sure I can do it, that's all. You have no idea how ashamed this makes me feel."

"Let's not go there, Cassie. The Divine Plan of God is open-ended. There are no closed doors. Every choice we make opens to the unconditional love of God. Either way, you're no less the person you are. This is the wonder of the Divine Plan of God."

"I think I understand," I said, smiling at his understanding. "But I also know that if I go public with the miracle of my unborn child I'll be given an incredible opportunity to grow spiritually; but I just don't know if I can take the heat. That's my dilemma."

David laughed. "Paul Mathew used to say that all the growth is in the hassle. I'm sure you can take the heat, Cassie. I think you just don't want to put your kids through anymore hardship, that's all."

"That's what makes it a test of character, doesn't it?"

Again, he laughed. David appreciated my dilemma. I had to ask him what he would do in my situation.

"Panic," he replied.

"See? It's not so easy, is it? Maybe if you tell me what proof you have that a fetus is not a little person it might give me the confidence I need to tell my story."

He sat back and stretched his legs. He closed his eyes, put his hands behind his head and thought for three or four minutes. I could almost hear the gears of his brain grinding out what he had to say, but in reality I think he was connecting with his *inspiration.*

"There are no coincidences," he began. "We were destined to meet for a reason, Cassie. Maybe karmic, maybe not; I don't know. Either way, the Atma brought us together to open up a larger channel for whatever it wants to give to the world. That much I'm sure of."

"I don't understand," I interrupted. "What do you mean, the Atma has brought us together to open up a larger channel?"

"One Atman is a wonderful channel for the Atma force, but when two Atmans connect in that special way, like Shams and Rumi did, they can become an incredible channel for the reconciling power of Holy Spirit to be introduced into social consciousness. I suspect we're being used by the Atma for a purpose far beyond our capacity to appreciate."

"Only if I choose to take Father McDuffy's challenge," I said.

"Yes. So, would you like to hear my proof then?"

"It's not scientific, is it?"

"Of course not. Science can't measure this truth yet. Have you ever heard of the neuroscientist Doctor Michael Persinger?"

"No, I don't think so."

"He's a professor at Laurentian University in Sudbury, just north of here. He's a hard-nosed skeptic who has what he believes to be scientific proof that the brain is responsible for creating paranormal experiences. He attaches electrodes to a subject's head and stimulates the brain, which simulates paranormal feelings and sensations. This is his scientific evidence for disproving the spiritual nature of man. It's all brain activity, he says. It's amusing watching him trying to pour the Great Ocean of God into his tiny teacup. That's what you would be up against, Cassie: a solid wall of scientific incredulity."

"I know. That's why I want to hear what proof you have that a fetus is not a little person. I need all the confidence I can get, David."

"Okay. What do you think Soul is here for?"

"I don't understand what you mean?"

"What does Atma-Gare tell us our purpose in life is?"

"Spiritual self-realization first, and then God-realization consciousness," I replied, wondering what David was getting at.

"Yes. Then we become co-workers with God. That's what the Divine Plan of God is all about. And how do we serve God, Cassie?"

I smiled. I knew that answer. It was engraved in my heart. My role model was my irrefutable answer. Her words came to me instantly. *"'All destiny leads to growth, love, and service,'* said Elisabeth Kubler-Ross. She devoted her whole life to helping people. We serve God by serving life, David."

"Yes, but each according to his own gift. This is the beauty of the Divine Plan of God. We're all individual Souls. We all have our own gift to give to the world."

"Oh God!" I gasped, cutting David off. *"That's so true!"*

"What?" he asked, staring at me. David must have thought I had just seen a ghost, but it was much better than that. *It was an epiphany!*

He was right. We all have our own gift to give to the world. That's how we complete our destiny in life. But I did not realize this until the image of the blind baby girl in Doctor Kubler-Ross's memoir came to my mind as he spoke.

A mother gave birth to a blind baby girl. Her heart was broken. Nevertheless, she hoped that one day her daughter would grow up and graduate from school and get a profession. Her doctors told her this was unrealistic and advised her to put her daughter into an institution. Then she met Doctor Kubler-Ross, who told her that no child was born so defective that God did not endow it with a special gift. "Drop all your expectations," Doctor Kubler-Ross told the mother of the blind baby. "All you have to do is hold and love your child like she was a gift from God." The mother replied, "And then?" And Doctor Kubler-Ross answered, "In time, He will reveal her special gift." Many years later Doctor Kubler-Ross read an article in the newspaper about Heidi. Heidi was the same blind infant girl. She was all grown up now, and a promising pianist who was performing in public for the first time!

Doctor Kubler-Ross looked up the mother who told her that it was a struggle to raise her daughter, but one day her daughter's gift for music emerged and it blossomed like a flower. She thanked Doctor Kubler-Ross for her love and kind words of encouragement. They had kept her hope alive and nourished her dream to come true.

I shared this story with David, but as I told the story I remembered something else from my mentor's memoir that confirmed that our purpose in life is to serve God by serving life. Doctor Kubler-Ross was one of the first professionals to study the near-death experience. She learned from people who had died and come back that when they went over to the other side they were asked the following question, "What services have you rendered?"

"That's how a person's life is tallied on the other side, by the services they have rendered life," I summed up for David. "So I agree with what the Atma teaches. We're born to serve life. That's the spiritual destiny of each and every Soul. *And I think I'm being called to serve life by telling the story of my unborn child!"*

David smiled at my burst of excitement. "Freedom and responsibility are the two gifts of the spiritually self-realized person, but freedom precedes responsibility," he replied, in his serious, get-to-the-point voice. "This is the curious nature of evolution. As we evolve through life, we ascend the ladder until we realize this mysterious unit of consciousness called the self. This takes place in the primordial life of man. This unit of self-consciousness separates man from the lower species. The lower species know, but primordial man now has a sense of knowing that he knows, and he begins to create personal karma because he has a sense of self. This means that he makes choices now. This is where free choice comes from, Cassie. The mystery is solved. Free choice does not come from God, as such; it comes from this evolved unit of consciousness that we call the self. The self no longer acts on instinct and impulse; it acts out of a dim sense of self-awareness and self-interest. This is how free will evolves, and thousands of lifetimes later man is free to make up his own mind. It's this freedom to choose born out of the long karmic evolution of man that leads me to conclude Soul enters the child after birth, and not before."

"I'm not sure I follow you," I said, with the eeriest feeling that I had just stepped into the inner sanctum of David Oakly's holy of holies.

"Let me walk you through it," he said in his soft voice, which I loved. "Karma governs life in these lower worlds. Karma is the law of cause and effect. The Living Atma Master has simplified karma. He calls it the Law of Return. We create karma with every choice we make. This is how we grow in our own unique self-identity. We are free to make the choices we make, so karma is predicated upon our ability to choose. Now, can you tell me what the difference is between the Atma and Soul?"

"I don't think there is a difference. If I remember correctly, the *Shariyatma* says that Soul is made up of Holy Spirit," I replied, mystified by his question.

"Yes. The Atma, or Divine Spirit, is the essence of life. Without Holy Spirit there can be no life. It is the primordial life force. Some day scientists will prove this. Divine Spirit creates life in the material worlds, and life grows and evolves by taking in the life force; but what is Divine Spirit, Cassie?"

"We're told in the *Shariyatma* that the Atma is the Body of God, aren't we?" I answered, feeling a little nervous.

"Yes, the Atma is the Body of God. But what does that mean?"

"I'm not sure," I said.

"The Atma is the consciousness of God, and the purpose of life is to give the consciousness of God a vehicle to become aware of itself. This is the unit of consciousness we call the self. The Atma creates life, and as life grows and evolves from the lowest life form to man it collects the life force. The more life force a life form collects, the more it evolves up the ladder of evolution. In the life form of primordial man, the life force reaches critical mass and becomes aware of itself for the first time. This dim sense of self-awareness is the birth of the self. With this dim sense of self-awareness, primordial man now has a dim sense of personal choice. Out of this dim sense of personal choice is born our karmic destiny. So contrary to what Christianity believes, this unit of self-consciousness that Father McDuffy calls a little person is not created at the moment of human conception; it was created eons ago through natural evolution. And from life to life to life this unit of self-consciousness evolves into a freethinking individual Soul. This is the pre-existent self that enters the body of the unborn child."

I gasped at David's wisdom, and I had to pause to reflect. I was curious about one thing. "Does the fetus have consciousness?" I felt compelled to ask.

"Good question. All life has consciousness, but only man has self-consciousness; as far as we know, that is. Some researchers believe dolphins have self-consciousness; but that's another subject. So the fetus does have consciousness, but it does not have self-consciousness until it is animated by the pre-existent self that chooses that body to be born into."

Nonplussed by his knowledge, I said, "You said that Soul enters the body after the birth of a child, didn't you?"

"Yes," he replied. "But let's be very clear here. By Soul we mean the pre-existent individuated spiritual self that has taken eons to evolve, not Soul the life force as some people believe. The aboriginal people of many countries for example believe that all of nature has a Soul. They speak of the Soul of a tree, the Soul of a rock, and the Soul of a mountain. This is the Soul of nature that individuates through evolution into the unit of self-consciousness that animates the body of the newborn child. It is the un-individuated consciousness of Soul, if you will, not the spiritual self. It's all a matter of correct perspective, Cassie."

"I think I understand that," I said, not really sure what I understood. "And it's the spiritual self that Father McDuffy calls a little person, then? The spiritual self is the identity of the self that has evolved through karma and reincarnation, isn't it?"

"Yes," he said.

"The fetus doesn't have a self yet, does it?"

"No. It's a biological entity that has life-consciousness but no self-consciousness. It only has self-consciousness when the pre-existent spiritual self enters the body of the newborn child," he answered, and slumped back in my nice, soft, Italian leather sofa chair to pause and catch his breath; but I was too excited to take a break.

"That's my question, then. You said that Soul enters the body after the birth of the child. Why after the birth and not before?"

He laughed. "This is all dialectical reasoning, you know that?"

"Yes, I know that. But it's the best explanation that I've ever come across. There's nothing in the Atma literature that explains this."

"There's no literature anywhere that explains it," he replied, sitting up. "This is one of those mysteries that one has to be initiated into. Before you ask, I can't tell you yet how I came to realize this mystery. Suffice to say that I'm as comfortable with my realization of the spiritual self of man as I am about how beautiful and exciting you are to me."

"Don't play with me, David!"

"I'm not. I find you very engaging, Cassie. Not to mention very beautiful. You're the most exciting Atman, let alone woman, that I've met yet!"

"You're not serious?" I said, taken completely by surprise.

David smiled, then broke into a hearty, titillating chuckle:

`Someone asked me,
What is love?
Don't look for an explanation.
Dissolve into me and then you know when it calls.
Respond. Walk out as a lion, a rose.
Inhale Autumn, long for Spring.'

That's a poem from my mentor, Cassie."

"Rumi?" I said. I was at a loss to say anything else.

"Yes. You have stirred my longing for spring, Cassie. It's been far too long. Far, far too long..."

"I too long for spring, David," I heard myself say, realizing that was the perfect response. I was about to say something else when my daughter came into the room.

"Are you guys still at it? Mom, I'm hungry," she said, in her plaintive little voice.

"Make yourself a snack, sweetheart," I said. "How about the boys, do they want something too?"

"Yeah. They asked me to bring them something. Can you make us a bedtime snack, please?"

"Alright," I said. "David, would you mind?"

"Not at all. I could use a snack myself," he said, and laughed.

We both got up and went into the kitchen. It felt like *deja vu*. I made up a plate of their favorite corn chips and salsa for each of my children, and an assorted plate of crackers, cheese, and olives for David and myself. Over our snack, I asked him to explain why he felt that Soul entered the baby after birth and not before as some people believed. But as much as I wanted to know, my mind had been distracted by his unexpected declaration of longing to be loved. I never saw that coming at all.

"First, let me ask you this," he replied, after he swallowed a bite of Old Cheddar cheese. "How would you define this unit of consciousness that we call the self?"

"The self is who we are. The self is Soul," I replied.

"Yes, that's what we say in Atma-Gare. I am Soul. You are Soul. We are Soul. But what does that mean, Cassie?"

"It means that we are all Divine beings," I said.

"Self-realized atoms of perception," David said.

"I beg your pardon?" I said.

"That's what the poet John Keats called Souls— atoms of perception that come into this world from God to create this unit of consciousness we call a self. I have yet to find a more concise explanation of the Divine Plan of God than the letter that John Keats wrote to his brother. He called his letter 'The Vale of Soul Making.'"

"David, you've made reference to the Divine Plan of God a number of times this evening, and in our previous conversation over lunch. I don't remember reading about the Divine Plan of God in the Atma literature. Where did you get it? The *Shariyatma?*"

"No, it's not explained in the Atma books. Not yet, anyway. This is one of those mysteries one is given when he's ready to receive it. I was granted entry into this mystery one day while I was hiking in Georgian Bay. It was a very strange week for me. My wife sued for sole custody of our daughter because she wanted to bring Samantha up in a lesbian relationship, and my Sufi teacher told me that he had taken me as far as he could. I had to find another spiritual teacher..."

David stopped talking. I felt him welling up with emotion. I felt an urge to rush over and hold him in my arms.

Snapping himself out of his emotional reverie, he continued. "I hiked the Bruce Trail for days until every muscle in my body ached. I pitched my tent overlooking the water shimmering brilliantly in the Georgian Bay sunset. I sat staring at the sun as it descended. The blazing orb of blood-red orange heavenly splendor mesmerized me. If you haven't seen a Georgian Bay sunset yet, I'll make sure you do one of these evenings. It's a natural wonder. I was so physically drained from my hike and so emotionally exhausted from life that I just let go and surrendered to the experience. That's when it happened. The face of the sun transformed into the face of a man. I learned later that this man was the Satma, the Living Atma Master who was to become my new spiritual teacher. The face came out of the sun and floated towards me, and as it approached me it manifested into a man who reached out for my hand and lifted me out of my body and we ascended to the *Anami Lok,* the Tenth Plane of Consciousness. This is the Body of God, the Great Ocean of Love and Mercy, the Divine Word of God that contains the sum of all teachings emanating from the Satman, the Creator of all that is and will be. This is where Souls are reproduced by God reacting upon Itself, and where the poet Keats ascended to catch a glimpse of the Divine Plan of God. Keats called these new Souls atoms of perception. He saw that these atoms were Souls that had to grow their own personal identity in life. The Tenth Plane is the heart and core of all life; but life begins here, in the lower worlds. These atoms of perception are sparks of Divinity that are sent into the material worlds to create their own identity, their own individual self. This is what Keats meant by 'Soul making.' The Satma let me experience these sparks of Divinity coming into the material worlds. Not only did I witness them evolving from one life form to a higher life form until they became units of individual self-consciousness in the life of primordial man, I experienced my own evolution from my inception in life when Soul first entered the life process all the way to my present lifetime. I experienced my evolving self from my first primordial human lifetime when I gave birth to my own self-consciousness all the way up the ladder of evolution to the moment when my Sufi teacher told me I was ready for my next, and final teacher; and then the Satma brought me back to my body and I found myself staring into an empty sky..."

I slumped back into my sofa. My head was ringing with the loudest Sound of Atma I had ever heard. It was like a whirling pool of water singing the magnificent Sound of God, the amazing HU. I can't explain it, but I *experienced* every word that David spoke. I *was* with him on his journey to the Tenth Plane, and I *knew*. I just *knew!*

The living room felt different. The Satma was present. I couldn't move. I was paralyzed by the experience. I stared at David. I saw a light around him. It was the most beautiful golden light of infinite wisdom that I have ever experienced, and his eyes shone with a love so pure that it filled me with a feeling of ineffable goodness!

David smiled. He reached over and picked up a wheat cracker and placed a piece of cheese on it. He took a bite and swallowed. It was all so natural for him. "Now I can tell you," he said, with a playful smile.

"What?" I asked, still dazed by his sunset experience.

"Why I believe Soul enters the child after birth," he said. "This spark of Divinity which has evolved through life to become an individual Soul has but one desire. Can you imagine what that desire is?"

I stared blankly at David. By the far-away look in his eyes I knew he had already detached himself from his sunset experience. In his normal voice, he said, "Soul's desire is to become totally self-realized. This is what drives every person in life. We all crave self-identity. We all long to be our true self. We all want to be whole. This is our spiritual destiny. In Atma, we call this spiritual self-realization and God-consciousness. Whatever it's called, it is Soul's pre-scripted need to become a God-realized Soul. But the only way to become totally self-realized is through the individual destiny of our own personal karmic life. No two Souls have the same karmic destiny, so no two Souls are alike. The Sufi poet Fariduddin Attar spells this out in his allegory *A Conference of the Birds,* which I'm translating from Persian into English with a man called Binny, a Sufi friend of mine. This means that the pre-existent spiritual self must be free and independent to pursue its individual karmic destiny. This is why Soul must animate the body of the child after birth, and not before."

"Why can't Soul enter the fetus while in the womb?" I asked.

"I've read many accounts of past-life regressions where this has happened, but it's only temporary," David replied, as though anticipating my question. "Soul just wants to get a feel for its new body to adjust to its new life, that's all. The pre-existent self must be independent of the mother's womb to continue its own karmic destiny in life. As long as the fetus remains in the mother's womb, Soul will not occupy that body because the fetus is part of the mother's karmic destiny, not the unborn child's. Two separate Souls cannot coexist in the same body, because each Soul has its own individual spiritual line of destiny that it must pursue. This is why in the Book of Genesis it's written that Soul enters the body when the child takes its first breath of life. As a matter of fact, Cassie, in one of the editions of *The Atma-Gare Journal* there's a story of a father who witnessed Soul's entry into his new infant's body after the child was c-sectioned from it's mother's womb. If you don't have that edition I can drop it off for you."

I slumped into the sofa with absolute relief. Climbers of Mount Everest must have felt as I did just then when they took their final step to the top of the world's highest mountain!

David stared at me. "Well?"

"Well what?" I asked, completely nonplussed.

"Does that satisfy your need to know?"

"What happened, David? Where did all of this come from? *I would not have believed it if I hadn't just experienced it!*"

"The Atma," he replied, smiling. "Somehow, in some mysterious way, no doubt as Rumi did with Shams of Tabriz, we connected so well that the Atma was free to reveal this information for the memoir you're going to write some day. Now, Cassie, I should be getting along. It is getting late, and I'm up at five every morning."

"Five? Why so early?"

"Why? Because that's *my* time. I HU every morning, read Rumi and some modern poetry for half an hour or so, and then I work on my own poetry before I go to work; and on weekends I work on my translation of *A Conference of the Birds.* In fact, tomorrow I have to go to Peterborough to see Binny. He's got a few more pages for me."

"I don't understand. If your friend translates it from Persian..."

"Binny gives me a literal translation," David said, anticipating my question. "I take his literal translation and render it into a reader-friendly transcription of the Sufi principles couched in the allegory. I'm working on an annotated translation. My goal is to demystify the allegory for the modern reader. Coleman Barks is doing the same thing with Rumi's poetry, and he's doing a wonderful job; but Barks can't quite grasp the *subtlety,* which is the soul of Sufism. This will be my contribution to the Path in the western world. This is my baby, Cassie; and I can't wait for the weekends to come around. Thank you for dinner. It's been quite an evening."

"Thank you for coming," I said, with my heart aglow.

I walked David to the door. He leaned over and kissed me on the cheek. It was the sweetest kiss I have ever received from a man!

"Sweet dreams, Cassie," he said, and walked off to his vehicle, a white cargo van with DAVID OAKLY RENOVATIONS, Wyedale, Ontario, and his telephone number on the panel in deep blue letters inside the green outline of a large oak, which in Atma-Gare symbolizes the secret order of Higher Initiates, "The Brothers of the Leaf."

Before I went to sleep I had to look up David's biblical reference. I found it in Genesis, Chapter 2, Verse 7: *"And the Lord God formed man of the dust of the ground, and breathed into his nostrils the breath of life; and man became a living soul."*

I turned off my lamp, snuggled up with my body pillow, played the evening over and over again in my mind, and drifted off into heavenly bliss.

Chapter 8
The Day After My Evening With David

Normally I sleep in on weekends, but not the day after my evening with David; I was up with the sun. I wanted to see the sunrise. I imagined David with me on my deck sharing a morning cup of coffee and watching the sunrise together.

The sun shone through the shimmering green of the newly foliaged maples and oaks that edged my property line, rising to the top of the trees, above the trees, and then it was suspended in the empty, silvery-blue horizon and shone for me alone. I felt blessed.

I could not get over the evening. I could not believe how we had connected. It was like nothing I had ever experienced before. It felt like a dream, but I knew it wasn't. David Oakly was too real for it to be a dream. *He was the most real man I had ever met!*

I put my hand to my cheek where he kissed me. I felt his tender lips all over again. I closed my eyes and saw his face. I wanted to call and thank him for the evening. I wanted to be with him. *I was in love!*

I sat in dreamy reverie for another half hour, and then I got dressed and did my morning HU. I took out my journal and my heart just poured onto the pages until the children called for breakfast. *"Please, Satma,"* I ended my journal entry, *"let it be so…"*

Sunday was family waffle day. I squeezed fresh orange juice for Patrick, who like his father only drank freshly squeezed orange juice, filled the other glasses with Calcium enriched Tropicana, and then I made a stack of Belgian waffles with whipped cream and fresh maple syrup that the children and I had recently purchased at our local Wyedale Maple Syrup Festival. We sat down to eat. Cindy was first to speak about the night before.

"So do you like him, Mom?" she asked.

"Yes, very much," I said, with an irrepressible smile. "Do you?"

"He's okay, I guess," she said.

"How about you guys? What do you think of David?"

"He's cool," Mark replied.

"Yeah, I'd say he's cool, too," Patrick added.

"He is cool, isn't he?" I said, with a grin from ear to ear.

"He's not as cool as dad," Cindy said.

"I know sweetheart, but I can see David again, can't I?"

"Why not?" Patrick jumped in.

"Yeah. Go for it, Mom," Mark said.

"Cindy, would you mind if I saw David again?"

"I guess not. He's not like dad, but he's okay."

"We're unanimous on this?" I asked.

"I'm okay with it, Mom," Patrick said.

"Me too, Mom," Mark said.

"Cindy? Are you okay with it?"

"I think so. Go ahead, Mom. I don't mind."

"We may be going hiking soon. That may mean a whole weekend with David. Are you guys okay with that?"

"Where you guys going?" Patrick asked.

"Algonquin Provincial Park, I think."

"You guys going to camp out and stuff?" Mark asked.

"Yes, I think so. I'm not sure."

"Cool!" Mark said.

"Can I come, Mom?" Cindy asked.

"Get real, Puppy Face!" Patrick said.

"Why not? I can come, can't I, Mom?"

"Three's a crowd, Puppy Face," Patrick said.

"I'm not a crowd! Can I come, Mom?"

"We'll see, sweetheart."

"No way!" Patrick said. "Tell her, Mom. You don't want her along, do you? She'll spoil it for you guys!"

"I can go if I want to, can't I, Mom?"

"How about we plan a family weekend together? David doesn't mind. What do you think of that?"

"Yeah! Let's do that!" Cindy said.

"So, can I go with David on my own this time?"

"I guess so," Cindy said.

"Thank you. So, Patrick; what did you think of David's philosophy about being your own person by doing what you love to do? Wasn't that something?"

"He's deep, Mom. I'll give him that," Patrick said, reaching for another waffle.

"Hey, Mom, did you notice David knew what troglodyte meant?" Mark said.

Trogs, which was short for troglodytes, was Mark's name for the half-ape humans in his first series of Shadow Man stories.

"Yes, I did; and I was quite impressed," I said, smiling proudly at my son.

"Yeah, me, too. David's got the Light, Mom. He's cool. I'm going to make him a Light Master in my Mythmaster Chronicles," Mark said, and took a bite of his waffle.

"I think David would like that. Can I share that with him?"

"Okay. Ask David if he Soul travels with Huzee, please? I have to know that if I'm going to make him a Light Master."

"I will. Alright, Cindy; I want you at the piano first thing after breakfast. Patrick, you have to study for your English test before you go anywhere today. And Mark, I want you to clean up your room today before you get into your story. And I want everyone's dirty clothes in the laundry room by eleven o'clock. Okay?"

"Okay," they said in unison.

After breakfast I did the dishes and then read my private Atma Discourse that had come in the mail during the week. As I sat in quiet contemplation, I got the urge to walk the Georgian Bay beach. I went downstairs and asked Cindy if she wanted to join me, but she was going to her girlfriend's house after she practiced her piano lesson. As I was about to leave, the phone rang. "It's for you, Mom!" Patrick hollered.

"Got it!" I said, and picked up the phone in the kitchen. It was David. My heart skipped a beat. "What a nice surprise," I said.

"I want to thank you for the wonderful evening," he said. "It was the most satisfying *satsang* I've ever experienced."

Satsang is an Atma word. *Sat* means true, or unchangeable, and *sang* means union, coming into contact with the Atma Sound Current, which is the creative life force that flows through life. *Satsang* is that special spiritual connection that Soul makes with the Satma, who is the Atma; and David and I had connected with the Atma all night long.

"It was a *satsang,* wasn't it?" I said, so excited that I wanted to scream with joyful abandon. "I still can't believe what we talked about," I said, trying to sound casual. "I have a few more questions I want to ask you, but they can wait. David, thank you for sharing your sunset experience with me. I watched the sunrise this morning. I haven't done that in years. It was absolutely divine. I would love to experience a Georgian Bay sunset with you. I'm free anytime," I said, and instantly flushed hot with embarrassment.

"I would love that, Cassie. So, what are your plans for today?"

"I was just about to go for a beach walk. Would you like to join me?" I asked, and the blood rushed to my face again.

"I'd love nothing more, but I'm just about to go for my long training run today, and then I have to drive down to Peterborough to see Binny. May I have a rain-check?"

"Certainly. Perhaps some evening?"

"That would be nice. About the hike. Whatever weekend suits you. Just let me know so I'm sure to be free. I'll leave it up to you, okay?"

"It's definite, then?" I asked.

"Yes. But run it by your children first. If they don't mind, we'll make plans. And if they want to come along, let me know so I can book a couple of cottages. Your choice."

I smiled at David's consideration, but I didn't tell him that I had already run it by my children. "I'm going to need camping equipment, aren't I?"

"I have camping equipment if we need it, but we can work that out some time this week. How about we get together this coming

Saturday? We can go out for dinner."

"That sounds wonderful, David."

"Seven?"

"Seven's fine."

"Good. I'll see you then. Thanks again, Cassie. Last night was one of the most wonderful evenings I've ever had. You're the only person I've ever shared my sunset experience with. I didn't overwhelm you, did I?"

"I'm still buzzing," I said, and laughed nervously. "I feel very privileged, David. Maybe when we get together I can share my experience with my unborn child with you. I may just be up to talking about it now."

"Only if you feel it's right," David said.

"Thank you for that," I said, deeply appreciating his consideration. "May I ask you a personal question, David?"

"Of course."

"It's very personal."

"Is it important to you?"

"Yes, very."

"By all means, ask me."

"Why me, David? What do I have that attracts you?"

Silence. The longer I waited for his answer, the more foolish I felt for asking. I honestly expected something clever, but David surprised me.

"It's not for lack of opportunities that I'm still alone, Cassie," he replied, in his soft, intimate voice. "I've had many occasions to get involved, but I've always stepped back. Why you? For one thing, you're an Atman. I refuse to get involved with another woman who does not share my spiritual values. The spiritual life is the most satisfying part of an intimate relationship, and I can't imagine not sharing it. I've been there, and I'd rather be alone than be with a woman who does not share my spiritual values. I live my life to the fullest, Cassie; so if I'm going to get involved it won't be with just any woman. Given how we connected last night, I think you're the kind of Atman I could get involved with, if I'm not being too forward..."

"Not at all," I jumped in, my heart racing. "Thank you, David. I needed to hear that. May I ask what kind of Atman I am to you?"

"Not all Atmans are birds of the same feather, Cassie. You soar like an eagle. Last night proved it. We connected in that special way that opened the floodgates of Soul. In all honesty, you're the most exciting thing that's happened to me since my divorce."

"Me, too," I said, through instant tears of joy. "Okay, David. I'm sorry for keeping you from your run. We can continue this Saturday evening."

"I'm looking forward to it. Have a nice walk, Cassie."

"And you have a great day, David. Thank you for calling."

"Bye now."

"Bye," I said, but I couldn't hang up the phone. I slumped into the chair with the phone in my hand. That was too much. *Not in my wildest dreams could I have imagined meeting a man like David Oakly!*

Chapter 9

A Lady With a Dog Named Clover

I put in a load of laundry and then drove down to the beach. I took my sandals off at the end of the boardwalk and walked barefoot in the soft, stone-free sand.

It was nothing like walking the Pacific Ocean beach front back home with the massive waves rolling into the shoreline and the fresh salt air pungent with seaweed, but this gentle stretch of Georgian Bay was the longest fresh water beach in the world and I loved the clean, sweet taste of the air, the soft, onshore breeze blowing in off the bay, and the feel of the cool, fine sand on my bare feet. Every so often I walked in the cold, refreshing water.

For such a beautiful stretch of beach I saw very few people, the occasional man or woman walking their dog, or a pair of lovers walking hand in hand. I met two lovers coming towards me and gave them a friendly smile. "Beautiful morning," I said.

"It certainly is," the silver-haired man replied, smiling proudly.

The blond, full-figured, much younger woman about the same age as myself gave me a satisfied smile and said, "Enjoy your walk."

"Thank you," I said; catching a hint of commiseration in her smile that led me to respond in my mind, *"Someday soon I'll be walking hand in hand too..."*

I welled up with emotion. A few feet further I stopped. I had to check my life pulse. *"Is it really happening?"* I asked myself.

My mentor came to mind. *"Everything happens for a reason,"* she said. I believed it. My abortion happened for a reason, as did my experience with Seana. When I visited Doctor Kubler-Ross in Scottsdale, Arizona just before she passed away she told me that her life had been mapped out for her before she was born; she just had to follow her heart to get to where she was supposed to go. Her words rang loudly in my mind: *"All destiny leads to the same path of growth, love, and service."*

Was it love's turn now? I knew that she meant love for all of life, and I tried to live my life with love in my heart for everyone, but it was my turn now. I knew in my heart that life was finally returning my love. *"Was David part of my destiny? We met by chance. All great romances begin that way, don't they? It has to be! Please, Satma..."* I pleaded.

I walked on slowly, letting my excited mind follow my heart's desire. I felt a sudden urge to walk in the water. It was invigorating, and I felt young again. *"God, it's been a long time since I felt this good!"* I exclaimed to myself.

Then Father McDuffy spoiled it. His reward popped into my mind to soil my mood. I tried to push it out of my mind, but it wouldn't go away. I had to deal with it. *"Is this the price I have to pay for love?"* I asked myself. *"Does love always have to come with a price?"*

"Satma," I said, in a loud whisper, "what should I do?"

I didn't expect an answer. I walked on. My life had changed since I joined Atma-Gare. I trusted Huzee implicitly. I knew that he was guiding my life, but I still had to make the decisions. He helped me to make the right decisions. All I had to do was listen. Watch and listen. The Holy Spirit of Atma speaks to us every single moment of every single day. We just have to listen for the silent voice of God. The signs are everywhere.

I stopped. I perked my ears. "Satma, I don't hear anything," I said out loud, and broke into a gentle laugh. It felt good to laugh at myself again.

Then my mood changed. *"Do I have to, Satma? Do I have to go into the lion's den? Is that the price I have to pay for love?"*

I walked on, feeling the cold water wash onto my bare feet. I looked down at my feet. I liked my feet. Everyone said I had beautiful feet. Kevin loved my feet. They excited him sexually. He loved to kiss and caress them. "Why do I have to pay for love?" I said out loud, snapping out of my reverie. *"Why do I have to tell my story, Satma? Why?"*

For some reason I connected my feelings for David with the miracle of my unborn child, and I could not separate them. The two events of meeting David and Father McDuffy's challenge happened so close together that they had to be connected in some way.

I had just met David in Minneapolis. When I got home I read Father McDuffy's ad in the *Gazette*, which awakened memories of my abortion that made me furious. *"This can't be a coincidence,"* I thought. *"Something's going to happen. I feel it!"*

But it was my choice to go public or not. David said it wouldn't matter to God if I didn't open that door, because every door opens to the unconditional love of God. It was my choice which door I opened. It was always my choice. I chose to have my abortion, and I paid dearly for it. *"The sole purpose of life is to grow,"* said my mentor. Well, I did grow. I grew so much that it made me ready for Atma-Gare. When the student is ready, the teacher appears. I wasn't ready when I dreamt of the Satma. I had to wait eight years to become ready. "Well, here I am, Satma," I said, out loud. "What do I have to do now?"

I walked on, reproaching myself for my little tantrum.

"I have to be thankful," I thought. Atma-Gare had opened up my world. I could not believe how open and free my inner life had become. I was free of everything that had kept me from living my own life when I was a Roman Catholic. I was finally free to be me; but now I was called upon to be counted, and this terrified me.

Did I have to move my chair closer to David's? Did he come into my life to give me the strength I needed to step into the lion's den? Was that why the Atma had brought us together? *"Everything happens for a reason,"* said my mentor.

The abortion issue had reared its ugly head again. The anti-abortion group of Wyedale spearheaded by Father McDuffy had erected a large billboard on Highway 93 that passed through the community condemning abortion as an act of murder. I was affronted every time I drove by the billboard with the big red X drawn over the picture of an unborn child curled up in fetal position in its mother's womb. Then came Father McDuffy's reward offer in the Wyedale *Gazette*, which made my blood boil. Every cell of my body screamed to respond to the priest's provocative challenge. But was it the right thing to do? *"Give me a sign, Satma,"* I pleaded. *"Any sign whatsoever!"*

I had read many stories of Atmans asking the Inner Master for signs to guide them in their decisions. One woman asked the Satma for the symbol of three pink elephants to confirm what she felt she should do after her husband's death. Should she stay, or relocate? She asked for a sign of pink elephants to affirm her decision to relocate, and she saw her first pink elephant in a greeting card in the drugstore, the second pink elephant in another store window, and the third pink elephant on a pink balloon that a child was carrying, and she saw them all on the same day. She quit her job, sold her house, and moved to a warm southern state.

I wanted a sign like that, but I didn't know what sign to choose. I walked on, thinking of a clear sign from the Atma to speak to me. "How about a girl with reddish hair named Seana?" I asked, out loud. "No. That would be asking too much, wouldn't it?" How about eagles?" I said, thinking of what David had called me.

"Not all Atmans are birds of the same feather," I repeated under my breath, and smiled. What did he mean by that? I had to ask him the next time we talked. I loved that he saw me as an eagle Atman. I soared to the heavens. And I did soar with him when he told me his sunset story. *What an experience!*

"God," I said to myself, as I reflected on my new life in Atma compared to my old life in Christianity. There was a whole world of difference. *"It's a separate reality,"* I said to myself, smiling at my play on Carlos Castaneda's book by the same title that I had read in my desperate quest to find myself. "I'm sure glad I didn't follow that psychic path," I said, under my breath. "Who knows where Don Juan would have taken me?"

Nevertheless the spiritual life of Atma is so far beyond the grasp of the ordinary person that I could not share it with just anyone. I had

114

learned that the hard way. The strange looks, the whispers, and the labeling finally forced me to be more discerning in whom I shared my new spiritual life with. I had to be absolutely certain before I shared my story.

I thought of Michael Haydon, who gave me my Second Initiation in Atma. He was a Seventh Initiate. "Love is the cornerstone of the Atma life," he said to me when I joined Atma-Gare. "To love, we have to be free to love. We can't love if we're tied up in knots by thoughts and feelings and ideas that imprison us. We have to let go of our past to embrace our future. You came into Atma-Gare because you're ready, Cassie. Don't let your past get in the way of your future life. You wouldn't be so keen on Atma if you weren't ready for it. You must learn to trust yourself. But more important still, you must learn to trust the Satma."

Michael didn't say it, but he meant that I had to let go of my Roman Catholic past. I stopped walking. "I have to trust myself," I said under my breath. "I have to trust the Satma."

That's what I hated about my Roman Catholic faith. I could not trust myself. I had to trust what I was told to believe by my faith. But my faith let me down. I could not let go of the guilt for taking my unborn child's life, and I tried to take my own life to make up for it. My guilt crushed my spirit. *My Roman Catholic faith crushed my spirit!*

There was no guilt in my new Atma life. "What did David say last night?" I asked myself, and stopped walking again. I reflected, searching my data bank. Like my father, I have a prodigious memory. "'Every choice we make opens to the unconditional love of God,'" I said, quoting David. I smiled at the thought. *"My God, he's wonderful!"* I shouted, and quickly turned to see if anyone was around to hear me. No one was.

I thought of my father. He would approve of David. David Oakly was his own man. My father had to be his own man also. That's why he left the Church. He could not stomach being told how to live his life. It was a mystery to me why he married my mother. My mother thought with her feelings, my father with his brilliant mind, and they fought. Short of calling Mother stupid, my father said she was "cognitively indolent." My father was obsessive about using the right word. *Le mot juste,* he called it, quoting the novelist Henry James. That's where I got my love for words, and my son Mark. He reads the dictionary for pleasure.

I inherited my mother's passionate Irish spirit, but I agreed more with my father. My mother felt her way through life. She did not stop to reason. That's why my parents argued all the time. My father would stop and think first, and if he didn't know the answer he would seek out a book and come back with ten different answers, and my mother would kneel and pray to Jesus to solve her problems. She couldn't think for herself. That's why my mother and I grew apart, too. I began to think for myself.

My father had one of the keenest minds I've ever come across, but he couldn't reason his way out of his depressions, which lasted for months at a time. He thought he could, and he read every book he could find on the subject; but his "black dogs of despair" were relentless, and they eventually devoured him whole.

My "black dogs" nearly devoured me too. *"Thank you, Satma,"* I said, quietly in my mind. "Thank you for sparing me going down that path," I said out loud, with an overwhelming feeling of gratitude that welled me up with tears.

The Satma was always there with me. I know he was. I met him in my dream long before I tried to take my own life. He was always with me, but I just did not know about the Inner Master then. I do now. "Thank you, Zee," I said, out loud; and then laughed to myself. Huzee was the Mythmaster. Mark called him Amazing Zee, and I trusted him implicitly.

The Satma is the Inner Master, and he's closer to us than our own heartbeat. He is the Atma, the consciousness of God. We just have to become aware of it, that's all. That's why I love my new life in Atma-Gare. I've grown so much spiritually that it startles me to see how small my world was before I found Atma-Gare, and I cannot imagine my life without it now.

I saw a large boulder jutting out of the water close to the shoreline, about knee deep. I walked out to it in the bracing water. I wanted to reflect upon my life in Atma-Gare. I sat on the rock, bent my legs, and held them in my arms.

I laughed. I could not fathom how people could be so foolish to accept on blind faith alone what Christianity told them to believe. I laughed at the thought, because I was one of those foolish people not that long ago. *"What happened to break that spell? Was it my abortion?"* I asked myself.

"Of course it was," I said out loud. My abortion brought my whole world to a head. It put me to the test, and though I thought I had failed, I had not. My pain was so great that it shattered the insidious hold that Christianity had upon my Soul.

That's what Michael Haydon meant when he said that the spiritual law of life makes one ready for the most direct path home to God. "By spiritual law of life, you mean what?" I asked him one Sunday morning after the worship service.

"Karma," he replied, with the light bright in his eyes.

"Could you elaborate, please?" I asked.

"We pay through personal suffering for refusing to give up what keeps us from growing spiritually. No karmic pain, no spiritual gain," he added, with a pleasant smile. I didn't understand him then, but I do now. I paid with the guilt of my abortion for refusing to give up my blind faith, which kept me from taking responsibility for my own life.

"It's a hard lesson to learn," Michael amplified. "Karma teaches one to take responsibility for his own life. There is no eleventh hour salvation in the real world of karma and reincarnation. That's just a myth man has created to comfort himself."

"I know. It comforted me most of my life. But it never felt right to me. Every time I went to confession and was forgiven my sins it felt like I had taken candy from the store without paying for it. It felt like I had cheated God. That's what salvation felt like to me."

But not anymore. After I joined Atma-Gare I began to feel the invisible chains of my Christian faith fall away one by one, until I began to see the difference between belief and consciousness. They weren't the same. They were worlds apart.

In Atma-Gare, I grew in spiritual consciousness. By practicing the spiritual exercises of Atma daily I shed the chains of karma that kept me bound to spiritual ignorance; that's why I love singing HU. It frees me from my past. It lets me be me.

Quietly, I started singing the Love Song to God. I sent my voice out over the gentle waters of Georgian Bay. I imagined the HU riding the choppy little waves to the farthest reaches of the horizon and beyond, touching everyone in its path with love.

I sang the HU for ten minutes, loving the sound of the pure Atma as it came through my body and out across the bay and into the world. So wonderful did it feel that I got the distinct impression that the HU is the purest form of love, which in my heart I knew it was.

"You've got it," I heard a quiet voice speaking to me.

Startled, I stopped to look around. I was alone. "Pardon me?" I said, now realizing that it was the Inner Master's voice. I laughed. *Amazing Zee had just spoken to me!*

Silence. Once was enough to confirm what I felt about the HU. Then it hit me. The Satma was playing upon my love for *My Fair Lady* again.

"She's got it!" I shouted, and jumped into the water and started splashing like an excited child. I splashed and splashed and splashed! *"And thank you, Mark!"* I shouted again, grateful for my son's unique relationship with Huzee, the greatest magician in the world!

After I had my fun I started walking back, thinking about how lucky I was to have such wonderful children. Patrick shied away from Atma-Gare, but Mark and Cindy were born to become Atmans. Patrick felt he had to be loyal to his father, so he kept his faith; but in my heart I knew he was also ready for Atma-Gare. He just had to find his own way to it, like I had to. That's what Patrick and I have in common. We're both stubborn.

It makes it touchy sometimes when we talk Atma in the house, though; but deep down Patrick knows he's an Atman. He's just too proud to admit it. That's why David almost brought me to tears when he told Patrick about the way of love, because that's what the path of Atma is all about. Patrick will be going to Simon Fraser University in Vancouver when he graduates from high school, so he'll be back home before he knows it.

After a great deal of angry recrimination the first two or three weeks in Wyedale, he finally accepted his new life in Georgian Bay and makes the most of it. Like his father, he makes friends very quickly. His friends call him a "chick magnet" at school. He likes that. But he doesn't have a steady girlfriend yet; despite all the calls and text messages he gets from girls, not to mention Facebook and Twitter. He's waiting to get his driver's license first.

Mark's different altogether. He spends hours on the Internet googling for information on the myths of the world for his stories, and he loves to play computer games. He's learning about computers on the inner planes. He's forever Soul traveling to schools on the inner planes where he's taught by Atma Masters how to use the computer for new functions that have not been dreamed of out here yet. Mark is so creative it scares me. His Mythmaster stories send chills up my spine. They're like a new kind of Atma teaching story for future generations. He calls his stories "gateways." He's like a little George Lucas with an Atma twist, and I know he's destined for greatness. And Cindy is visited by the great Atma Master Zak Tarzman in her dreams and during the day. The torchbearer of Atma-Gare takes her to different places on the inner planes where she's taught about the Light and Sound of God. She doesn't talk about her experiences, though. She has to keep them secret, and I respect her privacy.

We don't always HU together out of respect for Patrick, but we do the HU once a week at our family *satsang*. Patrick has allowed us that. I look forward to our family HU songs. They bond my children and me in a way that prayer never could.

Something magical happens when we sing HU together. The door to the inner worlds open up, and we often have Soul travel experiences during our family Love Song to God. We don't share them with Patrick, though. We used to, but this upset him. So we stopped.

I stopped walking again, thinking of Patrick. "I guess he came into our family to keep us humble, didn't he, Zee?" I asked the Satma, thinking out loud.

I thought of my old friends in Vancouver. Eva Stenson's husband Robert was a highly successful orthopedic surgeon at Vancouver General, and Eva was the Director of Nursing at St. Paul's Hospital where I worked. They had two brilliant boys who grew up to become medical doctors. She had two miscarriages trying for a daughter. Her doctor told her that it was too dangerous to try again, and they adopted an infant aboriginal girl who turned out to have Fetal Alcohol Syndrome. She was a very difficult child to raise, but they brought her up with more love, care, and attention than they believed they were capable of giving. She died of a seizure in her sleep at the age of twenty-three, three days after she got her first job.

"Becky humbled our family," Eva confessed to me one day over coffee in her Florida sunroom. "She taught us the gift of patience, which in turn taught us how to love; and then she left us. Cassie, she left a big hole in my life that I can never fill..."

I was into Edgar Cayce at the time, so I gave Eva some books on reincarnation. I thought they might help to put her daughter's death into perspective and help ease her pain, but she returned my books without reading them. I didn't see much of Eva after that experience. With so many of my friends, we simply grew apart.

Strangely enough, I see Eva in my dreams every two or three months. And I've seen her with her daughter BAtmay twice. We're still friends on the inner planes. Like David said, one day she'll be ready for Atma-Gare too.

An elderly white-haired lady and her dog walked towards me. The big brown Labrador was not on a leash, and it ran up to me and started licking my hand. He reminded me of Tiger, our own big Labrador whom we had to put down when a car hit him.

"He's very friendly," I said, as I stroked the big dog's head.

"Yes, he is," the lady said, with a friendly smile. "He's all I have now," she added, in a mournful tone of voice that told me she was a recent widow.

"You miss your husband dearly, don't you?" I said, opening the door that she had invited me to walk through.

"I still can't believe he's gone," she said, her eyes turning inward to all the memories of their life together. Catching herself, she stared at me and said, "How did you know I just lost my husband?"

"I just knew. I'm sorry for your loss. How are you coping?" I quietly asked.

"I'll never get used to it," she said, in that same mournful voice. "How can I? But he's not gone away. He still comes to me. I've seen him in my..."

She stopped in mid sentence. With a frightened look in her eyes, she forced a smile and said, "I shouldn't be telling you this. I'm spoiling your walk. I should be on my way. Come on, Clover. Let's let the nice lady finish her walk. Come on, precious."

Embarrassed, nervous, and frightened, the lady wanted to walk away but couldn't move her legs. I knelt down and rubbed Clover's head with both hands. "I know, I know, you just love to be touched, don't you? You love it, don't you, precious?" I said, as I gently stroked Clover's big brown head.

Our dog loved to be touched too. Tiger preferred to be touched to the table food scraps that he also loved. I didn't realize it until one day I came into the house and Tiger came lurching at me to welcome me home. I had a trying day at the hospital, and Tiger's welcome felt so wonderful that I knelt down and thanked him for his love.

I stroked Tiger over and over, feeling his love for me slowly dissolve my long day's stress. It felt so good to be loved without being judged that I suddenly realized what unconditional love really meant!

I stared into Tiger's big soulful eyes as they poured out his love for me, and I got the urge to say, *"I love you too, Tiger!"* That's when it hit me. That's when I *saw* Tiger. "Yes, you're here too, aren't you?" I said, now *aware* of Tiger's presence.

We had connected Soul to Soul. For the first time since we got him as a puppy, I acknowledged Tiger as another Soul and not just a family pet that we all took for granted. From that moment on he *was* Tiger, an evolving individual Soul like all of us, and I acknowledged his presence every chance I got. That's why Tiger loved to be touched by me more than anyone else in the family— *we had connected spiritually!*

That's when I learned that pets love to be touched. Through touch they feel accepted and loved and acknowledged for who they are. I also learned something else from Tiger that day. As frustrated as I was from my day at work, when I looked into Tiger's big soulful eyes as they poured out so much love for me that I was compelled to say, *"I love you too, Tiger!"* it suddenly dawned on me what "I love you" really meant.

In my love for our family pet I had acknowledged Tiger's evolving spiritual identity, and the doors of perception opened up to me and I realized that when we say "I love you" to someone, the three most beautiful words in the world, we acknowledge them for who they are and confirm their identity without judgment, and that's unconditional love!

I really missed Tiger. I continued to stroke Clover's head as I looked up at the lady who did not want to leave. I stood up and introduced myself. "I'm Cassie O'Shaunnesy," I said, giving her my hand.

"Oh, hi. I'm Marilyn Symonton," she said, shaking my hand. "And my dog's name is Clover," she added, patting him on the head.

"It happens all the time," I said, without judgment. "I'm a nurse, and I've heard many stories of loved ones coming back to comfort family members. I'm sure it was your husband who came to visit you, Marilyn. He loves you, and he just wants to make sure you're okay."

Somewhat startled, Marilyn's eyes widened. Then she started pouring her heart out to me. I was used to this from the bereaved, and I put all thoughts out of my mind and gave her my full attention as my mentor had taught me.

"Listen with your heart, not your ears," Doctor Kubler-Ross instructed me in her reply to my letter when I asked how she coped with the bereaved. *"Put everything out of your mind and focus all of your attention on what they are telling you. If you learn to listen with your heart you will hear the person behind the words, and you will touch their broken heart with healing love without saying a single word."*

As I listened to Marilyn I continued to pet Clover, who now sat by my side lapping up all of that touching love. My heart went out to Marilyn as she told the story of her husband's cancer and lingering death. At some point in her story, I felt that my listening touched her heart like an invisible hand just as I was touching Clover's heart with my physical hand, and the more Marilyn poured her grief out to me the more I felt her need to be touched with love.

I waited patiently for her to bring her story to comfortable closure, and then I gave her a nice, long hug. I didn't say anything.

Over the years I had learned that the silent hug is the most eloquent expression of love that one can give to a grieving person.

Marilyn held me tight in our embrace, and we did not let go until the moment felt right. Then I looked into Marilyn's teary eyes and said, "You're going to be fine. I promise you," and I quietly walked away.

I'm sure one day Marilyn will tell her friends about the lady she met walking the beach on the shores of Georgian Bay who must have been an earth angel, but however she looks back upon our moment together I know that the Atma touched her in that special way that heals a broken heart.

The Atma rewarded me also. As I walked away I felt so good for my service to life that the doors of perception opened again, and I instantly knew *the* secret of healing touch therapy. It was love, pure and simple!

"So that's what you meant," I said out loud, as I recalled my mentor's last letter. *"When all is said and done, the true healer is always love,"* she wrote. I believed her, but I had no idea of the literal truth of that statement until I met Marilyn and Clover on the sandy shores of Georgian Bay!

I *knew* in that spiritual way that needs no proof, that love is the true healer of life, and I walked in deep reverence for a long while. And then my thoughts pulled me back to David.

"Can I satisfy him," I asked myself, as the reality of a physical relationship hit me. It was so long since I had made love with a man that I felt like a nervous teenager. *"I'll bet he's a wonderful lover!"* I exclaimed, jumping right into my fantasy.

I couldn't wait for Saturday night. I had to make an appointment for my hair right away, and I had to have a manicure. "I should go shopping this afternoon," I said, panicking about what I was going to wear on our first real date.

I could not believe how nervous I suddenly felt. I jumped into the cold water again and splashed my face. I had to cool myself off.

I continued walking the beach, past the end of the boardwalk where I had started. I wasn't ready to go home just yet. I wanted to collect my thoughts. Too much was happening too fast, and I didn't want to be caught unprepared.

First things first. I had to think my way through Father McDuffy's challenge. I didn't have to respond. I wasn't a scientist, but I did have proof that a fetus is not a little person. I *knew* that it was a biological entity, but I did not have to respond.

David agreed with me, but he wasn't called to stand up to Father McDuffy's challenge. I was. I didn't understand my compulsion to tell the world about my unborn child. I certainly didn't have that compulsion before I read Father McDuffy's reward offer. From the moment I read it, I heard the Call. Everything that I stood for was put on the line, and I knew that I was the only person who could stand up to his challenge with an equal conceit; but I had to think of my career and my children. What would it do to us if I went public?

I walked in deep thought sorting out the consequences of my decision; but either way, I knew that I had to do something. I picked up a stick, wrote MY UNBORN CHILD in the sand and thought about my decision.

If I chose to stay silent, would I be able to live with myself? I didn't know. If I went public, what would this do to our life in Georgian Bay? I didn't know. I had to talk this over with David. I had to share my experience with him first. I had to get his reaction. I knew that I could trust him with my life!

I walked back to my car and drove home. I put in another load of laundry, put a pot roast in the slow cooker, got all of my vegetables and salad ready, and then I showered, changed, did my make-up, and drove to the newly expanded Georgian Mall in Barrie to check out the new stores for something to wear Saturday evening; I had to find something that made me look as incredible as I felt— *if that was possible!*

Chapter 10

Stumpy's Secret Truth

My abortion changed my life, and the way I thought about life; that's why I felt compelled by Father McDuffy's challenge to tell the world about my unborn child.

David was right. He confirmed what I knew in my heart. The Atma let me have my experience with my unborn child for my benefit, but also for the good of every woman torn by the moral question of abortion.

A woman is not a man, and no amount of explanation can bridge our differences. We don't think like men, we don't feel like men, we don't behave like men, and we certainly don't make love like men, and try as he may man will never understand just how important the abortion issue is to women. It is not only central to our basic identity as women, but it strikes at the very core of life itself because without us there would be no human race.

In spite of in vitro fertilization and all the advances made by modern science, we are still the baby-makers, and we have been used as baby-makers since time immemorial; but we've come into our own now, and we demand the right to our own body. It is no longer simply a question of freedom of choice, but of personal power.

Women hold the power to create life, but because society has evolved to the point where freedom of choice has become an individual right, women now threaten the very seat of man's power— the seed of life itself.

Despite his fine rhetoric and token gestures, man does not want to relinquish his power over women. It is his inherent right to use women to perpetuate the transfer of power from father to son; but now that women are free to choose to not be baby-makers, we threaten the family, society's most fundamental institution; and this terrifies man.

Man does not want to give women the power to control the process, because power is central to man's identity; and the Christian Church, with its male God and male priests has always come to the defense of man. But Christianity is running scared today. Society has outgrown Christian dogma, and a clash is inevitable. It's only a matter of time. This is why the abortion issue is so vital to the Christian Church. Abortion is a threat to the very core of Christianity's inflexible, dogmatic hold upon social consciousness.

Abortion is a simple issue of power. It was for this reason that I embraced the spiritual path of Atma-Gare. The Atma does not exercise power over my mind, my body, or my spirit. It gives me the freedom to be the person I want to be, because Atma-Gare is an individual spiritual path. It does not judge my life. I am free to grow at my own pace.

The idea of total freedom and total responsibility, which are central to the spiritual path of Atma, so terrifies the old religions of the world—Christianity, Judaism, and Islam—that they have gathered their collective wits to keep us from having the right to our own body.

The old religions want to keep women in their place, which has always been subordinate to men. They don't want us to have the power to have an abortion. They know that the moment they relinquish their authority over our body they will lose control over our mind, which they've had since the dawn of history. The old religions of the world know that if they forfeit their control over us they will become an effete force in society, which is why Islam is running scared today as women wake up to their inherent spiritual right to be free and why abortion is such a vital issue for Christianity; freedom threatens their existence!

And this is why my uncle Clancy reacted with such ferocity to my abortion that day. I threatened his very identity as a man in one of the most male dominated institutions in the world. My abortion was not a sin against God as I was told to believe by my Roman Catholic Church, but a sin against all Christendom, and my uncle Clancy had to defend his faith because he was an obedient servant of his Pope.

As a child, I loved my uncle Clancy. He was different from my uncle Timothy, whom I loved and admired more as a father figure; but as much as I loved Uncle Clancy, something about him always made me uneasy.

Uncle Clancy seemed to be so devoted to God that I felt sinful around him. I tried, but I could never get close to him. Uncle Clancy never hugged or kissed me on the forehead like my uncle Timothy did; he patted me on the head and admonished me to be a good girl, because God was watching me.

I grew up to fear sin. Even to this day I twinge at the thought of committing a mortal sin. But as I grew older and began to formulate my own thoughts, thanks to my father's incessant prodding, I began to ask questions that disturbed Uncle Clancy.

No longer could he pat me on the head and expect me to accept his word as the law of God. He had to respond to my probing questions in a way that forced him to reveal his blind obedience to the Church, and he resented me like he did my father for challenging him.

"Sin is an offense against God," he curtly told me one day over early dinner after Sunday Mass. Uncle Clancy often ate early Sunday dinner with us before Mother served dinner to our boarders. It was one of Mother's favorite family rituals.

"I understand," I said. I was not married to Kevin then, but I was nursing at St. Paul's Hospital and still living at home. "But what exactly is a sin, anyway?" I asked.

"I just told you," my uncle replied, in his haughty voice. "Sin is a transgression of God's law. Sin is an offense against God. Sin is a violation of the Ten Commandments. You haven't broken any commandment, have you?" he asked, with a devilish smile.

"No," I snapped back. I hated being treated like a child. "You haven't answered my question," I insisted. "I still don't understand what a sin is. Perhaps I don't know how to phrase my question properly, but I think what I want to know is this: who can say with certainty when a sin is a sin and not a sin? Do you understand what

I'm asking?"

I dared not tell Uncle Clancy, but that was my father's question that always got my mother started. She didn't that day, though. Mother let Uncle Clancy push me as far as he could, and she enjoyed listening. "The Pope is the Vicar of Jesus Christ, and he speaks for our Lord on earth," my uncle responded, with a huffy air of impatience. "So when the Pope tells us that it's a sin for women to have sex outside the sacred bonds of holy matrimony, he's speaking for our Lord Jesus Christ. A sin is what our Lord Jesus says it is according to his chosen Vicar. I am an ordained priest of our Holy Mother Church, of which our Pope is the Vicar of Christ, so when I tell you that it is a sin to have sex outside of the holy bonds of marriage I speak for the Pope and Jesus Christ. So a sin is what I tell you it is. Is that clear enough for you now?"

My uncle knew that Kevin and I were intimate. I had confessed my sin to him one Sunday morning before Mass several months earlier. I could not make my usual Saturday night confession with Father Bartholomew from another parish where I began to go when I was old enough to not want my uncles to know about my sins, but because I would never have heard the end of it from my mother if I missed communion on Sunday, I had to go to Uncle Clancy for confession before Mass, so he knew my dark secret.

I lost respect for my uncle that day. It wasn't fair of him to rub my face in it over dinner. But I asked for it. I knew that he knew I was having sex with Kevin. I just wanted him to tell me why it was so wrong to have sex outside of marriage when we loved each other.

Kevin and I both felt it wasn't wrong. The first time we made love we felt guilty, but after we made love a few more times we could not understand how such a beautiful experience could be a sin against God. Something wasn't right.

I could not broach the subject of love with my uncle. He was so cold and distant when it came to matters of the heart that I began to feel sorry for him. That's why I prodded him about sin. It was foolish, but I felt compelled to ask him. This was my father's side of me. I was like a dog with a bone. *I had to know why it was a sin to make love!*

Uncle Clancy enjoyed the hold that he had over me, and every person who confessed their sins to him. It gave him power, which he exercised in his own subtle way. But I was being pulled away from the Church by my spiritual hunger, which my faith could no longer satisfy. I continued to live in silent terror of mortal sin and eternal damnation, but the more exposed I was to the world outside my religion the more I questioned my faith.

I believed in heaven and hell, which were central to my faith, but as I questioned mortal sin I began to have doubts about eternal damnation. I could not fathom how I could be sent to hell for eternity for doing something that the Pope had decided was a mortal sin—like eating meat on Friday, which we could now do, or missing Sunday Mass which we could now attend Saturday evening instead. A perfect act of contrition would spare me from a fate of eternal damnation in hell, but that wasn't what bothered me. I really had no say in my own salvation. I was totally dependent upon my Roman Catholic faith, and that bothered me.

That's what attracted me to reincarnation. I had heard of the idea of living many lifetimes in high school, but I was too much of a Roman Catholic to entertain the idea of reincarnation seriously. I dismissed it with the same blind conceit that Christians have done for centuries. But the older I got and the more experiences I had, the more fascinated I became with the idea of reincarnation, and especially the idea of karma.

Karma put salvation squarely in my lap where I felt it belonged. I liked the idea of being responsible for my own salvation. Karma was the universal law of cause and effect, just compensation, and harmony. It was not a law instituted by man that could be changed at will. Karma affected everyone equally like the law of gravity, and it made perfect sense to me. Karma meant that I would be reborn into a new life according to how I lived my present lifetime, and the more I thought about karma and reincarnation the more appealing they were to me.

My abortion caused my break with Christianity. It was inevitable, but my abortion sped up my karma that led to my crisis in faith.

Something was happening around me that my religion refused to address. It became apparent to me that my Christian faith was out of sync with the rest of society. It seemed to me that the more society wanted to breathe in the fresh air of personal freedom, the more Christianity dug in its heels, and this terrified me on a visceral level.

That's why I felt compelled to tell my story to the world. It would help women to breathe more freely and live their own life. When Doctor Elisabeth Kubler-Ross began researching near-death experiences, she documented case after case of people who were asked on the other side what services they had rendered to life, and I knew in my heart that telling the story of my unborn child would be the greatest service that I could render!

I believed in equal opportunity for everyone, men and women alike. My abortion experience with my unborn daughter compelled me to make a contribution to woman's rights, but I was wedged between a rock and a hard place. I knew that the longer I procrastinated the more guilty I would feel, and there was nothing I hated more in my life than feeling guilty!

"What's your secret?" I asked one of my terminal patients the day after my walk on the beach. I had wrestled with myself all night long, and I had to make a decision.

Stumpy Stevens was an old bachelor in his eighties who had worked in the bush camps in the Kenora district in Northwestern Ontario most of his life. He came back to the family farm in Wyedale to live with his widowed sister, but he was diagnosed with cancer when he went to see his doctor for the pain in his stomach. His cancer had spread throughout his body and he was given less than two months to live, but he refused to be admitted to the hospital until he had to be. Stumpy had such an air of quiet resignation about him that he made me smile every time I popped in to see him, which I did several times a day.

"My secret?" he said, with a puzzled look.

"Yes, what's your secret, Stumpy?" I asked again.

"My secret? About what?" he asked, with a puzzled look.

"About you. Your life," I said, with a big smile.

I wanted to know how he could be so resigned about dying. We had talked about dying already, which I made a point of doing shortly after he was admitted, but he wasn't ready to tell me his secret yet. He thought for a moment or two, and then grinned when he made the connection. He motioned me with his thin arm.

I moved in closer, but it wasn't close enough. He wanted me to bend over so he could whisper his secret into my ear. "Dying's not so hard," he said, in a raspy whisper. I pulled back a few inches. "It's living that's hard. You wanna know my secret? I can tell you," he said, with an impish glint in his wise old eyes.

"Yes, please do," I said.

"Come closer," he said again. I pulled a chair over and sat by his pillow so he could rest his head back. He looked me straight in the eye and said, "No matter what it's gonna cost you, you gotta be who you are. That's my secret. I'm gonna die soon, but I lived life on my own terms. I'm not afraid to meet my Maker. I did a lot of stupid things in my time, but I never hurt nobody. I paid my own way, and I don't owe a penny to anybody. I never did. I always paid my bills. My mother told me three things when I left home. Don't hurt anybody. Pay your bills. And don't lie. That's how I lived my whole life. I never got married, but I don't care. I got my sister and three nephews and seven foster kids in Africa. That's my whole family. And I'll tell you something else, if you wanna know the honest truth. I never sold out. The way I see it, it's better to be alone like me than to be one of *them.*"

By the way he spit out the word, it must have meant something very personal. I had to ask. "What do you mean by *them,* Stumpy?"

Dying patients have nothing to lose. Once they accept that they are no longer for this world, they have license to speak their mind. That's why my mentor told me to listen carefully to every dying patient's last words. *"Ask them for their secret,"* Doctor Kubler-Ross said to me as her parting gift. *"Everyone has their own relationship with God. That's their secret truth. Ask them. I promise you, you won't get the same answer twice."*

That's why I asked Stumpy.

"You wanna know who *them* is?" he said.

"Yes, I do," I said. "Who is *them*?"

Stumpy's dark little eyes lit up like a light bulb. He was smiling inside so much that his whole countenance shone with his inner light. He was going to share his secret truth with me, the essential wisdom of his eighty-two year old personal relationship with God. If he could have gotten up to dance, I'm sure he would have because there's nothing more that a dying person wants than to tell the world that his life meant something.

This was the secret that my mentor passed on to me just before her own death. Doctor Kubler-Ross told me about this unique relationship that people develop with God over the course of their life. Her secret, born of years of helping people to die with dignity, was that *"a person's life is their own secret truth from God."* And Stumpy couldn't wait to share his secret truth with me.

He took a few labored breaths. *"Them* is those who run this world," he began, his low raspy voice taking on an ominous tone. "Civil servants, lawyers, and priests. They're the ones," he continued, speaking very slowly. He labored to speak, but his eyes were on fire now, and his face glowed. "The *we* people of this world. *We* this, and *we* that. They don't have the guts to speak up for themselves. They all hide behind the *we* mask. Indians, the whole lot of 'em. Always *we* do this, and *we* do that. They can't take responsibility for anything. And if they do stand up to be counted, it don't mean much cuz they ain't for real anyway. Indians, the whole lot of 'em. Sneaky, money-mooching freeloaders. Liars, the whole lot of 'em. They're all getting a free ride on the backs of hard-working, honest people. Just try and pin one of *them* down. You can't. All you get from *them* is a big pile of you know what. Don't be like *them*, Cassie. I know you're not. I can tell. I got a nose for this kinda stuff. You can't trust 'em. You wanna know how I know? I'll tell you the honest truth. You wanna know?"

I was spellbound. This was better than juicy gossip. It sounded like Stumpy was blowing the whistle on life's dirtiest little secret. "Please tell me," I said. "But take your time, Stumpy. Take a little rest first. Would you like a drink of water? Is your mouth dry?"

"No. I'm okay," he said, and smiled at me with his eyes.

"Alright. So tell me how you know *them,* Stumpy. I want to know."

"I can tell *them* by how they smile. It's not like you and me," Stumpy said, and then he gave me a deliberate facial smile.

"What kind of smile is it?" I asked. I was getting pretty good at reading false smiles myself, and Stumpy had me burning with curiosity.

"It ain't real," he said, and shut his eyes for a few minutes to rest. I waited patiently, eager to hear his personal truth. When he opened his eyes he had that devilish glint again, "A real smile comes from here," he said, putting his hand to his heart. "It comes from the Soul. *We* people don't have a Soul. They sold their Soul for the dollar. I tell you, the almighty dollar's gonna destroy this world. Mark my words, Cassie."

"Not just the almighty dollar, Stumpy," I said, sharing my own little secret. "It's also about status, security, and image. You'd be surprised how much power these things have over us. It's all about appearances today. It's not easy being true to what you believe. I'm proud of you, Stumpy. You give me hope in the human race."

"I'm proud of me too," Stumpy said, matter-of-factly. "I'm gonna die soon, maybe tonight; but I'm not afraid to meet my Maker. I had a good life. I never cheated nobody. And I never lied to nobody either. I got nothing to hide from my Maker. Not like *them*. I never saw so many friggin liars and cheaters my whole life till I got involved with the government. Lawyers are no better. All they do is take. Take take take. They don't give anything back. Indians, the whole lot of 'em. All they do is take. They don't work for their money. Two hundred dollars for one phone call. By the time he was through with me I had to pay five thousand dollars just to get what the government owed me. It ain't fair. I worked my whole life and I don't owe anybody a cent. Not a red cent. You wanna know my secret? You wanna know why I ain't afraid to meet my Maker? Give something back to life. That's my secret. That's what the good Lord put us on this earth for. He didn't put us here to take and take and take like *them*. That ain't how nature works. Nature takes and nature gives back. That's the way it's supposed to work."

"Take what, Stumpy? What does man take?" I asked.

"Oh, you know what I mean," he said, with a dismissive wave of his arm. "They always want something for nothing. Indians, the whole lot of 'em. I'm gonna die soon, maybe tonight, maybe tomorrow, so I don't care anymore. I got into trouble up north talking about Indians.

They've been taking for so long now they don't know how else to live. And they know it too. But I don't care anymore now. I'm gonna die, so what's it matter to me?"

Stumpy sunk into his bed. He got a big load off his chest, and he was exhausted; but I never saw a more satisfied look on a dying man's face. Even with that devilish glint in his eye, it was angelic, like he had just snuck through St. Peter's gate.

"I agree with you, Stumpy," I said, joyful for his secret. "But you know what? If we don't pay for what we get in life we're going to pay for it down the road."

"You got that right," he spoke up, with a sudden surge of new life in his frail body. "And they're gonna pay for it in spades too. Nature don't like cheaters. I never cheated nobody my whole life. My mother told me to pay my own way, and I did. I never got a free ride like *them.* Not once. Nature's gonna bite *them* one day, and you know where, eh?"

I laughed. "I admire you, Stumpy."

"You do?" he said, surprised.

"Yes, I do," I said, and kissed him on the cheek. Stumpy smiled back to let me know that he approved of me.

"On the whole, Stumpy," I said, hoping to get one last answer before he crossed over, "what do you think about life?" I had to know. Stumpy's answer might help me to make up my mind about Father McDuffy's challenge.

"It ain't too bad," he sighed, making one last valiant effort to share his secret with me. "I know I griped about a lot of things, but it ain't too bad really. The chickens always come home to roost. Can you get me a glass of juice? I feel kinda parched."

"Yes, of course," I said, with a grateful smile.

Stumpy liked orange juice, so I went and got him a little container of orange juice with a straw. I held the juice box for him to sip. When he had enough, I placed it down and said, "Thank you, Stumpy. I'm going to treasure what you shared with me. I think you're a marvelous man, and I'm very, very proud of you."

Stumpy did not reply. He just smiled at me. That was enough.

I finished my shift and drove to the store to pick up a few

groceries. The next morning I saw on the chart that Stumpy had passed away during the night, which didn't surprise me. We didn't expect him to die till the end of the week, but he was ready to cross over and I was happy that he did so peacefully.

"And what services have you rendered?" I heard the Gatekeeper ask Stumpy Stevens in my mind when he stepped into the Light.

"I paid my own way," I heard him say.

"Yes, but what services have you rendered?" the Gatekeeper asked.

"I sponsored seven starving little orphans," Stumpy answered.

"Step this way," said the Gatekeeper, and opened the gate that led to the Golden Temple of Spiritual Wisdom and the way of eternal life.

Chapter 11

My Brother's Revelation

My uncle Clancy is the oldest in my mother's family and my mother is the youngest, but only my mother, Uncle Clancy, and Uncle Jimmy are still alive. My uncles Terry and Michael sacrificed their lives to "the troubles." Uncle Jimmy, who owns and operates a small but successful whiskey distillery, lives in Belfast with his family. My uncle Timothy is my only living relative on my father's side. My grandparents on both sides have passed on.

My mother was a young woman when she came to Canada with my father and my brother Michael, stopping in Halifax first and then Vancouver where Uncle Clancy and Uncle Timothy lived and where she's been ever since. She married my father when she was seventeen, and at eighteen gave birth to Michael in Dublin. I came along five years later in Vancouver after two miscarriages, which made me very special to my parents.

My father was only twenty-three and working on his PhD in English Literature when he fell in love with my mother who ran away from home to work in Dublin. His pet name for Mother was Nora. It was ironic, but I didn't find out why until I read *Ulysses*. James Joyce was my father's literary idol, not for his writing alone, but for his contempt for the Roman Catholic Church which, ironically, my mother embodied heart and Soul.

My mother left Vancouver twice, each time to attend her brother's funeral in Ireland, and each time coming back stronger in her faith. After my father was hospitalized for the third time for his "troubles," as he called his internal conflict with his demons, my uncle Jimmy helped my mother to finance the purchase of a three story boarding house in False Creek, Vancouver's east end, and my brother and I grew up with strangers coming in and out of our lives. We were never bored, but we missed our father who came and went like our boarders.

My mother worked tirelessly in our boarding house, cooking and doing laundry while holding down two part time jobs to pay for our education.

My brother went into dentistry after he left the seminary, and I became a nurse. Michael married his hygienist. They have two boys and a girl, and by all appearances he's happily married. For Mother's sake, he goes to Mass at St. Stephen's in North Vancouver, which is uncle Clancy's parish, with his family every Sunday; but he's not a very good Catholic.

My brother stopped believing in his religion long before I did, which I did not know until after I had my abortion. I desperately needed someone in my family to understand why I had my abortion, and to my surprise Michael not only understood but also approved.

I called Michael up to talk about my abortion, and he invited me for a round of golf at his country club, the Mayfair Lakes Golf & Country Club, minutes from his office in downtown Vancouver. We had just shot the ninth hole and stepped off the fairway into a shady little grove to talk before shooting the second half of the course. I got very emotional.

Michael looked at me with that sad, melancholy look in his brown eyes that never seemed to go away, put his arms around me, and said, "I love you, sis, and I forgive you." He held me close to his big, strong body, stroking my back first with his warm comforting hand, and then he caressed my forehead and cheek, and when I finally stopped crying he looked into my eyes and said, "So what's the big deal, anyway?"

"I don't know," I said.

"Do you still feel guilty?"

"Yes."

"Why?"

"Don't you think abortion is murder?"

"No, as a matter of fact I don't."

"You don't? Does Mother know this?"

"She has no reason to know how I feel about abortion."

"She must have talked about my abortion with you," I said, surprised.

"She's talked about it, Cassie; but you know Mother. She talks, you listen. I tried to tell her how I felt about it last Sunday over early dinner, but she didn't want to hear me. She went on with Uncle Clancy about you as though you've become unredeemable. They blame Father, of course. Don't let them get to you, sis. You have the right to live your own life."

"That's what I keep trying to tell her, but she won't budge. Neither will Uncle Clancy or Uncle Tim. They all think my abortion and marriage break-up scrambled my mind. They do, Michael. They think that's why I left the Church. But I didn't. I left the Church because there's nothing in it for me anymore. *Nothing, Michael!"*

"I understand," Michael said, and grabbed my trembling hands and held them with both of his. "You don't have to justify your reason for leaving. I understand."

"Do you really?"

"Yes, I do. I honestly do."

"Do you still believe, Michael?"

"I go to church to keep Mother happy, that's all," Michael said, letting go of my hands. "I stopped believing long ago. The truth is, I'm not sure if I ever believed. I must have inherited Father's skepticism," he added, with a wry smile.

"You never told me. How come? When did this happen, Michael? Does Mother know about this?"

"Of course not. It would break her heart, so whatever you do..."

"Of course I won't," I interrupted. "So you're just pretending to be a good Roman Catholic, then? How can you, Michael?"

"To keep peace in the family," he replied.

"You rat! I tortured myself trying to convince Mother why I had to leave the Church and all along you had left. How long, Michael?

How long has this been going on?"

"What does it matter?" he asked, with a life-worn look on his face.

"It matters to me. How long, Michael?" I insisted.

"About ten years now," he said, with a shrug.

"You rat! Why didn't you tell me?"

"What for? You had to find your own way, sis."

"I know. *My God, if Mother only knew!"*

"And don't you dare tell her. That's her whole life, Cassie. Mother lives by the cross and she's going to die by the cross."

I slapped Michael on the arm. "How can you go to Mass every Sunday and live with yourself?"

"Let's not get righteous," my brother shot back, in that tone of voice I was so familiar with growing up and had learned to respect. "It was no less painful for me to leave the Church than I'm sure it was for you to abort your child, so why don't we just leave it at that?"

"I'm sorry. I didn't mean it that way. I didn't know; that's all. Why didn't you tell me? *Why, Michael?"* I said; feeling like I always did when I pushed myself on my brother.

"Like I said, you had to find your own way. It wasn't easy, Cassie. And it's not easy now. But I don't want to hurt Mother."

"I'm sorry. I didn't mean to pry. You're right; I had to find my own way. We all do, don't we?" I said, feeling my brother's deep love for me.

"That's the way life works, sis."

"Forgive me?" I pleaded.

"Of course I forgive you," he said, and hugged me again.

I felt good in my brother's arms. He was my hero, growing up. I looked up into his large, melancholy eyes and said, "I have to know one thing, Michael. I have to know, so please don't deny me. Did you lose your faith in Jesus, or just the Church?"

Michael stepped back. "Let's just say that I stopped believing what the Church has made of Jesus. It got so that I had to block it all out of my mind when I went to Sunday Mass. I'm good at it now, sis. I listen to Uncle Tim or Uncle Clancy's sermons and play golf in my mind. That's the only way I can stand to be in church. I was going crazy there for a while listening to their sermons. It was like forcing a square peg into a round hole. They were driving me out of my mind until I figured out a way to block them out. For a long time I thought of leaving the Church, but I couldn't for Mother's sake. So now I play a game of golf in my mind when I go to Mass. That's the only way I can deal with it. And Mother's none the wiser."

"Michael, I've been wrestling with my faith for years. Why in God's name didn't you tell me? I feel like you betrayed me!" I said, ranting like his little sister all over again.

"Don't take it personally, sis. Faith is a private thing. Look at what happened when I told you I was leaving the seminary?"

Suddenly it all came back. *"You nearly broke Mother's heart!"*

"And yours. Remember? That's why Mother doesn't need to know this."

"I love you, Michael," I said, with a sudden rush of guilt. "I wish I were as strong as you. I wish Mother knew you like I do. She has no idea, does she?"

"None. And let's keep it that way, please."

"I won't tell her," I said, and took a moment to collect myself. "Okay, tell me now," I said, in my firm, all grown up, sisterly voice. "I have to know why you really left the seminary. You can tell me the truth now, Michael.*"*

Michael laughed. "I love life too much to be a priest, Cassie," he said, with an ironic smile on his dimpled, strong-chinned face. "Maybe it was my uncles who discouraged me. Look at them, sis. Uncle Tim drowns his faith with booze, and Uncle Clancy hasn't opened up his mind to a new idea since he forfeited it to the Church when he took his vows. They're pathetic, both of them."

"I know," I said, sheepishly.

"I can take Uncle Tim, but not Uncle Clancy. When I get near him I feel like I'm being sucked into a black hole. He gives me the creeps. He was easier to talk to when I was in the seminary, but I still couldn't share his reason for becoming a priest. I thought then that he was serving God for the wrong reasons, and I still do. But that's his problem. The truth is, I left the seminary because I wanted to be a healthy, normal man. Uncle Clancy is not a healthy normal man. He's queer, Cassie. In more ways than one."

I stared at Michael in stunned silence. Michael waited until it sunk in. "Are you saying what I think you're saying?"

"Yes," Michael said.

"No way!"

"Yes, he is, Cassie."

"Oh God! When did you find this out?"

"At the seminary," my brother said. "More than anything else, that's why I decided to leave. I didn't want to risk my normalcy. I had problems with my libido, Cassie, as do all seminarians. After I found out about Uncle Clancy I began to see that it just wasn't healthy to suppress the sex drive with celibacy, and I was right. Look at all the priests today being charged for molesting children. It's not a healthy way to live, Cassie. That's why I left."

"One could argue that your faith wasn't strong enough," I said, just to get Michael's reaction to the question of personal faith.

"Yes, one could. One could sublimate one's sexual drive into one's service for God, but that was a risk I refused to take. I sacrificed my desire to serve God for my desire to live a normal life. Is that so bad? Is it so wrong to be a normal, healthy, sexual human being? I don't think so. Neither did Father. *'Welcome, O life!'* he shouted when I told him I left the seminary. *'Go out and encounter for the millionth time the reality of experience and forge in the smithy of your Soul the uncreated conscience of your own life!'* He was playing on Stephen Dedalus' parting words in Joyce's novel *A Portrait of the Artist as a Young Man,* and he was so proud of me that he went on a big bender to celebrate. The truth is, sis, I don't believe God loves me any less for leaving the seminary than if I had become a sexually frustrated priest. I may not be true to the Church, but I'm true to my own life. That's our father's legacy, and that's all that really matters to me."

"I'm proud of you, Michael. I really am," I said, with tears in my eyes. "Does Mother know about Uncle Clancy?"

"Maybe, but I don't think so. He's very good at hiding it. On the other hand, Mother can be a real ostrich sometimes. But why do you think Uncle Clancy is so involved with the AIDS crisis? Mother thinks he's a martyr for volunteering all his time to AIDS, but it goes much deeper than that."

"How could I have been so blind? Is this why you never got along with him all these years? Does he know that you know, Michael?"

"Yes, he knows. But that's not why I don't like him. I'm not a homophobe. I just don't like him. Father pegged him right. He's a nasty little creep who uses his collar to cover up his lie. Father called it his life-lie. He got that little psychological gem from one of Henrik Ibsen's plays. Uncle Clancy doesn't serve God; he serves himself. He always has. You have no idea how I feel when we go to his Mass with Mother. Every word of his sermon rings like a cracked bell. But I play my best game there. I have no handicap at St. Stephen's Golf & Country Parish for the Spiritually Handicapped!"

Stunned, I shook my head in disbelief. "And Uncle Tim? What kind of game do you play at St. Jude?" I asked, still in shock.

"Not too bad. I'm down to a two handicap. You see, sis, I have a wee bit of a problem with the Irish myself..."

"I know. And I wish you would do something about it. For Father's sake, please don't wait too long. *Please, Michael...*"

I loved my brother. I loved him more than anything. He was my best friend growing up. I turned to him for everything. But as much as I loved him, I didn't really know him. The water ran deep with Michael, and he was more like our father than he wanted to admit; but he certainly opened my eyes that day. He didn't go to Church because he was a faithful Catholic; he went out of love and respect for Mother, and I admired and hated him for it.

I could never do that. I was too selfish to care how my behavior affected others. That's why I had my abortion. After we shot the back half of the course I went straight to Uncle Clancy's to forgive him for feeling the way I did about him all those years, but that was a decision I would live to regret.

I was on cloud nine when I left my brother Michael, and I was certain that I would get my uncle to understand why I had my abortion and left the Church; but as high as I was, my uncle Clancy pulled me down so low that I went straight home and tried to take my life.

Michael was right. Uncle Clancy was a black hole. He pulled me so deep into despair that my head spun with so much guilt and shame that all I could hear as I swallowed my sleeping pills was his shrieking voice condemning me from every corner of my mind, *"You're a heathen just like your father! You murdered your own child, and you don't deserve to live for what you have done!"*

Chapter 12

The Depths of the Ocean

In all honesty, I don't know if I could have lived with the guilt of my abortion on my conscience for the rest of my life, but I know I would not have attempted suicide had my uncle Clancy not pushed me over the edge. I haven't spoken to him since.

I went over that day hundreds of times in my mind, but I never understood the destructive influence my uncle had on me until David revealed something to me one day in RAPER'S PARK in Meaford that opened up my windows of perception.

We were already four glorious months into our blossoming relationship. One drab October Sunday morning, which reminded me of my old Vancouver winters when the sun refused to appear for weeks at a time, David dropped by the house unexpectedly and invited me for a day trip to the Meaford Apple Festival in Grey Bruce County. He hadn't received his pages from Binny yet, so he was free to go for an early run, and he dropped by in his running togs.

That's what I loved about him. He had an instinct for perfect timing. "I'd love to go," I said, grateful for another opportunity to be with him. "But you have to stay for breakfast first. Sunday's waffle day, and we can't break family tradition."

David accepted and stepped into the house. He was wearing his skin-tight black leggings and yellow Goretex jacket over his hooded gray pullover. "I'll stay for breakfast, but then I have to go shower and change," he said, and took off his runners.

"You don't have to change for me," I said, giving his taut runner's body a prolonged, deliberate stare. David had the sexiest legs. His calves were so firm and taut, and his thighs so muscular that they made me quiver with excitement.

He gave me an unselfconscious smile. "Can I do anything?"

"Yes, please. You can squeeze some orange juice for Patrick."

"Do you think he would notice the difference if I didn't?"

"In a New York minute," I said. I had waited a long time to use that expression, but the moment it came out of my mouth it sounded pretentious.

"There's no fooling that kid, is there?" David said.

"He's as straight as they come. I don't know where he gets it from, David. My father, I think. He was obsessively truthful."

"And you're not?" David said, and smiled.

"I try to be truthful," I said, with a blush of embarrassment. I asked the children to vote, and it was two to one for regular Belgian waffles with strawberries and whipped cream. Cindy wanted blueberry sauce, but the boys won out. I took out a package of frozen strawberries, and a package of bacon for David and the boys, and then I took out my waffle maker and plugged it in to heat up as I made the batter.

David squeezed the oranges and set the table. Then he looked after the bacon and the strawberry sauce while I made the waffles. He also grated some of the orange rind into the strawberry sauce, which gave our breakfast a special zest. "Do you guys mind if David and I go to the apple festival in Meaford today," I asked them over breakfast.

"Why should we?" Patrick said.

"Cindy?" I asked.

"Have fun, Mom," she said.

"Thank you, sweetheart."

"Yeah, have fun," Mark said. "Hey, David; I've been thinking about what you told me, but I can't work it into my story. I need a real good villain to make it work."

"What kind of villain?" David asked.

"You know, the kind that nobody thinks is a villain."

David laughed. "Well, Mark; there's plenty of them around."

"That's for sure!" Patrick said, in that cock-sure way of his that reminded me so much of his father. "Why don't you make Mr. Hopkins your villain? He'd be perfect."

Mr. Hopkins was Cindy's figure-skating coach.

"He's not a villain," Cindy said.

"Yeah, right! He googles you girls more than Google surfs the net!"

"He does not! He's a really good coach, and I like him!"

"You can like him, sweetheart; but remember what I told you."

"I remember, Mom. He won't touch me. I promise."

"He better not!" Patrick threatened, and dug into his waffles.

"So you guys don't mind if I take your mother to the apple festival?"

"Go for it," Patrick said.

"Yeah, go for it," Mark said, following suit. Then, with that look on his face that he gets whenever he's struck by an idea, he focused his eyes on David. "So what do you think? You know the kind of villain I need for my story. What if I made him a walk-in?"

"What's that?" Cindy asked.

"That's a spirit who takes over another person's body," Mark explained, and then turned to David again. "I know. He could be just an ordinary guy, but he turns into a villain and nobody knows why. Then another person becomes a villain, and another, and another, and nobody knows what's happening. It's like a virus, but it's not. It's a host of walk-ins who come from another dimension to take over the world. That's when the Mythmaster comes to plug up the hole to the other dimension and saves the planet. What do you think?"

"That's brilliant, Mark. But the Mythmaster doesn't interfere in world karma, as such. So how do you propose he plug up the hole?"

"Yeah, right. Okay, I could have him teach his Atma Warriors how to plug up the hole with the vibrations of the almighty HU. That would work, wouldn't it?"

"Perfect. Give it a try and see where it takes you…"

My children liked David. He related to each personally, and he didn't favor one over the other. Before they went to Vancouver for the summer, David took us all for a weekend of hiking and kayaking at

Algonquin Provincial Park. He booked two cottages, one for himself and the boys, and the other for Cindy and myself, and the children loved it. They preferred kayaking to hiking, especially Patrick who kept challenging David to race and proudly beat him two out of three races. I didn't care what we did, as long as we were all together. Every moment with David was precious, but I never knew if his time with me was as precious to him.

This was my one and only concern in our relationship. As much as David wanted to be with me, his other priorities took preference, and this really bothered me. They seemed to hang over my head like a threat. David's business came first, because he had to have work to live and support his other interests, which I had no problem with, but he was so committed to his other interests that it made me jealous. His passion for writing poetry came second to his business, with an obsession to annotate his translation of *A Conference of the Birds;* and then his long training runs for his provincial marathons ate into the weekends and evenings, not to mention Mediterranean cuisine cooking classes that he attended in Mississauga every second Saturday. That left little time for me, and I resented it deeply; but I never let it show.

David ran home and returned within the hour. He drove my Honda Odyssey to Meaford. "Do you miss Vancouver?" he asked me, a few miles down Highway 26.

"Very, very much," I said. Regardless how I felt about David, I couldn't lie to him. David called this kind of basic honesty "emotional integrity." I had never heard that phrase before, but I knew what he meant. That's what destroyed my marriage. I wasn't emotionally honest enough with my husband, and this drove him into the arms of another woman.

"Do you miss the mountains?" he asked.

"Much more than I could have imagined," I replied wistfully as I glanced at the changing colors of the landscape, which was just like my home province of British Columbia in the fall, except for the spectacular mountains of the west coast. "But as much as I miss the mountains, I miss the Pacific Ocean more. Something about the ocean fills me with a wonder I can't explain, David. The ocean has a depth, a power, and a primordial resonance that speaks to my Soul. I like

Georgian Bay, mind you, but Lake Huron is not the Pacific Ocean. And I dare not tell you how much I miss my native city. From one of the most beautiful cities in the world to the little town of Wyedale, of all places. I'm still suffering from culture shock. But I guess that's the price one pays for listening to their heart, isn't it? And you, David? Do you like living in Georgian Bay?"

"Since we're being so honest with each other, I have to confess that it doesn't really make much difference where I live these days. My body may be here, but I dwell in a place I can't explain," he answered, in his far away voice.

"Don't I know it?" I said.

He caught my meaning. "It's not fair to you, is it?"

"It's who you are, David," I said, not wanting to put him on the spot. "I don't understand this about you, but it's who you are; and I have to learn to live with it."

" It bothers you, doesn't it?" he said, placing his hand on my thigh.

"Yes and no. Your honesty mystifies me, David. You remind me of the Pacific Ocean, if that doesn't sound too strange. I think your honesty has a depth like the ocean, and this both fascinates and frightens me. I can't help it, but that's how you affect me."

"Well, I have been to the Ocean of Love and Mercy," he said, and smiled. He was referring to his sunset experience when the Satma took him to the Tenth Plane of Consciousness, the Body of God.

"I can't imagine what that experience has done for you, but if it's responsible for you being so…what's the word I'm looking for?"

"Charming?" he volunteered, and laughed.

David could be cheeky without even trying. "You certainly are that," I said, with an ironic smile. "No. I'm looking for a word that captures your emotional integrity. The first time you brought up the subject of emotional integrity, I couldn't get it out of my mind. I kept thinking of the time I tried to take my own life. That's why I think I did it. I didn't have enough emotional integrity. If I had, I wouldn't have been pushed over the edge with my abortion. I would have been strong enough to deal with my guilt and shame. That's why I broke down. I didn't have enough emotional integrity. I thought I did, but I didn't."

I felt a sudden rush of shame and my body flushed hot with the memory of the whole experience. Had the bleak day transported me back to Vancouver? I didn't expect to be so revealing. Realizing what I had done, I fell silent, and David graciously said nothing for the next few miles. That was another quality about him that I adored. He thought before he spoke. Unless he connected with his *inspiration*. Then the wisdom just poured out of him.

"Authenticity," he finally said, with absolute confidence in his voice. "That's the word you're looking for, Cassie. I said something one day to my Sufi teacher that he saw to be false, and he said to me, *'The authentic life is the path to the complete life. But to be authentic you have to know your own falseness.'* Sam saw right through me that day. Why suicide, Cassie? Albert Camus wrote in *The Myth of Sisyphus* that suicide is the only philosophical question worth considering. I've never been pushed that far by life, but I've given this question a lot of thought over the years. Would you like to talk about it?"

"Yes," I said, to my surprise. I paused, realizing just how much I trusted David from the day I met him. "I still haven't come to terms with it." I continued, feeling a strong need to talk about my attempted suicide. "Would you like to hear how I came to that point?"

"Only if you're up to talking about it," he said.

"I'd like to talk about it, David. A lot of things were going on in my life, but the day I tried to take my life came as a complete surprise to me. I felt so good after talking with my brother about my abortion that I thought I had finally come to terms with it. Then I made the mistake of going to see my uncle. That's what pushed me over the edge."

"Your uncle the priest?"

"Yes, my uncle Clancy. I wanted him to understand me. That's all I wanted from him. My brother had just revealed to me that my uncle was a homosexual, and had been for many years. I thought that because I knew his dark secret and forgave him he would forgive me my abortion, but I was foolish for thinking such a thing. Instead my uncle turned on me with a vengeance I never saw coming. He made me feel so worthless that I felt I didn't deserve to live. I went straight home and swallowed a handful of sleeping pills."

David let out a wry snicker. He wasn't laughing at me. He was laughing at the irony of a servant of God making me feel worthless. He reached over and gently patted my thigh and then squeezed it lightly. "He raped you, Cassie. That's what he did."

"Raped me?" I said, with a frown.

"That's what that type does to people. Your uncle raped you of your precious self and took away your will to live. *Now, there's an experience!"* he exclaimed, and gave me a firm but gentle slap on the thigh.

"What do you mean?" I asked.

"Let me share something with you, Cassie," he said, turning to look at me. "Your uncle's rape was metaphorical. The woman I raped was real. But the two rapes are not dissimilar. In fact, I've come to see that most sexual rapes presuppose metaphorical rape."

Startled by David's revelation, I didn't say anything for a long moment. "Can you please explain what you mean by that," I finally said.

Again he turned to look at me. Staring into my eyes, a mischievous smile came over his face. "I'll tell you when we get to Meaford."

"Why can't you tell me now? You've piqued my curiosity," I said.

"You'll figure it out when we get there," he said, sounding very mysterious.

"I don't have a choice, do I?" I said, a little annoyed by his reticence.

He did not respond. He just gave me a quick look and another smile. We drove the rest of the way to Meaford in relative silence, enjoying the scenery along the way, especially from the community of Craigleith to Thornbury with the open water of the bay on one side of Highway 26 and cottages and new condominiums along the shoreline and the Blue Mountains on the other side of the highway where I promised the children we would be going skiing come winter. The anticipation of what David meant by metaphorical rape made me very anxious, as though I was about to enter into the private depths of his ocean.

We finally pulled into the community of Meaford, which was already bustling with locals and tourists. This was my first time to Meaford, so I didn't know what to expect at the apple festival. My first impressions were of a quaint little town with historical Victorian and Edwardian red clay brick buildings still proudly standing like the old guard amongst the modern commercial buildings like Tim Hortons, the coffee shop that has found its way into practically every town and city in Canada, and where David stopped to pick up take-out coffee and blueberry muffins for us.

Everywhere we looked the town was alive with scarecrows that adorned all the lampposts and street sign poles, two and three and four scarecrows hanging in various comedic positions, with dried corn stalks tied in bundles to the bottom of the posts, and bails of straw and pumpkins and more scarecrows sitting casually on the straw bails, in front porches, decks, lawns, store entrances and windows, everywhere we looked. Meaford broke the Guinness Book of Records in 2002 for having the most scarecrows in one place with a final tally of 2,041.

The community had such a festive fall atmosphere that the moment we pulled into town we felt transported into another time and place.

We had passed a number of tired old apple orchards and vibrant new orchards still laden with apples of all varieties waiting to be picked as we drove from Thornbury to Meaford, which was nestled on the shore of the bay and in the heart of the famous apple growing region, and I couldn't wait to experience my first apple festival in Georgian Bay.

As we drove downtown through Meaford we came to the junction of Bayfield and Sykes, which I couldn't help but notice because the street sign stared me in the face as David made a right turn, and which had a scarecrow holding onto the post for dear life. Twenty feet or so further stood the sign RAPER'S PARK, with three scarecrows sitting on a bail of straw beneath the sign gesturing in animated conversation.

David pulled into RAPER'S PARK, which was right on the shore of the bay and peopled with scarecrows everywhere, but the parking lot was almost full. He found a space and backed the Odyssey in so we could have a clear view of the open water of Georgian Bay. He kept the engine running to keep the heat on. Then he flipped the tab on our coffee cups and handed me mine, and a muffin. "Now we can talk about rape," he said.

With a bemused smile, I said, "RAPER'S PARK?"

David laughed. "Yes. Fred Raper was one of Meaford's early settlers. I believe he owned this property, and his wife donated it to the township when Fred passed away. I don't mean to imply anything by this, but I thought it would be more memorable to talk about sexual rape in RAPER'S PARK. A little levity for such a serious subject. You don't mind, do you?"

"You're something else, David Oakly," I said, shaking my head in disbelief. "No, I don't mind. As a matter of fact, whatever wisdom you have to share with me about rape will be impressed upon my mind now, won't it? *Especially with all these scarecrows!"*

The devilish glint in his eye told me this was his intention, which was something that he did often. David did everything with as much awareness as possible, and taking me to RAPER'S PARK confirmed what he meant when he told me that to live a full life one must learn how to live it *consciously,* emphasizing the word consciously to make his point.

I returned the smile, and said, "Well, I'm waiting."

"I raped a student at university," he said. Without giving me time to react, he took a quick sip of coffee and continued his confession: "We call it date rape today, but back then we all called it scoring. I scored by seducing a student who caught my fancy. Her name was Francine. But it wasn't seduction, Cassie; it was rape. We were students at Carlton University in Ottawa. We were both taking journalism, and we shared most classes. Francine was a virgin and did not want to give up her virginity. This made it all the more challenging. I took her out for a nice dinner and later in my apartment plied her with more wine and empty promises until she finally gave it up to me. I was never the same after that. I took something from her that night, but I lost more than what I took, and it took me years to get back what I lost."

David waited for me to respond, but I was speechless. I sipped on my coffee to give myself time to think. I stared out at the whitecaps as they rolled into shore with a silent splash. "Two things," I said, my voice a little shaky from his shocking revelation. "What did you take from her? And what did you lose?"

"She didn't want to have intercourse, and she did say no. She was a devout French Roman Catholic student from Quebec City, and her virginity was precious to her; but this excited me so much that I had to have her. I didn't think I was like that, but I was. It took me years to understand why I had to have her, but I figured it out eventually," David further confessed, with a tremor of remorse in his voice I never heard before.

"I'd like to know why you did it, but first tell me what you took from her and what you lost. It wasn't just her virginity, was it?" I felt compelled to ask.

"It was much more than that. Her virginity embodied the precious spark of her essential self. I traded off empty promises for her virginity. I raped Francine of her sacred self with fatuous lies. I ran into her on an assignment a few years later in Montreal and we talked about old times over a drink. She said something to me that changed my whole life. `I haven't trusted a man since that night in your apartment,' she told me. That's when I started my Soul-searching. So what did I lose? I lost my way, that's what I lost. I went into journalism because I had a burning desire to get to the truth of life, but how could I ferret out the truth when I lied to myself? My life was a lie, Cassie; and I thank Francine for waking me up. We have a saying in Sufism. `*To see the truth, you have to tell the lie from the truth in yourself first.*' Francine changed my life when she told me that I was responsible for her distrust of men. I raped her of her innocence, Cassie; and I hated myself for a long time."

Shuddering at David's brutal honesty, I said, "I understand what you mean by emotional integrity now. That goes to the very core of who you are, doesn't it?"

"Exactly," he said. "Consent. That's what rape is all about. Take away a person's consent and you rape them of who they are. A week after Francine dropped her bombshell, I met someone by chance—and I use the word chance loosely—who hooked me up with an Ojibwa shaman, and he told me in no uncertain terms that I had to go on a vision quest. I went back with him up north to Manitoulin Island and did the sweat lodge thing, and the spirit of a white wolf came to me in a vision. What a magnificent creature. The white wolf told me that I was ready for my path. That's how I found Sufism. But Sufism doesn't mean much without a human exemplar, so I had to find a teacher who had the power to transmit *Baraka*, the spiritual energy that awakens the secret within. *Baraka* is the Sufi word for the Atma force. The Sufis call *Baraka* the *subtlety*, which can only be known by means of itself. This means that the secret within can only be awakened by practicing the Work. Living the Work is what Sufism is all about, which they call the Path, just as living the Atma life is what Atma-Gare is all about. I found my teacher in Toronto, and he put me through the wringer. As I lived the Work, I awakened the secret within. This is how I made myself ready for the spiritual path of Atma-Gare."

David paused for me to digest everything he had just revealed, which was much more than I had expected; but I had to know one thing right away and summoned my courage to ask him: "What exactly did Sufism do for you?"

"Good question," he said, with a smile that lit up his whole face and cast the gloom out of the dreary weather hanging over the bay and his melancholy confession. He finished his muffin, took a drink of coffee, looked me straight in the eye, and said, "Sufism freed me from the hold that my primal self had over me. It freed me from the false spirit of personal ambition that drove me to become a famous journalist. It freed me of the stubborn intellectual pride that I came by honestly, blind obedience to convention, propriety, custom, and pretentious social status. It freed me from the awe and deference to higher-ups—all those empty suits with authority who love to throw their weight around; but most of all, Sufism freed me from my baser human instincts of lust, greed, envy, and blind, stupid anger. The Work taught me how to gather enough *Baraka* to be in the world but not of the world, just as Jesus taught his disciples. That's the secret of the mystical path of Sufism, Cassie."

"And your mystique!" I blurted out unexpectedly.

"Now you know," David sighed. "Having said this let me get back to your uncle Clancy. Actually, let's go back further to your life growing up a Roman Catholic. The Sufis will not accept anyone into their fold unless they possess a certain amount of this *je ne sais quoi* that they call *Baraka.* This is the secret within that some people have and most people don't. In Atma-Gare, we say that one has to be ready for the Atma teaching; but no one knows what this means really. To be ready means that one has enough *Baraka* to gravitate to the Way, be it the Atma path, the Sufi path, the way of Tao, Chi Gong, Zen or whatever cultural form the Way comes to that person; so the question is this: what exactly do we mean by *Baraka*?"

"I don't mind telling you this, David," I said, with a wry chuckle, "but I'm completely mystified by all of this. What is it, exactly?"

"Free will," he replied. "But to explain this, I have to give you a glimpse of the Divine Plan of God. Are you up to it?"

"How can I not be? *I live for these moments!"*

David laughed. "Good for you. That's why I'm falling madly in love with you, Cassie O'Shaunnesy..."

Wow! I certainly didn't expect that declaration. I didn't know what to say, so I just sat in stunned silence. I wanted to tell him that I was already madly in love with him, but I didn't dare jinx the moment; so I kept my mouth shut and waited.

"You're making my life complete," he said, leading me to believe that he was about to declare more love for me, but instead he jumped right back into his explanation of the Divine Plan of God. "Do you remember me telling you that the poet John Keats called Souls sparks of Divinity?" he asked, with that excitement in his voice that made me envious.

"Yes," I said, both annoyed and excited by his paradoxical behavior.

"These sparks of Divinity are atoms of God," he continued, his eyes sparkling like diamonds refracting the brilliant light of the sun. "Keats also called them atoms of perception." David was fully connected with his *inspiration* now, and I could feel his energy as he spoke. "These atoms of God are sent into these lower worlds to create their own identity. They do this through the natural evolution of life. This is why the Living Atma Master says that experience makes a person more spiritual. It's through experience that the atom of God gathers the life force, which the Sufis call *Baraka*. The more *Baraka* the atom of God gathers through experience, the more it evolves in spiritual consciousness. Spiritual consciousness is the essence of God, which is characterized by freedom; so the more *Baraka* the atom of God gathers, the more free will Soul will have. Do you see where I'm going with this?"

"Strangely enough, I think I do," I said. "I think you're going to tell me that free will is the secret within, is that it?" I asked, busting with curiosity now.

David laughed. "Yes, it is. This is why Sufis will only accept people with enough free will to live the Path. The complete life is what the Path is all about, but to find the Path one has to be spiritually mature enough to live it, and only those with sufficient free will can live the Path. This is what makes one ready for the Way, which today has come out into the modern world as the spiritual path of Atma-Gare."

"Thank you for sharing that, David," I said, very grateful to hear the most lucid explanation for why some people are ready for Atma-Gare and some aren't. "But what does this have to do with my uncle Clancy?" I asked. "I don't see the connection."

"It has everything to do with it. But first, your religion. You grew up Catholic, so you were told how to live your life, weren't you?" David asked, with that focused look in his eyes like he was on the hunt for another elusive truth.

"Completely," I said. "My Catholic religion was my life."

"This would offend a lot of Christians, but the truth is that there's not much room for free will in Christianity. Christians are told how to live their life or suffer the consequences; but because the secret can only be known by means of itself, Soul can only grow in free will by exercising its own free will. Your Christian faith wouldn't let you do that. But you dared to exercise your free will by exploring other spiritual teachings, did you not?"

I quickly made the connection. "Yes, I did," I said, bursting with excitement. I couldn't believe it, and I sat back in my seat to bask in my joy as I stared blankly at the dreary, overcast sky. I felt so good that I even forgave David for getting to me the way he did. "My faith wasn't satisfying my spiritual hunger," I said, as memories of all the times that I doubted my faith came to mind like the waves splashing onto the sandy shore. "That's why I had to look elsewhere. But it was more than that. I don't know how to explain it, but I had a dull ache in my heart my whole life until I found the Satma, the Living Atma Master. That's when I really began to satisfy my spiritual hunger..."

David reached over and held my hand tenderly. We stared at the open water and enjoyed the warm touch of our hands.

Then he let go and gave me a serious look. "Cassie, the ache in your heart was Soul's separation from God. Christianity wasn't bringing you closer to God fast enough. That's why you had to break away from your faith. Your ache was the Call of Soul to return back home to God. That's why you became a seeker..."

"That's why I was so restless!" I exclaimed again, suddenly realizing why I hopped from one branch of nursing to another. "That's why I couldn't stand still! I was bored and had to experience other branches of nursing! That's how I gathered *Baraka.* The more new experiences I had in the hospital, the more I grew in free will. I started out as a general nurse, then I went to EMERGENCY, then I trained for the O.R., then I did psychiatric nursing, geriatrics, and palliative care —*and all the while I was upgrading!* I got my Master's degree in nursing. I couldn't help myself, David; I had this need to grow in my profession. I was compelled to explore different branches of nursing because I needed to grow. And I explored different teachings to satisfy my hunger to be whole. My husband couldn't understand me. That's why Kevin left me. He said there was no more room in my life for him. He was right, but I didn't see it. I was too selfish to see it. I had to do what I felt compelled to do. *My God, so that's why I was driven to find myself! I was hungry for spiritual energy, wasn't I?"*

"Yes," David said softly, with the sweetest smile.

I couldn't resist the temptation. I leaned over and held his face in my hands and kissed him firmly on the lips. Then I pulled back, as he very often did when he kissed me, and said, "That's also why I had to wait eight years from my dream of the Satma to the day I joined Atma-Gare. I wasn't spiritually mature enough to live the life of Atma. I had to grow more. I had to experience more life. *I had to have more free will, didn't I?"*

Again, David reached over and grabbed my hand. I felt so touched by the energy that he sent through my body that it brought tears to my eyes. As much as I wanted to make a point about detachment by pulling back with my kiss like he often did with me, I could not hold back my emotions. "Thank you, David," I said, with tears trickling down my cheeks. "Thank you for being who you are. I think I'm falling madly in love with you, too."

"Now," David said, pulling his hand back, "let's get to the nitty-gritty here and reveal Christianity's dark secret!"

I shouldn't have been startled, but I was. I wiped my tears and collected myself. Then I turned to David and said, "I wish you wouldn't do that to me. These sudden shifts in emotion always give me whiplash."

David burst into laughter. *"Touché,"* he said, but I knew that he had just returned what I had put out. That was the difference between us. I did what I did deliberately to get even with him, but he just did it because that's who he was; and as much as I loved him for being so natural and spontaneously detached, I resented him also.

"So what's Christianity's dark secret?" I asked, very proud of myself for my quick recovery from the emotional whiplash but also ashamed for having invited it.

It didn't faze David, though. He continued as if nothing had happened. "I don't know if I should express it in this context," he said, very thoughtfully, "but it's the best way to reveal it. Let me reflect on this for a moment…."

I knew he was turning inward again, to his *inspiration*. He wanted to know if he was going to break the Spiritual Law of Silence for revealing what he was going to tell me about Christianity. We sat in silence, taking in the cold open bay and the choppy little whitecaps rolling into the shore peopled here and there with scarecrows bundled up in lawn chairs.

I couldn't get over how good I felt compared to the bleak

weather outside my warm, cozy Odyssey, and I chuckled to myself. In that moment of silence, I felt the separate reality of my inner world and my outer world, and suddenly I *knew* what David meant when he said that it didn't really matter to him where he lived. It didn't matter, because he was comfortable living in the inner, private world of his own reality; and that's what I both admired and resented about him. He didn't do it intentionally, but he made me feel like he didn't really need me in his private world; and I envied his spiriutal freedom.

David turned to me. Without cracking a smile, he said, "Rape may be too strong a word for Christianity's dark secret, but it comes close to explaining how it seduces Soul of its will to grow with empty promises of forgiveness and salvation. This is why there will always be conflict in social consciousness. This conflict is Soul's desire to grow in spiritual consciousness and Christianity's need to maintain its control over Soul. You outgrew Christianity, Cassie; that's why you broke away from your faith. It's unfortunate that you had to go through what you did, but when Soul hears the Call nothing can stop it from moving closer to God. It's written in the Divine Plan of God."

"I still don't understand what this has to do with my uncle," I said.

Speaking softly, David replied, "Your uncle made you feel so worthless that you didn't think your life was worth living, didn't he?"

"He told me I didn't deserve to live."

"It's hard to believe that a savior of Souls could do that to a person, let alone your uncle," he said, with disgust in his voice, "but the dark spirit of Christianity has no conscience. It kills the spirit of life just like I killed the spirit of Francine's innocence. She lost her trust in men because of me. Your uncle Clancy did to you what I did to Francine, only a thousand times worse. I raped Francine of her innocence, but not of her will to live. She can regain her innocence, but you could have lost your life. What your uncle did to you was unconscionable, Cassie. That's Christianity's dark secret!"

"I beg your pardon?" I said, not fully understanding.

"*'Kill them all, and God will know His own,'*" David replied, with contempt in his voice. I didn't say anything. I could tell that he was upset. I waited for him to explain. "The Cathars were a Gnostic

Christian sect living in medieval France who threatened the spiritual authority of the Roman Catholic Church. Being Gnostics, they knew the secret within and did not need the intermediary of the Church for salvation. They knew the Divine mystery, which was the same secret that Jesus awakened in his disciples. Imagine what this would have done to the authority of the Roman Catholic Church if it caught on? So the Vicar of Christ ordered to have the entire population of the Cathars murdered. Someone had the temerity to say, `Surely, they can't all be heretics?' and the papal legate who carried out the massacre said, *`Kill them all, and God will know His own.'* The dark spirit of Christianity murdered the Cathars, Cassie; and this same dark spirit exists in the Soul of every Christian in the world. You threatened the dark spirit of Christianity with your break from the Catholic Church. Despite himself, your uncle Clancy became the vessel for this dark spirit. It tried to destroy you because you threatened its existence with the light of your newfound spiritual freedom just as the spiritual light of the Gnostics threatened the Catholic Church; that's why your uncle did what he did to you. He couldn't help himself. Your uncle may have been blind to what he did to you, but it was deliberate evil. And this is exactly what you will set free this summer with the story of your unborn child in the *Gazette* and at the public forum on abortion. You are forcing this dark spirit of Christianity out from the unconscious mind of man into the clear light of conscious day..."

Astonished, I understood everything now and sat in satisfied silence. It was still overcast and dreary, with rain threatening, but David wanted to walk the main street to soak in the festive atmosphere at the heart of Meaford's downtown core, which we did; and then we drove to the arena and curling club on Collingwood Street to take in the craft shows.

All the streets to the arena and curling club were lined bumper to bumper with vehicles and several tour buses, with not a parking space in sight. An OPP officer directed traffic as a steady stream of people crossed the street back and forth from the arena to the curling club. David had been there before, and he pulled into the curling club parking lot that had been extended to an open, back-field parking lot attended to by volunteers wearing bright orange vests. There was an admission fee of five dollars per adult, which David paid; but it was well worth the admission to see over two hundred booths displaying their wares. The arena and curling club were shoulder to shoulder with people, but we took in every single craft booth, and David made a point of complimenting every person on the craftwork that excited his interest. "I just love people who love what they do," he whispered into my ear.

I bought three needlework doilies for my coffee and end tables, a set of hanging ceramic plates displaying gorgeous red apples to hang on my bare kitchen wall, natural soaps and scented candles, four jars of various chutneys, a jug of apple cider, three jars of apple butter, and a wonderful apple recipe cookbook that I couldn't wait to try out on the children, and a different apple recipe cookbook for David in the hope that he would try some recipes out on me.

David bought me a beautiful, stained glass, golden eagle in flight, which he said he would hang for me in my foyer window to greet me when I came home from work every day, and then he took me to *Captain's Corner* for a simple but satisfying dinner of fish and chips. On the way home we stopped at the *Goldsmith Orchard and Market* and I picked up a half bushel of Honey Crisp apples for the children's school lunches, a quart basket of plump fresh field tomatoes, broccoli, a dozen cobs of peaches and cream corn. For Thanksgiving dinner the following weekend, which I had invited David to, I picked up my sweet potatoes, a small basket of colored yellow and purple carrots, which I hadn't seen before, parsnips, and a butternut squash. For the children I also picked up fresh cantaloupes and strawberries. As I was picking up my vegetables David was also filling his cart. "Eggplants?" I said. "What are you going to do with them?"

"Well now, you'll just have to wait and see, won't you?"

"I can't wait. But I'm hoping you'll try one of the apple dinner recipes first."

"We'll be trying them all," he said, and laughed.

On the drive home, David stopped at KFC in the town of Collingwood and picked up a family dinner combo for the children. We didn't talk anymore about my attempted suicide. We didn't have to. David had given me the answer I was looking for!

Chapter 13
Making Love on the Persian Rug

When I found Atma-Gare—or, more precisely, when Atma-Gare found me—I had no idea that it would be so spiritually and personally satisfying!

The Holy Spirit of Atma found its way into every nook and cranny of my life, and I became so preoccupied with living the spiritual life that I had no time for a relationship. Besides, I would have preferred to get involved with a man who shared my newfound spiritual beliefs, and there weren't that many eligible Atmans to choose from.

We're a quiet minority. But there's a very good reason for this. This new religion of the Light and Sound of God is not for everyone. As David said, Atma-Gare is only for people mature enough to take evolution into their own hands. As much as I loved my new life in Atma however, I never denied the fact that I secretly wanted a new man in my life.

I had grown used to sleeping with a man in my bed every night, and I missed that. But long before my abortion and break-up with Kevin, my priorities were changing. I needed something else in my life, and my new life in Atma-Gare gave me that.

As satisfying as my life was with the challenges of my nursing career, our young family and endless horizon of possibilities, I lacked something that wasn't written into the script of my all-too-cramped life, and Kevin knew this; that's why I could never hold it against him for leaving me for another woman. I drove him away.

I loved Kevin and he loved me, but he could not write what was missing into the script of my needy life. Sadly, I didn't know myself what was missing. Ever since I could remember, I had a nagging feeling that I had lost something very precious, but I did not know what I had lost; and that was the wedge that drove us apart.

This feeling of loss was similar to the time I lost my engagement ring, only magnified a thousand times. I walked around for days feeling so guilty that Kevin had to go out and buy me another ring, but it wasn't the same thing. I had to have *my* ring. I found it eventually behind the flowerpot on my kitchen windowsill, and the feeling when I found it was similar to the joy that I experienced when I found Atma-Gare.

"I'm home," I said to myself under my breath in the public library room of the Collingwood Branch on Kingsway Street in Vancouver when I listened to the Living Atma Master Sri Herman Knecht on video talking about Soul's journey back home to God, so as much as I wanted to be with another man after my divorce, I wasn't lonely. I had the Satma to keep me company through this new and exciting chapter of my life.

I had much to learn, though. I did my HU chant every morning for twenty to thirty minutes; I went to Atma worship services every Sunday; I attended *satsangs* and Atma book discussion classes; I studied my private Atma Discourses; I read all the Atma books two and three times; and I welcomed the challenge of introducing my children to the wonderfully liberating spiritual path of Atma-Gare—to my mother's absolute horror!

But they were my children, and I did not want them to grow up like me. I wanted them to grow up to be freethinking individuals capable of making up their own mind about what to believe and not believe; and I made a practice of holding a family *satsang* once a week, which was one of the most satisfying parts of my new life in Atma.

It would have been nice if Patrick had taken to Atma-Gare as Mark and Cindy did so readily, but Patrick was his father's son and eventually wanted nothing to do with the religion of the Light and

Sound of God. He refused to even try to understand what it was all about, as though it was responsible for his father leaving me, and he went to his room whenever we did our family *satsang;* but the water ran deep in Patrick, and it didn't bother us that he didn't join Atma-Gare. He was an ancient Soul, and he would embrace the Atma in his own good time.

Nevertheless, my children were right. I was starting to get lonely. I needed a man in my life. Atma-Gare had taken the dull ache out of my heart, but it was time to satisfy those basic needs all women are born with and which had begun to surface again four or five months after we were comfortably settled into our new life in Georgian Bay.

I began to long for the loving glance, the tender caress, and the sweet little gestures of endearment that often mean more than a whole bouquet of roses. Most of all, I began to long for the musk of a man's body and the feel of his arms around my naked flesh.

I wanted to make love again. I wanted to experience the pleasure of having a man inside me. Kevin and I were wonderful lovers. But the more I became involved in my private life, the less we made love; and we began to grow apart sexually. I never saw it coming, but it was there in black and white.

I believe now that a good marriage needs good sex to keep it alive and fresh. Our marriage waned from year to year. My need to find the missing pages of my life began to override all of my other needs, and this drove a wedge in our relationship; so I can't fault Kevin for leaving me. My husband didn't have the same needs as me. He could not understand what drove me, and he began to call me strange.

But spiritual seekers don't respond to life as other people do. We listen to a silent imperative. We're attentive to all the signs and symbols that point us to where we're called to go to satisfy our longing to be whole. We don't heed the world's call to the good life, and this makes us strange in the eyes of the world.

It takes a long time to find the author of life's script, but when we finally find the Living Word or he finds us, as the case may be, we're given a new role to play. We no longer have to figure out what this play called life means; we *know* what it means, and we live life with the conscious purpose of becoming spiritually awakened Souls.

Ironically, as strange as we may appear to be in the eyes of the world, the more we grow in the conscious spiritual life the more the Atma dissolves our personal aberrations, and without realizing it we become more spiritually balanced with each passing day; so it's not really us who are strange. It's the world around us that's not in tune with life's script.

It takes a long time for the world to accept us for who we are, so I stopped being bothered by the labels people pin on us for being different. Nevertheless, we have to live in the world, so we have to appear to be the same just to get along in life. This is why we don't talk openly about Atma-Gare. The time's not right yet. But it's coming.

In the little farming community of Wyedale in beautiful Georgian Bay, I was given a golden opportunity to satisfy my desire to be with a man who shared my spiritual values, as well as the challenge of "proving" that a fetus is not a little person by telling the story of my unborn child, and I knew that's what the Atma was pointing me to when I told the wonderful lady in the washroom of *Geno's* restaurant back home in Vancouver that my heart had been scoured for the splendor of my new life. It was all coming together very quickly, and it felt like I was being swept up in a dream.

David and I fell for each other for reasons that went far beyond my limited comprehension. We connected in a special way at the Atma Springtime Seminar in Minneapolis, but I had no idea that he was as interested in me as I was in him. We finally got involved in a relationship, and even though it was never spelled out the way I would have liked, being together never ceased to excite me. Being with David completed my life, and I was star-struck.

I liked everything about David. And I just loved listening to him when he connected with his *inspiration*. He transported me to the higher planes of consciousness of the inner circle of life. I had found more than a friend and lover in David Oakly; I had found my own personal mentor. I felt like I was to him what he must have been to his Sufi teacher, so I believed in him implicitly when he told me that two people who connected in that special way make a much better channel for the *inspiration* to flow than one person alone; but the excitement of being with him went far beyond a romantic interest—*it nourished my spirit!*

I loved exploring different subjects with him. Whenever we connected in that special way, mysteries dissolved before my eyes. Like the time we were enjoying a Saturday evening snuggling on his couch in front of the fire in his new home after our first snowfall of the year. David had made one of his succulent recipes from his Mediterranean cooking class, *Canard aux Framboises,* and it felt so good, so right, and so natural to be in his arms after such a romantic dinner that I just had to ask him what he thought about the gay life.

Given how right life felt at that moment, it suddenly struck me very wrong that a person could be attracted to his or her own sex. "The gay life, David. Do you think nature or nurture makes one gay?" I asked, musing out loud.

"It could be both, and it could be neither," he replied.

"That's a strange answer," I said.

"Karma affects our genetic make-up, so it's quite possible that one may have a genetic predisposition to being gay; and this could be amplified by social conditioning and one's environment. No one knows for sure, Cassie. But I do know that past lives have a great deal to do with being gay," David said, as he played with my hair.

My ears perked up. "In what way?"

"Let's back up a moment," he said, and I knew by the tone of his voice that he was connecting with that mysterious fount of personal wisdom that he called his *inspiration.*

I had to ask David about this *gift* one day. He had already explained to me that he could tap into the Holy Current of Atma much more easily when someone believed in him, as I certainly did, but I was still puzzled. "David, can you explain something to me, please? I'm still puzzled by this connection with the spiritual current," I asked him when he dropped by the house one Saturday afternoon on his way home from his twenty kilometer training run.

I made him something to eat, and over coffee the subject of his special connection came up. David jumped in without hesitation, which confirmed what he had already revealed to me about his long runs automatically connecting him with his inner self. That's why he had such a passion for marathon running. Running made him whole, he said; so I knew that his *inspiration* had to do with his relationship with his inner self.

"The Atma Current is the God force that flows through life," he explained, with that focused look in his eyes. "Jesus called it the water of everlasting life. The God force is also called the Word, and the Word is the Way. The Way is the omniscient consciousness of life, and when one believes in a person it opens him up to this God force. This special connection lets Soul, our spiritual self, speak; because when one taps into the Atma Current he's connecting with the Soul Plane of Consciousness, which is that infinite fount of spiritual wisdom that I call my *inspiration*..."

"Are you saying that I believe in you in this special way?" I interrupted, just to be sure I understood him correctly. I wanted to hear David say that I was special to him.

"Yes," he said, with a smile that didn't quite assure me in the way I wanted to be assured. "But what makes our connection with the Atma Current so wonderful is that I believe in you in the same way," he explained, and smiled again. This time I felt it, and I knew that he did think of me in that way. "That's why I fell for you, Cassie. The moment we shook hands in Minneapolis, I knew we were meant to be together by the way we connected."

My heart fluttered. "Thank you for sharing that," I said, and kissed him.

"You're welcome," he said, and quickly pulled back to that place where he was alone with the Alone, and which I was beginning to resent because it shut me out. "Now, to be absolutely clear about this connection with the Atma Current, it all depends upon how spiritually resolved one is that determines the spiritual clarity of what comes out of a person," he explained, with that same kind of far-away look that my son Mark gets when he's struck by an idea for one of his stories. "The less spiritually resolved one is, the more one taints the message. In other words, one has to put his ego aside if he wants Soul to speak freely. This is why I love Rumi. He was so open to the God force that he became intoxicated with the sweet bliss of God-realization consciousness. That's why his poetry is so full of love."

"I think I understand," I said; "but what does it really mean to believe in a person in this special way? Do you mean in the way that Christ's disciples believed in him? *"'He that believe on me, as the scripture hath said, out of his belly shall flow rivers of living water,'"* I said, quoting from John's Gospel to make my point.

David was surprised by my quotation. "Yes. But this kind of belief in a person is not limited to spiritual teachers alone. It can also be belief in anyone who inspires confidence in people. The more you believe in a person, the more you will draw out of that person. This is why we should love our children. It brings the best out of them. It's magic, Cassie. *Pure magic!"*

"I know," I said, smiling at David's show of emotion. I had witnessed this magic with David many times since we met in Minneapolis, and I definitely believed that my children flourished much more when I gave them love and encouragement, not to mention my plants which I talked to on a regular basis; but I was still mystified. "Is this what makes some people charismatic, then? Politicians, for example; or artists, movie stars, and gurus?" I asked. "Do they connect with this magical life force as well?"

"In effect, yes; but as I said, it all depends upon how spiritually resolved a person is. The less spiritually resolved one is, the more inflated their ego will be. This can make a person very charismatic. Like movie stars, artists, musicians, and cult leaders," David explained, and then paused. He waited a minute or so before continuing. "My Sufi teacher said the wise man learns not to identify with the *Baraka* that he transmits. But that's easier said than done. It's very easy to fool yourself, Cassie. Cult leaders do it all the time."

"What do you mean?" I asked.

He caressed the back of my neck. It felt wonderful. I thought it was going to lead to something, but he stopped. "Whether Jesus said this or not, no one can be sure. He said, *"I am the way, the truth, and the life; no man cometh unto the Father but by me."* If Jesus said this, he identified so strongly with Holy Spirit that he fooled himself into believing that he was the way, the truth, and the life; but he wasn't. Spirit is the way, the truth, and the life. Jesus was just a channel for Holy Spirit. That's the tragedy of the Christian religion. It has made of

Jesus the sole savior of the world with this saying, and doing so Christianity has led the world down the proverbial path. That's the root source of Christianity's spiritual conceit. If it weren't for this declaration, who knows where Christianity would be today."

That's why he mystified me. David stood apart from whatever came out of his mouth when he let Soul speak. He did not identify with his *inspiration*, so it never went to his head. His ego served him, not he his ego; and I loved him for it!

"Back to your question," he continued. "Being gay comes down to a question of personal choice, however agonizing that choice may be. I don't believe there is a gay gene. Not yet, anyway. Maybe some day, giving the proliferation of the gay life style; but even if there were a gay gene, it wouldn't negate the fact that one may have an innate predisposition to being gay because of his past lives. When Soul has a series of lifetimes in the same gender, say four consecutive lifetimes as a woman, when it crosses over in its next incarnation to the male gender the subconscious memory of four consecutive lifetimes as a woman will have an inordinate influence upon his male psyche. This is why some men feel like a woman trapped in a man's body, and vice versa."

I couldn't believe it. That made perfect sense to me. "Have you shared this with anyone else?" I asked, so excited that I had to pull back and look into David's eyes.

"No. But I think it's common knowledge among some Higher Initiates."

"Do you think it's true?"

"Yes."

"How could you prove it if you had to?"

"With past-life regressions, I would think. Regress a gay person who believes that he's a man trapped in a woman's body or a woman trapped in a man's body and see what happens. I think he or she would get a real surprise. Coincidentally, Cassie, I've been toying with the idea of writing a narrative poem based on this very premise."

"Why don't you? That would make a fantastic poem!"

By the way David smiled, I knew something was up. "Let me share something very personal with you. Something I would have to draw upon if I were to write this poem. It's about my own innate gayness, if you will."

"Hold that thought!" I exclaimed, startling David. "Can I ask you about your ex? Did she ever tell you why she was attracted to women?"

I don't know why I asked him that, but I had to know.

David laughed. "All she told me was that she had a lesbian experience in a private school in Lausanne, Switzerland that she never got over. She said she was going back to her roots. I tried to talk her out of it, but she said she couldn't get the sexual satisfaction from me that she got from a woman. She said she felt more complete making love with a woman. But I don't know whether to believe her or not. My ex has an inordinate capacity for self-deception. That's her character flaw. Maybe that's why I married her," David added, with a snicker.

"I think I understand that," I said, as my uncle Clancy came to mind. "I'm sorry for interrupting. You were saying?"

"Alright, my unconscious gayness," David said, with another self-conscious snicker. "I was a practicing Sufi at the time. One technique that I had to master was to *non-identify* with my desires, sexual or otherwise. I didn't have to become celibate, but I chose to do so for this particular exercise. My Sufi teacher said that this technique would be more effective if I remained sexually active, but I didn't think I could do that. This is an extremely difficult technique to master, but it's one of the most effective techniques for gathering *Baraka.* I managed to live my celibate lifestyle for a full year when it began to have a strange effect on me. We had a junior male reporter on staff that began to arouse me. For the life of me, I could not fathom why he aroused me. Just seeing him sent shivers up my spine. I had never had those kinds of feelings before. I shared these feelings with my teacher. He told me to *identify* with my desire for the cub reporter, but not to play it out in real life. Play it out in your mind, he said. Identify with your desire for him, and then *non-identify* with your desire, which meant that I had to give in to my desires in my mind and then *detach* myself from my desire. Allow him to arouse your senses, my teacher said; and then *detach* yourself from all the feelings you have for him.

Do this until you gather all the sweet honey, meaning *Baraka*, that you can out of this experience, he instructed me; and he gave me that Master's look that not only challenged me to try this impossible exercise, but it energized me with *Baraka*. I can still feel the power of his look. It still gives me strength to take on the impossible whenever I'm challenged by life.

"It took three months of excruciating daily effort to exhaust my attraction for this young reporter, but the more I *identified* and *detached* myself from him in my mind, the more I felt my desire for him lose its hold on me. It was like squeezing a stress ball in my mind. Finally, one day my desire for him ceased to be. I had extracted all the *Baraka* out of my desire for him and it no longer had a hold on me. None whatsoever. I had killed my desire for him completely, and it disappeared from my psyche. I told my teacher, and he very proudly said, 'Welcome to the Path, David. You have done the impossible and transformed yourself. If only the world knew what Jesus meant when he told his disciples to be in the world but not of the world.' Believe me, Cassie, this is much easier said than done!"

I just loved it when David shared his private life with me. It was so fascinating and out of the ordinary that he made me feel privileged. It also explained his lovemaking!

I had only made love with two men in my life before I met David, the first man in my second year at university, and only one time because I was so mad at my mother for accusing me of living the loose life at university that I went to a party and did it with the first man who hit on me just to spite my mother, and then I made love with Kevin. When David and I made love for the first time totally naked on the sun-baked rock where he had his sunset experience as we enjoyed the glorious sun setting over Georgian Bay, not in my wildest dreams could I have imagined that making love with a man could be so perfect!

I was aroused. I put my arms around David and pulled him into the couch on top of me. "I want you, David. I want you so much it hurts!" I said, with tears in my eyes.

We kissed, and fondled, and caressed, and made love on the Persian rug in front of the fire, like two angels lost in a paradise of infinite bliss!

Chapter 14

The Strange World of David Oakly

David Oakly made such a powerful impression upon me at the Atma Springtime Seminar in Minneapolis that the first thing I did when I got home was get together with my Atman friend in Barrie. "Well?" I said, after I shared my exciting news with Grace over a cup of coffee at Tim Hortons on Bayfield Street, only two blocks from her house.

"Well what?" she said, just to tease me.

Grace Iverson was a dynamic lady in her young fifties who always brought homemade baking treats to our worship services for fellowship. She had to take an early retirement from a successful career in management to care for her husband who had advanced MS. She also had three children, but hers were older than mine. Julia was married and living in Toronto, her son Eddie was in Florida studying marine biology, and Sara was completing high school; but Grace was the only Atman in her family. They were all Catholic, which made it difficult to share with her family what she called the golden season of her life.

We took such an instant liking to each other that we both concluded it had to be a past-life connection. We had a standing luncheon date after our monthly worship service, and we emailed each other two and three times a week. I shared my dream experience with the Satma on our first luncheon date, and she shared her incredible experience with Kati Sada, which inspired Grace to join Atma-Gare.

Kati Sada is a female Atma Master of the Ancient Order of Gare Adepts whose true age is beyond belief. She's said to be hundreds of years old. Like all Atma Masters, Kati Sada serves God by helping others find the Satma, the Living Atma Master. Like many Atma Masters, Kati Sada works behind the scenes in life, and Grace never shared her experience with Kati Sada with anyone outside of Atma-Gare. "No one would believe me," she told me over our first luncheon.

Grace spoke fluent French, so she was sent to Paris to work out the details of a merchandizing contract for her company. On the train to Geneva, where she was going to visit a close friend before returning to Canada, her female seat companion noticed the book she was reading, *The Art of Happiness,* by the Dalai Lama and Howard C. Cutler. Grace was exploring Buddhism at the time. The lady glanced at Grace's book and gave her a friendly smile.

"Did you attend the Buddhist convention in Paris?" she politely asked.

"No," Grace replied. "I was there on business."

"You know," said the lady, with another glance at her book, "he's not the real Master. There are those who say the real Master is a man living in the United States."

She then got up, smiled at Grace and walked away. She never returned to her seat, and Grace never saw her again.

"Do you think I could get back into my book?" Grace said to me, with a look on her face that revealed her astonishment. "I couldn't. I left it at the station in Grenoble!"

Back in Canada, Grace saw a poster in the window of her favorite bookstore *Books and Crystals* in Barrie, where she had purchased her book on Buddhism. It advertised an introductory talk on Atma-Gare, and she felt a very strong tug to go to that talk.

"I had to go," she said. "I can't explain why. I just had to go."

As she browsed through the books on Atma-Gare for sale at the introductory talk in the Georgian Room at the public library in Barrie, she saw some pictures of Atma Masters. As she went through them one by one, her heart jumped when she saw a picture of her seat companion on the train in France. It was the Atma Master Kati Sada. "Hey," Grace said to me, "how could I not join Atma-Gare after that?"

"Well?" I said again. "Tell me everything you know about David!"

"I'm surprised you haven't met until now," she mused, genuinely perplexed. "Isn't that curious?" she added. "I never thought to tell you about David Oakly. I wonder why that is? I'm sorry I didn't tell you about him, Cassie. He's definitely the most eligible Atman bachelor in the whole area, that's for sure..."

"I don't doubt that for a moment!" I said, so excited I could hardly wait to hear all the details. "We know that the Atma has its own agenda, Grace, but David walked into my life last Friday in the Book Room at the Convention Center and there has to be a reason for that, so let's have it; is he seeing anyone?"

Grace laughed. "He's something else, isn't he?"

"Grace, is David seeing anyone?"

Grace gave me her close-friend look, which always betrayed her love for me. I loved her as much as I loved my best friend Carol in Vancouver, and I thanked the Satma for finding me such a good friend so quickly when I moved to Georgian Bay.

"David was seeing Anoria Dupont, but I'm sure they broke up," she said, betraying a gleeful smile. "We don't see much of David at our worship services. I think he goes to the services in Toronto because his daughter lives there."

"His daughter? Tell me he's divorced! Please tell me, Grace!"

"Yes, he is," she said, with another gleeful smile.

"Do you think he's still seeing Anoria?" I fearfully asked.

"I don't think so, but I can find out for sure if you want," she said.

"Of course I want!" I exclaimed, and quickly looked around to see if anybody was staring at me. Some people were, but I didn't care. I waved to them.

Grace smiled at me. She had the most sincere smile of anyone I knew. Her whole face radiated when she smiled. But that didn't surprise me. Grace was a giving person. Apart from caring for her husband whom she adored, she volunteered three afternoons a week at the animal shelter in Barrie and was responsible for our monthly Atma newsletter.

"I'll ask Joan tomorrow. I have to drop by her store to pick up my new quartz crystal. I got a Golden Healer pendant for my husband. Joan hears all the Atma news at her store. She knows David pretty well. They both write poetry and share a common interest in Rumi."

"David quoted Rumi to me in Minneapolis," I said excitedly. "Would you ask Joan tomorrow and call me after work? I have to know everything about him. I can't get him out of my mind, Grace. He got to me!"

"You?" Grace said excitedly. "He's had every single female Atman in this whole area chasing after him, and one or two married ones too! The only one I know who made it past his front door is Anoria. David's a tough catch, Cassie. You're going to have your hands full. He's not like any Atman I've ever met. I think he's a Higher Initiate, but sometimes I get the feeling he's more like an Atma Master in disguise. He's a very intriguing man..."

"I know!" I exclaimed. *"*That's the effect he had on me too, and I only met him for a few minutes at the seminar! Should I call him?"

After a thoughtful pause, Grace said, "I wouldn't, Cassie. I'd wait and see what the Atma has to say. I don't want to say it, but if it's meant to be, it'll happen on its own."

"But I can't get him out of my mind!"

"He does have that effect on you, doesn't he?" Grace said, with a smile in her eyes that understood my interest in men again. "When I met him in Newmarket during our Arahata training course, I was so taken by him in our little discussion group that I blurted, *'I want to be you!'* I couldn't believe I said that."

"What did you mean by that?" I asked.

"I don't know. I think it was David's whole attitude about the spiritual life of Atma. Something he said just got to me. 'The Atma is life,' he said. 'Once we realize that, all the pieces fall into place.' Something clicked, and I just blurted out, *'I want to be you!'* I was so embarrassed. But you'll never guess what he said to me."

"What?" I asked, dying to know. I was so giddy I felt like a schoolgirl.

"He looked deep into my eyes, and in the sweetest possible way he told me to live my own life. 'I'm flattered, Grace," he said, 'but if you want to be me, you're missing the whole point of the spiriutal path of Atma.'"

"Wow! That's so true, isn't it?"

"Well, it sure woke me up, I'll tell you!"

"So what do you think, Grace? Should I set my sights on him?"

"I wouldn't push it, Cassie. David's not that kind of man."

That's what intrigued me. He wasn't like any kind of man I had ever met before, both in and out of the Atma community. There was much more to him than met the eye. But I knew in a little corner of my heart that the key to unlocking the mystery of David Oakly's character could be found in something he said to me in Minneapolis: *"The journey of Soul through life is a journey of the alone to the Alone."* Those puzzling words bounced off my mind like an echo from somewhere beyond my comprehension, and I knew that if I wanted to understand David I had to penetrate that mystery; but I couldn't go there. Try as I may, I could not fathom what he meant by "the alone to the Alone."

David Oakly certainly is alone. Even when we're together I feel his aloneness. But what mystifies me is that he does not always make me feel like he's alone. Only sometimes, when he gets that far-away look in his eyes. Then he's so alone that I feel shut out. But he does have an aura of aloneness about him all the time, like the lonely fur trapper Jeremiah Johnson. That's why everyone at the worship service in the library that day in Newmarket was staring at him. David Oakly *was* a lone wolf Atman. He was a part of our circle, but he wasn't part of our circle; and I will never stop regretting not moving my chair in closer to his. It was a missed opportunity, and I hate myself for it.

That little incident became the metaphor for our relationship. He sits alone, and I want to inch my chair closer to his; but I don't know how.

David Oakly is so far outside the box that he never ceases to surprise us at our Atma functions. Like the time Edgar Smallwood shared his little Atma protection story with us. It was late winter. Edgar's car broke down on his way home to Newmarket from an evening *satsang* class in Alliston. By "chance" another Atman who left a few minutes after him decided to take a different route home because she was nudged to pick up munchies for her husband to snack on while he watched his hockey game on TV. She happened to see Edgar standing by his car on the side of the road. His cell phone was dead. He was stranded and didn't' know what to do, so he asked the Satma for help and sang HU.

A winter storm was moving in fast, and Edgar couldn't thank the Satma enough for sending a fellow Atman to his rescue. "If I hadn't been nudged to buy some snacks for my husband, I wouldn't have gone that way," Tara said. "The Atma must have sent me to help Edgar."

She belonged to the CAA and called on her cell phone for help. They dispatched a tow truck immediately, which took Edgar's car right to his dealer and then gave him a ride home just as the storm began to break. "That's how the Master protects his chelas," Edgar said, with a proud smile on his face.

Everyone loved this story because it confirmed for us how the Holy Spirit of Atma works every moment in our life to guide and protect us. Then David burst the bubble and all that warm fuzzy Atma love changed into stark, naked awareness. "That's a nice story," he said, very casually. "Incidentally Edgar, do you have a membership with the CAA?"

"No," he replied, with a look of surprise.

"I see," said David, and fell silent.

Edgar wasn't quite sure what David was getting at, nor did anyone else until Grace jolted in her chair. *"Oh!"* she exclaimed. "You're talking about karma, aren't you?"

David smiled. "The Satma certainly came to Edgar's aid, but I think it was as much a test as it was spiritual protection," he replied, but didn't explain any further.

After the worship service, David invited me to *Mama's,* an Italian restaurant that served an all day buffet that he wanted to try. "What was Edgar's test?" I asked him.

"The Atma's always testing our integrity, Cassie," he said, after sampling a meatball, which he chewed very slowly. By the look on his face there was something about the taste of the meatball that he had to figure out. "Edgar was so excited because the Atma got him out of his little jam that he failed to see the door the Satma had opened for him."

"What door?"

"It's parsley," David said, with a satisfied look. "Parmigiano Reggiano and Italian parsley. That's the taste I want for my meatballs." Smiling proudly at himself, he finally answered my question: "The Satma opened up a door to test Edgar's honesty, but he blew it."

I stared blankly at him. He saw my confusion.

"Edgar got a free ride on someone else's ticket, Cassie. But there are no free rides in life. You know that. We pay for everything we get in this world. I'd be curious to know if Edgar continued to have car trouble after that experience."

"You mean that's how karma would make him pay for his free ride?" I asked, to confirm my understanding.

"Exactly," he said, and gently forked another meatball.

"Edgar failed the test, didn't he?" I asked, just to be certain.

"Like I said, he got a free ride on someone else's ticket. If he had the integrity he thinks he has, he would've paid CAA back for the towing charges," David replied, and put the whole meatball into his mouth as if to make a point about karma.

I enjoyed watching him eat. There was something different about the way he relished his food. I couldn't put my finger on it, but I could tell by the expression on his face as he chewed and swallowed his food that there was something more going on. It wasn't just the flavor that he was savoring; it was something else that I couldn't see.

I waited for him to swallow his meatball and then I said, "But Edgar is a Higher Initiate. He should know better, shouldn't he?"

"So? Higher Initiates are tested also, aren't they?"

"All I meant was that he should have seen it, shouldn't he?"

"He couldn't, Cassie. He's a peacock Atman. He doesn't have the sight of an eagle Atman. Edgar loves the look of his own feathers too much."

I remembered David's comment about Atmans not being birds of the same feather, and I smiled. I wanted to ask him what other kinds of Atmans there were, but I was too embarrassed. I should have made the karmic connection with the CAA, but I didn't. Grace made the connection, and she wasn't a Higher Initiate either. I changed the subject, reserving my right to bring it up again when I had more confidence. I just wanted to break the ice with him at lunch.

The opportunity to ask him finally came up at Algonquin Provincial Park. My children were thoughtful enough to let us go on our own the first time so David and I could get to know each other, and at some point on the hiking trail David stopped to give me a breather.

We found a shady spot under a gnarled old maple tree, which for some strange reason brought my father to mind, and we sat down to rest. I took a well-deserved drink from my bottle of spring water, and boldly said, "So, David, what kind of Atman is Anoria Dupont?"

"An owl," he replied, without batting an eye.

I didn't know what to think of that, but I didn't want to ask him. I took another drink, trying to appear casual. "And Sandra Smallwood?" I singled out Edgar's wife because she was a Higher Initiate who had a habit of monopolizing the time at Atma functions with her personal problems. Again without hesitation, he said, "A love-starved chicken Atman."

"Why chicken?" I asked.

"She's forever scratching for ground," David explained, giving me a look that I'm sure his Sufi teacher must have given him many times, and I knew instantly not to play games with this man. "Sandra can't stop justifying herself. Her *shadow* has too much power over her personality. But being a Higher Initiate she's too stuck on herself to see it. That's why she obsesses about her problems. Now don't ask me about any more Atmans. It's not nice to label people. It creates a psychic barrier and makes it more difficult for them to grow spiritually."

"What do you mean by that?"

"Nothing. So, are you feeling better now?"

"Yes," I said, knowing very well that he was referring to my emotional insecurity and not my tired body. "I think we can continue now."

As we ascended the trail I locked my arm into his and boldly said, "I have to know what other kinds of Atmans there are. Blue Jay Atmans? Seagull Atmans? Crows? Chickadees? Sparrows? What,

David?"

He laughed. "Probably all of those and more. But the ones I keep seeing are the parrot Atmans. *They just love to parrot the Living Atma Master!"*

Startled by his comment, I dared not say anything for fear of saying the wrong thing. David was dauntless. He certainly had his own mind, which was why he intimidated Atmans, especially Higher Initiates like Stephanie Werner.

David showed up at my front door one Sunday morning all dressed up in casual beige slacks and a short sleeved, white polo shirt, all ready to go. He had forfeited his morning work on *A Conference of the Birds* and gone for an early run instead because he wanted to take us to the worship service in Orillia, which Stephanie Werner was officiating. The Orillia Atma community had found a wonderful new location for the worship services at the Leacock Care Center, and David wanted to attend the inaugural service because he loved the satirical writings of the Canadian humorist Stephen Leacock whose spirit was said to haunt the Leacock Care Center and museum named after him, and He had also promised to take the children to Webers for their famous charbroiled burgers after the service.

Stephanie Werner was still a very attractive single woman in her middle fifties, but she was twice divorced, childless, and petless since a neighbourhood dog killed her Siamese cat. She was a Higher Initiate, an Atma cleric, and managing editor of a woman's magazine in Toronto, and by her body language and the way she spoke I knew she was a high achiever.

"Welcome," she said, as we walked into the worship service room at the Leacock Care Center. It was spacious and well lit from the large windows. "I'm Stephanie Werner," she said, giving me her hand. "I'm a Atma cleric from Toronto, and I'm a Sixth Initiate. I'm going to be officiating the first worship service here this morning." Then she gave me a perfunctory hug, and Mark and Cindy as well, but she deliberately walked away from David to greet another couple who had just walked through the door. I couldn't believe my eyes.

"A peacock for the Leacock room," David said to me in a whisper, and broke into a gentle laugh. I was beginning to understand his effect on Higher Initiates.

That was the fourth or fifth time that I had heard an Atma cleric from Toronto announce their level of initiation, which was shameless. It sounded like they had come from the big metropolitan city to the remote northern boonies to share their great spiritual wisdom with us lowly country Atmans. This is what Grace meant by the Toronto vanity, which she knew very well from twenty-four years of working in downtown Toronto.

I witnessed this Toronto air of self-importance in Barrie. A silver-haired Atman in her late sixties, who was wearing a flamboyant flowered shawl over her left shoulder with an air of cutting-edge fashion, and her forty-something stuttering bachelor son were invited to give a talk at our worship service. "I'm so and so," said the lady, "and I'm a Higher Initiate from Scarborough. That's my son Harry, and he's a Higher Initiate also. We're both Higher Initiates from Toronto, and we're going to talk to you today about spiritual survival in our times..."

I got the feeling they had just come down from the Mountain to share their great spiritual wisdom with us ignorant Souls. I was incredulous.

I watched Stephanie Werner as she greeted other Atmans when they walked into the room. She was consistent, reminding me of my ex-husband's friend's wife Lilian Gotlieb, a hen-pecking physiotherapist who had rendered her unsuccessful art dealer husband to a brooding malcontent, and yet Stephanie, who even looked like Lilian Gotlieb, was a Sixth Initiate.

I had to ask David about this. It puzzled me how one could be a Higher Initiate in the most conscious spiritual path in the world and still be so full of themselves.

"It can be a real problem for some," he explained to me one Saturday evening over a cup of tea. I had invited David for dinner, but he had to complete a roofing job in Stayner to beat the weather and didn't drop by till after eight. He and his worker put on the last row of shingles just as the wet snow began to come down. I had already eaten with the children, so I warmed up a plate of roast lamb with rosemary, baby potatoes, braised endive, and a fennel and orange salad that I had made especially for David from my new cookbook, *The Ultimate Italian Cookbook* by Carla Capalbo, which he enjoyed and thanked me for after apologizing again for having to work so late. And then we sat in the living room with a pot of herbal tea.

"The difficulty many Atmans have understanding this attitude that some Higher Initiates have is that they assume ego is supposed to disappear in direct proportion to one's level of initiation," he explained, with the light of *inspiration* now shining in his eyes. "The higher one climbs the spiritual ladder, the less ego one is supposed to have. But if that were the case, why would some Higher Initiates drop out of Atma-Gare and go back to the world? Why was that Atma Master whose name one dare not mention stripped of all his initiations?"

David was talking about the previous Living Atma Master who left Atma-Gare and started his own spiritual path. Not once since I had joined Atma-Gare was his name mentioned. This was a dark stain on the modern history of Atma-Gare, and we had to live with it. "I think only the Satma knows the answer to that," I replied.

"No doubt. Didn't the Living Atma Master write in one of his books that heaven must be won anew each day?" David said, and took a sip of tea.

"I don't recall, but that sounds like something he would say."

He took another sip. "What must be won anew each day, Cassie?"

"One's spiritual consciousness, I would think."

"Yes and no. Here's what I think. The operative word in this whole dynamic is the self. What is this unit of consciousness called the self? Is it mineral, vegetable, animal, or spiritual? Or all of these? The self is the mystery of life. In Atma we say, I am Soul, we are Soul, which is cut and dry because Soul is life; but it doesn't explain what the self is. To say that the 'I' is Soul doesn't explain what the 'I' is. 'I' is the operative word here. It takes billions of years to give birth to this unit of consciousness called 'I'. This 'I' is the individuated consciousness of God, which takes the universe all the creative energy of the evolution of life to give birth to. It's no small mystery, Cassie. All of science and religion lead to this mystery."

David finished his tea and refilled his cup. His clear blue eyes, which had taken on that special light of enlightenment, shone with a radiance that illuminated his whole countenance, and my living room.

He had come in exhausted from his roofing job, cleaning up before dropping over; but as tired as he was, the moment he connected with his *inspiration* he came alive. It never ceased to amaze me how quickly he could be energized by the Atma force. He told me that it was like a runner's high, but incomparably better.

"My Sufi teacher Sam the Man is a very skilled tradesman," he continued, sitting back in my soft leather sofa chair and crossing his legs. "Apparently he was a scholar before he took up the trades. In the basement room of his house where we held our classes, he had one wall full of Sufi sayings, all categorized for specific experiences. The first saying on this great wall of Sufi wisdom was written in bold letters. `HE WHO TASTES NOT KNOWS NOT.' At the heart of Sufism lies the mystery of the *subtlety*, the energy of God the Sufis call *Baraka*. This energy is the Atma force, which we are linked up with when the Satma initiates us into the Atma Stream of life. This is what makes Atma-Gare the most direct path to God—this linkup with the Holy Atma Current that runs through life. Sufism does not have this advantage, because only the Satma, the Living Atma Master, can link Soul up with the Atma Currrent. One may link up himself, but this rarely happens. Sufism is all about mastering the art of gathering this *subtlety,* because without *Baraka* this unit of God-consciousness we call the self cannot grow into the God-conscious Soul that it is pre-destined to become. So, what am I saying with all of this?"

David paused. I didn't think he wanted me to respond, but I felt inspired, too. "The self is Soul, but it's also the ego, isn't it?" I said, feeling very sure of myself.

"Yes," David said, and smiled. I think I threw him off track, but he welcomed the new direction the Atma had given him with my unexpected question. "The ego is the human dimension of this unit of God-consciousness that we call the self," he continued. "Since *Baraka* is the energy that the self needs to grow, it follows that the whole ethos of the Sufi teaching would be how to gather *Baraka*. In Atma, all we have to do is practice the spiritual exercises like the HU song. With the

HU, the Atma flows directly into our life. This is an extraordinary gift, Cassie. Few Atmans realize just how extraordinary the HU song really is. So the more Atma force, or *Baraka,* that one gathers, the more one will grow in spiritual consciousness, or in this unit of God-consciousness that we call the self. In the Sufi tradition, *Baraka* is best gathered by *doing*. The more one *does*, the more one gathers this life force. This is why my Sufi teacher became a tradesman, and why I also took up the trades with my teacher. The tradesman is always *doing*. The American poet Gary Snyder expressed the joyful wisdom of *doing* best when he said that there is '*a relentless clarity at the heart of work*'. This is why I love to run. I run for this relentless clarity at the heart of my run. Snyder also said something else that speaks to Sufism. '*When you get it right, pass it on.*' It took me a long time to get it right. I loved journalism, Cassie. I loved the chase of a good story. It was a foxhunt for me. The catch was so unbelievably sweet it made all the frustration and anxiety worthwhile. But I was ruthless. I would do anything to get my story. I was a predatory journalist, as most journalists are; but then I had a casual drink one afternoon with Francine, the student I raped at university, and my whole life changed."

Again, David paused for a drink of tea. He sipped it slowly and sat back. I waited with bated breath for him to continue.

That's what I loved about David. He was so open with his life that he made me feel like a tomb. At one Atma Worship Service in Barrie the cleric Dona McDirmit, whom David called 'a little lamb Atman' because of her innocent reliance upon the Satma, said to him, "You're so open your eyes just shine. *I could just hug you!*" David hugged her instead.

"Do you remember me telling you that some sexual rapes presuppose metaphorical rape?" he continued, with a different look in his eyes.

"How can I forget RAPER'S PARK?" I replied.

"No, of course you wouldn't. Well, raping Francine Peltier woke me up to the type of person I really was. I had no idea I was a metaphorical rapist until she told me that she no longer trusted men because of me. I knew that what I had done to her was wrong, but I refused to own up to it. I called her rape 'scoring,' as we all did back then, but by whatever name we call it a stinkweed will always smell like a stinkweed. I lied to myself, Cassie. I repressed my true feelings for what I had done to Francine, but they exploded in my face when she told me that I had killed her trust in men. I began to hate myself, and I knew I had to change my life. That's when I connected with an Ojibwa shaman and went on a vision quest."

"How did you connect with this shaman?" I asked, remembering that he had told me it was a very strange coincidence that led him to Sufism.

David's face brightened at the memory. "Right. I was walking down Bay Street in downtown Toronto thinking about what Francine had said to me when a street person hit me up for spare change. Absent mindedly, I said, `Why don't you get yourself a job?' I was so disgusted with myself that I took it out on the homeless man. But what he said to me was so out of context that I was jolted into paying attention. *Why don't you get yourself a shaman?* 'he snapped back, and walked away."

"What a curious thing to say," I said.

"Wasn't it? I got to the restaurant and sat down for lunch. As I was eating my soup a man walked up to me and said, `You look like you could use some company.' I didn't care, so I invited him to sit down. Actually, there weren't anymore chairs available and he called the waiter to ask if he could join me; but however this stranger came to me, the end result was that he was a cultural anthropologist doing research on native spirituality. `Have you ever been on a vision quest?' he asked me. I flippantly replied, 'Maybe that's just what I need at this time in my life.' I don't know if he saw through my sarcasm or not, but he said he could hook me up with an Ojibwa shaman. A bell went off and I made the connection with the street person who told me to get a shaman. It was destined, Cassie. That's how I got my life turned around. That street person was an Atma Master. And the white wolf that came to me during my sweat told me that I had to find a spiritual path, but the wolf also said something that puzzled me for the longest time. It wasn't until I was deep into Sufism that it began to make sense."

"What did he say?" I asked, all excited.

"*'All creatures must kill to survive,'* said the spirit wolf, *'but how man kills to survive determines whether he is a man or still a creature.'* I asked the spirit wolf what the difference was. *'That's your puppy,'* the wolf replied."

"Your puppy?" I said, puzzled.

David laughed. "Yes, my puppy. It took years before I understood what the spirit wolf meant. The rapist is still a creature, Cassie. The rapist is driven by his animal nature. He lusts for *Baraka,* and the only way he can get it is by taking it from others by force. All creatures need the life force to survive. *Baraka* is the life force. *Baraka* is more than that. It is the way, the truth, and the life, as Jesus said. It is the Word, the omniscient consciousness of Holy Spirit. It is the I-consciousness of God. And the self needs *Baraka* to satisfy its primal need to grow. The self has to grow. It cannot help itself. Its sole purpose in life is to grow into a spiritually self-realized, God-conscious Soul. However, the self is a very complex entity. The self splits in two as it evolves through life. The self begins as a unit of human consciousness, but the more *Baraka* it takes in from life to life the more spiritual it becomes. This is how man came to believe that he has an immortal spiritual nature. The human aspect of this unit of self-consciousness becomes aware of its spiritual essence as it evolves, so now the self has to nourish both its human nature and its spiritual nature. And herein, Cassie, lies the elusive mystery of ego. It is the human aspect of one's self that experiences life, and it is the human aspect of one's self that has to be transformed so the spiritual self can grow and be liberated from its human self. This is where all the salvation teachings come into the picture. This is what Jesus brought into the world with his gospel of salvation. His teaching is all about liberating the spiritual self from its human self. Didn't Jesus say, *'He who shall lose his life shall find his life?'*"

"Yes," I replied, awestruck by David's wisdom.

"Well, the more I practiced Sufism the more I found myself. I had to walk the talk to find myself, Cassie. That's Sufism in a nutshell. Why? That's the question I had to answer. I knew that my life was wrong. I was as much my father's son as I was my mother's, and I knew I had to change my life or I would end up just like my father."

"What do you mean, like your father?" I asked, burning with curiosity.

"My father's a stern, cold-hearted man. He lost his Christian faith in his twenties and he's been a recalcitrant atheist ever since. He's not a happy man, Cassie. He can't make peace with himself or the world. He's a die-hard skeptic, cynic, and pessimist all rolled up into one, and not an easy man to get along with. I couldn't, anyway."

"And your mother?" I asked.

A melancholy look came over David's face and he didn't speak for a long while. I waited patiently. "She's a reluctant agnostic," he finally said, and forced a smile. "My mother wants to believe in a loving God, but she can't bring herself to do so."

"Why not? What's stopping her?"

"It's a long story," he replied.

"Give me the short version. I'm very curious, David."

He thought for a moment, and then said, "Okay." He took a sip of tea and put his cup down. "I had an older sister who was killed by a drunk driver when she was twelve. My mother went to her church after my sister got killed and prayed to God. She wanted to know why God had taken her daughter away from her. She knelt in her church for seven hours straight, but she heard nothing, felt nothing, and saw nothing. She walked out of her church and never stepped inside another church again."

"Never?"

"Not even for weddings or funerals. My mother told God that day that as far as she was concerned he no longer existed for her."

"Is that why you call her a reluctant agnostic?"

"Yes. She wants to believe, but her pride won't let her."

"*Wow!* That's some heritage, David!"

"Isn't it? After my sister's death, my mother stopped loving me the way she used to. She couldn't risk another broken heart should something happen to me. That's how she coped with life. I was two years younger than my sister, so I grew up in a very complex family dynamic. I hungered for my mother's love, and I did everything I could for my father's approval. It's no wonder I became a metaphorical rapist."

David fell silent. Memories of his family had taken the light out of his eyes. I reached out for his hand. He took it, and I pulled him to the couch where I was sitting. I hugged him. We held each other for a few minutes, and then David kissed me and got up, poured another cup of tea and sat back down in the easy chair. Softly, he began to sing HU. I joined him.

A few minutes later, we brought the Love Song to God to a gentle close. David had a big smile on his face. So did I.

"Metaphorical rape?" I said, now that the light was back in his eyes.

"My father's very good at it," David said, with a wry, reflective smile. "He doesn't know he does it, but the more I practiced the Sufi disciplines the more aware I became of this predatory human instinct. That's where I got it from, Cassie, my father. He's unconscionable in this habit. My father is so skilled at appropriating another person's will that one can hardly notice it until one day, like my mother finally did, you feel so smothered by him that you can't breathe. He sucked the life out of us. That's where he got his energy from."

I gasped. That was exactly the same effect that my mother had on me. I can't remember the number of times that I couldn't catch my breath with my mother. I hyperventilated so badly sometimes that I had to leave the house to get away from her. My father left permanently. "Are your parents divorced?" I asked.

"No. But they live separate lives in the same house. Like I said, it's a complex family dynamic. As Tolstoy might say were he alive today, every family is dysfunctional in its own dysfunctional way. It doesn't bother me anymore, Cassie. In fact, I find it all quite amusing now that I've outgrown my family consciousness."

"That's how I feel about my family!" I exclaimed.

"I have to thank Sam the Man for that. Once I caught the scent of the *subtlety*, I couldn't stop growing. My Sufi teacher told me that some people have more of this *subtlety* than others. When one has enough *subtlety*, he has what the Sufis call the secret. When one wakes up to the secret within, he has caught the scent of *Baraka,* and he can't help but seek out the source of *Baraka*. This is how the Sufis explain man's hunger for God. This hunger for God is Soul's hunger for *Baraka,* because only through *Baraka* can one find God."

"I can't get over how well versed you are in Sufism," I said, entranced by David's knowledge of the secret Sufi teaching. "How long did you practice Sufism?"

"It's not the length of time that makes one a good Sufi, Cassie," he replied, and reached for his tea. He finished his cup and excused himself. When he came back, he continued from where he left off. "As Sam the Man used to say, once you catch the secret it's all a matter of *doing.* I managed to catch the secret early in my Sufi life, and I thank my father for that. Because of what I did to Francine, I did some serious Soul-searching. When I began to practice the Sufi disciplines, I began to wake up to the warped personality trait that I inherited from my father, and I caught the secret immediately. I don't want to mystify you anymore than you already are, Cassie. The secret is difficult to put to words, but that's what I'm trying to do with my poetry and annotated translation of *A Conference of the Birds.* I'll give it my best shot for you, though. That's the least I can do for such a lovely dinner."

"Thank you," I said. " I really would like to know, David."

"I know you do. But bear in mind that this is all privileged knowledge not meant for public consumption. I'm breaking the rules here, but I'm taking my lead from Rumi. Okay, let's call the *subtlety* nectar. Bees go out and gather nectar from flowers. Sufis go out and gather *Baraka* from life. What's the bee's secret? Study the bee. He goes out and works the flowers. He flits tirelessly from flower to flower to collect nectar. The Sufi learns from the bee how to work tirelessly to collect what he calls the sweet nectar of life. How does he do this? The secret is so simple it will shock you. The bee does not steal the nectar from other bees; he goes out and works for it. Neither does the Sufi steal the sweet nectar from life; he works for it like the bee. He is tireless in his efforts to gather *Baraka* from every flower of his experiences. Why work for it, you ask? The answer is simple, but impossible to see. Because stolen *Baraka* is not the same as the *Baraka* that you gather through your own efforts. Stollen *Baraka* doesn't belong to you, and it has to be paid back to life. That's God's law. That's karma. But earned *Baraka* is yours forever. This is the inscrutable secret of the Sufi teaching—*the secret knowledge of how to gather the sweet nectar of life from whatever one does, just like bees gather honey!"*

Pausing to rest, David stretched out his legs and put his hands behind his head. He shut his eyes for a minute or two, and then continued: "My father learned to steal *Baraka* from people by raping them metaphorically. They hated him at the paper where he worked, but they respected him because he was more right than wrong. Many people do this, Cassie. It's a natural predatory instinct that keeps the spiritual self of man trapped in its human consciousness. I could never fathom why my father was so damn cynical his whole life. Now I know why. He's been conditioned by his own predatory instincts to trust no one. His predatory animal consciousness rules his life. The predatory consciousness has been refined by evolution, but however refined it may be it's still a predatory instinct, and its sole purpose is to prey upon life to nourish man's fundamental need for more self-consciousness. This is the mind-boggling mystery of ego, Cassie. Ego is the 'I' of the self, and it's insatiable in its appetite for more self-consciousness. It will do anything to get it, and as long as man is trapped by his predatory animal consciousness he lives only to grow in ego consciousness. This is why egoists are never satisfied. There's no end to the appetites of the ego consciousness. These appetites will destroy one before they can be completely satisfied. So what does the Sufi do? He learns how to gather *Baraka* from the richest and most rewarding flower in the world— *his own ego!"*

David had tapped into a source of wisdom that simply astounded me, and I stared at him in awe. But I still did not understand something. "I'm following you the best I can, David, but I'm still having trouble with this concept of metaphorical rape."

"I know," he said, smiling at my bewilderment. "It's not easy to capture, Cassie; but we all do it, especially men. We've always been predatory hunters. We still are. We all feed off each other's subtle energies. That's life in the first stage of evolution. Watch people. Study their behavior. Listen to how people talk to each other. See if you can tell the difference between a person who gives another person his space and the person who deprives another person of his space. Let's call a person's space one's sense of self. Now listen to people. When they talk to people, do they allow them their sense of self, or do they refuse them their sense of self? And if they refuse them their sense of self, see if you can catch how they try to take away that person's sense of self. It's very, very subtle. For example, do you remember Stephanie Werner's service last Sunday? Remember how she insisted that we all move our chairs in closer to her because she liked to have a tight circle. She used the excuse that it was more cozy and friendly, but in reality she was imposing her will to nourish her ego with the *subtlety*. We were comfortable, but she wanted to have her way with us because she was feeling insecure and needed our energy to prop up her ego, so she insisted that we move our chairs in closer together. She was the cleric, and she used her authority as the cleric to get her way. That's a subtle form of metaphorical rape. She asserted her will to appropriate the *subtlety* from us to feed her ego, and she succeeded. Everyone moved their chair in closer but me, which only added fuel to our personality conflict; but I did not acquiesce for reasons which I hope will one day wake her up to the hold that her ego still has over her. She may be a Sixth Initiate, Cassie; but Stephanie still has a lot of work to do on her ego. Another thing. Did you notice how reluctant everyone was to move their chair in closer to her? It was a gratuitous request for the benefit of her manipulative ego, and it raised a red flag. That red flag was our own natural instinct to not be preyed upon by others. It's all about *Baraka*, Cassie; the subtle life force that ego needs to grow. I know this is all very metaphysical, and difficult to grasp; but like I told you in Minneapolis, '*the declaration's better than the secret.'* Does this help you to understand what I mean by metaphorical rape?"

"Yes," I said, flabbergasted by David's explanation. I wondered why he had refused to move his chair closer when Stephanie asked us, and now I knew why. His explanation sent shivers up my spine. "Still, David," I said, "I'm not sure I understand why some Higher Initiates can be so full of self-importance. Can't they see their own ego?"

David broke into laughter. "Why do you think it took me so long to see my own insidious character flaw?"

"Are you referring to your father's personality trait?"

"Yes. I was too close to myself to see it. To see yourself, you have to stand back from your own ego. But how do you stand back from who you are? It's damn near impossible to do. But if we can't do it on our own life will shock us out of ourselves with an unexpected experience, usually a tragedy of some sort, because we're all driven to grow spiritually. It may not seem to be very significant, but what Francine said to me that afternoon over a double shot of scotch shocked me enough to see myself for what I had become, and I did not like what I saw. I was a bastard. I was one of those men that women love to hate. But the Sufi life separates one from the self he thinks he is. The metaphysics of the self are abstruse. That's why Sufism focuses on *doing*, not analyzing. *Doing* gathers *Baraka,* and *Baraka* raises one's level of spiritual consciousness. As one raises his consciousness, he sees his human self more clearly."

"But surely a Higher Initiate should be able to see his own ego?" I interjected. "Why can't they? Aren't they high enough?"

"Good point. Ego adapts, that's why. There is only one way to stand apart from one's ego, and that's to create a special place in yourself which ego cannot inhabit—your own sanctuary from life. If you can do that, you will overcome the creature within."

"Creature?" I said, taken aback by that image. "What creature?"

"The self that is not what it is," David answered, with a big grin.

"You're losing me," I said, feeling a little frustrated now. As much as I loved him for his *inspiration*, when David overwhelmed me my battery would overcharge. I had to be very careful or sparks were sure to fly. "I want to follow you, David, but you can't keep going into warp drive on me. Remember, I'm only a Third Initiate. Is this special place your talking about what you meant by the journey of the alone to the Alone?"

David sensed the change in my voice. He stood up, came over, and gave me a long, tender, and very passionate kiss on the mouth that made my head spin.

"What was that for?" I asked, as he made for the front door.

"You're an eagle Atman, that's why," he said.

"I don't understand," I said, following him to the door.

"You will some day," he said, and pecked me goodnight on the cheek.

Did he notice that I had enough of his super-charged spiritual energy for one night? Or had I inched my chair closer to his? That's what it felt like.

Chapter 15

The Secret to David Oakly

I was too hyper to sleep. I sat in my bedroom after I recorded my evening with David in my journal. I had to buy more notebooks. I was filling them up quickly since we became involved. I reflected on our incredible evening, and for the first time in our relationship it dawned on me what made David Oakly so different from every other Atman I had met.

The one quality that defined Atmans as I had experienced them since I joined Atma-Gare was their uniqueness. No two were alike in the same way that most people are alike. We're all the same insomuch that we're initiates of the Audible Life Stream, the creative spiritual current that runs through life, and we all have the Satma's love, guidance, and protection; but our spiritual identity makes us all unique.

"Atmans are more spiritually self-realized than most people," said David one hot July afternoon when he took me on a day trip to introduce me to Georgian Bay. "Our spiritual personality makes us unique, not our human personality," he added, and opened up another door to the mystery of human nature.

I took my July journal out of my drawer to remind myself of our conversation. It didn't occur to me that he had distinguished himself from other Atmans that afternoon in the shade of the big locust tree at the roadside park in Craigleith, but upon reflection I saw it.

I was feeling sorry for myself that day. I missed my children and I called David on his cell phone just to talk with him. It was after one and he was supposed to be working on his own house. He had just sold the house he was living in and had thirty days to have his new house ready to move into, and I didn't want to disturb him. I caught him as he came in from his long run. "It's nothing important, David. I just wanted to talk with you, that's all," I said.

"I'm glad you called, Cassie. What's up?"

"Oh, nothing much. I'm just sitting here missing my children."

"Are you in a funk?" he asked.

"Yes, I am. I'm not going to lie to you, David."

David paused before replying. "Would you like some company?"

"You're working on your house today."

"Give me an hour, okay?"

"What about your house? Aren't you supposed to start painting today?"

"Life's all about timing, Cassie. See you in an hour," he said, and hung up.

I was still in my pajamas. I quickly showered and dried my hair and put on a pair of shorts and top and then did my make-up. Two minutes to the hour, the doorbell rang. I opened the door and David said, "How about we go for a day trip somewhere?"

"I'd love that. Where to?"

"Let's do the scenic route along the shores of Georgian Bay. Through Wasaga Beach, Collingwood, and maybe the Blue Mountains. How does that sound?"

"Fantastic," I said, feeling much better already.

We took my Odyssey, but David drove. Wasaga Beach only has sixteen thousand people, but summers teem with young people coming up from the Greater Toronto Area to spend time on the beach, and it took us thirty-five minutes to negotiate our way through the beachfront traffic; but I wanted to see all the action.

"Oh, to be young again," I said, as young women in skimpy two-piece bathing suits paraded their curved tight bodies down the sidewalk in front of *Pedro's* gift shop.

"Youth is such a wonderful thing. Too bad it's wasted on the young," David said, and broke into a private chuckle.

"Bernard Shaw! My father quoted him all the time!"

"Feeling better now?" David said, his eyes smiling.

"Much better, thank you. I wish you could have met my father, David. You would have liked him. I know he would have liked you."

"Why?" he asked.

"I don't know if I should tell you," I said, playfully.

"Okay. Your choice," David said.

"Now I have to tell you!" I exclaimed.

David laughed again. "I'm listening."

"It's who you are, David. My father admired independent thinkers. He used to say to his first year students, 'One man's wisdom may be another man's nonsense, and one man's nonsense may be another man's wisdom.' That was his motto."

"Great motto. But it's incomplete."

"Oh?"

"How can you tell one from the other?"

"That's the dilemma, isn't it? My father tried to figure that out his whole life, but he couldn't. But you know what, David? I did."

"You did?" he said, with a surprised look on his face.

"Yes. I found Atma-Gare. That's my yardstick for wisdom."

"Touché!" he said, and slapped me proudly on my thigh. On the way out of the Beach he pulled into *Lorna Dune's* at the junction of Mosley and Highway 26 for a soft ice cream. I asked for mine in a wafer cone and dipped in chocolate.

"I'm spoiling myself today," I said.

"Then I'll spoil myself too," he said.

"You're doing that just for me?" I said, begging for all I could get.

"Resonance, Cassie," David replied, and stepped out of the van.

"What did you mean by resonance?" I asked, when he handed me my cone.

He took a bite through the chocolate dip and took two licks before answering. "The day will unfold gracefully if we're in sync," he said.

I think I knew what he meant, but I didn't pursue it. I was so happy he had taken the rest of his Saturday off for me that all I wanted to do was enjoy our time together.

We drove through Collingwood and down Highway 26 to the Blue Mountains, but David didn't drive into the Blue Mountains as I expected; he continued down 26 until we came to the Northwinds Beach Park just off the highway on the shores of Georgian Bay.

He pulled in, but the parking lot was full. "Huzee, we need a parking space," David said, addressing the Satma, and we just waited in the middle of the parking lot.

I didn't say anything. Within minutes a man and woman came walking up the bank. They got into their car and pulled out.

David backed up for them to drive out of the parking lot, and then he pulled into the empty space, switched off the ignition, and said, "Thank you, Huzee."

I wasn't sure what had just happened. We got out of the van and found an empty bench under the shade of a locust tree. A huge weeping willow by the shore cast such a large canopy of shade that there were four park tables under it, and they were all occupied with people in shorts and bathing suits having a wonderful, carefree picnic. I looked around and saw that all the tables in the shade of all the willow trees along the grassy bank of the park were occupied, and the beach was sprinkled with people and chairs and umbrellas and I was so happy that David had brought me that I got up and kissed him on the cheek. "Thank you," I said.

"You're welcome," he said, and I sat back down.

David cast his gaze about, taking in the scenery of the bay and all the people who had driven up from the city who were enjoying a little respite from the hustle and bustle of their busy urban lives, and then very thoughtfully, he said, "What makes us different, Cassie?"

"You and me?"

"Us and them."

"We're Atmans," I said.

"Yes, we are; but what makes us different from the rest of the world?"

"Are we so different, really? Sri Herman says that Soul equals Soul. That makes us all spiritual equals, doesn't it?" I replied, sensing David's *inspiration* stirring.

"Yes, we are spiritual equals; but only insomuch that we're all made of the same energy of God. We're all Soul, as Atmans are fond of saying, and Soul equals Soul; but we're all atoms of God evolving through life for the purpose of realizing our divine nature. All these people are Soul, and each one has his or her own personal karmic destiny; but what they don't know is that they also have a spiritual destiny. Not only do we know we have a spiritual destiny; we also know what it is. That makes us different."

"But just because we know our spiritual destiny doesn't really make us different, does it? They're going to find out eventually. It may take a few more lifetimes, but everyone will find out that they have a spiritual purpose in life."

David put his right arm on the bench, and turning to me crossed his legs. Looking deep into my eyes, he smiled and said, "It's all a matter of degree, isn't it? The acorn seed is a potential oak tree. The Latin phrase is *in potentia*, I believe. We're all acorn seeds, Cassie. We're all in the process of becoming spiritually self-realized, God conscious Souls; but at what point in our evolution do we become conscious of our spiritual destiny?"

"That's easy," I said, with a proud smile. "When we find the Wayshower."

"True. We need the Living Atma Master to initiate us into the Atma Stream of life; because that's the only way we can break the cycle of karma and reincarnation. So we have two lines of destiny, then," he explained, as the gentle waves lapped the shores of the bay like soothing background music to our conversation. "We have our pre-scripted destiny, which is spiritually driven, and we have our personal destiny, which is karmically driven, and at some point in our evolution our two lines of destiny will have to come together, or coincide. The Atman has finally come to this point of self-coincidence in his evolution. That's what makes us different from all these people here. They're not conscious of their spiritual purpose in life."

"Self-coincidence?" I said, puzzled by the phrase.

"Yes. Our personal or karmic destiny will have to coincide with our spiritual destiny one day, because it's written in the Divine Plan of God. Atmans have evolved enough to bring their personal destiny into agreement with their spiritual destiny. This is self-coincidence, and this is what separates us from the rest of the world."

"What about Sufism?" I asked, wondering if that spiritual path could bring our two lines of destiny into agreement like Atma-Gare. "Doesn't Sufism bring one's personal destiny and one's spiritual destiny to the same point of agreement?"

"It can, if the Sufi path takes one to the Living Atma Master," David said. His eyes were bright with the light now, and his face began to radiate with that glow I had begun to associate with his special connection with the creative life stream, and I couldn't help but smile at him. "That's why Sam the Man had to let me go. He could do no more for me, so with his blessing I stepped out into the world to look for my new spiritual teacher."

I smiled again at David, because I don't think he was aware of how easily he shifted from his everyday self to his inner, *inspired* spiritual self. This is what made it exciting to be with him. It didn't matter to David where we were, or what we were doing, whenever he had an opportunity to talk about the spiritual life, he magically shifted to a spiritual perspective.

"But didn't Sam tell you about Atma-Gare?"

"No, he didn't."

"Did he know about the Living Atma Master?"

"Yes, he knew. But he wouldn't tell me. He trusted me enough to let me find my own way to Atma-Gare," David replied, with a private chuckle."

"Why wouldn't he tell you?" I asked.

David didn't answer right away. He took a long look at the people splashing in the water, walking the beach, talking, sitting, laughing; and then with a touch of wistful sadness, he said, "It's a fact of life that those to whom the teachings of Atma are given have less appreciation for the teachings than those who earn them. People who come to the Atma of their own volition are more likely to stay compared to those who are handed Atma-Gare on a platter. That's why Atma Masters seldom introduce people directly to the Atma teachings. `By indirections we find directions out,' said Shakespeare."

I understood what David meant. Grace's experience with the Atma Master Kati Sada proved it. She didn't tell Grace who the Living

Atma Master was. "There are those who say that the real Master is a man living in the United States," she said. Grace was given a shove in the right direction by Kati Sada, but that's what Atma Masters do. When Soul is ready for the Atma teaching, it falls into what David called the consciousness of affinity.

"And by that, you mean?" I asked him on our weekend getaway to Algonquin Provincial Park when he revealed to me that Sufism had transformed his consciousness enough to have an affinity with the spiritual current of life.

He thought before speaking. And then he explained one of the most profound mysteries of natural evolution that I had only seen hinted at in the *Shariyatma*. But like most Atmans, I didn't know what that meant until he broke it down for me. "The Atma is the Way; the Atma is life; ergo, life is the Way," he said. "It's a simple syllogism."

Puzzled, I said, "Are you saying that life is the Way of the Eternal?"

"Yes. Every experience that we have in life brings us closer to our true self. It's that simple," he said; and by the time we ended our getting-to-know each other weekend of hiking the Algonquin trails, which was like an exciting, two-day metaphor of what he explained to me about the Way, I came to understand that life itself is the spiritual path back home to God; but sitting on the bench at Northwinds Beach Park that hot July afternoon he took me deeper into the mysteries of the Way of the Eternal, and I listened with rapt attention. "The consciousness of affinity is that place in one's evolution when Soul begins to resonate with the laws of life," he explained. "This consciousness of affinity is responsible for all those surprising little coincidences that pop up out of nowhere in one's life. This is the most exciting stage of one's spiritual journey, Cassie. Soul has begun to wake up to the spiritual consciousness of life. At this stage one has come to the end of the Exoteric Circle of Life, the long first stage of evolution, and finds himself at the gateway of the Mesoteric Circle, which is the next stage in our spiritual evolution through life."

"You mean there are stages to spiritual evolution?" I asked, totally engaged in our "dialectical discourse," as David described our *inspired* talks.

"Yes," he said. And then he introduced me to the Divine Plan of God, which I had not read about anywhere, let alone in the Atma literature. "The atom of God does not come from God into the life process with an individual self-consciousness, or sense of self, if you will. It's like the acorn seed. It is the seed of its own God self, and it is planted in the lower worlds to grow this God self. This is the essence of the Divine Plan of God. Life was created by God to serve God's need to grow. The *Shariyatma* tells us that nature will only evolve man so far, and no further; so when man has reached this point of evolution he has no choice but to take evolution into his own hands. He is driven by his pre-scripted spiritual destiny just as the acorn seed is genetically driven to become an oak tree. This is where natural karmic evolution meets conscious spiritual evolution, or where the Exoteric Circle of Life meets the Mesoteric Circle of Life. This is where all those exciting coincidences that point one in the right direction take place, because one has evolved a spiritual consciousness of affinity and is now guided to his spiritual destiny by the omniscient guiding force of life. I know this is all very esoteric, but does it explain it for you?"

"I think so," I said, awestruck by David's grasp of the Divine Plan of God. "Where did you get this knowledge? I don't remember reading this in the *Shariyatma*, or any other Atma book for that matter. Where, David?"

He gave me his mystic Mona Lisa smile. David seemed to know a secret that no one else in the world knew, and this secret was reflected in his smile.

"From Rumi," he said, his smile fading as he spoke but leaving its radiance behind like an afterglow. "Of any poet in history, Rumi was the most connected with the Holy Current of God. Coleman Barks, the popular translator of Rumi's poetry, is mystified by how spontaneously Rumi composed poetry; but this shouldn't surprise Atmans. Rumi's teacher was Shams of Tabriz, who was the Living Atma Master of his times. Shams initiated Rumi into the Holy Current of God. Shams was to Rumi what Father in heaven was to Jesus. Rumi and Jesus were so connected with the Holy Current of God that the water of everlasting life just poured out of them. With Rumi it came out in his mystifying poetry, and with Jesus it came out in his gospel of salvation. In both cases, it was the Way of the Eternal revealed according to the unique spiritual personality of each man."

My mind was racing to find the right words. I didn't want to pry, but I had to know. "David, how did you get to be so knowledgeable on this subject?"

"What subject?"

"The Way of the Eternal."

"I'd have to credit two things," he replied. "My Sufi training, and my writing. Actually, we can't forget the Holy Current of God. The Atma is the source of all my *inspiration*, Cassie, and the most important factor in my knowledge of the Way of the Eternal. My Sufi training brought me into the Mesoteric Circle of Life where the Holy Current of God pours out of the Higher Worlds, but I had to find a way to tap into this infinite source of spiritual wisdom. Rumi instructed me here. He tapped into this oceanic fount of truth with his poetry, so I put to the test my favorite Rumi saying, '*He who tastes not, knows not.*'"

David stopped talking, letting me come to my own conclusion. It took several minutes, but I finally did. "You began writing poetry?" I asked, a little hesitant.

"Yes," he said, and laughed. "It's one thing to write journalism, but quite another to write creatively. I made a discipline of writing one poem a day for one month, then two poems a day for two months, then three poems a day for three months, then four poems a day for four months, and then five poems a day for five months. And then I wrote one poem every day for one year. By writing poetry every day I learned how to connect with my *inspiration*. That's how I came upon the idea that opened up the floodgate to the ocean of infinite spiritual wisdom."

"What idea?" I asked, now bursting with curiosity.

"To dialogue with the *Shabda Dhun*," he said.

"What?" I asked, even more mystified.

"*Shabda Dhun* means the Voice of that which gives life to all. It's the Voice of Atma, or Divine Spirit, if you will," he explained.

"*You dialogue with the Atma?*" I said, incredulously.

He laughed. "No, not like you think. It's not like the Holy Ghost and I have a conversation. It's more a question of being open to what the Atma has to say. What comes through in my writing is the Voice of Atma. Jesus called it the water of everlasting life, and I call it my *inspiration*."

"How do you do that?" I asked, oblivious to everyone around me now.

"I write personal essays. I've cultivated a creative technique that taps into the ocean of infinite wisdom. That's where I get most of my knowledge on the Way of the Eternal. And before you ask, my technique is simple enough. I use my daily life as my entry point into the mystery that has captured my interest. I just let my *inspiration* flow as I write in my journal. I may not get my answer in my first try, but with each entry that evolves into a personal essay the Atma gives me more insights, which I then connect to get the answer to my query. Like the mystery of suicide. I was intrigued by suicide, so I explored it by writing about it. It's a creative technique. Like a Socratic dialectic. That's all it is. Novelists use it all the time."

I knew David was right, because whenever I journaled our conversations I got incredible new insights. I tapped into something deeper. That's when I realized why he was so different from other Atmans. He could tap into this fount of infinite wisdom almost at will in our conversations, which always transported me to the higher worlds. That's why he could be so intimidating.

I witnessed this at the inaugural Atma Worship Service at the Leacock Care Center when Stephanie Werner's ego got bruised. David offered everyone a different perspective on her talk, and she was rattled enough by him to change the subject entirely.

It was obvious that Stephanie and David didn't see eye to eye, but I knew it wasn't David's doing. He simply refused to be played by her.

We did our HU song, which we always do when we begin our worship service, and then Stephanie gave her talk. "The goal of the Atma life is to become a co-worker with God," she began, very confident in her thin voice. "We serve God by serving life. That's how we become a co-worker. Every life that we have lived has prepared us to serve God. My talk this morning has to do with how to best serve God. I drove all the way up here from Toronto today to serve the

Atma, because I am a co-worker with God. This is how I serve God. I serve the Atma community. We help the Satma, the Living Atma Master, by bringing the message of Atma out into the world. Are there any non-Atmans here this morning?"

A young couple from Washago put their hands up.

"Wonderful. Is this your first introduction to Atma-Gare?"

"No," said the young lady, her voice a little nervous. "We're taking a book discussion class in Huntsville on waking dreams."

"Waking dreams are an important part of Atma-Gare," Stephanie replied. "I just gave a talk on waking dreams last month in Kitchener. But my topic today is Spiritual Destiny. I remember one evening after doing my spiritual contemplation I asked the Satma how I could serve the Atma, and he told me to be all that I can be. That's why I became an Atma cleric. When I got my Fifth Initiation, I didn't have time to be an Atma cleric. My magazine took up so much of my time that I hardly had a personal life. But it didn't satisfy me the way I needed to be satisfied. Something was missing in my life. I asked the Satma what I had to do to satisfy my longing, and he told me to be all that I could be. At first I thought he meant my profession, but he didn't mean that at all. After four or five more months of long days at the magazine, I still felt empty. I had to do something. That's when it hit me to become an Atma cleric. I did. And you know what? I don't have that empty feeling anymore. Being an Atma cleric gives me all the satisfaction I need at this time in my life. It also gave me my Sixth Initiation. I'm still the managing editor of our magazine, but I serve God now by serving the Atma community. That's how I have become a co-worker with God. We all have to find a way to bring the message of Atma out into the world. That's what our spiritual goal in life should be…"

She went on for a few more minutes, and then she asked us for ideas on how to be a co-worker with God. David spoke up. "If I may, Stephanie," he said, and I knew by the sound of his voice that he was going to rub her the wrong way, "are you saying that the spiritual destiny of every Soul is to become a co-worker with God by helping the Satma to bring the message of Atma out to the world?"

"That's exactly what I'm saying," she replied, emphasizing her words.

"That's admirable," David said. "However, I have a different take on what it means to be a co-worker with God."

"Oh? And what would that be?" she asked, in a sarcastic tone.

"The answer lies in what the Satma told you," David replied, with a confidence in his voice that demanded everyone's attention. "Be all that you can be. Isn't that what Huzee said when you asked him how you could serve the Atma?"

"Yes," Stephanie said, a little doubtful of herself now.

"I have no doubt that you made the right choice for yourself by becoming an Atma cleric," David continued, and we could tell by his voice that it was coming, "but that doesn't apply to everyone."

"Why not?" Stephanie shot back defensively.

"Not everyone is cut out to be a messenger for the Atma," David calmly replied. "My understanding of the Atma life is that we best serve God by being the most that we can be in what we do. A nurse who serves her calling with all the dedication, care, and compassion that she can bring to nursing would be serving life by being all that she can be in her profession. She doesn't have to go out and bring the message of Atma to the world. She may not want to. That's her choice. Another Atman may be a schoolteacher. Being the best teacher that he can be would be how he serves God. If I may borrow a phrase from the poet Gary Snyder, *'When you get it right, pass it on.'* Being all that we can be in what we do is what being a co-worker with God means to me, because the more true one is to what he is and does—be one an engineer, a social worker, or chimney sweep—the more open one is to the Atma. This is what characterizes the genius of individual talent. Michelangelo, DaVinci, Beethoven, Mozart, Shakespeare, William Wordsworth, Rumi, Newton, Einstein, Lincoln, Mahatma Gandhi, Doctor Kubler-Ross; all these great people connected with the Holy Current of God through their own individual talent and passed it on to the world. Surely what they gave to the world is a little taste of the Divine, don't you think?"

Stephanie did not answer. She changed the subject. "Does anyone here have an Atma experience that they would like to share?"

As we all stood in line at Webers on the 400 Highway after our worship service at the Leacock Care Center, I asked David what it was about him that bothered Higher Initiates like Stephanie Werner. He whispered into my ear, *"My balls."*

I knew what he meant, but waiting in the unbelievabley long queue at Webers was not the place to explore it further. When it finally came to our turn to order, David placed the order for us, and Cindy said to him, "Can you order a burger and fries for Patrick?"

"Maybe we should get him two burgers and fries. What do you think?"

"Yeah. One burger's not enough for Patrick," Cindy said, and smiled proudly.

"How about you, Mark? One or two burgers?" David asked.

Mark thought for a moment. "I'll have two, please."

David looked at me and smiled. I was as surprised as he was, but said nothing.

We finally got our charbroiled burgers, fries, and cold drinks and ate them in the van with the doors open. Mark kept his second burger for later. On the drive home I asked Mark what he thought of the discussion at the service.

"With David and Stephanie?" he asked.

"Yes," I said. "What did you think?"

"I liked it. But it was no contest. Stephanie's a foot soldier, Mom. She's not an Atma Warrior. David blasted her puny thought forms with his Light. That's why I made David a Lightmaster in my story. You want to read my story when I finish it, David?"

"I certainly do. What do you call your story?"

"Karma Buster. But I might change it."

"I love it. How did you come to choose that title?"

"That's what Lightmasters do, don't they? They blast karma with the Light and Sound just like you blasted Stephanie's mind karma today," Mark said, with that casual spiritual prescience that never ceased to amaze me.

David laughed. "What about you, Cindy? What did you get out of the service?"

"I'm going to be all I can be," she replied.

"And what's that?" David asked.

"A healer," she said.

"A healer?" David asked, surprised as I was. "Why a healer, Cindy?"

"I'm not supposed to say."

"Why? Is it a secret?"

"Yes."

"An Atma secret?"

"Yes."

"You don't want to break the Law of Kamit?"

"Yeah; but we don't call it the Law of Kamit anymore. It's the Law of Silence."

"Whose 'we,' Puppy Face?" Mark asked.

"Zak Tarzman and Huzee," she replied.

David turned to me and smiled. "What would people think if they heard us talking like this? What do you think, guys? Funny farm time?"

"Yeah, right! As if we're the crazy ones!" Mark said, impersonating his brother.

When we got home I asked David to join me on the deck for a few minutes. "I have to ask you something," I said.

"Anything your heart desires," he said.

"If you only knew what my heart desires," I thought to myself. We almost felt like a family, but not quite. I still had a long way to go before I "bagged him," to use Grace's expression. It wasn't that David wanted our relationship to be on his terms, nor did I want it to be on mine; it just had to find its own level. Patience was my byword.

"Balls," I said, with a self-conscious smile. "That's a coarse metaphor, David; but it's very true. I know that's what bothers some Atmans about you, but why?"

David looked at me with a guilty expresssion. "I'm sorry, Cassie. I didn't mean to be so coarse. I forget myself sometimes. I'm a tradesman, and I slip into my tradesman's earthy vocabulary without realizing it. How about we use the word gonads instead?"

"I'm much more comfortable with that," I said, giving him a big smile.

"Good. Well, not to take anything away from them because they certainly have earned their spiritual accomplishments, but what bothers some of these Higher Initiates about me is what I call my *sanctuary*. Let me tell you one of my favorite Nasrudin stories."

"Nasrudin?"

"The Mullah Nasrudin is a Sufi folk hero. Actually, he's the physical embodiment of the Sufi Path. He's a practical joker, but much more than that. His exploits are used by Sufi teachers to free one from the constraints of his lower self. The Mullah Nasrudin would be to Sufism what the koan is to Zen Buddhism, only much more entertaining and instructive. To put it simply, the Sufis use the adventures of the Mullah Nasrudin as teaching stories."

"And what does the Mullah Nasrudin have to say about your gonads?"

With a twinkle in his eye, David replied, "In this particular story the Mullah was a magistrate. A woman came to him with her son and asked him to formally forbid her son from eating sugar because she could not afford to keep him in sugar. Nasrudin told her to come back in seven days. When she returned, he postponed his decision for another week. `Now,' he said to the youth when they returned, `I forbid you to eat more than such and such a quantity of sugar every day.' The boy's mother asked Nasrudin why he needed so much time to give a simple order. The Mulla replied, `Because, madam, I had to see if I myself could cut down on the use of sugar before ordering anyone else to do so.' Stephanie Werner, like Edgar Smallwood, his wife Sandra, Chris Mahony and every Higher Initiate who finds me a threat are bothered by the simple fact that I can stop eating sugar anytime I please. Does that help?"

In a flash I saw through the mystique of David's sweet mystic smile. *"That explains everything!"* I exclaimed, to David's surprise.

"What?" he asked.

"So the secret to David Oakly lies in this place you call sanctuary?" I said, unable to contain my excitement. "I think I know what you mean, but I have to be absolutely certain. Please explain it to me."

David couldn't get over my excitement and just stared at me. "Yes, that's the secret to David Oakly," he said, with a big grin. "My *sanctuary* is the home of my alone," he explained, and then glanced at his watch. "I have to run, Cassie. I have to meet someone in a few minutes about a kitchen he wants me to renovate. We can pick this up another time, okay?"

I didn't realize until the first few months of our relationship how skilled David was in the trades. He did everything himself when it came to renovating. He practically built his new house alone. But he was neither boastful nor modest about his accomplishments. It was an incredible place to be, and it puzzled me.

At first I thought it was because of his family upbringing. His parents must have been the inspiration for his *sanctuary*, but I couldn't be sure. The more I thought about it, the more I attributed the mystique of his aloofness to his Sufi training. What he had shared with me about his attraction to the cub reporter sent chills up my spine. *What incredible discipline!*

It was two-thirty in the morning, but I was still too hyper to sleep. I had so much energy that my ears were ringing. This always happened whenever David and I connected in that special way. I would hear the Sound Current for hours after he left.

The Sound Current is the Audible Life Stream; the all-embracing spiritual force of God that makes up all the elemental substances, including the component parts of Soul, and it can be heard and seen with spiritual vision. It's the creative life force, and David's *inspiration.*

I often heard it when I did my HU chant, and almost every time that David and I got together; especially when David connected with his *inspiration* like he did after dinner. He had given me such a boost of energy that my ears buzzed with the Sound of God. The humming was so loud that it felt like I was standing under a main power line.

I made a cup of hot chocolate. I wanted to reflect some more. I wanted to inch my chair closer to David's by understanding him better. I opened my journal at random and read one of his *inspired* comments that I had gotten into the habit of highlighting in yellow: *"The path to spiritual mastership is the path of self-reliance."*

David said this at an Atma Worship Service in Barrie. The guest speaker was a Higher Initiate from Peterborough, David's hometown. He knew Bob McLean before Bob joined Atma-Gare.

Bob Mclean's talk was one of the most fascinating Atma stories I had ever heard. He gave us a brief history of how he had come to Atma-Gare. As a child, Bob could see Atma Masters who came to him in their Atma Sarup, or Soul body. Whenever he went out into his back yard he saw a golden net enveloping his yard, and four Atma Masters came out of the sky to talk to him; Fedar Farad, Jivan Nuri, Rak Tarzman, and Paul Mathew. The first time he saw the Atma Masters, Zak Tarzman asked him how he liked his new life. He didn't. Bob's family was poor, and it made Bob very sad. He lived in a small house that didn't have an indoor toilet, but he remembered where he had come from, a palatial home on the other side; and he was confused and angry. He recalled the white marble columns and beautiful garden surroundings of his other home, and he couldn't understand his new life. But Bob liked his back yard, because it had a golden net that domed his whole yard; and he loved the Atma Masters who came to visit him. His parents thought he had a vivid imagination, and they didn't believe his experiences with the Atma Masters.

As Bob grew older, his spiritual sight faded. He lost the connection with the Atma that he had as a young boy, and the rest of his story had to do with how he lost his way in life. He began to drink and do drugs. He was so depressed one day that he wanted to take his own life, but he remembered his childhood and the special gift that he had to Soul travel through pictures and this pulled him out of his suicidal despair. Bob could look at a picture and Soul travel into the picture and experience the reality of that picture. One day he was looking at a picture of Jesus in the Garden of Gethsemane. As he stared at Jesus, he felt himself being pulled into the picture and he talked to Jesus, but Jesus didn't look like the man in the picture. Jesus told Bob that portraits of him were what artists thought he looked like. Bob asked Jesus why he could not see the golden net anymore like he used to when he was a boy. Jesus told him that he had to look for the golden net now. He asked Jesus if he could take him to the golden net. Jesus said it was not his place to do that. He told Bob that he had to go out into the world to look for the golden net. In his room, and at the point of taking his own life, Bob remembered the Atma Masters who came to him as a young boy. He called to them for help. He heard a voice. It was the Atma Master Paul Mathew. He said to Bob, "To find the answer that you're looking for, you have to go to the mountains." Bob was startled by the voice. After he collected himself, he had a strong desire to move to British Columbia to see the mountains, and he finally moved.

One evening in Vancouver Bob saw an Atma-Gare poster with a picture of Atma Masters. There was something familiar about them. A young man came up behind him and said, "What do you think of that?" He was an Atman, and they were holding an introductory talk on Atma-Gare in the building across the street. Bob attended the talk and found his golden net, which he recognized was made up of the golden threads of Atma wisdom. He became a member of Atma-Gare and reconnected with the Audible Life Stream, the Holy Current of God.

Bob summed up the moral of his incredible story: *"We have to claim our spirituality. That was the lesson that I came to learn in this lifetime."* Which was why David maintained that we have to earn the Atma teachings through karmic resolution. "Like Paul Mathew said," David quoted, "'we just keep coming back until we get it right.'"

Before Bob told his incredible story a woman came up to David and asked him a question. Janet was new to Atma-Gare, and she was bothered by something a former Atman had told her about Paul Mathew, the man who introduced Atma-Gare to the modern world in 1965. This former Atman told her Paul Mathew had plagiarized the Atma teachings from a guru he met in India. Janet was disturbed by this, but David reassured her that Paul Mathew was not a plagiarist. " Paul was a master compiler of the spiritual teachings of Atma that were scattered throughout the world in the various religions, teachings, and traditions," he explained to Janet; "and Paul's mandate from the Satma was to go into the world and collect all these scattered threads of golden wisdom so the world could have the whole teaching of the Way of the Eternal. He wove these threads of spiritual wisdom into one golden tapestry and called it Atma-Gare, and we no longer have to go from path to path to find our way to wholeness because the Atma is the most direct path to our true self. So don't be disturbed by these detractors. Just listen to your own heart, Janet. That's the only voice you need to hear."

She did, and as she listened to Bob's incredible story about how he found the golden net of Atma wisdom her heart told her that she was on the right path and she made a point of standing up and thanking Bob for sharing his story with us. "You spoke to my heart," Janet said, "and I'm going to reclaim my spirituality too."

Janet had tears in her eyes. We were all moved. Then Bob asked us the question, "When you lose what you believed in, how do you find a new belief to live by?"

Everyone agreed that we should look for spiritual signs, because they point us in the right direction; but then David surprised everyone. "How do you keep from spinning the interpretation of a sign to what you want it to mean?" he asked.

Henry Sanderson, a Higher Initiate from Richmond Hill, turned to David and in a superior tone of voice said, "You have to be brutally honest with yourself, that's how."

"I'm no stranger to brutal honesty, Henry!" David retorted, with the swiftness of a mongoose and in a tone of voice that I had never heard before. It was so categorical that it sent a chill up my spine. "Brutal honesty doesn't ensure a correct interpretation of the signs," David continued, his eyes focused on Henry with such fierce intensity that Henry recoiled in his chair. Henry had struck a raw nerve. "I know people who will go to their grave as slaves to their own uncompromising sense of brutal honesty, and they would be no less a fool than you," David struck back with mongoose precision. "My parents being two such people. No, Henry, I'm afraid it's not enough to be brutally honest. *It's simply not enough..."*

A deadly silence descended upon the room like a cold, merciless guillotine. David had opened the door to a mystery that went beyond all of us. No one dared speak.

"You have to surrender to the Atma," a nervous voice finally spoke up, breaking the unnerving silence. It was Nora Burnaby, a little blond Atman from Orillia, whose starry-eyed love for the Satma always made my heart smile. "That's how you know what the Atma is trying to tell you," she said, and giggled her nervous little laugh.

Everyone agreed, but it still bothered David. He respectfully but firmly said, "I'm coming from a different place, Nora. I don't disagree with what you say, but the path to spiritual mastership is self-reliance, not Atma-dependence. We have to trust the Atma completely before we can surrender to the Atma completely, but how do we do that? The Living Atma Master tells us that we grow spiritually by exercising our own spiritual muscles. But we can only do that by making our own decisions. To be a master in our own right we have to have total trust in ourselves. The difference between surrendering to the Atma and walking the path to spiritual mastership lies in the fine line between self-reliance and Atma-dependence. True, we have to claim our own spirituality, as Bob says, but once we claim it we have to exercise our own free will to walk the path to spiritual mastership, because the more we trust ourselves the more Atma-centered we will be. This is a paradox that will boggle the mind of anyone who dares to push the logic of the Atma life to its conclusion. This is why I don't look for signs anymore. I just do what I have to do to live my life and I let the rest take care of itself. But then, Atma-Gare is an individual path, isn't it?" David added, with an ironic smile.

Everyone was shocked by David's no-nonsense spirituality, but in that moment of stark realization, which felt like he had just sliced the proud head off our Atma community's spiritual conceit, starting with Henry's, it suddenly dawned on me that I had to have the courage to trust myself totally to inch my chair closer to David's, and I smiled to myself at my secret discovery. I put my journals away and tried to get some sleep.

Chapter 16

The Spirit of Our Times

My children were in Vancouver for July and August. They were only gone three days and the house felt so empty that I almost panicked. I had to find a way to calm myself.

Kevin didn't know it, but they would not be around to receive the direct fall-out from my open letter to the Wyedale *Gazette*. The children knew that I was going to respond to Father McDuffy's challenge, and they wished me luck before they left; but I asked them to respect my decision and not discuss this with their father.

I had resolved to write my letter to the paper. I knew it wasn't the scientific proof he was asking for, but a personal response to Father McDuffy's challenge would cause people to look at the abortion issue differently. That's all I wanted to accomplish.

I was alone out there. I had David's moral support, but I could not lean upon him; nor could I lean upon our small Atma community. It was nice to know that there were people who shared my spiritual views, but I had to see this through on my own.

It was my test. I was the one who had "murdered" my unborn child; I was the one who had experienced the miracle of my unborn child; and I was the one who would be twisting in the wind from the fallout. I couldn't put my friends through that. I had to firm up my resolve to expect the worst. *But it did not happen as I expected!*

We always imagine the worst, and when it doesn't come we don't know whether to be relieved or disappointed. I honestly did not know how to feel. My open letter to Father McDuffy had been out for three days, and I heard nothing except for David's call Wednesday evening, the day the paper came out. He had picked up the *Gazette* in the morning and called me on his cell phone from Creemore, where he was working late on a bathroom-tiling job.

After telling me how much he liked my letter, which I did not show him before I submitted it to the *Gazette* and Barrie *Examiner*, he said it was exactly what had to be said to shed new light on the issue. "It read like the Atma guided your hand," he added, which was true. "You don't have to go through this alone, Cassie. Call me anytime."

I knew David would be there for me, but I hoped I would be strong enough to deal with the fallout on my own. I expected the worst at the hospital, because most of the staff was Christian, but not one person made a comment about my letter. It had been out for three whole days, and still not one single comment. *It was the strangest thing!*

I got looks, and my staff whispered with the odd glance at me, so I knew they were talking about my letter, but no one came up to me directly. It was the most bizarre experience of my life, and the only thing I could come up with was that the miracle of my unborn daughter Seana must have stunned the community into silence. It was too much for their Christian minds. That was the only possible explanation that I could think of.

The *Gazette* came out on Wednesday, and it was Saturday morning when I got my first response to my letter. I was in my kitchen having a cup of coffee and anxiously waiting for the storm to break. The phone startled me. "Here it comes," I said, and braced myself.

"Hello. Is this Cassie O'Shaunnesy's residence?" It was a woman's voice, elderly and feeble.

"Yes," I said.

"Oh good. My name is Elizabeth Bartley. I used to live in Wyedale. My parents had the Bartley Farm there for years. My brother's running the farm now and I live at the Grove Park Nursing Home in Barrie. I get the *Gazette* every week. I get pretty lonely here, and it's nice to read about people I know. I had to call you, dear. Your letter made me cry."

"Oh," I said, not knowing what to say.

"You see, dear," the lady said, with what sounded like tears in her voice, "I had an abortion many years ago. I never told a single soul. I lived with my guilt my whole life. I never got over it. I read your letter many times. I believe in miracles. I had to call to tell you that I believe you, dear. Your letter has given me new hope."

"Thank you," I said, at a loss for words.

"I dreamed about my baby many times," Elizabeth continued, with a sense of urgency in her faltering, teary voice. "I often wondered what life would have been like for him. My baby was a boy, you know. He came to me in my dreams for two years. Then he stopped. I know why now. I think he went to another family, just like your baby Seana did. I want to thank you for your letter, dear. I know I didn't kill my baby now. His Soul is not stuck in Limbo. My little baby's Soul has another body, doesn't it? I believe your miracle, dear. Your letter has made an old lady very happy. I don't have that burden anymore. I didn't condemn my little baby's Soul to Limbo, did I? I want to thank you from the bottom of my heart, dear."

"You're very welcome, Elizabeth," I said, choking back my tears. "I'm grateful for your call. You're the first person to call me about my letter, and I could not have asked for a more heart-warming response. I wrote my letter for you, Elizabeth. Bless your heart for calling."

"You're very welcome, dear. You have a nice day now."

Knowing seniors as I do, I expected Elizabeth to go on talking for a good while longer, but she didn't. It must have taken her so much courage to get that out of her system that she was probably exhausted. I received one more call Saturday. It was from Cindy. She was calling on her cell phone from her grandfather's cabin cruiser. Kevin had taken the children boating for the day. Cindy loved being with her father, but she missed me as much as I missed her. Her call cheered me up even more than Elizabeth Bartley's call. And Sunday I decided to stay at home instead of going to the Atma Worship Service in Barrie in case someone called. I waited all morning on tenterhooks.

Finally I got two calls, one right after the other, while having lunch. The first woman told me that she was a Catholic her whole life and had never heard of reincarnation. It was too much for her to imagine living more than one lifetime, but she wanted to know where she could get more information on reincarnation. The second call came from a Baptist mother of four children who thought I should be locked up for my crazy story. "You better get some professional help, lady," she said, and hung up.

In all honesty, I was grateful for that call. It confirmed my worst fears. I could enjoy the rest of my day knowing that my letter would affect everyone differently, and it did not matter to me as long as it didn't jeopardize my career.

I had a right to my beliefs, and I had the right to freedom of speech, so I didn't really have anything to fear; but I knew hospital politics well. Anything could happen. I just had to wait and see how it all played out. But waiting frayed my nerves.

Laurie, one of my younger nurses, came up to me Monday morning and said, "By the way, Cassie; I read your letter in the *Gazette*. I didn't know what to make of your experience, but I agree with you. We should have the right to choose. I think this anti-abortion thing is a farce!"

Later in the day Doctor Jordon, our local family physician who had practiced in Wyedale for almost fifty years, made a passing remark. "Quite a letter, Cassie," he said, with a wink and a smile on his loveable, scarred face. He never mentioned it again. Later in the day, a young assistant from physiotherapy said, "Did that really happen, Cassie?"

"Yes, Beverly, it did," I said.

"Wow! I wish I had an experience like that!"

I laughed. I didn't expect that, but she didn't pursue it. I hoped she would, just so I could break that awful silence, but it didn't happen.

I waited every day for something to happen, but nothing did; and I didn't know whether the issue had been put to bed, as David humorously suggested, or whether this was the lull before the storm. I felt it was the lull before the storm, and I braced myself. Then I read in the next issue of the *Gazette,* which to my astonishment did not have a single letter responding to my letter, that Father McDuffy had set a date for an open forum to discuss abortion. The public was invited to air their views, and he issued a challenge for me to attend.

I knew Father McDuffy from his hospital visits. He was a tall, white-haired, blue-eyed, handsome-looking senior. If you took away his white collar and put him in a Brooks Brother's suit and tie, he would look like a polished, well-seasoned politician. We exchanged pleasantries, and nothing more. I had nothing to say to priests and ministers anymore.

Like most Irishmen, Father Terrence McDuffy could be very charming. All the patients liked him, except for one crusty elderly man who said to me with what sounded like disgust in his voice, when Father McDuffy walked by his room, *"There goes Poker McDuff!"*

I turned to look, but he had already passed by. "Who?" I asked.

"Poker McDuff!" my crusty patient repeated.

"Oh, Father McDuffy," I said.

"I don't call him Father. *He don't deserve to be called Father."*

"Oh? Why not, Jim?" I asked.

"Cuz he's not what everyone thinks he is, that's why."

"What do you mean?" I asked, very curious now.

"He's been playing poker with the boys every second Friday night in the back room of the taxi stand for years, and he's about as single as a rooster in the hen house. *That's Poker McDuff for you!"* Jim said, with disgust in his hoarse, tobacco-chewing voice.

I laughed. "Well, he is a man, Jim."

"You got that right! So what's he doing trying to save lost Souls? He should be looking after his own Soul, that's what he should be doing. He came in here yesterday to save my Soul. He asked me why I stopped going to church and he wanted to hear my confession, but I told him where to go!"

Again, I had to laugh at Jim. He expressed exactly what I felt about priests now. "So you're a Catholic, Jim?"

"My whole life. I go to church sometimes in Barrie when I visit my daughter, but I don't go to his church. *I can't stand that rooster!"* he spit out again, only this time tobacco juice came flying out of his mouth as well, and that upset him even more. *"Gosh darn it!"* he said, and wiped his mouth with the back of his hand.

"Now look what you've done, Jim," I said, giving him some Kleenex tissue from his bedside table. "You know you're not supposed to chew tobacco in here. I told you the last time you were here, didn't I? Now we have to clean up this mess. I should charge you extra for this, you know."

Jim wiped his mouth with the tissue. "Put it on my bill," he said, and guffawed.

I admired the crusty old farmer. He was right, too. Father McDuffy did project an image of a tall, lanky rooster with a vain, proud strut. He did have a long face and aquiline nose that looked like a rooster's beak, and his thick flock of snowy white hair combed tall on his head did resemble a rooster's crown.

"So tell me, Jim; do you believe in heaven and hell?" I asked, as I removed the tobacco-juice-splattered bed cover.

"I believe in heaven, but I don't believe in hell," he replied, and frowned. His forehead was furrowed seven rows deep. My son Mark called men who frowned like that Klingons. "I don't think God would do that to anybody. Those priests just use hell to scare people, that's all. It's not right, and they should stop doing it. It scares the kids."

"I agree with you, Jim; but Christianity is built on this idea of eternal punishment in hell. I think it's wrong, too. I think it scars people for life."

"I know it does. So what do you believe in, kid?"

"Do you really want to know?"

"Yeah, I do. You're different. You kinda speak your own mind, don't you? So, what do you believe in?" he asked again.

"Have you ever heard of reincarnation, Jim?"

"Yeah," Jim replied, without batting an eye. "I knew a man who told me he hated to come back to this world. Nobody believed his stories, and I never made heads or tails of them, but he wasn't crazy. I know that for a fact. He was one of the best mechanics I ever met. He knew his work better than anybody. He could strip a motor in no time flat. He could fix anything that came into his shop. But he was different. He told me he lived in Spain in a past life, and another time he lived in Russia. He said he was a woman that time. He wasn't crazy, but I didn't know what to make of his crazy stories. Why? You believe in that stuff too?"

"Yes, I do. I think we live many lives."

"If that's true, how come we live so many times?" Jim asked, furrowing his brow.

"Life is a big school, Jim. We come here to learn our lessons, and then we move on. But it takes a long time to learn our lessons, doesn't it?"

"Move on to where? Heaven?" he asked, with another pensive frown.

"I guess you could call it that," I replied.

"How come we have to come back to learn? Can't we learn it one time and get it over with?" Jim said, waxing philosophical, like all country people seemed to do.

I laughed. "I wish it were that easy, Jim."

"Yeah, I know what you mean. Look how long it took me to learn the couple things I know. So when can I get out of here?"

"We have to run a few more tests, Jim. If all goes well we can sign you out Monday."

"Good. I have to get back to my chores. I have lots of work waiting to get done. I have my first crop of hay to cut. I have—*hell, I got lots to do!*"

"Alright, Jim. I have to go. I'll send one of the girls to change your bed."

The day after my conversation with Jim, one week before I wrote my letter to the *Gazette,* David dropped by the house for a surprise visit on his way home from his after-work run. I got him one of Patrick's Gatorade sports drinks from the fridge and asked him about something that had puzzled me for years. If anyone could tell me, I knew he could. "David, do you think society has outgrown Christianity?" I asked.

David took another sip of his energy booster, paused, gave me a prolonged, unblinking stare, and then said, "There are three levels to social consciousness: the Exoteric Circle of Life, which is the outer circle and first stage of human evolution; the Mesoteric Circle, the middle level and second stage of evolution; and the Esoteric Circle, the inner, secret third stage of evolution. Christianity came from the inner circle of life, where Jesus studied the secret teachings of the Way. As his teaching was introduced to the world at large, meaning the first stage of human evolution, it got watered down so much to appease the exoteric level of social consciousness, it lost it's purpose. Nevertheless, Christianity is here to serve the spiritual needs of all those Souls that need a crutch to lean on. Christianity will never go away, Cassie. It can't go away. It's here for a reason. It's all part of the Divine Plan of God."

A feeling of anger possessed me and my body stiffened. I wanted Christianity to go away after what I had experienced. "What possible reason could Christianity have for telling people they will be damned to hell for eternity if they don't accept Jesus as their savior?" I said, showing my emotion. I think this idea of eternal damnation is so dark ages that it would be ludicrous if it weren't so tragic!"

David laughed at my emotional outburst. "It's not like Christianity has a choice, Cassie. Christians believe in their theology, however dark ages it may be. Salvation from eternal damnation is central to Christian dogma. How can that ever change?"

"I don't know. All I know for sure is that the grass roots has trouble buying into eternal damnation these days," I said, thinking of my crusty patient Jim. "On the other hand," I added, with a self-conscious blush, "it wasn't so long ago that I bought into it. I guess it bothers me that Christians have to live their life in fear, that's all. I don't know what I'm going to do, David. I want to respond to McDuffy's challenge, but I don't know if it will do any good."

"I don't know what your story is, Cassie; but I would guess you had an experience with the Soul of your unborn child. If you go public with it, no one knows what kind of reaction you will get. Speaking as a former journalist, I know you can never take people for granted. Just when you think you have them figured out, they surprise you. I'd be curious to see what reaction you get. I'd love to see where the zeitgeist is these days. I think your story would make an interesting barometer."

"Zeitgeist?" I said, wondering what he was getting at.

"The zeitgeist characterizes the moral tendencies of an age," David said, and took another long drink and finished the rest of his booster. Satisfied, he said, "Out of curiosity, what do you think the spirit of our times is trying to tell us?"

I smiled at the memory that David had stirred up. "My father once told me that if I wanted to see where society was headed, all I had to do was read the contemporary poets. He said poets have antennae which pick up signals from society that no one else can pick up. You're a poet, David. What signals are you picking up from society?"

"Not just poets. All artists. But I asked you first. Tell me, then I'll tell you."

"I can only tell you what I feel," I said, once again thinking about Jim who spoke for the grass roots. "I feel the zeitgeist today speaks for the moral ambiguity of society. I think society is torn between the past and the future. That's why I think this abortion issue has reared its ugly head again. I think people are torn between personal freedom and spiritual responsibility. I think Christianity is our past and Atma-Gare is our future..."

"May I?"

"Yes, please."

"I agree. World religions like Christianity, Judaism, Islam, and even Buddhism speak for the past and early stages of human evolution, and Atma-Gare speaks for the future and final stage of human evolution, but we don't all evolve at the same time. Soul evolves according to its own karma, so every religion plays its part in life. They're all going to be around until society outgrows them. But we won't see that in our lifetime."

"So what do you think the zeitgeist is telling us, then?"

"Society is waking up to a new God, Cassie," David said, with that focused look in his eyes that I had begun to notice, and a change in his voice that commanded my full attention. "This spiritual awakening is shocking the social psyche, and people are scrambling for safe ground to stand on. I think the spirit of our times is characterized by the fear and anxiety that comes when society wakes up to its own conscience. People are waking up so quickly to what we're doing to our environment that society is experiencing the first stage of the grieving process—denial. Society is waking up to its own karma, Cassie. That's the zeitgeist today."

I was delighted to hear David make reference to my mentor's

five stages of grieving, the other four being anger, bargaining, depression, and acceptance. It made our special connection more special. I had to pursue it. I wanted to connect with David more intimately.

"Denial?" I said, with a thoughtful pause. "As you know, David, Doctor Elisabeth Kubler-Ross is my role model. She's been my mentor from the day I met her in Seattle when I took her course. I've made a serious study of her books on death and dying, which I've been privileged to put to practice in my work, and I think we're talking about anticipatory grief here."

"Anticipatory grief? I'm not sure I've heard the term," David said.

"People grieve because of loss, but anticipatory grief is the beginning of the end in our mind. It's fear of the unknown and the pain that we're going to experience. Most of the time in grief we're focused on the loss of our past, but in anticipatory grief we occupy ourselves with the loss ahead. I think that's what you're referring to, isn't it—the loss that we're all going to experience if we don't do something about our environment?"

"Wonderful! That's exactly what I think characterizes the zeitgeist today—*fear of future loss!*" David said, with an excitement that warmed my heart.

David looked at me with the sweetest smile, and I knew that I had just connected with him on a deeper level that inched my chair a little closer to his.

Chapter 17

The Deep End of the Pool

The Ministry of Community and Social Services supervisor for Wyedale and the surrounding area works out of Barrie, but Brian Stewart has his home in Wyedale, a fifteen-minute drive from Barrie. Simcoe County Social Services has an office in the new wing of the Wyedale Community Hospital, which Brian uses three days a week.

I met Brian Stewart before his third wife passed away. During the last stages of her cancer, he broke down, and not more than one month after her death he asked me out for dinner. I declined. He asked me out a second time, and I declined again. Then he asked me out for coffee just to talk. "I don't think it's a good idea, Brian," I said.

"Just to talk," he pleaded, playing upon my sympathy.

"We've talked already, Brian," I replied.

"Why won't you talk with me, Cassie?" he pleaded.

"Brian, please let's not mix words. I would love to sit down and have a real nice talk with you, but we've already done that. Your wife is gone, and you have to deal with your loss. You need time to grieve, Brian."

"All I want to do is talk," he insisted.

"I'm sorry," I said.

"You'll change your mind."

"I don't think so."

Brian singled me out to be his crying shoulder. His anger was so deep that it was difficult to get through to him, but I listened. He read something more into my listening, and I didn't want to encourage him. I knew his type, and it was all about him.

Brian wanted to blame someone for his loss. It wasn't fair to him, and his anger was impulsive and unpredictable. He blamed his wife for leaving him just short of his fifty-fifth birthday and early retirement. He became more resentful, and his anger more toxic. As a colleague I respected Brian, but I certainly did not want a relationship with him.

Before I moved to Georgian Bay I chanced upon the social activist June Callwood's remarkable book *Twelve Weeks In Spring.* One of my patients was reading it. She looked up from her book and said to me, in no uncertain terms, "This is your cup of tea, Cassie. You have to read this book." She gave me the book and I was so moved by the Margaret Frazer story that it planted the seed of one day establishing a hospice house for AIDS patients.

The day after I read the Margaret Frazer story, I got the strongest urge to quit my job. I had no idea where this urge came from. It had not once crossed my mind to leave St. Paul's Hospital, but I couldn't fight the urge. I had that same urge every time I was called to a different branch of nursing and to study for my Master's degree, and I never regretted my decisions, but this urge to quit my job was inordinately more powerful; so I went on the Internet that night and learned that the Wyedale Community Hospital in Georgian Bay had just posted an opening for the position of head nurse. *"Move,"* said a voice in my mind.

Startled by the voice, I sat up.

"What?" I asked.

"Move," said the gentle, but firm voice again.

Startled, my senses went on red alert. I waited for the voice to speak again, but it didn't. I waited anxiously for the longest time, but nothing happened. I knew that it had to be the Satma's voice, so I applied for the job in Ontario just for the fun of it.

When I was granted an interview I knew that the Atma was calling me to Georgian Bay; so I flew to Toronto and drove up to Wyedale for my interview.

My resume impressed the newly appointed Hospital

Administrator, who had been hired by the hospital board to get their house in order. I was granted my second interview before returning to Vancouver, and I was awarded the position.

I shared my dream of establishing a hospice home for AIDS and other terminally ill patients with Bob Deacon, the veteran new administrator of the Wyedale Community Hospital, who knew June Callwood personally and stood up for her when she was falsely accused by a black woman of being racist, and he was very encouraging.

"Once you get settled in," he said, "we can put together a steering committee to look into it. We could use a hospice house in this area. I like the idea. I can call June and pick her brain; but bear in mind, Cassie, these things take time, patience, and serious funding."

Brian Stewart was a member of our Hospice House Committee, and he was instrumental in getting a wealthy widow who owned three farms that only grew potatoes for Hostess Potato Chips to bequeath her two-story Century home on five acres of prime land to our committee on condition that we name our hospice house after her son Colin who died of AIDS.

We called our project Colin House, modeled after Cayce House that June Callwood was instrumental in founding. Bob Deacon took a line out of Callwood's biography to be the motto and inspiration of our project: *"When you dream, do not be realistic and fix your dream to what exists and is possible. Fix your dream to what should exist and should be possible."* When Bob Deacon gave me that quotation, I knew that I had a formidable ally in my CEO.

I was acquainted with Brian Stewart for three or four months before we learned that his wife had terminal cancer. It shattered his life. Irene, Brian's wife, was the most forgiving woman I had ever met. She was only forty-four when she died, but one month before she crossed over to the other side she told me something that took my breath away. "I hear you believe in reincarnation," she said to me, as I made my first round that morning.

"Yes," I said, but I didn't have time to talk. "Would you like me to come back at the end of my shift and we can talk about this?"

"Would you, please?" Irene asked.

"It would be my privilege," I said, and when my shift ended I picked up a coffee and joined Irene by her bedside. She asked me to close her door and post the no visitors sign.

Irene was raised a strict Episcopalian, but she stopped going to church in her early twenties. She shared the three experiences that pulled her away from her faith.

Her first two experiences were vivid past-life recollection dreams. She did not know what to make of them, but she knew that it was herself in another life.

In one dream, Irene was a scullery maid in London, England; and in her second dream she was a Nazi during the war. This dream became a recurring nightmare that haunted her all of her married life. She was a doctor at the Ravensbrueck women's concentration camp in North Germany, and her husband Brian Stewart was a prisoner.

Irene's third remarkable experience was with her son Brian junior, who left home at sixteen to get away from his father. As a boy, he had imaginary friends.

Irene did not believe him. One day, she saw him talking with two very strange men in his bedroom. One man had short-cropped hair and a dark beard, shiny dark eyes, and he was dressed in a knee-length maroon colored robe. He appeared to be about thirty-five years old, and he was carrying a wooden staff. The other man was elderly with long white hair and beard. He had a gentle smile, and he was dressed in a long white robe.

Startled, Irene stared at the strange men standing at the foot of her son's bed. The man in the white robe said to Brian junior, "Would you like to introduce us to your mother?"

Her son did, and Irene never again doubted Brian junior's experiences with Zak Tarzman and Fedar Farad. She did not know they were Atma Masters, nor did her son, but they continued to visit him until he turned seven, and then they left. The memory of those men never faded from her mind. Facing her imminent death, she recalled her experience with her son's spirit friends. From her description of the two men, I knew who they were.

"Those men were Atma Masters," I said to Irene. "The word Atma means Holy Spirit. Atma Masters are Spiritual Masters who help us in our journey through life. They're like guardian angels, but they're not. They're great spiritual beings. I had a similar experience with an Atma Master. My daughter Cindy is visited regularly by the Atma Master Zak Tarzman, so it's not uncommon, Irene. Would you like to know more about Atma Masters?"

She did, and I told her all I knew. I introduced her to the Satma, the Living Atma Master, and to the spiritual path of Atma-Gare, and then I gave her the HU song to help her through her final days. She thanked me, but she did not share this information with her husband, who did not believe in any of this "weird stuff."

The Satma had arranged for me to be with Irene when she *translated* to the other side. *Translate* is the Atma word for dying, because Soul shifts its consciousness from its physical body to its subtle bodies when the physical body dies, just as the meaning of a word is translated from one language to another.

Irene and I were singing the HU song when she left her earthly body. She was so feeble she could hardly sound the word, but the HU was her last breath on earth. The moment she left her body I saw Huzee, the Satma, the Living Atma Master, walking hand in hand with Irene through an open field of beautiful purple daisies. I could not have been happier for her, and I cried with joy at her passing.

Doctor Kubler-Ross came to mind, and I smiled at her profound, albeit humorous view on life: *"If anything, people should mourn when someone's born and has to start the whole nonsense of living all over again."* I was happier for Irene's passing.

Irene had a very difficult life with her husband Brian. She accepted his emotional abuse with stoic resignation because she had the haunting memory of how she had treated him in their past life together. Still, that did not excuse his cruel behavior.

Brian was a self-serving, insensitive man. A civil servant most of his life, he knew how to use the system. He could make exploitation look like an act of charity. That's why he volunteered for our Hospice House Committee when he learned that his wife had only a few months to live. It was part of his strategy to win me over.

When Irene died, she left a huge hole in Brian's life. He had to fill it quickly before it devoured him. Brian was deathly afraid of being alone, and he continued to press me for a date. His phone messages and emails began to disturb me.

"How can I get through to you, Brian?" I said, trying to make light of what I knew could become a serious situation.

"Cassie, once you get to know me, I guarantee you'll like me," he said, and laughed to hide his fear of rejection.

"I like you, Brian," I said, "but I don't want our relationship to get complicated."

I knew Brian's type from years of working with civil servants. I knew that he could be a formidable ally, which he proved to be on our Hospice House Committee, but I also knew that when a civil servant turns on one of their own they can make their life miserable, which a friend of mine experienced, and I was always on my guard with them.

"Trust no one who works for the government," my father used to tell me. "Their first allegiance is to the system."

I could not refuse Brian when he volunteered for our Hospice House Committee, but something about him triggered my survival instincts, so I made a point to not encourage him; but this only made him more persistent. When he couldn't win me over with flattery, he played upon my sympathy by telling me about his first two marriages.

He was young when he married his high school sweetheart, but they broke up because they were too immature for marriage. His second wife stopped loving him, and he could not stay in a loveless marriage. He did not want to divorce his wife for their daughter's sake, but he said he had to get on with his life. He painted a nice picture of himself.

I listened, but I didn't judge. Curiously enough, I learned from one of my nurses that Brian had dumped his wife for the woman he was having an affair with, and his daughter never spoke to him again. Brian blamed his wife for his daughter's estrangement. "It's never their fault," said the nurse.

That's what attracted me to David Oakly. He was the exact opposite of Brian Stewart. David accepted absolute responsibility for his own life, and I was more attracted to him even than Brian was to me, but in a very different way.

Brian cornered me in the stairwell on the way out of the hospital so I had to confront him. "Brian, you're an intelligent, reasonable man, so I know you'll understand me when I tell you that our friendship will not go beyond what it is. Why do you persist in asking me out, Brian?"

"Because I find you very attractive," he replied, very sure of himself because we were all alone in the stairwell.

"Thank you, Brian," I said; "but that doesn't give you license to pursue me. I've made myself very clear. Why do you persist?"

"I don't know. I can't help myself. I think you're the most fascinating woman I've ever met, and I'll do whatever it takes to win you over," he replied, with that wolfish smile that made me shudder. "So what do you say we go to Tim's for a cup of coffee?"

"I have children to care for, Brian. Thank you, but no thank you."

"How about we go for a cruise on my boat this weekend? We can cruise up to Parry Sound, have a nice lunch at *Wellington's Pub & Grill,* and let it all hang out. What do you say, Cassie? That'll give us a chance to get to know each other."

I gave him a pleasant smile. "Thank you, but no thank you, Brian."

"Some other weekend, then?" he insisted.

"No, Brian," I said, getting annoyed.

"Why not? Tell me why not? Am I not your type?"

"No. I'm not your type, Brian," I said, now frustrated.

"How do you know that? You don't really know me, do you?"

"I think I know you well enough to know that I'm not your type."

"What's my type, then? Tell me that," he insisted.

"Not me, Brian," I said, not wanting to get personal.

"Come on, Cassie. Do me this one favor. Tell me, why aren't you my type? You haven't gone over to the other side, have you?" he said, pretending moral indignation.

He turned my stomach. I knew it would only be a matter of time before he got nasty, because they always do, so I had to win him over quickly.

"If you want to know the truth, Brian," I said, taking the edge out of my voice, "I'm not anybody's type because I don't want a man in my life right now. I'm in a really good place since my divorce, and I want a chance to explore my life on my own terms now. That's not asking too much, is it? I like you, Brian. I have no doubt that you would be a very nice man to be with, but it's my turn now, and I don't want to miss this opportunity. I've never been closer with my children than I am right now, and I just don't want a man in my life. I'm sorry, Brian. So please, no more emails and no more messages. If you ask me out one more time, I'm going to sic my children on you," I added, and forced myself to laugh.

"Bring them on!"

"Brian..."

"I have no chance, do I?"

"No," I repeated.

"Maybe in a couple of months?"

"No. I need my space. Please, no more. Okay?"

"Alright. But you can't blame a guy for trying, can you?"

"No," I said, and we parted on what I hoped were good terms. But I could not trust Brian, and I puzzled over his fascination for me which I knew could become a fixation.

That night, I recorded my stairwell encounter in my journal, hoping to make sense of Brian's behavior. "I wonder what Doctor Kubler-Ross would make of him?" I mused to myself. "She's a psychiatrist. She would know."

An idea flashed across my mind. I chuckled, then sat back and let my mind go blank. I did a silent HU, which became audible within a few minutes. I sang the Love Song to God softly with my eyes closed and my heart open to the Inner Master's guidance.

As I sang the Love Song to God I imagined myself Soul traveling to the inner worlds on the waves of the Holy Current of Atma. I imagined that I had an inner-dimensional tracking system like the GPS I have in my Odyssey. I imagined myself Soul traveling to my mentor's new place of residence on the inner planes. I imagined myself knocking on her door. The door opens, and she smiles and gives me a big hug. She invites me into her house. I tell her about my situation with Brian Stewart.

"What did I tell you, Cassie?" Doctor Kubler-Ross replies. "The purpose of life is to grow, is it not? Did I not tell you that the ultimate lesson in life is learning how to love? *Love this creep from a distance!"* she shouted at me.

Her voice startled me back into my body. I sat for two or three minutes, totally amazed by my unexpected Soul travel experience. Once I calmed myself, I laughed at my mentor's delicious sense of humor. I closed my eyes again.

I thought of Brian's wife. Irene had told me how her husband had treated her from the first year of their marriage, which was another reason why I wanted nothing to do with him. Irene wanted to make it up to Brian for the horrific experiments that she performed on his body, but she never revealed this to him. I was the only person who knew about their past life together at the Ravensbrueck concentration camp in Germany.

"I cried myself to sleep many nights," she confessed to me. "I suffered his abuse for years. God gave me a chance to make up for what I did to him in the concentration camp. I know this sounds crazy, Cassie; but my husband taught me how to forgive. Brian was a young woman in that lifetime. You can't imagine what I did to her body. That's why I put up with his abuse all these years. He doesn't know, Cassie. But I'm free now. I'm free . . ."

Free for now, I thought to myself. But what was Brian's spiritual lesson? Shouldn't he have forgiven her for her cruelty in the concentration camp? How could he forgive her? He didn't remember their past life together. Was that fair? I was puzzled by Irene's story. I had to ask David. If anyone had an answer, I knew he would.

My opportunity came sooner than I expected. By coincidence my friend Grace Iverson, with whom I had a standing luncheon date after our Atma Worship Service in Barrie, could not attend that Sunday, so I invited David for lunch. I was surprised to see him, so I asked why he had decided to attend the service.

"I had the strongest urge to come," he said, with a bright twinkle in his eyes. "I was going to work on my house this morning, but when the Atma called, I listened. Now I know why," he added, with an encouraging smile.

My heart raced. I broke into nervous laughter.

"What's so funny?" he asked.

"Oh, I was just thinking of this man I know from work," I said, using the opportunity to ask him about Brian Stewart.

"Is this man in the world and of the world?" David asked.

His peculiar question took me off guard. I had to stop and think for a moment. "Yes, he's very much in and of this world," I finally said.

David laughed. "I know the type, Cassie. I used to be one."

"You? I can't imagine you being anything like this man!"

"Why? Because I've turned my life around?" David said, and took a drink of water. He took another glance at his menu, then back at me. "This man has the same opportunity as any person to turn his life around also. This is the beauty of the Divine Plan of God. There are as many entry points to spiritual growth in one's life as there are dead ends. It all depends upon one thing. I think I'm going to load up on carbs. I'm going for a long run later."

I could not get over how quickly David excited my curiosity. I looked into his highly intelligent, clear blue eyes when I spoke. "Depends on what?" I asked.

"Love," he said, with what sounded like casual indifference. "I think I'm going with the Fettuccine Alfredo and Garden Salad. I love their pasta here. Now, love, Cassie? How do we give love and receive love? That's what opens and shuts the door to spiritual growth, doesn't it? Take love out of the equation and the world will shut its doors in your face. Give love to the world, and doors will open everywhere you go. That's what the Atma life is all about. Sufism taught me this lesson. I was very much my father's son, Cassie. I was born with that chauvinist conceit that most men are saddled with, and I took advantage of my smug male superiority. But I went too far. I crossed the line one night at university. That's what forced me to change my life."

"How?" I asked, surprised by David's strange confession.

He did not answer for a moment or two, but I noticed a deep frown come over his face. "I'll tell you some day. How about you? What changed your life, Cassie?"

The waitress came to take our order. David ordered Oven-Baked Garlic Cheese Bread and his pasta and salad dish. I had only glanced at the menu, but I knew *East Side Mario's* made a wonderful Grilled Chicken Caesar Salad, and I ordered that.

"Will there be anything else?" the waitress asked.

"No, thank you," I said. My mind was on David's question, and the moment the waitress left I said, "My abortion changed my life, David. It changed my life completely."

"Yes, I imagine it would. So have you decided to respond to McDuffy?"

"I'm still torn. David, can I ask you something personal?"

"Certainly," he said.

I took a deep breath, wondering if I should ask him. David sensed my concern and gave me an encouraging smile. "I had a patient who died of cancer two months ago. She had one of the most beautiful deaths I have ever witnessed. The Satma was with her when she left her body. I saw him crossing her over to the other side. Her husband has asked me out repeatedly since her death. I have no desire whatsoever to go out with him. He's a nice man in public, but I know something about his private life. I get a creepy feeling when I'm around him. You're a man, David. Maybe you can tell me. What do you think it is about this man that makes me feel so creepy? I would really like to know."

"Define creepy," David asked.

"I don't know if I can. I just feel very uneasy around him."

"How do you feel with me?" David asked.

"Just the opposite. I would trust you with my life."

"Why would you trust me with your life?"

"I don't know. I just would."

"You say this man has the opposite effect on you?"

"Yes," I said.

"You wouldn't trust him with your life?"

"No, I wouldn't. He's the type that uses people."

"He's a taker, then?"

"Very much so."

"That would make me a giver?"

"Yes, I would say so," I quickly agreed.

"Good," David said. "What did I just say about love? Didn't I say that how we give love and receive love opens and shuts doors for us?"

"Yes," I said, wondering where he was going.

"Is this man a giver of love, or a taker of love?" David asked.

"He's a taker of love. Is that why he makes me feel so creepy?"

"You're a giver of love, Cassie. That's obvious. You have that special quality that Sufis call the *subtlety*. That's the mysterious substance that attracted you to Atma-Gare. However you came by the *subtlety,* people sense that you have a lot of it, and they want it. This creates that mysterious dynamic that exists between those who have the *subtlety* and those who don't. This man wants what you have, but he's not willing to earn it the way you do—through honest effort and integrity of character. His type just wants another person's vital life force, especially if they have a lot of it; and they'll do whatever they can to get it."

With that, David gave me a smile that confirmed the encouragement I saw in his eyes. "I know how to give love, David," I said; "but how does one take love?"

"By force, guile, deceit, lying, cheating, manipulation, any which way they can, except by earning it through honest effort and integrity of character," he replied.

That was Brian Stewart to a tee.

The waitress brought our order and David offered to share his Garlic Cheese Bread. I was off bread since I met David, but the aroma of the warm garlic bread won me over. I took a small slice, ate it slowly, and digested the bread along with David's uncanny wisdom.

"I want him!" I screamed in my mind.

"Past lives," I said, focusing my attention back to the point. "This man I'm talking about was married to the woman who recently died of cancer. They had a past-life relationship, which she remembered but he didn't. She lived her life to make up for what she did to him in their past-life relationship. She was a doctor in a Nazi concentration camp and she did horrible things to the woman who became her husband in this life. She let her husband abuse her because of what she did to him in their past life. Do you think that was fair, David? Should she have let her husband abuse her because she did terrible things to him in their past life?"

David thought for a moment or two. "If that's how she felt she could redress the karma that she created with him in their past life, who are we to judge whether it's fair or not? Maybe he would have tortured her if he remembered what she did to him in their past life in the concentration camp. Who knows?"

"You're right," I said, surprised by his answer. "Can I ask you another question?"

"By all means," he said.

"Do you think we had a past life together?"

"Probably. Why do you ask?"

"I don't know. I just think we did," I said.

"Why?" he asked again, his eyes sparkling.

"I can't put my finger on it, but I just do," I said, blushing.

"Well, if we did have a past life together the Atma must have a good reason for keeping us in the dark about it," he replied, with such nonchalance that I suspected he knew more than he was letting on. "But that's probably because it makes the dynamic of our relationship that much more alluring, as it does for all couples who come together for karmic reasons. That's just the way it is, Cassie."

I wanted to tell David just how alluring he was to me from the moment I met him at the Convention Center in Minneapolis, but I dared not. "David," I said, in my most casual voice, "don't you find the world shallow now that you're an Atman? I know I do. I could never go back to what I was. Could you?"

He swallowed a forkful of fettuccine. "There's an old Buddhist saying," he answered, with a light in his eyes that pierced my heart, "that may put this feeling into context for you: '*Before enlightenment, you chop wood and carry water. After enlightenment, you chop wood and carry water*'. Cassie, the world is only shallow for people who swim in the deep end of the pool. Man evolves through three stages in life, and one day even the shallowest person will find his way to the deep end of the pool. He has to. It's written in the Divine Plan of God."

My face glowed with the love I suddenly felt burning in my heart for him, and I knew in that moment that David would be the man I wanted to spend the rest of my life with. "I believe that," I replied, repressing my feelings. "Like my mentor Doctor Elisabeth Kubler-Ross told me when I asked her if she felt I was on the right path nursing, *'All destiny leads to the same path of growth, love and service,'* she said, and I never forgot that. David, I'm really happy you were nudged to come to the worship service today."

"Now we know why, don't we?" David said, with a twinkle in his eyes.

"Yes, we do," I said, blushing with embarrassment.

Chapter 18

A Letter to the Satma

David's question over lunch about responding to Father McDuffy's challenge found its way into my heart, and I could not stop thinking about it.

I didn't want to show it, but I was terrified of the stigma I could suffer if I told the story of my unborn child. At the same time, I could not deny the voice in my heart that was shouting at me to breathe fresh air into the suffocating issue of abortion that Father McDuffy and his anti-abortion group were stirring up. Just thinking about it made me hyperventilate. I had to sing HU to calm myself.

Some call it feminine intuition, but the voice in my heart was more than that. I was five years old when I began calling my inner voice my teacher, which was not silent then, and seven years old when my mother told me that I had the gift like my grandmother.

My grandmother could see a light around people. My mother told me that grandma Molly could see into a person's Soul by reading the different colors of their light. She told my mother that the darker the colors around a person were, the less she could trust them; and the brighter their colors were, the closer they were to God. I could not see a person's aura, but I could hear a voice speaking to me in my head.

My mother thought I had my father's illness, but when I told her some of the things my teacher said to me she began to see that I had a special gift just like grandma Molly's second sight. It was different from my grandmother's, but it was a special gift too.

"You must not tell anyone about your special gift," my mother told me when she could no longer deny that I had it. "People will think you're possessed by the Devil, so promise me you won't tell anyone about your gift. Promise me, Cassie," my mother pleaded.

I promised. But as I got older my teacher spoke to me less and less. And gradually I stopped hearing my teacher altogether. I knew my teacher was a man. I could hear his voice in my head as though he was speaking to me on the telephone. Sometimes he told me stories.

My teacher was the Satma, the Inner Master. I know now that he speaks to us through thoughts, ideas, insights, nudges, feelings, signs, symbols, coincidences, waking dreams, the silent little voice in our heart, and sometimes in his own voice like when he told me to move to Georgian Bay, and I was doing my best to hear what he was telling me to do about Father McDuffy's challenge.

As I drove home from lunch with David at *East Side Mario's* after the worship service in Barrie, I longed to hear my teacher's voice again like I used to when I was a child living in our boarding house. My longing was so intense that it triggered a vivid memory of my childhood nightmares and the man who helped me, and my heart started racing madly at my realization. I couldn't believe it. *After all those years it finally dawned on me that the nice man in our boarding house who helped me was the Satma, my spiritual teacher!*

From the day a strange and sinister man moved into our boarding house I began to have nightmares. They got so bad that my mother had to take me to our family doctor, but he found nothing wrong with me. Doctor Peterson said I had a wild imagination, and he gave my mother a prescription for me to take before bedtime, but the nightmares continued.

When my mother brought me back to Doctor Peterson I told him that the strange man in our boarding house was a bad man and that I kept dreaming of him. The dream was always the same. I was tied on an altar in a wooded clearing in the middle of the night. There was a big fire burning. The man from our boarding house was dressed in black and naked men and women danced around us and the man stabbed me with his knife and I always woke up terrified and screaming.

I asked my mother to tell the bad man to leave, but he had paid his rent in advance for three months. He was a traveling salesman. He stayed at our house three days a week. Every time he stayed I had nightmares. Then another man came to our boarding house and my nightmares went away.

This other man was my teacher who spoke to me in my mind. I didn't know he was my teacher then, nor did I make the connection when I joined Atma-Gare. I had completely forgotten my childhood nightmares until my drive home from lunch with David at *East Side Mario's*. Whatever it was about our conversation, the Holy Spirit of Atma had pried open that part of my psyche that stored my terrifying childhood dreams.

I met our new boarder in our sitting room on the day he moved in. He had a notebook on his lap and he was writing in it. "Hi," I said. "My name is Cassie. I live here all the time. Are you our new boarder?"

"Yes," he said, and smiled at me. He had a beautiful smile that filled me with love and made me feel safe. "I've come to live with you for a little while," he said, sounding like an Englishman, but he wasn't; he was American, from Kentucky.

"What's your name?" I asked.

"My name is Paul," the man said, and his face lit up again. He was not a big man, and he sounded just like my teacher. I asked him what he was doing, and he told me he was writing a story. "Do you like stories, Cassie?"

"Yes," I said.

"What kind of stories do you like?"

"I like Dr. Seuss stories," I said. Then I told our new boarder about the bad man who stayed in the room at the end of the hall upstairs and how he scared me in my dreams.

Our new boarder said, "He won't scare you anymore, dear."

"Can you stop him, please? He kills me with his knife. I told my mother, but she can't tell him to leave because he paid his rent and my mother needs the money to pay our bills. I don't like him. I'm scared to go to sleep..."

"He won't scare you anymore. I promise," our new boarder said.

The sound of his voice and the love in his eyes made me feel so safe that all my fear went away. "What's your story about?" I asked.

"It's a story about my teacher," he said, with another big smile.

"I have a teacher too. What do you call your story?" I asked.

"Seeker By The Lake," he said.

The next day the bad man came home, packed his bags and left our boarding house. He did not ask for a refund on his rent, and he never returned.

When I got home from lunch with David I rushed straight to my bedroom to look at Paul Mathew's photo that I had hanging with other Atma Masters on my bedroom wall at the foot of my bed, and I was transfixed by Paul's face. *He was my childhood teacher!*

I was so excited I didn't know whether to cry with joy or scream hysterically. I could not believe I had met the Satma, the Living Atma Master, when I was a little girl and that he was my teacher! The memory had completely left me. I broke into tears..

Cindy came into my bedroom. "Mom, you're crying," she said.

"Yes," I said, and wiped my eyes.

"Why Mom? Did another one of your patients die?"

"No, sweetheart. I'm just happy, that's all."

"You're crying because you're happy?"

"Yes," I said, and pulled my daughter into my arms. "I love you Puppy Face. I love your cute little nose and your cute little freckles and everything about you. I love you so much precious! Don't ever forget that! *Don't ever forget that...*"

What was I going to do? Could I stigmatize my children with the miracle of their unborn sister? I knew I had been called to serve life, but could I put them through the humiliation I felt certain would follow if I went public with my abortion experience?

It was enough that two of my children were Atmans. They had learned not to talk about their spiritual beliefs, which were so different from orthodox religions that they invited open ridicule, but if I went public with my miracle story their spiritual beliefs would be out in the open. What would that do to them? Would they be strong enough? People can be very cruel if you're not like them, especially children. I honestly didn't know what to do.

I asked Cindy if she could give me some private time. She looked away for a moment or two and then turned to me and said, "Mom, Zak told me to tell you it's okay to cry. He loves you, Mom. He said whatever you do, it's okay."

I smiled. My daughter had a special gift too. "Thank you, sweetheart. You tell Zak that I love him too, and I'll do what I feel is right. Okay?"

"Okay," Cindy said. Then she added, "Zak said you have to make your own footprints in the sand. I don't know what that means, Mom."

I didn't either until I thought about it. When it came to me, I smiled and said, "That means I have to walk my own path, sweetheart."

"Zak is laughing, Mom!"

"Thank you, Zak," I said, addressing the invisible Atma Master who spoke to Cindy like my childhood teacher used to speak to me.

It encouraged me to know that I was not going to be alone if I went public with my miracle story, but I wasn't going to do so unless I had my children's blessing. I decided to consult them. I would tell them the whole story. If they felt I was doing the right thing to stand up against this new surge of pro-life advocacy, I would step into the lion's den and respond to Father McDuffy's challenge with an open letter to the Wyedale *Gazette*.

Patrick was playing street hockey with his friends in town, and Mark was in his room working on his new story. I decided to tell them after dinner. I sat them down in the family room after dessert and told them the whole story of their unborn sister Seana.

"I have to write my letter to the paper," I said, choking back my tears. "If I don't stand up to Father McDuffy and his anti-abortion group, I won't be able to live with myself. But I won't write my letter if you don't want me to. I love you, and I don't want to do anything that might make your life more difficult. What do you think I should I do?"

Patrick was first to speak. With a big puff of his chest and in a deeper voice than normal, he said, "We're the O'Shaunnesys, Mom. We're different. We're not afraid of what people say about us. I promised dad I would look out for you, Mom. If you want to write your letter and tell your story, it's okay with me. I got your back, Mom."

"Thank you, Patrick. What about you guys?" I said to Mark and Cindy.

"It's okay, Mom," Mark said. "What can they do, anyway? It's a free country, isn't it? We can believe what we want, can't we? Besides, you're an Atma Warrior, Mom. You got the Light. And you got the Silver Shield too. Nobody can harm you, Mom."

"Thank you for reminding me about the Silver Shield, Mark. We can also use the White Light for protection. You know how funny people can be when it comes to our Atma beliefs. People are afraid of what they don't understand."

"So what?" Patrick said. "I don't understand all this Atma stuff either, but I'm not afraid of it. Maybe they won't be afraid either, Mom."

I smiled. "Thank you, Patrick. You're very wise for your years."

"You're welcome," he said. "Can we go now?"

"In a minute. What about you, precious? What do you think I should do?"

"I don't know. Can I ask Zak?" Cindy said.

"Please do," I said.

Cindy turned her head and looked up. "What should Mom do?" she asked.

We all waited with excitement. Cindy started to laugh. "What?" I said.

"Zak made me laugh, Mom."

"But what did he say I should do?" I asked.

"He said he loves you no matter what you decide."

"I love you too," I said, smiling at the invisible Master.

Patrick was getting nervous, and said, "Can we go now, Mom?"

"Yes. You can go…"

I should have known to trust my children, and I should have known better than to expect a miracle from Zak Tarzman. It was my decision to go public with the miracle of my unborn child, and I decided that I had to listen to my own heart.

I put in the last load of laundry after I cleaned up the kitchen and went to my bedroom with a fresh cup of green tea to journal my day.

As I journaled my lunch with David and my shocking childhood recollection of Paul Mathew, who was the Satma, the Living Atma Master who brought Atma-Gare to the modern world, I got the strongest nudge to write a letter to the current Living Atma Master. I did a quiet HU, and then I poured my heart out in my first letter to the Satma:

Dear Huzee,

This is not my monthly initiate report. It's a personal letter. I have a big decision to make. Probably the most important decision of my life. I'm exaggerating, but it feels like the most important decision of my life, and I want to tell you how I feel about making it. I'm still not a hundred percent sure I'm going to make it. That's why I'm writing you this letter.

Please pardon my rambling. I want to speak to you from my heart. You know that my heart has a mind of its own, so whatever comes out I'm not going to censor it. I have to get it all out. I can't keep it inside anymore. I tried, but I can't. It's just too big for me.

I love you, Satma. Thank you for your protection. I made a very difficult life-changing decision to move my children away from their father and grandparents and all their friends, but I know this is where you want us to be. It's been a big challenge for us. The children have made new friends and are adjusting better than I hoped, and I seem to fit in well at the hospital with both the administration and staff, and I thank you for that. I bring the Holy Spirit of Atma to my work, and the Atma does what it has to do to bring the Light to my little corner of the world. I'm just serving life like my mentor Doctor Kubler-Ross.

Satma, I have to decide what to do about Father McDuffy's absurd challenge. Yes, I believe it is absurd. How can anyone prove in the cold light of pure science that Soul exists before the life of the unborn child? It's not possible, is it? I don't think so. Science hasn't evolved enough yet to weigh and measure the spiritual self of man. And what is the spiritual self of man if not that "little person" who will take over the life of the unborn child? Do you see my dilemma? I'm stuck between a rock and a hard place.

I know that Soul exists prior to the life of the unborn child because I know that reincarnation exists. Soul is who we are, and we live many lifetimes so we can grow in spiritual consciousness. That's what we're here for, isn't it Satma? Soul is not created at the moment of human conception like Christianity believes, because Soul is eternal.

Father McDuffy's challenge is so ludicrous it hardly deserves a response; but someone has to respond. Not just anyone can respond though. I have to respond. That's why I'm so torn up about this. I don't know what to do.

Can we look at this rationally, Satma? How can the immortal Soul of man be created out of the finite and mortal matter of man? Is it possible that mortal matter can conceive an immortal Soul that pre-exists its mortal body? That's absurd. But that's what the logic of Christianity implies. How can mortal matter create an immortal Soul that will by its very nature pre-exist its finite, mortal body? Where's the logic in this kind of reasoning?

I guess what I'm saying is that if the spiritual self is eternal it has to exist beyond the boundaries of space and time, which our mortal physical body is restricted to. So either the "little person" created at the moment of human conception is not eternal in the sense that we all understand eternal to mean, or the eternal nature of the "little person" begins at the moment of conception as Christianity wants us to believe, and that's a pill I cannot swallow.

Christianity wants us to believe this just as it wants us to believe many things that defy reason. Like Jesus dying for the sins of the world. How can Jesus wipe away the karma of the whole world with his death on the cross? That's nonsense.

But I don't want my letter to turn into a diatribe against Christianity. I've been down that road, Satma; and I don't want to stir up those negative emotions again. I would rather that they resolve themselves on their own now. Besides, I've since grown enough in Atma to respect what other people believe. Or have I?

This letter is about what Father McDuffy believes, and what I believe, which goes against what Father McDuffy and his group believes. They want to start a movement they hope will catch on so they can re-legislate the law on abortion and make it illegal, but that goes against what society has fought so hard for. So as much as I respect what other people believe, we have a dilemma here.

What bothers me most about this whole abortion issue is how smug the anti-abortion people are. Father McDuffy and his little group are so sure that a fetus is a "little person" that they cannot see beyond their belief. But what is a "little person," Satma? Isn't a "little person" a who and not a what? Isn't a "little person" a human body with self-consciousness? Isn't that what a person is?

Where did self-consciousness come from? Father McDuffy would have us believe that self-consciousness is created at the moment of human conception, but this can't be scientifically proven one way or the other, so why must society bow to a belief that cannot be proven either way? That's not right, is it? We have a right to our beliefs too, don't we?

Women are free to have an abortion because society has chosen the rights of women over the rights of the fetus. This was a democratically legislated decision. But this anti-abortion movement cannot live with this decision. This is Christianity all over again. It always wants to tell us how to live our life, and that's not right.

This abortion issue is one of those moral dilemmas that crop up in an evolving social consciousness, like gay marriages, to name another. But we have to plow our way through, don't we? Well Satma, the Atma let me have an experience that proves I did not terminate the life of my unborn child when I had my abortion. I terminated the life of the fetus that my husband and I conceived when we made love, but I did not terminate the life of the "little person" who was going to be our daughter Seana. I did not, and I have proof.

But that's my dilemma, isn't it? I have proof that is mine alone. I'm sure there are other women out there who have had a similar experience, but I have to decide whether to share my experience or not. What should I do, Satma?

I should make up my own mind, shouldn't I? That's how one becomes a spiritual master, isn't it? We can lean upon the Atma, but like my new friend David Oakly said, the more we lean upon ourselves the more Atma-centered we will be. It's a paradox, but it's true. David said that we are true to the Atma when we are true to ourselves. So, Satma; what should I do?

The ball is in my court, isn't it? I have to ask myself the question that I've been putting off ever since I read Father McDuffy's ad in the *Gazette*. Do I stand up for what I believe is right for women, or do I remain silent about the miracle of my unborn child? Like Kevin's father likes to say, I have to fish or cut bait, don't I?

Satma, thank you for finding me a role model in Doctor Elisabeth Kubler-Ross. Her courage, perseverance, and integrity have inspired me to seek out my own destiny in this life. I'm a divorced mother of three beautiful children, a registered nurse, and a happy Atman. I am the sum of all my parts; but I can be more, can't I?

My mentor was so much more than the sum of her parts. Doctor Kubler-Ross has added immeasurably to our understanding of death and dying. She has given death the dignity it deserves, and she taught the world how to grieve. This was her service to life.

Eureka! That's what makes a person greater than the sum of their parts! Our service to life exceeds the sum of our parts. It's the fruit of who we are, isn't it? This is why people are asked when they cross over, what services have you rendered?

That's it. Life all comes down to service, doesn't it? This is why Doctor Kubler-Ross told me that all destiny leads to love, growth, and service!

I know it does. But how will I answer when I cross over? Will it be enough to say that I served life by being the best mother and nurse that I could be? That's not enough! I want my life to be more than the sum of my parts. I want my life to stand for what I believe. I have to step into the fast currents of life that will take me to personal wholeness so that when I cross over I will have my answer ready: *I served life by being all that I could be!*

I have to, Satma! I have to take up Father McDuffy's challenge! Someone has to, and that someone is me! Thank you for listening to me, Huzee.

And thank you, Doctor Kubler-Ross. Thank you for taking me into your heart when I needed someone to believe in me. I know what I have to do now to be more than the sum of my parts. I have to give more. *I have to tell the story of my unborn child!*

That's all I have to say.

All my love,

Cassie Patty O'Shaunnesy

Chapter 19
A Special Kind of Honesty

After I wrote my letter to the Satma I sat back in my reading chair and closed my eyes. My decision to go ahead with the story of my unborn child put me in a strange state. I felt spent from committing to my decision, but strangely energized by it. I had never felt anything like this before. I did a quiet HU, letting my mind wander...

I was a young Yankee soldier in the American civil war, positioned on my knee with my long rifle to my cheek in the middle of a canon-blasting, rifle-popping wet and muddy battlefield pungent with an acrid sulfurous smoke and hazy fog at the height of the war between the proud, stubborn Greys of the South, and the equally passionate, stubborn Blues of the North. We fired at our own people from a distance, and then with fixed bayonets we charged with blind fury and fought hand to hand to the death. It was devastating for both sides. There were bodies everywhere soaked in blood and dirty, black mud. At long last, our enemy retreated and we paused for respite. I thought of Michael. Did he survive?

Michael was my best friend. Twice he had saved my life. I had to find him. I panicked when I saw his body. I went closer. Thank God he was still alive. He had been shot in the leg and played dead.

Michael and I had enlisted together. We shared the same conviction with equal passion. It was morally repugnant to own people like chattel. It went against God and nature. We fought for the emancipation of the slaves and I know we won that battle and the next two, but I couldn't see where they took place. In the third battle I lost my left arm and was sent home to Detroit, Michigan.

Michael's leg wound healed and he fought to the bitter end of the war. He survived intact, came home, and we married our fiancés in a double ceremony, had three children each, and remained best friends for the rest of our life. We were such good friends we were closer than brothers.

On my deathbed, I promised Michael that we would meet again one day. He gave me the sweetest smile. I recognized the smile. I was right. We did meet again. *Michael Elliot Davenport was David Oakly!* I was so excited I jumped out of my chair and paced my bedroom. I couldn't believe it! I knew we had a past life together, but I never dreamt...*"Thank you, Satma,"* I said excitedly, and sat down and tried to compose myself; but I couldn't. "Should I call David? What should I do?"

Suddenly I wanted to be with David. I wanted a romantic relationship with him. I felt so weird that I had to stand up and pace the room again. *"No,"* I said, *"I can't tell him!"*

But then I quickly thought, David would understand. That was then; this is now. Maybe I should tell him. *"I don't know what to do!"* I said, in frustration.

I sat down and closed my eyes again. I did another HU, slowly letting my breath out and relaxing myself as I sang the Love Song to God. The more I relaxed the calmer I felt, and the less anxious I was. After ten or twelve minutes I was calm enough to reflect on our past life together. I asked the Satma to bring me back to our past lifetime again. I let my mind wander blankly, back to my dear friend...

We were in Michael's drawing room. Michael had a beautiful three storied brick and stone Victorian home, as did I. We were both successful businessmen. Michael had taken over his father's publishing house, and I inherited my father's family furniture factory. We made a habit of retiring to our drawing room after Sunday dinner with our families for a glass of our finest Spanish port wine and our best cigars, and we discoursed for hours.

We had a unique friendship. We both believed that with thoughtful discourse we could reason our way through any problem and find our way to life's purpose. It was Michael's turn to choose the topic of the month. *"Integrity,"* he began, excitedly. As natural as integrity was to the evolution of man, he contended that it had to be cultivated in order for the race to surpass itself. "What would man's life be without integrity, Horatio?" he asked me.

Well-prepared, I replied, "Small, petty, and mean."

"I agree. But let's be clear on what we mean. A man's character is small, petty, and mean when it suffers a paucity of integrity. Am I correct?"

"Yes," I readily agreed.

"Excellent. It is my deepest contention, Horatio, which I have given considerable thought to this long month, that this noble virtue is firmly rooted in a generosity of spirit. We agree that a paucity of integrity makes man small, petty, and mean. The opposite would be equally true, would it not? Study a man's character and tell me if there is not a generosity of spirit in the heart of he who bears the stamp of this noble virtue."

"Not necessarily so, my good friend," I countered, after two or three long puffs on my heavenly cigar. "Intellectual integrity does not necessarily spawn a generosity of spirit. I have met great thinkers with a plethora of integrity but a paucity of generosity. And one or two, I might add, were downright mean-spirited creatures. It would seem to me, dear friend, that the integrity you speak of addresses the Soul of the man and not the mind of the man."

Michael laughed, *"You have found me out, honest friend!"*

And so we discoursed month after month and year after year. Even on my deathbed we continued our discourse on the eastern idea of returning to live life over again that our own American transcendentalists Henry David Thoreau and Ralph Waldo Emerson had explored with passionate interest. I contended that it would be so, and I declared my belief to Michael: "I promise you, dear friend, one day we will meet again in another life. I know it will be so as the night follows day." Indeed, our whole lifetime of discourse was framed by the inherent idea of reincarnation in one of our favorite Emerson quotations, which we did not fully fathom until our whiskers had turned gray: *"Be not a slave of your own past. Plunge into the sublime seas, dive deep and swim far, so you shall come back with self respect, with new power, with an advanced experience that shall explain and overlook the old."*

So it wasn't a coincidence that David and I both found Atma-Gare, the ancient spiritual teaching of reincarnation, and even less of a coincidence that finally we met at the Convention Center in Minneapolis at the Atma Springtime Seminar. Our past-life friendship ran so deep that we were closer than friends, and I knew in my heart that our love for each other was destined to blossom into a romantic love. I knew the moment we shook hands. But it felt strange. It felt as though if we became lovers we would be violating some unwritten cultural taboo. In all honesty, I didn't know what to make of my attraction to David now!

I certainly did not feel anything like my old American-English Horatio Charles Penseworth self. I felt very much the passionate Canadian-Irish woman Cassie O'Shaunnesy, and I very much had all the desires of a woman. There was nothing kinky about my feelings for David Oakly. They were natural heterosexual feelings that I had before I found out that we were such close male friends in our past life together. It's no wonder then that we're not allowed to remember our past lives, I thought to myself. We would be different people if we were allowed to remember. We wouldn't know who we were. *"God, reincarnation can be so complex!"* I exclaimed out loud.

I wondered if David knew the answer. He seemed to know so much about this secret knowledge of life that he inspired my total confidence. Did that have something to do with our past-life friendship? I went to sleep on it, and in the morning I called him.

David had already left for work, so I left a message on his voice mail to drop by the house anytime in the evening if he was free. "I have a burning Atma question I would like to ask you," I said, hoping to excite him enough to drop over. I also wanted to tell him that I had decided to write my open letter to the *Gazette* as well as the Barrie *Examiner* since I had learned that Father McDuffy had put his challenge out to the larger public.

"A word to the wise, Cassie," David cautioned upon hearing my news when he dropped over after dinner Tuesday evening, carrying a box of assorted pastries from the Wyedale Bakery that I placed on the coffee table and forgot about because I was so anxious. "Buffer your experience with your unborn child with all the details of your average, normal life that you're willing to share. It will lend credibility to your story," he proffered.

"What do you mean?" I asked.

"It's basic journalism. I learned this writing a weekly column for five years. If you want the public to believe you, you have to write to their comfort zone. Your experience will be so far outside their comfort zone that if it stands too much on its own they won't be able to identify with you. Write your letter in such a way that you come across as an ordinary woman who had an extraordinary experience. That's the safest way to put yourself out there."

"Thank you for that, David. I had no idea how I was going to write my letter. That sounds like good advice. Would you be willing to read my letter before I submit it?"

"Certainly," he said.

As David and I talked I was dying to tell him about our past life relationship, but I had to bite my tongue. "I wanted to ask you something about reincarnation," I said, getting to the point of my invitation.

"Right. Your burning Atma question. What about reincarnation?"

"Why do you think we're not allowed to remember our past lives?" I asked.

"I'm sure there are a number of reasons, but I would think the major reason would have to do with free will," he replied, and then got up, picked up the box of pastries, walked over and slid open the French doors to the family room. "How are you doing, guys?" he said, poking his head inside.

"Fine," Patrick said. "You?"

"Good. How about you, Mark?" David asked.

"Great," Mark replied.

"And how is everything in your world, Cindy?"

"Pretty good," she said.

"You watching a movie?" David asked.

"Yeah! *Harry Potter and the Half-Blood Prince*," Mark replied.

"I haven't seen that one yet. Would you guys like a little treat to snack on while you're watching the movie?" David asked, and the children perked up. He handed the package to Mark and said, "There's three of each for you. Enjoy."

"Thanks, David," Mark said, followed by Cindy and Patrick.

"You're welcome," David said, and closed the doors and sat back down. "As I was saying, we don't remember our past lives because it would interfere with our free will."

"Free will?" I said, feeling a little foolish.

"How can I explain this?" he continued, thinking I didn't get his point. "Take a habit like smoking or drinking, or an addiction to drugs. These habits can control one's behavior. As free as one may be, his life is actually controlled by his thousand and one habits. In Sufism we say that man is not one self, but many little selves who all want to take control of the personality. My Sufi training woke me up to this disconcerting truth. And the whole point of the Sufi way of life is to coalesce all of these little selves into one self. This is the Sufi way of saying that we have to bring our karmic destiny into agreement with our spiritual destiny. But if we were allowed to remember our past lives how free would we be to align the course of our karmic destiny with our divinely encrypted spiritual destiny? Not very free, would we?"

"Are you saying that we have two destinies?" I asked.

"Yes. We have two lines of destiny," David said, and then fell silent and gave me a long, penetrating look as if considering whether to tell me more.

His stare made me nervous. "Well, are you going to tell me?"

He laughed. "Alright," he said, and leaned his body into the sofa chair for comfort. He crossed his legs and gave me a big, contented smile. "We have two lines of destiny, Cassie. One karmic and one spiritually encrypted. Our karmic destiny is our personal line of destiny, which is determined by our free choice; and our spiritual destiny is pre-determined by the Divine Plan of God, which calls for our karmic destiny to be brought into agreement with our spiritual destiny. But this can only be done of our own free will. There's no other way of doing this, despite what religions like Christianity tell us.

258

This means that we have to grow in spiritual consciousness enough to want to coincide with our pre-ordained spiritual destiny, which is to become spiritually self-realized, God-conscious Souls. Do you follow?"

"This is all new to me, David," I said, awed by his knowledge.

"It was all new to me too. To make my point," he continued, with that focused look in his eyes that excited my curiosity, "I met an Atman in Sedona a few years ago who told me he had several very meaningful past-life regressions. He went into his regressions with the specific intention of finding out why he was the way he was in his current lifetime. He was convinced that his current life was powerfully influenced by some of his past lives, and he was right. The Satma allowed him to recall those past lives that had the most influence on his current lifetime, and he told me that had he not been an Atman with the Satma's protection he would not have been able to deal with the awakened consciousness of some of his past lives. One lifetime in particular overwhelmed him. He was so sexually obsessed in that lifetime that he had to summon every ounce of moral courage to not let that past life overpower his personality. And even then he had to ask the Satma for help. So imagine what the awakened consciousness of a Hitler, Stalin, or Vlad the Impaler would do to a person. It would be impossible to exercise the free will we need to change the course of our karmic destiny and bring it into agreement with our spiritual destiny. That's why the Divine Game Plan was written this way. We don't remember our past lives because each life we live has to be free to choose its own karmic destiny. True, we have unconscious influences from our past lives; but on the whole we're free to choose our own personal destiny. Does that answer your question?"

"You amaze me, David. That makes perfect sense. And it also explains something that I would love to share with you, but I can't," I said, with a self-conscious blush because I shouldn't have brought it up at all.

David looked so relaxed and comfortable on my new white Italian leather sofa chair that memories of our past-life friendship rushed to my mind. We had spent so many hours in our drawing rooms discussing the great ideas of literature, poetry, philosophy, science, politics and world religions that it was only natural for us to continue our friendship on another, more intimate level. *I wanted so much to tell him!*

"David, I apologize," I said, blushing with embarrassment. "I was so anxious to hear what you had to say about past lives that I didn't even offer you a cup of coffee. You will have a cup of coffee and some apple strudel, won't you?"

"Only if it's *a la mode,*" he said, and cracked a smile.

"I believe we can manage that," I said, and went into the kitchen to put on the coffee. I took out the second apple strudel that I had picked up at the Wyedale Bakery, which had been recently purchased by a German couple from Kitchener who introduced a variety of new pastries and wholesome breads, and sliced two portions. I added two scoops of Vanilla ice cream to David's and one scoop to mine. The children had already eaten theirs after dinner.

As I carried the tray with our coffee and apple strudel into the living room, the thought suddenly came to me that I was being too familiar with David, and I had a moment of acute self-consciousness. "David, did I take you away from your plans this evening?"

"No. I did what I had to do," he said. "Actually, Cassie, it was nice to hear your voice on my answering machine. I was wondering all day long whether you were going to respond to McDuffy's challenge or not."

"I honestly didn't know until last night. We had a family conference, and the children have given me their blessing. That was my first consideration. I don't want to hurt my children, David."

"Of course not. Do they know what you're going to write?"

"Yes. I told them the whole story last night after dinner."

"Good. As long as it doesn't come as a surprise to them. Who knows how the public will receive your letter? It's a toss-up, Cassie."

"Do you think so? I honestly don't know, David. The more I live the Atma life, the more removed I seem to be from the mainstream. And yet, the closer I seem to be to the very source of life itself. It's a strange place to be."

"How so?"

"I think it has to do with my work. Especially my terminally ill patients. My mentor Doctor Elisabeth Kubler-Ross told me that she learned more about how to live her life from her dying patients than from the living. It was her contention..."

I stopped in mid-sentence. *Contention* was a word that David and I repeatedly used in our past life discourses. David stared at me. "It was her contention?" he repeated.

"Yes," I said, snapping out of my reverie. "She contended that her dying patients were closer to the source of life than the living."

"In what way?" David asked, with wide-eyed curiosity.

"I've experienced the honesty of the dying, David. It's not like any other kind of honesty," I said, my mind drifting back to our friendship in our past life together.

"Fascinating. Can you elaborate?"

"That's it!" I exclaimed, to David's astonishment.

Bewildered, he stared at me. "What?"

It was the way we talked, not exchanging trivial information like most people do, but actually discoursing, exchanging thoughts, ideas, and feelings that defined our friendship and what attracted me to David from the moment we met in Minneapolis and what attracted me even more now. That was our past-life connection! Our karmic bond! *"We were close friends in a past life in the states, David,"* I blurted out. *"Very close friends!"*

David did not react to my emotional outburst. He reflected for a moment. "I'm not surprised. I'm very comfortable with you, Cassie. Is this why you invited me over?"

"You have found me out, honest friend!" I instinctively replied, and instant tears filled my eyes and trickled down my flushed cheeks.

It was an automatic response. I was so overwhelmed by the consciousness of our past life friendship that I had to release my emotions with tears. David did not move. I felt he wanted to come over and hold me, but he waited for me to collect myself.

I had made a complete fool of myself. I excused myself. A few minutes later, I returned. David waited for me to explain.

"I think you're right, David," I said, with a lump in my throat. "It's not fair to our current life to remember our past lives. It's much too hard. I'm sorry. I shouldn't have brought this up. I hope this doesn't jeopardize our friendship."

"On the contrary, it might just be the incentive I need. Look, Cassie. You've very emotional now. It couldn't have been easy to come to your decision to respond to McDuffy, and I can appreciate that. You need time to collect yourself..."

"I do, but please don't go."

"Are you sure?"

"Yes. I'm very emotional right now, for a lot of reasons; but I'd like you to stay. I trust you, David. Like I told you over lunch Sunday, I would trust you with my life. I didn't know why when I told you that, but I do now..."

I stopped in mid sentence again. I couldn't believe it. It didn't matter if I remembered our past life together or not, my feelings didn't lie. That was the point I had started to make about Doctor Kubler-Ross. I laughed nervously to release my anxiety. "We were talking about that special kind of honesty that dying patients have," I said, composing myself as I thought of my mentor's parting words just before she died. The memory brought new tears to my eyes. I wiped them with my napkin. I waited a moment. "David, most dying patients will open up to you if you give them half a chance. They have nothing left to lose, and they want to go out on a triumphant note. It's as though they've been granted a final curtain call, and you just know when they open up they're going to let go of something they've been holding onto their whole life. That's what makes their honesty so special. Doctor Kubler-Ross called this honesty the unvarnished truth of life. One patient told her just before she died that she would rather not have lived at all because she never got to live her own life. Her husband wouldn't let her. Doctor Kubler-Ross's own father didn't want her to become a medical doctor. He wanted her to become his bookkeeper. She went against his wishes, which was not an easy thing to do in those days, and she became a doctor. She had to fight incredible odds to live her own life, and she had to fight her whole life for her own identity. That's why she's my role model. It's because of her that I have to tell the story of my unborn child. It may not add up to a hill of beans, as my father's favorite actor Humphry Bogart would say, but I want to make my own contribution to this whole contentious abortion issue. This is what this special kind of dying-patient honesty is all about. I want to unburden myself of this truth, David. Like my mentor told me when I visited her in Scottsdale, Arizona just before she died, *`The trick is to be this honest when you're alive. Then dying will be a piece of cake.'"*

"*Touché,*" David said, and by the look that I saw in his eyes I knew that I had just inched my chair a little closer to his.

My Unborn Child

Chapter 20
A Blue Bottle of Spring Water at Galileo's

I stared at the face in my dresser mirror. It was me, Cassie Patty O'Shaunnesy, but the mother of three young teenage children and one abortion who stared back felt like a school girl again. It was really happening. I was more nervous than my first prom! I glanced up and read a poem by Richard Allen that I had taped to the corner of my mirror. I read it every morning to start my day. I read it now to calm myself before David picked me up for dinner:

...as you face your death
it is only the love
you have given
and received
which will count...
if you have loved well
then it will have been worth it...
but if you have not
death will come too soon
and be too terrible to face.

I thought of Rena Osborne, a cancer patient at St. Paul's Hospital in Vancouver. Rena was thirty-eight years old when she died her terrible death. She was married to a hockey bum who lived his drunken life in the glory days of his youth.

Kenny "Flash" Osborne never broke out of the minor leagues into the NHL, but the more he drank the more excuses he found for not making it to the "big time," and this took a heavy toll on Rena and their two boys.

Rena slaved for years in the hot dry end of the kiln in the plywood factory where she worked to support her family because her husband could not hold down a steady job. His drinking and bad temper always got him fired. But Rena would not abandon him. She had married him for better or worse, and she was going to prove to the world that she could change the man she had married for love, but she didn't.

Rena's life became the nightmare of the bad-tempered alcoholic's wife, and her anger festered until it began to rot her insides. By the time her doctor caught the cancer it was too late. She lay in her bed cursing her husband and fighting back the irreversible pain of dying.

For a whole week I tried to reach out to her, but she had built such a wall of anger around herself that nothing could get through. "You're crazy," she said to me, when I tried to inform her of Doctor Kubler-Ross's studies on the after-life and her belief that we would be born again. "This is all we got, lady! So don't give me that load of crap!"

Rena talked the rough talk of her working class culture. Twice she tried to commit suicide by slashing her wrists, and both times was rushed to emergency by her family, and still she could not leave her alcoholic husband.

"Flash" had a hold on her. Rena called it love, and she died holding on to the illusion that had cost her life. "I want that bastard to watch me die," she said, but on the day of her death her husband was so drunk and belligerent that security had to escort him out of the hospital. Rena's sons were so humiliated by their father's behavior that they left also, which they would live to regret. Their mother died alone a few minutes before I went back to check on her.

I had gone earlier to give her a shot of morphine, but she still refused to take it. She was so weak she could hardly speak. Tears of pain streamed down her cheeks. Regardless of what I said, she refused.

It was her wish to die in pain like she had lived.

"Please, Rena," I pleaded.

"Shove it," she said, with tears in her tormented eyes.

"For God's sake, be reasonable," I begged her.

"God? What God? Get out of here. I want to die the way I lived."

She got her wish. She died full of anger and pain. It was her way of getting even with the gods that had been so cruel to her.

I looked at myself one last time in the mirror and said to the adventurous woman with the short new hairstyle staring back at me, "Never hold a grudge. Learn to forgive. Love with an open heart. And never lie to yourself."

The doorbell rang. It startled me. I got up and went downstairs to the living room. My children were anxiously waiting for me.

"Wow!" exclaimed Mark. "You look fantastic, Mom!"

"Yeah," Patrick confirmed. "You really do, Mom!"

"Cindy? What do you think?" I asked my daughter.

I was wearing an emerald-green print sleeveless dress which I picked up at *Melanie Lyne* at the New Georgian Mall in Barrie, a simple gold-braided chain with my Atma pendant and complimentary bracelet, laced panties and bra from *La Vie en Rose,* and matching clutch purse and new shoes. I was blushing and very nervous.

"Let me check. Turn around, Mom," she said, giving me a critical look. "Once more, Mom."

I turned around once more. The doorbell rang again. Mark went to answer it. I waited for Cindy's comment. "You're hot, Mom!"

"Really?"

"You are, Mom!" Cindy said.

"Thank you, sweetheart. Alright," I said, and waited for David to enter.

He looked too good to be true. He had on a short-sleeved, light-green polo shirt that instantly drew my eyes to his well-toned, tight upper body, and beige, elegant but casual slacks. He was carrying a bouquet of red roses. "Hi, David," I managed to say.

"Flowers for the beautiful lady," he said, as he handed them to me. "Doesn't your mother look lovely?" he added.

"She's hot!" Cindy proudly exclaimed.

"I agree," David said, his eyes taking me all in.

I was so nervous I didn't know what to say. "Thank you for the roses, David. They're gorgeous. I'll just put them in a vase," I said, thankful for the opportunity to catch my breath. I went into the kitchen and took out my best crystal vase and added the package of nutrients that came with the roses, arranged them, and added the water.

David graciously gave me his arm after I proudly placed the roses on my coffee table in the center of the living room. "Shall we?" he said.

"Hey David, you're not taking Mom out for dinner in your work van, are you?" Patrick yelled up from the couch. "That's not cool!"

David laughed. "I washed it this afternoon," he said.

"No way! Mom, take the Odyssey!" Patrick shouted.

I looked at David. "Only if you drive," I said.

"If that's what they want," David said.

"Yeah, that's what we want," Patrick said. "Mom's a classy lady, David. She deserves the best. Right, guys?"

"Right!" Mark and Cindy replied in unison.

David had the perfect opportunity to show his wit, but he didn't. He looked at me and winked. Then he said, "See you guys later," and he drove our new family van to *Galileo's* on the waterfront in Barrie, where he had made reservations on the patio.

Being a Higher Initiate in Atma, David only drank alcohol occasionally to be sociable, a beer now and then with tradesmen he worked with, and a glass of wine for special occasions. He asked me if I wanted wine for dinner, and I said, "Only if you join me."

"Yes, certainly," he said, and ordered a half carafe of white house wine. And for dinner, I thought it would be a nice gesture for David to order as well. He selected the escargot as an entrée, and Galileo's Atlantic Baked Salmon, with herbs, orange juice, and brown rice, served with steamed broccoli and carrots. I smiled, but made no comment.

Before the waitress brought the wine, she placed the most beautiful, frosted, deep-blue glass bottle of spring water on our table. David looked at me and I at him, and we broke into laughter at the obvious message of the Golden-tongued Wisdom of Atma.

Blue is the color that symbolically speaks to the Satma's presence. The Satma often manifests as the Blue Light of Atma to people around the world, especially to Atma chelas during contemplation, or in their dreams, and water speaks to spiritual truth. The message of the deep-blue bottle of chilled water told us that the Satma was with us and that refreshing spiritual truth was on the menu, and David and I could hardly contain ourselves.

David poured two glasses of the cold spring water, picked up his glass, and held it up for a toast. I picked mine up and he said, *"Baraka bashad."*

Baraka bashad is a spiritual blessing. It means, May the blessings be, and I knew that was David's way of telling me that we should not try to direct our relationship but rather to let the Atma, the omniscient guiding light of life, direct it for us.

It was the perfect toast; but I couldn't resist, and I replied with my father's favorite toast, "Here's looking at you, kid!" I said, and clicked David's glass again.

"And you," David said, and took another sip of water. Then he placed his glass down and picked up the blue bottle and stared at it long and hard. "I was fortunate to have the Sufi teacher I had," he finally said, with a sudden change of mood. "I don't know what I would have done without him."

"Oh," I said, surprised by David's melancholy tone.

He held up the bottle for me to look at. "You see this bottle, Cassie? It symbolizes the truth that the seeker seeks. The strange thing about truth is that it refuses to be found unless you drink it in like water. *'He who tastes not knows not.'* That's what my Sufi teacher taught me how to do. He taught me how to taste life. That's why I'm so grateful to him."

I wasn't quite sure what David was referring to. He set the bottle down and took another drink of water. Picking up the bottle again, he said, "Some truth was very hard to swallow." He sounded distant, sad.

I wanted to respond with my own experience, but I chose not to. "How did your Sufi teacher teach you to drink in truth?" I asked instead.

David snapped out of his melancholy reverie. "Should we be

talking about me, Cassie? This must be a big night for you. Don't get me wrong. I don't mean because you're having dinner with me. I mean..."

"I know what you mean, David. And yes, it is a big night for me. I'm as nervous as a school girl!"

David put the bottle down and reached for my hand and held it gently in his strong, workingman's hands. "Don't be. You're a very beautiful woman, with all the seasoned maturity that any reasonable man could possibly want. I'm honored, Cassie."

"Thank you, David. The feeling's mutual. I've never met a man like you before, and I'd very much like to get to know you better. I don't mind if you tell me about your Sufi teacher. I honestly don't. You've piqued my curiosity."

"Just as Sufism piqued mine. Maybe it's because I came to Atma-Gare by way of Sufism that I feel the way I do about this path," he said, again with a melancholy tone in his voice. "In Sufism, we call the Atma force *Baraka*. As I've already mentioned once or twice, *Baraka* is that mysterious *subtlety,* the essence of life which Sufi students are taught to catch by living a secret way of life that would astound people. My Sufi teacher was a master tradesman, Cassie. He taught me how to catch the *subtlety* through the trades by working on myself."

"By working on yourself?" I asked, very intrigued.

"Yes. That's the key to the Sufi life," David replied, as he glanced at the deep-blue bottle of spring water. "Unless one knows how to work on himself, he will always be subject to the natural influences of life. My teacher taught me how to break the hold that these forces had over me. I thought I was a freethinking, self-determining individual, but I was wrong. I was governed by patterns of thought and behavior that I had inherited from my family and created out of my own needs, wants, and desires. My Sufi teacher liberated me from myself, Cassie. That's why I'm so grateful to him. Once I broke out of the prison of my own captivity, I began to grow into the man that you see today."

David paused, sat back in his chair, took a sip of wine, and softly said, "I love your dress, Cassie. You look gorgeous tonight."

My face lit up. I was hoping he would say something. "Thank you, David," I said, "It was my second choice. Cindy didn't like my first choice."

"And I love what you've done with your hair," he added, to my delight.

"Thank you. A new hairstyle for a new life in Georgian Bay," I said, with a nervous blush. I had waited years to cut it short, and David gave me the perfect excuse to try something different. I was so excited I was beside myself.

"Let's talk about that, Cassie," he continued. "What kind of life would you like to have here in Georgian Bay? Or, if I'm not being too forward, what kind of life did you leave behind in Vancouver? I'm curious to know about that first."

The waitress appeared with our entrée of escargot in a hot garlic butter sauce and freshly baked mini French crusty rolls wrapped in a checkered, blue and white napkin in a wicker basket. The hot garlic sauce wafted to my nostrils. "Enjoy," she said, with a pleasant smile.

I took a sip of wine, looked at David, and replied, "I could have had a full, satisfying life in Vancouver. I know that, David. I loved my job, my family is there, and I love Vancouver. It has to be one of the most beautiful cities in the world, and I miss it terribly. But I was called here. I don't know why. I got a very strong inner nudge to go on the Internet one night for a job search. It had not once crossed my mind to look for another job, but I could not deny my nudge. As the Atma would have it, the Wyedale Community Hospital had just posted an opening for head nurse that same day. I heard a voice telling me to move. It was the Satma. *'Move,'* he said. He told me twice. How could I not apply? This is where the Atma wants me to be. I'm not going to second guess the Atma, but I'm almost certain it has to do with Father McDuffy's ad in the *Gazette*. I think the Atma wants me to go public with the story of my unborn child. I really think that's why I'm here, David."

David looked into my eyes for a long, embarrassing moment. "You're an Atma Warrior, Cassie. I knew that from the moment we met. There are those whom the Atma chooses, and there are those who choose the Atma. Those who choose the Atma are Warriors. Don't ask me why. It just is. It's as though one has had to fight for every inch of one's spiritual ground. That's why Atma-Gare is so precious to the Atma Warrior. I get the feeling that you've had to fight for every inch of your spiritual ground. Am I right?"

"You have no idea what I went through to break the hold that my Christian faith had on me, David," I replied, welling up with emotion. David had sprung free my past, and I had to fight back my tears. "I went though hell, David."

"I thought as much. I didn't want to say anything to you, Cassie, because it's your decision; but from the moment you told me you had an experience with your unborn child that proves McDuffy wrong, I knew the Atma wanted you to respond to his challenge."

"Did you really?"

"That's what an Atma Warrior does. They fight the Atma's battles in the battlefield of everyday life. You've been called," he said, and broke into a gentle laugh. I was so moved I could not reply. "Shall we?" he said, looking down at his escargot.

We ate our escargot in thoughtful silence, dipping pieces of the freshly-baked bun into each empty little crevice in the ceramic plate to soak up all the garlic butter sauce, sipping our wine between bites and soaking up the relaxing patio atmosphere while waiting for our main course to arrive. "And here," the waitress said, placing our plates down, "is our chef's very own Galileo's Atlantic Baked Salmon. Enjoy."

"Thank you," David said, with a grateful smile.

"Atma Warrior?" I finally asked. I couldn't get the phrase out of my mind. "If I am, David, then I've been training my whole life to become one."

"Of course you have," he said, and laughed.

"What about other Atmans? Those whom the Atma chooses? What kind of Atmans are they? Foot soldiers, as my son Mark would say?"

"Very good, " he said, with an ironic look. "That's exactly what they are. In their own foot-soldierly way, they bring the Light and Sound of God to the hungry masses. But it's the Warriors who are called upon to stand up to the Kal's assaults on spiritual freedom.

McDuffy's challenge is a frontal assault on women's freedom, and I think the Atma has called upon you to respond. That may very well be why you're here in Georgian Bay."

The Kal is the negative side of the God force when it splits into its positive and negative currents as it leaves the Soul Plane and enters into the Lower Material Worlds of the mental, causal, astral, and physical planes. Kal is better known to man as Satan, and his mandate from the Supreme Deity is to keep Soul chained to karma and reincarnation until it is ready to return to the Higher Worlds of God.

I thought it was a strange coincidence that David should call me an Atma Warrior, because that's exactly how I felt about my mentor Doctor Elisabeth Kubler-Ross, the third child of a set of triplets who had to fight her whole life for her own identity.

I had to share that with David. "Funny you should say that about me, because that's exactly how I see my role model, Doctor Elisabeth Kubler-Ross," I said, excited to share this very private part of my life with David. "Her autobiography *The Wheel of Life* is by far my favorite book, and that includes all the Atma books that I have read. She has given me more inspiration than any other person in my life; because she had the courage to fight all those forces that denied her the right to her own life and destiny. You know, David, sometimes I get the feeling that life conspires to keep people from being who they want to be..."

David burst into laughter. *"Touché!"*

"I'm right, aren't I? Like my role model, I had to fight all kinds of resistance to do what I felt I had to do to fulfill myself. I was always accused of being selfish, and maybe I was; but what else can one do when they are driven to live their own life?"

"It's not an easy place to be when one hears the Call of Soul," David said, his eyes bright with that certain light of spiritual wisdom. Then he stopped in mid-thought and put a piece of salmon into his mouth. "Lovely," he said, and resumed the conversation. "It's written in the Divine Plan of God, Cassie. The atom of God is here for one purpose, and that's to realize its own identity. You're right. Life does conspire to keep us from satisfying our most basic need for self-identity. Just as grass has to break through asphalt to grow, so does

Soul have to break through the heavy crust of social consciousness to realize itself. It's never a question of not satisfying our most basic need, Cassie; it's always a question of when will Soul be ready to break through the asphalt of life."

I tasted the Atlantic salmon. "What makes Soul ready? Life experience?"

"Exactly. Do you like the salmon?" he asked.

"It's not Pacific salmon, David," I said, with an ironic smile.

David looked at me, and then laughed. *"How did I miss that?"*

"But I love your choice of salad dressing," I said, delighted that he picked up on my humor. "The balsamic vinaigrette works very well with the *Atlantic* salmon," I added.

David appreciated my humor, and laughed again. "Thank you. And we certainly can't beat the beautiful atmosphere, can we?" he said, playing along.

I broke into nervous laughter.

"What?" he asked.

"I was just thinking of something my mentor wrote in her memoir," I said, and put my hand to my chest. *"'Everything happens for a reason,'* she said. *'There are no accidents,'* Like your choice of restaurants," I said, glancing at the blue bottle of spring water. "This was meant to be, David. *I'm sure of it!"*

David laughed. "Your mentor's right, Cassie. I haven't quite figured out the significance of the restaurant's name yet. I chose *Galileo's* for the food and relaxing atmosphere, but maybe your response to McDuffy's challenge might be as great a threat to Christianity as Galileo was. We'll have to wait and see. In any event, from what I know about your mentor I'd say that she was an Atma Warrior no less than Galileo, Gandhi, Mother Theresa, or my favorite Atma Warrior, Abraham Lincoln. An Atma Warrior is an Atma Warrior, and the battle is always the same—*a battle for human freedom!"*

I kept glancing at the blue bottle as David spoke, and I felt myself drinking in big gulps of spiritual truth. When he exclaimed *"a battle for human freedom,"* I knew that Father McDuffy's challenge went so far beyond the issue of the rights of a fetus over the rights of women that it made my head spin, and I had to take a quick breath to calm myself.

"Are you okay?" David asked, noticing my odd behavior.

"I don't know. I feel dizzy. I think I just caught a glimpse of something much bigger than myself," I replied, and took a drink of water. "This may sound strange, but I just had an incredible vision of the future."

"No kidding? What did you see?"

"It's this abortion issue," I heard myself reply, my head still spinning. "It has to do with much more than a woman's right to her own body, or the right of the fetus to life. It has to do with Soul's purpose in life. What are we here for, David? Didn't you say that the atom of God is here to realize its own identity? Isn't that what the Divine Plan of God is all about?"

"Yes," David said, with wide-eyed curiosity.

"This abortion issue is not just about rights, David; it's about the age-old battle for spiritual freedom," I heard myself say, as the words poured out of me. "The negative forces of life will do whatever they can to keep Soul trapped in the cycle of karma and reincarnation. I just caught a glimpse of this battle for spiritual freedom. Abortion is the battlefield, and Father McDuffy has to keep the illusion alive that a fetus is a little person. He's Kal's agent, and he has to fight to keep Soul trapped. That's his mandate. And if I'm the Atma Warrior that you say I am, I have to fight to free Soul from the illusion that a fetus is a little person. It's no wonder that my head is spinning, David. I just caught a glimpse of what my response to Father McDuffy's challenge will do for every woman in the world!"

This was too much. David was right. *Galileo's* was the sign that I had asked the Satma to give me on my beach walk, and I knew that I had to respond to Father McDuffy's challenge just as Galileo had to stand up to the Roman Catholic Church with his proof that the earth revolved around the sun and not the sun around the earth. *Galileo's* was my sign to stand up for the truth that Soul pre-exists its human body and that it's not created at the moment of human conception, as Christianity believes! *Galileo's was the sign I had asked for!*

I stared into David's eyes, wondering what he thought of me now. I had never felt like this before. But it honestly didn't matter to me, because I just *was*!

David took a sip of wine. He stared at me for the longest time, but it didn't bother me. I was so content just *being* that nothing mattered to me. Still holding his glass, he leaned into the table to get closer to me. "There are two kinds of knowing, Cassie; mental and spiritual," he said, in a serious tone of voice. "Mental knowing is intellectual understanding, and spiritual knowing is spiritual understanding. Up until this moment, you had an intellectual understanding of what the abortion issue is all about. How could you not, being an Atman? You knew that Soul pre-exists the fetus. You knew that Soul lives more than one lifetime. You knew that Soul has to break out of the recurring cycle of life and death. You knew all of this intellectually. What just happened now, courtesy of the Satma and his Blue Bottle of Spiritual Truth, is that you had a spiritual realization of your own knowledge. This is why you feel dizzy. I've had this experience also. I know exactly how you feel, Cassie."

I listened, not caring whether David was right or not about what I had just experienced because I could not get past the feeling of just *being*. All I wanted to do was to just sit there and *be. It felt absolutely divine!*

I don't know how long I sat like that. I finally snapped out of my experience and noticed David staring at me with a big grin on his face. "You're back," he said, and laughed.

I took another drink of water. I looked into David's eyes. "I can't explain what just happened," I said, still reeling from my experience. "I have never in all my life felt so wonderful. I was *me*, David! *I was me!"*

Again, he laughed. "I know the feeling, Cassie. If you want, I can explain what just happened to you."

"You can?"

"Yes. But only because Sam explained it to me."

"Sam?" I asked.

"My Sufi teacher," David said.

"Your Sufi teacher was called Sam?"

"Sam the Man. That's what we called him. Sufism is all about centering oneself in one's true self. Sam is centered. By working on himself according to the secret tradition of Sufism, Sam transformed his consciousness and became what nature intends every person to become—fully self-realized. What you just had a taste of, Sam experiences all day long. This is my goal too, Cassie. This is what it means to be a fully evolved human being. You *are* you, and that's all that can be said about this incredible experience. In Atma-Gare, we call this the Atmashar state of consciousness."

"You mean you can hold onto this experience?" I asked, astonished by David's explanation. "It can't be done, can it?"

"Sam said it can be. The Living Atma Master, or any Atma Master for that matter, is Atma-centered. That's what you just experienced, Cassie. You were given a taste of *being* the Atma. This is the mystery of the spiritual path of Atma-Gare—becoming the Atma. This is what the Fifth Initiation in Atma is all about. It's the key that opens the door to this mystery of your spiritual self. The more you become your true self, the more you become the Atma. Your decision to respond to McDuffy's challenge was a call for you to stand up for who you are. In your decision, you became so completely yourself that you realized the Atmashar state of consciousness. You just experienced the Being of all beings, Cassie. You just had a taste of spiritual self-realization consciousness. You just experienced your true self—*Soul!*"

"Wow! So this is what being Soul feels like?"

"Exactly," David said, with a joyful smile. "The only way to *be* Soul is to be as completely yourself as you can be. This is the key to the higher worlds of God. This is the key to Atma-Gare, Cassie. Unfortunately, most Atmans don't realize this. They expect the carriage to pull the horse."

I didn't know what David meant by that, nor did I want to know just then, so I made a mental note to ask him later. I giggled nervoulsy.

"What?" David asked.

"This is like high school," I said.

"There is that element to it, isn't there?"

"Do you remember your first date, David?"

"Yes," he said. "Do you?"

"Oh yes! And I was just as nervous then as I was when you came to my front door this evening," I said, and broke into nervous laughter

again.

"And now? Are you still nervous?"

"Yes and no."

"Am I your first date since your divorce?"

"Yes."

"There you go, then. It's only natural, Cassie. Please don't be nervous with me. You'll only make me nervous."

"Okay. Let's talk about you, then. After all, aren't first dates about getting to know each other?"

"I'll tell you anything you want to know about me."

"You will?" I said, surprised.

"Yes. Ask away."

"Okay. What's your favorite pastime?"

Without thought, David replied, "Living."

"Living?"

"Yes, living," he said, with a cheeky smile. "Living can be a real challenge when you do it consciously. That's my favorite pastime. Living life fully and consciously."

"How ironic! That's almost the same as my motto. *'Live life fully and honestly,'* said my mentor. *I don't believe it!"*

"What else would you like to know about me? Anything. You have special privileges with me this evening."

"Anything?"

"Yes."

"Okay. Who's your favorite author?"

"Rumi, the Sufi poet."

"Who's your favorite Atma Master, if you have one?"

"Paul Mathew," he said, which I suspected.

"Why?" I had to ask.

"Because he was an Atma Warrior *par excellence.* "

"I think so too. Why do you think so?"

"Paul Mathew had an enormous amount of ego consciousness to resolve," David said, and put his fork down. "Shades of his ego remained in Paul's personality when he became the Satma, the Living Atma Master. Did you ever hear the story about the time he was giving Atma-Vidya readings?"

An Atma-Vidya reading is the ancient science of prophesy; the means of delving into the past, present, and future by the adepts of Atma-Gare.

"I don't recall," I said, eager to hear anything private about Paul Mathew.

"He was supposed to give an Atma-Vidya reading for a famous movie star. Cary Grant was supposed to go to Paul's house for the reading, but he called and asked Paul to go to his house instead. Paul was put out by Cary Grant's attitude of self-importance and said, `Who does he think he is if I am who I think I am?' Paul had just received the Rod of Atma Power. He had just become the Satma, the Living Atma Master. `*Who does he think he is if I am who I think I am?*'" David repeated, and broke into a hearty laugh. "Did you hear the shades of Paul's ego?"

"Yes," I said, smiling more at David than the story because that's exactly how I saw David. The shades of his own ego were always present, but his ego did not possess him the way it possessed other men. I wanted to thank him for sharing that with me, but instead I said, "Paul Mathew is very special to me because he came to me when I was a little girl. But we're not going to talk about me now. I have another question for you, David. When you cross over to the other side you're going to be asked this question: What services have you rendered? What do you think you will you reply?"

David's expression changed. He sat back in his chair to think. I thought he would have had his answer ready, but he didn't. He poured the rest of the water from the blue bottle into his glass and took a long, slow drink, then another and emptied his glass as if to say he needed all the spiritual truth he could get to answer. "If at all possible," he said, "I would like to make a contribution to the *Shariyatma* with my realization of Soul's purpose in life. Atmans are trying to pull the horse with the carriage. They place too much emphasis on Soul and not enough on the perfection of the self. To answer your question, Cassie, I'd like my service to be a clear understanding of how God becomes more God through the evolution of the self of man. I want to answer the great riddle of life that the torchbearer of Atma-Gare Zak Tarzman posed to his disciple Paul Mathew when he told him that man is as important to God as God is to man. That's the service I would like to render life."

"Wow!" I gasped. "Well, if anyone can do it I know you can," I said, smiling in awe at his heroic ambition. "I think I know all I need to know about you, David Oakly. You can ask me anything you want now."

"Wonderful," David said, and his face relaxed. He took his last sip of wine and looked me right in the eye and said, "Will you go out with me again?"

My heart jumped. *"How wonderful you are, David!"*

"I take it that's a yes," he said, with a boyish look on his adorable face.

Smiling demurely, I said, "Call me."

"I intend to!" he said, and we both burst into laughter. After dinner David took me for a walk along the waterfront, and our romance became a reality.

Chapter 21

On the Night of the Winter Storm

"Once a Catholic, always a Catholic," said my mother, almost as a curse after I left the Roman Catholic Church. Another one of her favorite sayings while I was growing up was, "Keep your faith, and pray to Jesus every day." But I stopped praying to Jesus after my last confession, and I lost my faith completely after my last conversation with Uncle Timothy.

As all Catholics, I grew up believing that the one true religion was my Roman Catholic faith and that all other religions were false. I was also taught to believe that the Pope was infallible in matters of my faith, and that to question my faith was to commit the sin of Lucifer. My family accused my father of the sin of Lucifer, which they said I had inherited from him, but the more life forced me to question my faith the more doubtful I became.

St. Paul was responsible for the proliferation of Jesus Christ's gospel throughout the world, but it was the crucifixion of Jesus that made Christianity the world religion that it is today. Without the crucifixion there would be no Christianity, so the whole truth of my faith was founded upon the death of Jesus upon the cross for the salvation of the world.

Jesus was the Son of God. He was conceived by the Holy Ghost and born of a virgin mother. God asked his only begotten Son to sacrifice his life to wash away the stain of original sin from the world. Jesus obeyed the will of his Father and died on the cross to save us.

That's what I was told by my Catholic Church, and that's what I grew up to believe.

I loved my savior Jesus. He suffered and died on the cross to save us from eternal damnation. I prayed to Jesus every day of my young life. But as I grew older I began to listen more to my teacher and less to what my Church had taught me to believe.

I don't remember my conversations with my teacher, only snippets now and then. I remember how gentle he was when he spoke to me, and how he always wanted me to decide for myself. "And what do you think you should do, Cassie?" he always asked me.

I no longer believe that Jesus is the only begotten Son of God who died for the sins of the world. I believe that Jesus was a mortal man who became a Spiritual Master. But I could never reconcile my feelings for Jesus, and it wasn't until I met David Oakly when I moved to Georgian Bay that my conflicted feelings about the savior who had such an enormous influence on my life began to be resolved.

"David, do you remember what you said on our first date at *Galileo's*, something about the carriage pulling the horse?" I mused, for something to say while he made hot chocolate for us in the kitchen of his new house. I was soaking in the glowing warmth of his fireplace as I studied the artwork that David had finally arranged on his living room walls.

I just loved the colors of the house, a harmonious blend of various shades of green and gold accented with a soft creamy white on the doors, windows, and trim; they created a warm, inviting space. David had a natural talent for decorating, and a very keen eye for art. When he showed me some of his artwork, I marveled at the originality. David made a habit of taking in three and four studio tours in the Georgian Bay area every summer looking for that one piece of art that caught his eye, and regardless the cost he would buy it. He also made a habit of getting to know every artist that he collected and cultivating a relationship with him or her because he wanted to stay abreast of the creative consciousness of our times. I stared at the piece above his fireplace. It was a portrait of David that he had commissioned from an artist whose self-portrait arrested David's attention. Lance Henrikson, according to David, was a lifelong student of Jungian psychology who was fixated on capturing the *shadow* in the portraits he was commissioned to paint. Lance never revealed this to his clients, but they all found his portraits to be very personal, intimate, and revealing. David told me that he studied Lance's self-portrait, discovered his secret, and asked to have his portrait done.

When I first saw it hanging over his fireplace, I thought it was a bit much; but not after David explained that he hung it in his living room to remind him of his *shadow*, the dark side of his personality which Lance Henrikson had subtly captured in his face.

David did not sit for his portrait. Lance took a dozen digital photographs of his clients, and then through computer technology cropped one composite photograph with the two left sides of the face and one composite photograph with the two right sides of the face. The photograph with two left sides of the face was a composite of the *shadow* side of his client's invisible personality, and Lance always drew three sketches for his clients to give his clients a full-spectrum perspective of their personality, and then he painted one portrait with the aid of his three sketches, which gave his portraits a physiognomic depth that amazed his clients.

I didn't like David's portrait. There was a cold look in his eyes and the faint trace of a sneer on his lips that bothered me, but as I got to know David I began to appreciate Lance Henrikson's talent for capturing the soul of his client's character.

I stopped staring at David's portrait and sat down on the couch and focused on the glowing, warm fire. We had taken a chance on the weather to go cross-country skiing at the Wye Marsh Ski Trails, but we had to cut our outing short because the snowstorm moved in much sooner than we expected. I called the children just in case I got snowed in at David's.

I don't know why I asked David that question. It popped up out of the blue, as though it was time to be resolved. It puzzled me at *Galileo's*, and it puzzled me when it popped up on the night of the winter storm. "I'll be right there," David said, and a minute or so later came in with a tray of hot chocolate and almond biscotti. "Yes, I remember," he said.

I was very comfortable with David now, despite the feeling that our relationship had not quite yet found its own level of commitment, and I wanted to know what he meant by that cryptic comment. I dipped my biscotti into my hot chocolate, took a bite, and broke into a gentle laugh. David looked at me. "What?" he said. "Don't you like it?"

"No, it's fine," I said. "I was just thinking about the carriage pulling the horse. Why would I think of that now?"

"Perhaps the Atma wants you to know now," he said.

"You mean I wasn't ready at *Galileo's*?" I said, now more mystified than ever. "I know I got my Third Initiation since our first date, but I couldn't have grown that much in spiritual consciousness, could I?"

It came as a complete surprise to receive the pink slip in the mail for my Third Initiation in Atma a few weeks after my open letter to the Wyedale *Gazette* and Barrie *Examiner*, and only three days after the open forum debate on abortion, because I had only been a Second Initiate for three years, but it didn't come as a surprise to David.

Over a celebration dinner at The Red Lobster in Barrie, he said to me, "The more you serve the Atma, the more karma you resolve. It's *ipso facto*."

"I know we earn our initiations, but are you saying that I resolved more karma than I normally would have by taking the stand I did on the abortion issue? I feel I did, but what do you think?" I asked, hoping David would confirm my feelings.

"As I said, the more you serve the Atma, the more the Atma serves you," he replied, with a satisfied smile. Then, a few seconds later, he said, "On second thought, Cassie, I think it's more a question of the good karma that you created by taking the stand you did. It lifted you to the Causal Plane where you received your Third Initiation. You gave the public an entirely new perspective on the abortion issue, which forced them to step outside the box. You freed them of their fixed mindset and earned the karma for your Third Initiation."

"Probably both," I heard myself say, which I knew was an Atma-inspired thought. "We burn off karma by serving the Atma, and we create good karma by serving the Atma. It's a win-win situation!"

David laughed. "You're almost there, Cassie."

"Where?" I asked.

"That special place where you can see the difference between the horse pulling the carriage and the carriage pulling the horse."

That brought back the memory of our incredible first date at *Galileo's,* which I will always remember as our Blue Bottle Date. Just as I was about to ask what he meant by that cryptic comment, someone I knew from the hospital spotted us and came over to say hello.

Irene McDonald was a lab technician, and she had taken her husband out for dinner to celebrate his promotion to management in his company.

I never got a chance to ask David again until it came up on the night of the winter storm. David took a bite of his hot-chocolate-soaked biscotti, and said, "You've grown much more than you realize, Cassie."

The wind howled fiercely and the snow pelted against his Great Room window. The first real Georgian Bay winter storm had moved in, and I snuggled into David's body with a strong desire to burrow so deep that I wanted to become one with him. David fondled my hair.

"So, how does the carriage pull the horse?" I asked.

He let out a big sigh. "That's a big question, Cassie," he said, and put his hands behind his head to not be distracted. "Let's back up, all the way to the time of Jesus Christ. What does the world know about Jesus, anyway? I read that somewhere in the world a new book on Jesus is published once a week, but what does the world really know about the man called Jesus? And was that his real name? Paul Mathew wrote in his little book *Notes to a Chela* that his name was Yahevau, and that the Atma Master Fedar Farad gave him the name Jesus. He also gave Jesus his Second Initiation in Atma at the Mukti monastery in northern Tibet where Jesus is said to have stayed three years. So whom do we believe? The historians? The theologians? Archeologists? Do we believe St. Paul, who never met Jesus personally but who made him the most famous savior in the world? Or do we believe Paul Mathew, who met Jesus on the Mental Plane of Consciousness where Jesus now resides? Who do we believe, Cassie?"

"I don't know," I said.

"It doesn't matter who we believe, because until one is initiated into the Esoteric Circle of Life he will never penetrate the mystery of Jesus Christ."

"What do you believe about Jesus?" I asked.

"I'll tell you, but first tell me how you felt growing up. You were raised Roman Catholic. How did Jesus affect you growing up?"

"Why do you ask?"

"I'm building a canvass upon which to paint the picture you asked me to draw," David replied. "How did you feel growing up a Roman Catholic?"

After some reflection, I said, "At first I felt safe. I felt special being a Roman Catholic, because I was told it was the one true faith. I had a special relationship with Jesus. I said my prayers to him every night. I went to Mass every Sunday, and I received Holy Communion faithfully. This made me feel very close to Jesus. I even wanted to become a nun when I grew up, but that's when I heard the voice in my mind for the first time. I didn't know that it was Paul Mathew. He was just a voice in my mind that became my teacher, and he asked me what I wanted to do with my life, not what my mother wanted me to do. 'What do you want to be when you grow up, Cassie?' he asked me, and I told him I wanted to be a nurse."

"When did you start to question your faith?" David asked.

"When? I don't really know. It was a gradual thing. I began to feel less and less satisfied by my faith. I wasn't getting as much out of going to Mass on Sunday. The sermons got more and more boring; I went to confession less often; and Holy Communion stopped giving me the feeling it once did. I don't know, David; it just wore thin on me, that's all."

"Then why did your abortion devastate you the way it did?" David asked, which took me completely off guard.

"Why?" I said, startled awake, which happened often when David and I talked. It was like being shocked into another perspective. "Because I suffered the classical guilt that all Roman Catholics suffer from, that's why," I said, with stark awareness. "I may have been losing my faith one Sunday Mass at a time, but deep down my religion still had such a powerful hold on me that it nearly destroyed my life.

Despite all the books that I read and all the different paths that I explored, my faith was like an anchor that kept my ship from sailing. I might still be stuck in that fetid pool of stagnant water had I not had my abortion. I'm still too close to my experience to appreciate how my abortion cut my anchor line, but I know that one day I'll be thankful for all the suffering that my religion put me through!"

"You make my point exactly," David said, placing his arm around my shoulder. I was so emotional that I reached for his free hand and held it with both hands. I felt so safe I didn't want to let go. "Two things," David continued. "One, the unconscious way of life, which every person is subject to until they are evolved enough to take their spiritual destiny into their own hands; and two, the conscious way of life. It may come as a surprise to you, but religion belongs to the unconscious evolution of the human race, not the conscious evolution. Religion is sown in the Exoteric Circle of Life, not the Mesoteric Circle. Religion is the fertile ground that nourishes the spiritual self of man until it is ready to be harvested. That's the central metaphor in Jesus Christ's teaching, isn't it? He went into the world to harvest those Souls who were ready to take spiritual evolution into their own hands. That's what makes Jesus the most famous savior the world has ever known. No savior's message has ever reached as many people as Jesus Christ's gospel of salvation..."

"Why?" I interrupted. "What makes Jesus Christ's gospel so popular?"

"Jesus addresses the plight of the masses, that's why. He speaks to the heart of every person who is ready to be liberated from the fetid pool of stagnant water, as you put it. The living conditions in those times were appalling under Roman rule, but the message that Jesus brought spoke to the heart of man not the mind. The heart is the seat of Soul. His message was embraced with such passion that it overwhelmed Jesus. He did not expect the reaction that he received. What the world doesn't know about the teaching that Jesus revealed in his gospel of salvation is that Holy Spirit will flow out of the messenger in direct proportion to the world's need, and the world at the time of Jesus was desperate for a savior. Despite himself, Jesus was deified by a people hungry for a savior. The world drew the Christ

Consciousness out of Jesus, but the world misunderstood his message of conscious spiritual evolution. Jesus came from the inner circle of life to give all those Souls who were ready to be harvested the secret to their spiritual destiny, and to this day no one has ever explained the esoteric power of Christ's sayings; and that, Cassie, continues to baffle me."

"Can you?" I asked.

"What? Explain Christ's sayings?"

"Yes," I said.

"It's the same teaching that I lived under the guidance of Sam the Man. Yes, I can explain Christ's secret teaching. But what would be the point?"

"It would clear up a lot of unresolved issues for me."

"Oh," David said, realizing how important it was for me. "Certainly. I thought you meant for me to explain it for the public. I don't think I'd bother trying to do that. The public can only digest so much, and no more. That's why the Living Atma Master has chosen to reveal the secret teachings of Atma through the imagery of simple stories. People can identify with simple stories. They don't have to think so much. That's why the Mullah Nasrudin is so popular in Sufi lore. He provides the simple imagery that speaks to the heart of the secret teaching. So, what's this secret teaching that is so difficult to convey to the outer circle of life?"

"Are you asking me?"

"Yes," David said.

"Well, from everything that I've studied I would say it has to do with the transformation of consciousness. Isn't that what the spiritual exercises of Atma are all about? We transform our consciousness by burning off karma with the spiritual exercises of Atma, and the more karma we burn off the more spiritually self-realized we become. That's it, isn't it?"

David bent over and gave me a long, lingering kiss. I held his head to prolong the kiss, but he wanted to complete his thought. I hated it when he did that.

"That's good," he said, oblivious to the effect that he had on me. "All you have to add to that is the Satma, the Dream Master, and the

Atma initiations. But the public won't buy it. It's too esoteric for the average person. Jesus revealed this when he said that his teaching was for those who had ears to hear and eyes to see. Jesus was referring to the level of a person's consciousness. If a person couldn't hear the inner meaning of what he was saying, he wasn't ready for the secret teaching of self-transformation. Like Nichodemus. He couldn't fathom what Jesus meant by being born again. How can a man return to his mother's womb? he asked Jesus. He took Christ's sayings literally, as does everyone in the outer circle of life. Only those Souls who have had enough life experience to awaken their spiritual senses will hear the inner meaning of the secret teaching. I'll be honest with you, Cassie. It came as a surprise to me when I began to hear the Word..."

"The Word?" I interrupted.

"Yes, the Word. That's the best description for the secret teaching that comes from the inner circle of life. It's the Atma, Cassie. Holy Spirit, the Sound Current, the water of living truth, *Baraka,* or the *subtlety* as I was taught. It's the same reconciling power of God that brings the lower nature of Soul into agreement with its higher nature. This is the secret of Christ's sayings, and the secret of the Way. This is the mystery that the outer circle of life cannot penetrate because society is not evolved enough yet to hear the inner meaning of Christ's words. To hear the meaning of Christ's words, you have to hear the Word within the words, and this cannot be done until one is ready to be harvested. It's that simple."

"You were about to tell me when you started to hear the Word," I said, curious to know all about David's secret life. "Can you tell me?"

"Of course I can tell you. *'The declaration's better than the secret,'* David said, and laughed. "Well, for the longest time I couldn't fathom what Sam meant when he told us that all those sayings on his basement wall were tools of the Sufi trade. Each saying served a specific purpose, but it took a long time to come to that realization. You see, Cassie, the Sufi secret lies in the esoteric knowledge that the spiritual self is made up of two separate selves, one human and one spiritual. Once you grasp this concept the puzzle of Christ's sayings begins to make sense. Christ's sayings were tools also, just like the sayings on Sam's wall. These special sayings have the power to transform one's consciousness. This is why the Sufis call them tools. What does a carpenter do with his tools? He measures, cuts, and hammers. He builds. He constructs. And if he's remodeling an old house he has to deconstruct first, doesn't he? He has to take apart what's there so he can rebuild the new part. You have to die before you are reborn. That's the essence of the Sufi teaching. As the Sufis say, *`you have to die before you die.'* It's the same with Jesus Christ's teaching. The sayings of Jesus deconstruct the lower self and reconstruct the lower self so it becomes like the higher self. *`Be ye perfect even as your Father which is in heaven is perfect,'* said Jesus."

David stopped talking to give me time to digest this esoteric wisdom, but I had one question that I had to ask and it couldn't wait. "David, my abortion was the deconstruction part of my life, wasn't it? My abortion tore down the Roman Catholic part of my personality. That's why it was so painful, wasn't it?"

"Yes," he said, and stroked my forehead. "You had to experience that for your spiritual self to grow. You've been a nurse for some time now. You must have experienced the change in some of your cancer patients. Being Atmans, we know that karma is responsible for what befalls us. Cancer is a karmic disease. Some professionals even call it a personality disease. These people don't know how close they are to the truth, because karma is created by the type of life one lives, which speaks to the personality. Like smoking, for example. Now here's the crux of the mystery, Cassie. The personality is the 'I' of Soul's lower self. If the 'I' of the lower self is not big enough for our spiritual self to grow it has to be deconstructed and then reconstructed into a larger 'I'. This is what Sufism is designed to do. This is what Christ's teaching is designed to do also. The personality that cannot allow the spiritual self to grow has to be deconstructed and reconstructed into a larger, more expansive personality that will allow Soul to grow. When man can't do this on his own, life will do it for him with his own karma. This is why people get diseases like cancer. Their personality needs to be deconstructed and rebuilt for Soul to grow. The world is mystified by miraculous cures. Why do some people experience a miraculous healing and others don't? The answer is simple. People who experience miraculous healings have learned their karmic lesson. They have a shift in their personal paradigm, if you will. They have changed their attitude about life, about themselves, and about God even. Change your attitude and you change your life. Your abortion forced you to change your attitude about life, did it not? You had to break down that part of your personality that kept you from growing spiritually. It's unfortunate that you had to experience that, Cassie, but that was life's way of forcing you to grow spiritually. The world cannot see it, but karma is the most merciful of God's laws. Karma is man's best friend, even when it comes in the guise of diseases like cancer, the death of a child, a house fire, the loss of a job, divorce, or what have you. Karma happens *for* us, Cassie; not *to* us. Without karma we would never grow. We'd be stuck in the same life forever. God, what a thought..."

I couldn't believe it! It was as though the howling wind had pierced my ears and I *heard* the Word for the very first time. *"Wow!"* I exclaimed, totally blown away by David's spiritual wisdom.

"What?" David asked, surprised by my outburst.

"Karma is man's best friend!" I exclaimed again, and sat up straight to look David in the face. "Do you realize how powerful that is?"

David laughed. "Of course I do. That's the same reaction that I had many times with Sam the Man. I don't want to give myself more credit than I deserve; but sometimes you make me feel like my Sufi teacher."

"What do you mean by that?"

"Sam told me that the function of a Sufi teacher is to open up the mind of a seeker so he may recognize his own destiny, but you're an Atman, and a Third Initiate at that, so you're definitely not a seeker; you're a doer. But we do seem to have the kind of relationship that I had with Sam when I was his student. I suspect it's because the teacher, the teaching, and the taught all share one thing in common— the *subtlety*. That mysterious essence that we call the Atma force. The Atma is the Word. The Word is in me, as it is in you, and the Word always flows from the greater to the lesser. This is why the Sufis say that a seeker has to have a certain amount of the *subtlety* to attract a teacher. This is what Jesus meant when he said that for some it was given to know the mysteries of the kingdom of heaven, and for others it was not. And this curiously enough opens the door to the tragic flaw of Christ's teaching; a flaw so imbedded in the psyche of man that it's become virtually irreversible."

Startled by David's comment, I stared wide-eyed. "What flaw?"

David stopped and listened to the howling wind. "Cassie, you can't go home. It's getting worse out there. Phone the kids and tell them you're staying over."

"I completely forgot," I said, feeling embarrassed. "I always get caught up in our talks. Give me a minute, please," I said, and called home. I explained that I was staying over at David's, and then said, "Patrick, there are four packages of DiGiorno's rising crust pizzas in the freezer. The pizza pans are in the drawer at the bottom of the stove. Put two pizzas in the oven at 350 degrees. Check them in thirty minutes. If the bottom is crusty, they're done. Got that?"

"Got it," Patrick said.

"Okay. I'll see you tomorrow, then."

"Okay, Mom. What are you guys doing for food?"

"David's going to surprise me."

"Can we have some of the chocolate cake you baked this morning?"

"Just one piece each."

"With ice cream?"

"One scoop each. No more."

"Yeah, right. Is that it?"

"Yes. Where's Cindy?"

"Right here. You want to talk to her?"

"Yes, please."

"Hi Mom. What's up?"

"I have to stay at David's tonight, sweetheart. The storm's getting really bad. Patrick's going to put the pizza on for you guys. I'll see you tomorrow, okay?"

"Okay, Mom. Can we have some cake, too?"

"Yes, dear…"

I joined David in the kitchen. He had already started dinner, with a glass of wine for us waiting on the counter. I loved the space of

David's house, especially his kitchen.

It wasn't a large kitchen, but it was very functional. Women love a functional kitchen, and this helped to make David's new house very marketable. He had ample cupboard space, with a pantry built into the maple cupboards, as well as a bookshelf stacked with David's growing collection of cookbooks and DVDs—Jacques Pepin, Julia Childs, Lydia's Italy, Molto Mario and others that he ordered from PBS. There was a working island with a marble tiled countertop where he was preparing Pasta Puttanesca and veal for dinner.

I asked if I could help, but David wouldn't hear of it. He just loved cooking. "This recipe is from Molto Mario Batali's cookbook," he said, as he chopped the garlic.

David planned to live in his new house for one to two years, depending upon how his contracting work went; and then he would sell it and build another. It had taken him three houses to own this new house outright, and every house that he built now would finance two more new houses, and he planned to build five more and then retire from contracting and devote his time to writing poetry and annotating his Sufi translations.

I asked him to explain exactly what he meant, and he said, "I want to make the esoteric wisdom of the Way accessible to the exoteric mind of man. That's my dream."

On the only available wall space in the kitchen, which was painted a soft, receding harvest gold that made his kitchen cheerful anytime of year, especially in the middle of a winter storm, he had hung an art piece that I had not seen before. I took my wine with me and studied it, but I couldn't make out the writing at the bottom of the piece. It was in another language. "This is new, David," I said.

"I just got it last weekend. Binny finally finished it."

It was a copper engraving with thirty embossed rays of sunlight emanating from an embossed sun, and attached to the end of each ray of light was a flying bird with its head positioned towards the sun. There was writing at the bottom of the symbol, but it wasn't English. I guessed it to be Persian. Probably a Sufi saying.

"What does the writing say?" I asked, as he chopped a red onion for his veal, tomato, basil, and onion recipe that I was looking forward to because veal was one of my favorite viands, to use David's word. Kevin and I had eaten Pasta Puttanesca at *Geno's* back in Vancouver, and I had prepared it at home; but not David's Sicilian recipe with capers and anchovies, and I was looking forward to it as much as the veal. Both recipes seemed right for the snowstorm that had moved into Georgian Bay from the northern states.

"That's my favorite Sufi saying," he replied.

"Don't tell me. Let me guess. *He who tastes not knows not.*"

David laughed. "But do you know what the symbol means?"

"No. I don't have a clue," I said.

"Obviously you haven't read *A Conference of the Birds* yet, have you?"

"I haven't had a chance, David."

"You might as well wait for my translation, then. That's the symbol that Binny and I have worked out for the book cover of my translation of *A Conference of the Birds.*"

"What does it mean?" I asked, eager to know now.

"It symbolizes the number of birds in the allegory that completed their journey home to God," David said, as he stirred the garlic and onions in his pan for the veal. "The sun symbolizes God, and the thirty birds the hardy Souls who looked into the Face of God."

"Oh!" I said, making the connection. In a flash of insight, I saw that David was one of those hardy Souls who had looked into the Face of God when he saw the Satma's face in the sun and was taken to the Anami Lok, the Body of God. "This piece symbolizes your Georgian Bay sunset experience, doesn't it?" I asked, to verify my insight.

"I can't get anything by you, can I?" he said, and grinned.

"I like it. Not as much as your portrait..."

"What's wrong with my portrait?" David said, feigning hurt.

"Oh, nothing really," I said, with a devilish smile.

Thankfully, David didn't pursue it. He concentrated on his dinner. I enjoyed watching him working in his kitchen. He reminded me of a head bartender I knew when I was working my way through university. David was a natural multi-tasker, and he moved around in his kitchen like a master chef in a five star restaurant.

Dinner was ready within the hour, and it was simple and

delicious. "That's the secret to good food, Cassie," he said. "Simple ingredients, and one very special spice."

"What special spice?"

"Love," he said, his face lighting up.

"Have you always loved cooking, David?"

He laughed. "Not at all. My mother's a bland cook. My father's a meat and potatoes man, and my mother wasn't allowed to venture into new culinary domains. No, Cassie; it was my Sufi teacher who got me interested. He told me that I had to find a hobby that I would learn to love, and to learn everything that I could about it. Sam's hobby is photography. I enjoyed trying out different restaurants when I was working for the *Star*, and I fell in love with Mediterranean cuisine, especially Italian. So I decided to make cooking my hobby."

"Why would Sam tell you to get a hobby?" I asked, knowing very well by now that Sam the Man was no ordinary person.

"You're not going to believe this..."

"Oh yes, I will," I interjected. "When it comes to you and Sam and Binny and Sufism, I'll believe anything you tell me!"

David laughed. "Alright, I'll tell you. Sam told me that a hobby opens up the channels to the creative forces of life. Photography is one of Sam's pipelines to *Baraka*. His love of photography opens him up to the creative life force, and my love of cooking does the same for me; but there's also an esoteric dimension which I'm not sure I should reveal."

"If you don't, I'll never speak to you again!"

Smiling, David explained the most ingenious spiritual technique that I had ever heard of in my life, not that I had heard of many; but it arrested my attention: "'*He who tastes not, knows not*,' said Rumi; and cooking has become my metaphor for life," David said, speaking in a lower, almost secretive voice. "Every time I try out a new recipe, I create a new opportunity to collect *Baraka*, the life force. You see, Cassie; I love the taste of food, the magical blend of ingredients that create new taste sensations. And every time I try a new recipe that I love, I *non-identify* with that dish when I'm eating it. This is a Sufi technique of *conscious detachment*. This way all the consciousness of pleasure that I experience with my senses while eating, I transform with the technique of *non-identification* and store it, as Jesus would say, in heaven where the thieves and moths and rust can't get at it. In a word, I've learned how to nourish my spiritual consciousness simply by cooking exciting new recipes and then *non-identifying* with them when I'm eating. But again, this is such a difficult technique to master that only he who has had a taste of it will know what it means. This is why Rumi's saying *he who tastes not knows not* has become my favorite motto."

"You never cease to amaze me, David Oakly!" I exclaimed.

David didn't react to my emotional outburst. He waited a moment, and then very casually said, "Why don't we finish the conversation we began before dinner? I was about to make a point about Christianity's tragic flaw."

"What were we talking about? I don't remember."

"Your abortion. How it changed your life."

"My God!" I exclaimed again as I realized that I had completely forgotten that we were talking about my abortion. *"How you so easily transport me to another world!"*

"We don't have to talk about it if you don't want to," David said, once again not reacting to my emotional outburst.

Collecting myself, I said, "I have to talk about it, David. I want to understand why I did it. You were saying that I had to have that experience to grow spiritually..."

"Yes," David said, and got up from the table and grabbed my hand and led me to his comfortable second-hand couch by the warm, cozy fire in his gas fireplace.

The wind howled ferociously now and the snow pelted against the windows, but I smiled because I welcomed any excuse to spend a night with David. "That's the way life works, Cassie," he continued when I was snuggled into his body. "We get the experiences we need to break up the karma that keeps us from growing spiritually, and you had to have your abortion to break free of the hold that your Christian faith still had on you. But I explained that. You wanted to know what I meant about Atmans putting the carriage in front of the horse..."

"I remember now!" I exclaimed again, and sat up to look David in the face. David smiled at my excitement. "I was going to make my point with the tragic flaw of Christianity," he said, and pulled me back into his warm body. "To understand this tragic flaw, I have to tell you about what the Sufis call the 'work self,'" he explained, fondling my hair. "This is a transitional self that one creates when he deconstructs the personality of his lower self. It's a neuter, or buffer self if you will; and its purpose is to absorb the psychic shock of deconstructing the lower self. That's the tragic flaw of Christ's teaching. It short-circuits this buffer self and goes straight from deconstruction to reconstruction of the lower self. Jesus reveals this in his famous saying, `He who shall lose his life shall find his life, and he who finds his life shall lose it.` Sam had me work this lethal tool for one whole year, and believe me, Cassie, this was the most excruciating year of my apprenticeship with Sam the Man!"

I paused before replying. "I think I understand the analogy, David," I finally said, "but I don't quite follow what you mean by this buffer self. Is it a separate self, like a dissociated personality?"

"No, nothing like that. It's a conscious self that one creates through esoteric effort. Had you a buffer self, you wouldn't have been so traumatized by your abortion," David explained, and I could tell by his voice that he was connected with his *inspiration,* which he had probably done while eating dinner in that esoteric way because I could see it in his face as he ate. "A buffer self is a transitional self," he went on, his quiet voice resounding with spiritual certainty. "It's a disciplined, spiritually conscious yes-no part of one's new personality that bridges the lower self with the higher self that Christ's teaching does not provide. If you recall, Jesus had a saying that went like this, `Let your communication be Yea Yea, Nay Nay, for whatsoever is more than these cometh of evil.` That's Christ's teaching in a nutshell. It's one or the other for Jesus. There's no buffer self. That's the tragic flaw of his teaching responsible for all the fanaticism in Christianity. For Christians, one is either for them or against them. This mindset is fixed in their psyche. When Bush declared war on terrorism, didn't he pronounce that one was either with him or against him? Where's the buffer self? Where's the comprising self? Where's the room for reasonable negotiation? There isn't any room with this Christian mindset. This is why you took the public by surprise with your letter to

McDuffy. It never occurred to anyone that there was a third side to their Christian either/or mindset on abortion. Your open letter was no less devastating to Christian dogma than Galileo's proof that the earth is not the center of the universe. You struck a mortal blow to Christianity with your letter."

Wow! It was like thousands of years of wax had been removed from my spiritual ears, and I couldn't stop *hearing* the Word in David's every single word!

"Are you with me so far, then?" he asked.

"All the way!" I had never been so excited with David as I was at that moment. All of my conflicted feelings about Jesus had been resolved at once, and I felt light-headed.

Of course David would have to smile his irresistibly sweet smile, which made my toes curl with excitement. And to top it off, he bent over and pecked me lightly on the cheek. I couldn't take it. I hiked him down and kissed him so firmly on the mouth that he had to come up for air! Needless to say, we made love on his Persian rug.

David could have restrained himself, but he chose not to. As he explained to me, "Making love is like eating. It's neither yes nor no for me, Cassie. I have the freedom to say yes to no, and no to yes. That's what defines the buffer self."

"I'm not made that way," I said. "It was yes-yes for me, and if you would have said no, I wouldn't have spoken to you for six months!"

David burst into laughter. "And well you shouldn't! That's what makes you who you are, Cassie. Life is an individual journey, so I don't expect you to be like me, nor anyone else. I've fallen for you because you are who you are, and I love who you are!"

"That's the nicest thing anyone has ever said to me," I said, and kissed him tenderly on the cheek. "Thank you, David."

"You're welcome," he said. "Should we continue, or would you like to just snuggle up and fall asleep in my arms?"

"I want both!" I exclaimed.

"Let's just cozy up and rest for a while, then. Later we can have a cup of hot apple cider or tea and we can complete our discourse."

Memories of our past lifetime flashed before my eyes. That's what my dearest friend Michael used to say all the time. We would take a break and complete our discourse later. This was an unbelievable night!

At my request, David made a pot of green tea and we continued our discourse on the tragic flaw of Jesus Christ's teaching. The storm outside was getting worse. I had never heard wind howl with such ferocity before. Out of the blue, I blurted, *"That's the wind of change blowing out there!"*

"Why did you say that?" David asked, with a look of curiosity.

"I just had this insight that it's the wind of change," I said, full of excitement. "It has to do with what you're saying about the tragic flaw in Christ's teaching. The wind out there is ferocious. I've never heard such a wind. I think what you're saying about Christ's teaching *is* the ferocious wind of change. I can feel it, David. Do you see what I'm saying?"

"Perfectly. But I didn't make the connection. If the Atma has made this connection for you, I don't doubt it. The fact is, something has to happen. Christianity can no longer satisfy man's spiritual hunger. The personality of the world is too small for the Soul of the world, and it has to be deconstructed and reconstructed for the Soul of the world to grow. If the Holy Spirit of Atma spoke to you, then the howling wind outside speaks the spiritual wind of change that's going to take place in social consciousness."

"It spoke to me, David. I heard it loud and clear. The tragic flaw that you discovered in Jesus Christ's teaching is going to bring about the wind of change that's going to deconstruct the Christian personality. *I know it!"*

"To be honest with you, Cassie, I don't know. It may or it may not, but it doesn't really matter to me one way or the other. I live my own life and let the world take care of itself. What will be will be, as the old song goes. So, to complete my thought on the flaw in Christ's teaching. I confess that I'm not certain that Jesus deliberately short-circuits the process of freeing Soul from its lower self by telling man that he has to die to his life to save his life, but his crucifixion seems to point to it. Let me explain..."

"Before you do, tell me why you think Jesus died on the cross," I interrupted. "We know he didn't die for the sins of the world because that's not possible. Karma is a personal responsibility. So why would Jesus sacrifice his life on the cross?"

"That's what I was about to tell you. I suspect Jesus used his own life to speak the message of his teaching, which can be summed up in his saying, *'He who shall lose his life shall save his life.'* Sam the Man brought this to my attention, but it wasn't until I put Christ's sayings to the test that I began to see what Sam was pointing to. Let me see if I can make sense of the drama of Christ's life within the context of the secret teaching, because outside the context of the secret teaching of self-transformation, it doesn't make any sense at all..."

"What do you mean by outside the context?" I interrupted, to not lose the thread of David's subtle thought. I felt privileged listening to David, like I was his only student.

"Outside the context would be the literal understanding of Christ's teaching," he explained. "The world has been led to believe that Jesus sacrificed his life to wash away the stain of original sin. When one is baptized in Jesus, he is saved. The Son of God died for the sins of the world, and unless one accepts Jesus as his savior he cannot be saved. That's the heart of the literal exoteric message of Christ's teaching, but the Word within the words of Christ's teaching speaks otherwise. The Word tells us to work out our own salvation, which St. Paul expressly said in one of his letters to his followers..."

"With fear and trembling!" I excitedly interrupted.

"Yes. Work out your own salvation with fear and trembling," David calmly said, completing the quotation. "Why fear and trembling? Because it takes courage and hard work to deconstruct the personality, that's why. What does that entail, anyway? Just what does it mean to deconstruct the personality? Can you guess what that involves, Cassie?"

I smiled at the image that flashed across my mind. "It's like a complete makeover. But it's on the inside, not the outside. It's a personality makeover, right?"

David laughed. "That's a nice analogy. Yes, it's a complete personality makeover. This is what Jesus Christ's teaching was intended to do, but his death on the cross threw a wrench into the gear

300

box. The Sufis *know* that the lower self of man has to be transformed for the spiritual self to be realized. That's the heart of the Atma teachings also, but only in Atma-Gare we have the most direct method to accomplish this goal. We have the Satma and the spiritual exercises of Atma. This makes it so much easier. Nonetheless, the goal is the same: to free Soul from its lower self. This lower self is the consciousness of our human self. Sufism is clear on this point. Soul is held hostage by its lower self. It's not entirely correct to say that our lower self holds our spiritual self hostage, because this is just the way the evolution of the self unfolds. So along comes Jesus with his message of spiritual liberation. He is so overwhelmed by the reconciling power of Holy Spirit that he sacrifices his life on the cross to get his message out to the world that he is the way, the truth, and the life and only through him can one be saved. Jesus used his death on the cross to speak the message of dying to one's life to save one's life, but his death was supposed to be taken symbolically, not literally. His death on the cross was supposed to speak the secret teaching of self-transformation through the sacrifice of one's lower self, but the world did not hear the Word in Christ's teaching, and the end result is this tragic flaw in the most confused spiritual teaching in the world next to Buddhism."

"I think I'm clear on this," I said, deliberately avoiding the subject of Buddhism because I didn't want to open that door. "But just to make sure, David, let me see if I understand you correctly. Soul is who we are, right?" I asked, feeling more like his student than his lover.

"Yes. Soul is our spiritual self. We all began our journey through life as spiritual atoms of God. But we did not have self-consciousness when we came into the world. The Divine Plan of God is designed for the atoms of God's Body to go through the evolutionary process of life to create this unit of God-consciousness called the self. This unit of self-consciousness, which takes billions of years to create through natural evolution, is a new 'I' of God. Creating a new 'I' of God is how God grows. When the atom of God gives birth to its own self-consciousness, which happens in the primordial life of man, it will continue to evolve through the creation and resolution of its own karma. Because the atom of God now has a self, it is the personal karma that the self creates that determines the distinct nature of the self. This is why no two Souls are exactly alike. We are all individuals because of our own individual karma. But as the self evolves from lifetime to lifetime it begins to sense its own divine essence. The evolution of the human self inevitably gives birth to its own spiritual self. This spiritual self is our real self, because our human self is merely the medium for the atom of God to realize its God self. This God self is the realized self-consciousness of Soul. This is why in Atma we say that we are Soul. But Atmans are blissful in their ignorance of the process that brings the God self into being. This is what I meant by putting the carriage in front of the horse. But let's not go there now. Let's complete this thought on the tragic flaw of Christ's teaching first, okay?"

"By all means," I said, in awe of David's esoteric knowledge.

He took a drink of tea, and continued. "To explain the tragic flaw in Christ's teaching, imagine three concentric circles. The inner circle is the Esoteric Circle of Life, where Soul is self-realized and God-conscious. The middle circle is the Mesoteric Circle of Life, where Soul lives a conscious spiritual life for the purpose of becoming spiritually self-realized. The final circle is the outer, or Exoteric Circle of Life. This outer circle of life comprises the vast majority of mankind. Now imagine a truth seeker who begins his spiritual journey in the outer circle of life, working his way to the middle circle of life, and then all the way into the inner circle of life where the Word comes from. Let's call this seeker Jesus. He works his way through life all the way through the middle circle to the inner circle where he becomes a God-realized man. He then decides to come back to the outer circle of life to teach the world how to get to the inner circle. He teaches the world with the Word that is contained in his sayings. He knows from having lived the secret teaching that only by living his sayings can one die to his life to save his life. This is Christ's way of deconstructing the personality for Soul to realize its divine nature. Jesus is a serious savior. He decides to convey his message of dying to one's life to save one's life by sacrificing his own life on the cross, but the world interpreted Christ's death on the cross to mean the sacrifice of the Son of God for the salvation of the world. In a word, man has been led to believe that he can go from the outer circle of life straight to the salvation of the inner circle without going through the middle circle. And that, Cassie, is Christianity's tragic flaw!"

"Wow," I said. "So that's why I was torn from my faith! It's wrong, isn't it? *The whole Christian dogma is wrong!"*

David laughed. "Yes. It's wrong. The middle circle is the most important stage of Soul's journey through life. It's here that we deconstruct the personality and reconstruct it for Soul to realize its divine essence. Christianity completely bypasses the middle circle of conscious evolution by taking Soul out of the outer circle straight to the salvation of the inner circle with Christ's death on the cross, without all the work involved in the middle circle. It's to the middle circle that St. Paul speaks when he tells us to work out our own salvation with fear and trembling. Christianity says that all one has to do to be saved is to be baptized in Jesus Christ. Christianity believes salvation is a gift granted by God with Christ's death upon the cross, but Christianity is completely wrong. Do you see the tragic flaw now, Cassie?"

No sooner did David complete his thought than the fiercest blast of wind stormed the house and practically shook it off its foundation. It startled both of us. I instantly grabbed David and held him. *"What was that?"*

"The wind of change," David said, and laughed.

I did too, but nervously. I couldn't help myself, despite how terrified I felt. I held David tightly. I felt so safe holding him that I didn't want to let go. "David," I said, fearing the worst; "the wind won't blow your house over, will it?"

"No way! I built my house on a solid foundation," he said, and laughed. I knew he was referring to one of Jesus' sayings, and I joined him. "Alright, now I can bring this discourse home. You asked me before dinner what I meant by putting the carriage in front of the horse, didn't you?"

"Yes. But I'm not sure I want to hear it now."

"Why not?"

"It might just blow your house down."

"It just might do that," David said, with a smile.

"Is it that powerful a truth?"

"I believe it is."

"So what does it mean then to put the carriage in front of the horse?"

"That's just my way of saying you can't bypass the middle circle of life, that's all. This is the most important stage of Soul's evolution through life, and it can't be bypassed. Let the carriage symbolize the God-realized state of the inner circle of life, and let the horse symbolize the conscious work of the middle circle of life that Soul has to do to realize its divine nature. Soul is who we are. Soul is our spiritual self. But how does Soul become aware of its divine nature if not through the unit of self-consciousness we call 'I'?"

"I'm not following you," I said.

"How many times have you heard Atmans say, I am Soul? I hear this all the time at Atma functions. This perception has become the mindless mantra of the Atma community. I am Soul, we are Soul, and Soul exists because God loves it; and all we have to do is realize that we're already perfect. Atmans believe it's that simple. Just do your spiritual exercises and you will realize that you're already spiritually perfect. That's the mindset. I have no problem with the truth of this perception. What I have a problem with is the emphasis on Soul instead of the 'I' of Soul. Do you see the distinction?"

I reflected for a moment. "I'm afraid I don't," I confessed.

"Let me give you the context, then," David said, very patiently. "Do you remember me telling you that Soul's journey through life is a journey of the alone to the Alone?"

"Yes," I said, all excited again. That was *the* mystery that I was waiting for David to clear up for me. I just couldn't fathom what he meant by that.

"Alright. The atom of God goes through life to create its own identity. The atom of God is the seed of its own perfect self, just as the acorn is the seed of its own perfect oak tree. The atom of God evolves through life to become a unit of God-consciousness, which must go through the middle circle of life to realize its divine nature. To get to the inner circle, the 'I' of God has to go through the middle circle where it is made so pure that the atom of God becomes aware of its divine nature. It's this purification of the self that I call the horse, and the carriage is the divine nature of God. If you will, the carriage is the God self. So the horse pulls the carriage all the way to the inner circle where the atom of God becomes aware of its God nature. Do you see what I mean by the subtle distinction between Soul and the 'I' of Soul? Just as Christians believe that salvation is a gift granted by God, so do Atmans believe that they are already spiritually perfect. Atmans place their emphasis on Soul, not on the individuated 'I' of Soul. It is the 'I' of Soul that has to pull the carriage into the inner circle of life, not the other way around. It is the 'I' of Soul that has to take the initiative and do the hard work. Atmans expect Soul to pull the 'I', but we can't just give it all up to Soul as Atmans are wont to do. This attitude takes away the initiative for self-reliance and makes one Atma-dependent. It robs the Atman of the inspiration to be creative and self-reliant. This is why Zak Tarzman said that the true man of God does not ask God for help; he solves his own problems. How can someone exercise his spiritual muscles if he depends upon the Atma to do everything for him? This is why the Atma community isn't growing as it could be growing. This Atma-dependent attitude chokes the flow of Atma. Soul is perfect unto itself, but the 'I' of Soul has to be purified for Soul to realize its own perfection, and this takes initiative, creativity, and self-reliance, not blind Atma-dependence. It's a subtle distinction, Cassie, and one that Atmans may find too intimidating for their lazy liking; but this is how I've experienced my own journey to the inner circle of life. And at the risk of sounding messianic, I speak from the consciousness of the Alone."

I had to catch my breath before I spoke. "You got this from your sunset experience, didn't you?"

"In a manner of speaking, yes."

"What do you mean?"

"I got it, but then I had to earn it. That's the difference between putting the horse in front of the carriage and the carriage in front of the horse," David replied.

The wind stopped howling. I listened. I heard nothing. Absolutely nothing. It was dead still outside. It felt so eerie that a cold chill ran up my spine!

David felt my body quiver. He put his arm around me and I snuggled into his taut, muscular body to calm myself. He held me close, stroking my arm softly. He held me in quiet, soothing silence, and I gradually drifted off into a deep, restful sleep.

Chapter 22

My Complete Life

My life changed forever after the night of the winter storm. I stopped seeing a distinction between the rest of the world and myself, which was there from the moment I became a member of Atma-Gare. The wind blew down my wall of distinction, and I no longer felt separate from the rest of the world. I was *me*, and the world was what it was, and the only difference was that I *knew* who I was and the rest of the world did not, and I felt like I had been set free from that part of myself that kept me from being complete.

"Before enlightenment, you chop wood and carry water. After enlightenment, you chop wood and carry water," said David, but I never really understood this until after the night of the winter storm. That's what David meant by *hearing* the Word. "The Atma is life; the Atma is the Way; ergo, life is the Way. The Atma is the Atma and life is life for most Atmans, and the Atma magically appears in life as if out of the blue," he said, but after that night I no longer saw the Atma as being separate from life. Life was the Atma for me at every level of its manifestation, from the smile of a newborn infant to the devastation of Hurricane Katrina.

It was difficult, if not impossible to express. I tried to capture it in my journal, but not until I witnessed what David did at the Atma Worship Service in Peterborough did I come to see my new relationship with life. What David did that morning made me realize that I had also given it all up for the Atma, but I only did so by risking everything to live my own life—just as my mentor Doctor Elisabeth Kubler-Ross had done!

I didn't know it, but my own life was the spiritual path that I had always been on. I *was* my own path to my true self, and on the night of the winter storm something magical happened to make me aware that I was never separate from my own life. *That was my moment of enlightenment!*

I was forever pursuing my own life as if it existed out there somewhere, in the foreseeable future, always chasing myself like the rest of the world; but something happened on the night of the winter storm to change all of that. It finally came out in my journal late in the evening when David and I came home from the Atma Worship Service in Peterborough. It was almost midnight and I didn't want to disturb David, but I had to call and tell him. He picked up the phone on the second ring.

"I've just connected the dots, David," I said, all excited.

"What dots?" he asked.

"The Big Dots!" I exclaimed, and waited for his reaction.

After a moment's pause, he said, "Well, are you going to tell me?"

"Our love-making on the night of the storm," I said, and waited.

"Oh?" he said, sounding very intrigued.

I laughed nervously. That was the most romantic night of my entire life. David held back his orgasm to satisfy me. *"Oh my sweet God!"* I screamed in ecstasy. David released his hot volcanic seed inside me with the most explosive climax that any man could possibly have. It took several weeks for the *subtle* energy of David's essence to work its way into my consciousness, and when it did I not only felt different, but I began to *see* life differently, and day-by-day I felt more complete, more connected, and more whole until one day I *saw* all life as one and I had to tell David that I had finally connected the dots.

"Life is, and I am!" I exclaimed to him on the phone. His mystical secret had become a part of me, and my life had changed forever!

Marlene Anderson, the Atma cleric who gave a talk on gratitude at the worship service in Peterborough that David and I attended the same day he introduced me to his parents, was a short, overweight divorcee and mother of two teenage girls.

I picked up a copy of her book after the service and read one or two stories every evening for a week before going to bed and recognized it as a copycat of the *Chicken Soup for the Soul* books. Marlene however saw her book on the cutting edge of the new spirituality finding its way into social consciousness, and she was very proud of herself. "These are original Atma stories, but I use the word Holy Spirit instead of Atma," she told me when she signed her book on the hood of her car after the service. "This book could change your life."

"Oh, really?" I said, with an ironic smile…

"Good morning. My name is Marlene Anderson," she cheerfully introduced herself at the service. "I'm a Sixth Initiate and Atma cleric from Toronto. I'm also a proofreader for Clarence Publishers in Toronto, and a publicist for new authors. I have my own book published. It's called *Old Recipes for the Hungry Soul.* I'm currently working on volume two. I'm also a professional speaker on spiritual topics like dreams, past lives, and Soul travel, and I teach creative writing classes.

Today, I'm going to talk to you about gratitude. I love talking about gratitude. It's one of my favorite topics. In fact, gratitude is the theme of my second volume, *New Recipes for the Hungry Soul.* But first, we're going to HU to open up our Atma pores..."

David and I smiled at Marlene's unselfconscious Toronto-the-only air of self-importance. We closed our eyes and sang HU…

As we sang the Love Song to God my thoughts drifted back to the night of the winter storm. I could not get our lovemaking out of my mind. I had never experienced making love like that. It was perfect. David held nothing back. It was unbelievable. Never in my life was I so sexually satisfied!

I had heard that men who practiced tantric sex could control their orgasm, which was a fantasy that most women would die for, and I had experienced it with David. It was so thoroughly satisfying that it made me feel complete. "This is how every woman should feel after making love," I thought to myself as I softly sang HU.

David was complete. That's what made him so different from anyone I knew. When Marlene brought the HU to a close with "May the blessings be," I opened my eyes and turned to David, and smiled. *I was so in love with him!*

Marlene began her talk on gratitude, but my mind was still on David and our lovemaking on the night of the winter storm. I always enjoyed making love, but as wonderful as making love with my husband was, it was nothing compared to David. Making love with Kevin was satisfying, but it always left me wanting.

That night with David I was so satisfied that I had no desire for more. And what made it even more magical was how I felt the next day and every day since that night. It was like all the separate pieces of my life had been arranged to fit into one complete perfect whole— *which was me!*

"There's something different about you," Karen, one of my senior nurses, said to me two or three days after that night. "Are you in love, Cassie?"

"Why do you say that?" I asked.

"I know you're not pregnant, so it must be love. Do I know the lucky man?"

My smile gave me away.

"Let's hope he's a good one. There aren't too many out there," Karen said.

"Oh Karen, don't be so cynical. There's a good man for every good woman. It's the law of natural balance," I replied, with an irrepressible smile.

"I only wish that were true," she said, and went back to work.

Karen, like most women, was unfulfilled. After two marriages and several abortive relationships, the last one being with Brian Stewart who hit on her after he gave up on me, Karen was still chasing her own life to fill the big hole in her life; but after that night of the winter storm with David I no longer had that driving need to chase after my own life.

My attitude changed. From that night on I felt so centered in who I was that I no longer felt a need to affect my own life. I just *was,* and my relationship with my staff improved immensely. And my love for my children changed also. I seemed to be less possessive, less intrusive, more tolerant, understanding, and forgiving; and they noticed it, too. "Mom, what's gotten into you," Patrick said to me, one week to the day after that magical night.

"What do you mean?" I asked.

"You're not going to send me to the penalty box?" he said, almost in shock.

"Patrick, you're not a kid anymore. You should have known better. Mark is Mark, and he likes to do things his own way. Don't do it again, that's all I ask."

"Yeah, you're right, Mom. I won't bother him anymore."

"Good. Apologize to your brother so we can get on with our lives, okay?"

Patrick just stared at me. "Okay, Mom."

I couldn't believe it myself either. I thought at first that it was love, like Karen said, but it went beyond love because it went against my nature to look at life through rose-colored glasses. It was something much more than love. It was a fundamental change in the nature of my being, and I know this change took place when we made love that night.

Marlene Anderson finished her talk and asked us if we had any gratitude stories we would like to share. I put up my hand. "I have one," I said.

David turned and looked at me. I didn't know why I put my hand up. I didn't know what gratitude story I was going to share, but the words just came out of my mouth of their own accord. "I'm grateful for the abortion I had when I lived in Vancouver. It changed my life forever, and I'm so grateful for the change that I can hardly express it. I just felt I had to share that with you."

"In what way did your abortion change your life?" Marlene asked.

"It freed me from the hold that my Roman Catholic faith had on me," I replied. "But more important, it brought me to Georgian Bay where I was able to use my abortion experience to help serve the Atma by serving life."

"Oh?" Marlene said, her ears perking up for a possible story for volume two of her series. "How did you serve the Atma with your abortion?" she asked.

"By letting people know about reincarnation," I said. "My abortion experience gave me the opportunity to talk about the eternal nature of Soul. The Atma must have wanted this information out there, and I'm grateful for the opportunity to be of service. I've always had a lingering shame for aborting my child, but not after I went public with my letter to the newspapers in response to this new Christian anti-abortion movement in Georgian Bay. I'm not proud of my abortion, but I no longer feel any shame, and for that I'm very, very grateful."

"Wonderful. Could we talk about your experience after the service?"

"If you like," I said.

After two or more gratitude stories from other Atmans, Marlene brought her talk to a close. "Gratitude. That's the spiritual key to a successful, happy life. Remember, the more you give to the Atma, the more the Atma will give to you. That's the Law of Gratitude. So make a habit of being grateful. That's how we serve the Atma and become Spiritual Masters."

After the service Marlene stood by the door to thank everyone for attending. The donation box was sitting on the table beside her that displayed Atma literature for newcomers, and she made sure everyone made a donation to help pay for the room. I only had three twenty-dollar bills in my purse, and there were only a few loonies and toonies in the box, so I didn't feel comfortable taking out change. I normally donated ten dollars at each service. Marlene smiled at my twenty-dollar donation, but when David put in a five-dollar bill she made an obvious frown, and then very boldly said, "Is that it?"

"I beg your pardon?" said David.

Marlene glanced at the donation box, and repeated, "Is that it?"

Without batting an eye, David took out his wallet, opened it, and took out three one hundred dollar bills and placed them into the box. He then put his hand into his front pocket and took out two folded bills, a ten and a twenty, and placed them also into the donation box. He reached his hand into his pocket once more and took out all of his change, one loonie, two quarters, a nickel, a dime, and two pennies. He placed them all into the donation box as well. He looked down at Marlene, who was five inches shorter than him, and said, "When you're willing to give it all up for the Atma, then you will be ready for Mastership. *Baraka bashad,"* he added, and walked out the door.

Marlene, never at a loss for words, was struck dumb.

I stepped in closer and gave her an Atma hug. In a soft whisper, I said, "I'd love to share my abortion story with you, Marlene, but I think I'll save it for my own book someday. But I will buy a copy of your first book. I'll be waiting outside for you."

On the drive to David's parents after I purchased a copy of Marlene's book, he said to me, "I guess you have to treat lunch, Cassie. I'm all tapped out."

I burst into laughter. *"I love you, David Oakly!"*

"But do you think she got it?" he asked.

"I doubt it," I said, still in awe of David's shocking gesture. "It's one thing to know what it means to give, but quite another to do it, isn't it?"

"Exactly," he said, and made a left turn to his parent's old-fashioned, unprepossessing red brick, three-bedroom bungalow in a quiet, heavily treed cul-de-sac. We walked up the sidewalk and up three cement steps to the front door. David rang the doorbell.

His mother answered. As tall as David, she was lanky and looked austere. She wore a metallic chain around her neck for her glasses, and her gray-brown hair was neatly styled with every hair in place. She was neatly dressed in black slacks, a starched white blouse, and a deep-red cardigan sweater buttoned half way. I expected them to hug, but she didn't show that kind of affection for her son. David introduced me. "I'm very pleased to meet you, Mrs. Oakly," I said, giving her my hand.

"Oh please, call me Vera. Come in," she said, giving me her limp hand.

David's father was in his den reading his paper. David told me that his father read the local *Tribune* four times every day; the first time to catch the big political news and any editorial *faux pas*; the second time to catch all the juicy human interest stories, with a special fascination for regional gossip; the third time to catch anything that he might have missed the first two times; and finally he lingered through the sports pages like a man having dessert after a full, three course meal. David opened the door and we stepped into his den, which reeked of nicotine.

"Dad, I'd like you to meet someone."

"Who?" his father responded, without turning to look.

"A very good friend," David said, hoping he would turn around, but he didn't take his nose out of the paper. He was having dessert.

We waited, but his father still didn't respond. David walked up to him, pushed the paper down so he could look his father in the face, and said, "Dad, I'd like you to meet someone. You can spare us a minute, can't you?"

"I suppose," his father said, and wheeled his chair around. He gave me a critical look, and said, "You're David's good friend?"

I couldn't help but stare. He was missing one leg. I caught myself, and said, "Cassie O'Shaunnesy. It's a pleasure, Mr. Oakly."

"Likewise," he said, and fell silent.

I didn't know what to say, and just stood waiting for something to happen; but nothing did. Mr. Oakly made no gesture to shake my hand. Resting his hands on top of his newspaper on his lap, his right thumb and two fingers stained a dirty yellow with nicotine, he stared at us as though challenging us to say something, but we didn't. It was the most awkward few moments of my life. Finally David broke the silence. "You can go back to your paper now," he said, and his father rolled his wheelchair back to where it was and resumed reading. David and I went into the living room and joined his mother. I felt very strange. Like something had just been taken away from me.

"I only made lunch for three," his mother said, unapologetically. "You should have told me you were going to bring a friend."

"We're not staying for lunch. I'm taking Cassie to *Binny's Diner*. I'm going to meet an old friend of mine there," David said.

"Let me take your father his lunch, and then we can get our business out of the way," she said. "Cassie, would you excuse us please?"

"By all means," I said, and David and his mother went into the kitchen. David brought me a cup of fresh coffee while I waited. David told me that his father always had fresh coffee after lunch, so his mother had it ready. I thanked David, with a nervous smile.

Aldous Oakly refuses to be called Al. He was one of the few surviving World War II veterans left in Peterborough. He lost his right leg during the Battle of Dieppe, which was a disaster for the Canadian soldiers. Nearly one thousand Canadian soldiers died when the Allied forces invaded the German-occupied port of Dieppe on the northern coast of France on August 19, 1942, and nearly two thousand were taken prisoner. Lucky to come out alive, Aldous Oakly was never the same after he lost his leg. The government paid for his education after the war, and when he retired as a copy editor at the Peterborough *Tribune* he only left the house to go to the Royal Canadian Legion for his daily quota of beer.

"He used to drive to his local branch of the Legion before he lost his license permanently for drunk driving," David explained, "but he still puts on his prosthesis and goes by taxi five days a week. He drinks his three beers and returns by taxi for dinner. Mom has dinner ready precisely at five-thirty every day, but she never eats with dad. They eat separately, and they sleep in separate rooms. They never talk, except for household matters; and he smokes only in his den. That was the only condition that mom placed on dad, or she would have left him."

"And I thought I grew up in a dysfunctional family," I said to David after he shared this with me on the way to *Binny's Diner.* "My God, David, I'm surprised you still have your sanity," I added, unable to refrain myself. "Your father's something else."

"It wasn't always like this, Cassie. They weren't bad parents. They went their separate ways after my sister got killed. My mother withdrew more into herself, and my father no longer got his way with her. They just fell into their separate routines. They've been like this for years."

"Do you keep in touch?" I asked.

"I phone every week or two, and I drop in every so often. Maybe three or four times a year. We're not close, Cassie."

"That's an understatement," I said, and laughed because I knew that David wouldn't take it the wrong way. He pulled into the parking lot at *Binny's Diner.*

It was an old building with white vinyl siding and gray trim with a black and white sign above the front window and door that read, "BINNY'S DINER."

By the size of the parking lot and building, I expected the diner to be much bigger, but it could only seat about two dozen people. It was about half full when we walked in.

David led me to a table and we sat down. I couldn't help but notice all the artwork on the white walls, striking copper etchings that caught the light and your attention the moment you walked into the diner.

"That must be Binny's work," I said to David, glancing at the copper etching of a man leading an ass loaded with a pile of books on both sides of its back. At the bottom it was scribed, *"The Scholar's Dilemma,"* in florid lettering that made it look like Persian writing.

"Yes," David said, with a big smile. "That's one of Binny's Mullah Nasrudin series. He has dozens of them that he rotates in his diner every two or three months before he sends them to various galleries. They tell the story of the Sufi path in copper art," David added, and laughed as he glanced at the etching again. "That one there is my favorite." David pointed to the etching on the wall above the empty table across from us.

"What does this one mean?" I asked, pointing to the one above our table.

With a big, satisfied smile, he said, "The ass represents the intellectual with all his books, and the man leading the ass with the rope is the Mullah Nasrudin."

I got the point instantly, and laughed. Then I turned to David's favorite. There were three symbols etched on the copper plate: a man on his hands and knees with his head pointing to the ground as if looking for something, a house, and the sun in the sky; and it was titled, *"The Key"* in the same florid lettering.

"Why is that your favorite?" I asked.

"I love that one, Cassie. It's Nasrudin at his finest. That's the Mullah Nasurdin's house, and he's looking for the key to his house on the ground in front of his house, but he lost the key in his house."

"Then why is he looking for it outside?" I asked, perplexed.

"Because the light is better outside," David said, with an ironic smile.

Puzzled, I said, "I'll have to think about that one."

Just then a frizzy white-haired man walked up to our table. By his step, the look in his steely bright eyes, and the energy that he emanated I felt it had to be David's teacher, Sam the Man who for some reason I had assumed David wanted to introduce me to.

The olive-complexioned man, who appeared taller than he was, put his left hand on David's shoulder, smiled, and gave me his free hand to shake. "You must be Cassie. I'm the man they call Binny."

Surprised, I didn't say anything for a moment or two. We shook hands, and then I said, "I thought for sure you were Sam, David's old teacher."

"Sam the Man? No. He's still in Toronto," Binny said, with an excited twinkle in his dark, charcoal eyes. "What made you think that?"

"I really don't know," I said, feeling a bit foolish. "You weren't by any chance one of Sam's students, were you?" I asked.

Binny smiled, and so did David. "Sam was Binny's student," David said, and the two men broke into laughter.

"Why don't we get you some lunch first, then we can talk," Binny said, smiling at my confusion. "What's it going to be?"

Binny was the owner and chef of *Binny's Diner*. He had two full-time waitresses for his steady clientele of locals, and a short-order cook in his late forties, a metallurgical engineer who by chance had lunch at Binny's Diner one day and was so fascinated by the copper art that he quit his job and became Binny's student. Not only was Binny passing on the ancient secrets of the Sufi path to his short-order cook, but the ancient skills of copper artwork as well.

According to David, Binny didn't want to get rich. He just wanted a little restaurant to live out the rest of his life and pass on the *subtlety* to his patrons. But his real passion was transmitting the secrets of the Sufi path through the exploits of the Mullah Nasrudin in copper art, which he had been doing in various art forms for over fifty years.

Binny was a puzzle to his customers. They came to *Binny's Diner* for the good, simple, home-cooked food, which was not only hardy and reasonably priced, and blessed with Binny's *subtle* energy, but mostly they came to talk with Binny. He was inscrutable to his regular customers, but they all loved him. They didn't know why they loved him; they just did, and they always came back for more of his hardy soups and arcane, mystifying wisdom.

"How old is Binny?" I asked David, after we placed an order of Binny's Sunday Special, Cream of Broccoli Soup and Pastrami on Rye.

"Eighty-six," David said, to my astonishment.

"He doesn't look a day over sixty," I said. "That's why I thought he was Sam the Man. What's Binny's secret?"

"He loves what he does, Cassie. He's had this restaurant for twenty-two years now, and he's just as happy today as the day he bought it."

"What did he do before that, teach Sufism?"

"He still teaches, but we really don't know what he did before he bought the restaurant, aside from his copper art, that is. Sam doesn't know. He thinks Binny was into finance. A broker of some sort, but he's not sure. Binny doesn't reveal too much about himself. But he does have a family somewhere."

"Somewhere?" I asked.

"Yes. He says in the old country, but who knows? The only thing we know for sure about Binny is that he's not what he appears to be. He's a Sufi in the true sense of the word."

"I don't know what that means," I said.

David's eyes told me to stop and think. I did, and soon I realized that David was not what he appeared to be either.

David was a journalist who became a Sufi who became an Atman, jack-of-all trades and house-building contractor, a poet, a translator of Sufi poetry, a passionate marathon runner, a collector of eclectic art, a hobby chef with a love for Mediterranean cuisine, and next to the Living Atma Master the best teacher I ever met.

I trusted David implicitly, even though I knew that tomorrow he could pick up and leave me with no regrets. I knew that the man they called Binny and Sam the Man were exactly like the man they called David Oakly. It was to the nature of their remarkable spiritual make-up, and the only way to understand them was to become like them.

"A true Sufi is not what he appears to be," he went on to explain. "Paradoxically, he's exactly what he appears to be. Binny is a cook, a waiter, a translator of Sufi literature, a brilliant copper artist with works in various galleries here and Europe—wall art like these you see here, free-standing sculptures, candelabras, lanterns, wall clocks, and even copper jewelry, all with an esoteric Sufi motif that mystifies all of Binny's collectors; and he's also the owner of this modest diner. He is what he is, but he's more than what he is. He may have been a broker, but he was more than a broker. Whatever a Sufi does, it does not make him merely what he does. He is more than what he does. It's this something more that makes a Sufi what he is. Can you guess what this something more is?"

"If you would have asked me this a few weeks ago, I wouldn't have had a clue," I said. "But now I think I know. I can't put my finger on it because it's so elusive, but I think this 'something more' is that certain *je ne sais quoi* that is more than the sum of one's life. I think this 'something more' is what completes one's life, David."

David gave me his sweet Mona Lisa smile, but said nothing. Binny brought our lunch on a tray and a folder of new translations of *A Conference of the Birds* for David to work on and pulled up a chair to join us. David turned to him and very casually said, "Cassie's got it, Binny. She's finally found the key to her house."

Binny burst into an unexpected fit of raucous laughter. *"Good for you, Cassie!* David had all the confidence in you. So, how did it all come together for you?" he asked, with a smile on his face that shone like a bright moon in a dark sky.

"I don't know," I said, feeling like I had just stepped into a private chess game with two Grand Masters. I felt I knew what they were referring to, but I wasn't quite sure. I reflected for a moment or two and then decided to throw caution to the wind. That's what David would have done. "In all honesty Binny, I think it all fell into place for me this morning at our Atma Worship Service. Would you like to hear what David did?"

"If what David did at your service put your star into alignment with the Great Constellation of Life, I certainly want to hear," Binny said.

"That's exactly what happened!" I exclaimed, catching the spirit of those two remarkable men. "I didn't realize it until just now, but his gesture spoke the secret of my life," I added, trying to contain my emotions.

"What secret?" Binny asked, giving me a pensive frown.

"Me! The secret of Cassie Patty O'Shaunnesy!" I exclaimed, surprising myself.

Binny and David burst into laughter. "I told you that she found the key to her house," David said, which only refueled their joyous laughter.

I still didn't know why they were laughing, but the spirit was infectious. "This may be amusing now, but it's taken me my whole life to put the pieces together," I said, trying to restrain myself from laughing also. "And I wouldn't have been able to connect the dots without David's help. He's been—well, let's just say that he's the catalyst of my life."

"Excellent! So you've solved the mystery of your life, then?" Binny said.

"No, I haven't. But I'm no longer mystified, if that makes any sense."

"It makes perfect sense!" Binny said, slapping his knee. "So, what did this man they call David Oakly do at your Atma Worship Service that put it all together for you?"

"He donated five dollars at the service, which the Atma cleric frowned upon because she felt he should have given more. So what does our man they call David Oakly do? He takes out his wallet and empties all his money into the donation box. And he empties out his pocket and puts all of that money into the donation box also. David donated over three hundred dollars just to teach that Atma cleric a lesson —*and now I'm stuck with lunch!"*

Binny slapped his knee again and keeled over with laughter. When he stopped laughing, he turned to David and said, *"But did she get it?"*

"She's a Higher Initiate, Binny. It may take time to sink in."

With that, they both burst into uproarious laughter. Then Binny got up and took down the copper etching called *The Key* and with the most radiant smile gave it to me. "A little gift for you, Cassie. Nasrudin welcomes you to his world of spiritual wonder."

I never felt so privileged in my entire life than to be in the company of those two remarkable men at that moment. Then Binny put his hand on my shoulder, smiled his mystic smile, and said, *"Lunch is on me, Cassie!"*

My Unborn Child

Chapter 23

Love on Line One

I felt my father's presence as I drank my freshly ground Maya Earth Coffee Saturday morning. It wasn't even five o'clock yet, but I was slept out. I had a trying day at work Friday, and I went to bed shortly after dinner. "What is it, Father?" I asked.

I didn't hear anything. As I sat in the quiet of my cozy kitchen, a feeling of warm love began to envelop me, like a blanket draping around my shoulders. "Is that you, Father?" I implored. "Are you here?"

My coffee cup was empty, but I didn't want to refill it for fear of disturbing the warm blanket of love around me. I sat and listened for my father's voice. Love welled up inside me like a rising tide. I could not hold it back. I had to let it out. *"I love you too, Father…"*

Tears came to my eyes. I thought of David's mother. She also suffered from depression. I had only met her once for a short time after our worship service in Peterborough, but it was obvious that she had shut her heart to love. I felt sorry for her.

I had no doubt that Vera Oakly was a decent person, but she had no love left in her. My father never tired of telling me how much he loved me. He said that his love for me kept his demons at bay. In the end he could not fight them off, and I never got over the feeling of guilt that my love for him was not enough to save my father from himself.

Guilt was my personal demon, and it began to possess me again.

From my father's suicide to my abortion to my attempted suicide, rushes of guilt began to flood my mind and I began to get that suffocating feeling again. I began to hyperventilate.

I took a few deep breaths. "You want me?" I said, addressing my rapacious demon. "You're going to have to go through the Satma to get me!"

I took a few more deep breaths, and then I began to chant HU. Quietly at first, then gradually I began to sing the Love Song to God in my natural voice. It filled my kitchen with the presence of the loving Atma force, and I felt my guilt flushing out of me with each long drawn-out HU that I sang. It felt wonderful!

I gave my father the HU chant to practice, but he never did. He didn't believe in "voodoo spirituality." I wasn't aware at the time of the healing power of the HU, but I trusted the Satma. My father would have nothing to do with my new spiritual path. He was trapped by his own mind. So was Vera Oakly. She had found a place in her mind to block out the pain of her daughter's death. That's what my father and David's mother had in common. They had both retreated into their own mind to escape from the hardships of everyday life.

I loved my father too much for my own good. I read all the literature that I could find on his debilitating disease with the hope of curing him, and I always made sure that he never ended up on the street, which came close to happening several times. I dreamed of him living a normal life, free of the demons that haunted him, but my dreams were shattered the day he took his life. I broke down at the funeral chapel and cried my heart out for my father.

To survive the pain in my heart, I took my cue from my mentor. *"Everyone goes through hardships in life,"* Doctor Kubler-Ross wrote in her first, and most cherished letter to me. *"The more pain you go through, the more you learn and grow. And when you learn your lessons, the pain goes away."*

I no longer felt the pain of my father's death. I suffered sharp pangs of guilt every now and then, which I quickly gave to the Satma to deal with for me, but I could not help but wonder what my father's karmic lessons were. He hadn't learned them. If he had he would never have taken his own life. David's mother hadn't learned her karmic lesson from her daughter's tragic death either. If she had she wouldn't be so embittered by life. And David's father. His anger was so deep that it had soured him on life completely.

The pain does not go away until we learn our lessons. That's why my childhood teacher, Atma Master Paul Mathew said that we would just keep coming back until we got it right. But what is the point of all these karmic lessons?

"The ultimate lesson," wrote Doctor Kubler-Ross, *"is learning how to love and be loved unconditionally."* I never tire of hearing that.

Our family dog Tiger loved me unconditionally, and I learned from him how to love unconditionally also. I try to love my children unconditionally, but it's hard. I try to not attach myself to my love for them, but I don't know how to do that yet. I think David knows how to love unconditionally. I think that's how he loves me. And it scares me.

Suddenly I got the urge to talk with the Satma. I went upstairs to my bedroom for my journal. I refilled my cup with my weekend treat of organically-grown, freshly roasted and ground coffee and sat down at the kitchen table, did a short HU, and began writing my letter to my inner spiritual guide:

Dear Huzee,

I'm sitting in my cozy kitchen enjoying my freshly ground coffee and thinking about my father, David's parents, my children, and the karmic lessons that we're here to learn in life, and I'd like to talk to you about love.

I love my children. I love my career. I love my new position here in Georgian Bay. I love serving life with my profession. I love my freedom in Atma-Gare. I love David Oakly. I love him more than I want him to know. I love my brother Michael. I love my mother. Not as much as I loved my father, but I can only love my mother so much. Didn't Zak Tarzman tell us that we should treat the spiritual life like the economic life and invest our love wisely? *"Love is everybody and everything,"* he said. That's the principle of love. I understand that now. I know that the Atma is love. I also know that the Atma is life. So I know what Zak means now when he said that love is everybody and everything.

Zak Tarzman also said that we should be very discriminating in our love. He made a distinction between the different kinds of love in *Talks with the Master*. Warm love is emotional love, and we should only give it to those who will not abuse our love. That's hard to do at first. But life teaches us to be discerning in whom we give warm love to. I no longer give my uncles the warm love that I used to give them. They don't deserve my warm love anymore. I give them neutral love instead. That's what Zak Tarzman said we should do.

Neutral love is good will, kind thoughts, forgiveness, and understanding. It's the kind of love where we give people the freedom to learn their own lessons in life. I would like my children to learn their own lessons, but I can't be that neutral. I love them too much!

Our dog Tiger taught me how to love unconditionally, but I can't do that yet. It doesn't have to be much, but I always expect a little something in return for my love. That's my lesson, isn't it Satma? I have to learn not to expect anything. That's what it means to give love without conditions, doesn't it?

David has learned how to do this. He doesn't expect anything in return from me. It sounds cold, but it's not. I've never met a more generous person in my life. What's his secret, Satma? How can he love me with more passion than I have ever experienced and be so detached at one and the same time? Maybe David's love for me is a perfect blend of warm love and unconditional love. Is that the magic elixir of his love?

I may have discovered his secret, Satma. His friend Binny shares the same mystifying secret. They think I have it also. I'm not sure I do, but I may have had it there for a moment at *Binny's Diner.*

It's the secret of giving, isn't it? If I understand this secret, it has to do with that mystical exchange between the giver and the spiritual principal of life. They call it the *subtlety*, but it has to do with the secret of love. That's why Binny gave me his piece of art and treated us to lunch. He's mastered the secret of giving love.

I'm not sure what I'm getting at Satma, but when David put every cent he had on him into the donation box at the worship service my doors of perception opened and I *knew* that unless one is willing to give completely to the Atma he will never be completely himself. I *knew* this. And I know that I have done this also, but only differently.

Maybe not so differently. Maybe it comes down to the same thing. Maybe the more we live our own life, the more completely we give our life to the Atma. Maybe that's what David meant when he told Binny that I had found the key to my house. That's why Binny gave me *The Key.* I went all the way with my own life, Satma. When I went public with the story of my unborn child I put myself on the line for the Atma. That's when I caught up with my life and became whole. But I had no choice. That was the fruit of my life. Like David said to me when we went on the studio tour in the Town of Blue Mountains and he introduced me to his artist friend Lance Henrikson and commissioned him to do my portrait, "What does the acorn seed do when it becomes an oak tree?"

"What?" I asked.

"Nothing. It just *is* an oak tree," he replied.

David puzzled me until I wrote my open letter to the Wyedale *Gazette* and Barrie *Examiner*. By doing nothing, David did not mean that the oak tree stops being an oak tree. On the contrary, the oak tree lives the life of an oak tree producing acorn seeds year after year after year. This is how the oak tree serves life. My letter to the public was how I served life, Satma. That's what David meant by just *being.* By just *being,* we serve life with the fruits of who we are just like the oak tree serves life with its fruit.

Doctors heal people, artists paint, musicians play

music, dancers dance, architects design buildings, carpenters build, and nurses tend to the sick. We do what we do in *being* who we are. Just *being* who we are is our own fruit, isn't it?

There is something so pure about just *being* who we are that it's holy! David calls this purity "the relentless clarity at the heart of work." That's why David fascinates me. He lives his life just *being* who he is in everything that he does. He does not affect his own life like everyone I know. He just *is*!

I stopped affecting my own life too, Satma. I have finally caught up with my own life, and now I just *am,* too. It's a magical place to be! We all have our karmic lessons to learn in life, and mine is to learn how to love unconditionally. Like I said, I know how; but I just can't do it yet. I hope to, soon. Maybe you can help me.

I love you,
Cassie Patty O'Shaunnesy

I shouldn't have been surprised, because it happens with every initiate report that I write, and my letter was much more than my initiate reports. The Holy Spirit of Atma responds with new experiences. A few days after I wrote my letter, I began to see life differently.

It started with the lights over our nurse's station. I had been after maintenance to replace the one fluorescent tube that had burned out and the other flickering tube for three weeks, but when I went to work on the Monday after I wrote my letter to the Satma both tubes had been replaced and a soft white light flooded our workstation.

It was a waking dream. The Atma had spoken. I had more spiritual light in my life, which I took to mean that I would see life more clearly. *And see I did!*

From the moment I sat at my station flooded by the new soft white light, I began to notice something different in the way I saw my nurses. Not just my nurses, but the doctors, patients, visitors, secretaries, housekeeping and kitchen staff—everyone. It wasn't what

I was seeing as such, but what I sensed about everyone.

I could tell just by looking and listening to people where they were at in their spiritual journey through life. *I knew their level of consciousness!*

At first I had to stand back to collect myself. I didn't know what was happening to me. I noticed it with my nurse Karen when suddenly I sensed something about her that I didn't want to see before. She had come to a spiritual impasse in her life that had begun to embitter her, and everything that she said and did was colored by her discontent.

This happened again with my nurse Pauline. Her inner life was an open book to me. I could not see the specific details of her life, but I just *knew* where she was at in her journey through life. She was standing in the doorway of a much more satisfying personal reality, and her world was about to open up to her. Everything she said and did was colored by optimism!

It happened again with my nurse Nancy. I took an instant disliking to her from my first day of work. As we spoke, a window on her private world opened up, and I saw such bitterness that it made me shudder; and I *knew* that I had to love and forgive her to help her grow out of her negative frame of mind.

After talking with Karen, Pauline, and Nancy I had to be alone to figure out what was happening. I took my clipboard and went to the cafeteria to reflect for a few minutes, but the same thing happened with Connie who worked in the cafeteria. I sensed her inner world also.

And as I reflected on what was happening, I connected the dots with the new light at our workstation and realized that the Inner Master had opened up my spiritual sight. It was like my powers of intuition had been amplified, and I could see with the eyes of Soul!

This happened all week long with everyone I talked to, and with each day I *saw* deeper and deeper into a person's life. It was like I had acquired another sense. I called David on his cell phone Friday afternoon and asked if he was free to drop over in the evening. "I have something I have to share with you, David. It's very important."

"How can I say no?" he replied.

Shortly before eight, David rang the doorbell. Cindy answered.

David gave her the two packages that he had picked up at the Wyedale Bakery before he went for his daily run. "A little treat for you guys," he said, and handed her the two boxes of pastry. "This one's for you and your mother; and this one's for the boys," he said.

Patrick and Mark, whom David never called by their nicknames, loved cinnamon rolls, which were also called sticky buns in Ontario; and the Swiss chocolate brownies that the new owners of the Wyedale Bakery made were my weakness, and Cindy's eyes lit up when David gave her the packages. "Hey Mom, David got us some treats! We got brownies!"

"Did you thank him?" I asked.

"Thank you," she said. "Can we have some, Mom?"

"Yes; but put them on a plate, please. And save some for tomorrow," I said, shaking my head at David. "You're going to spoil them if you keep bringing over treats every time you visit." But no sooner did I say this than I *saw* David's inner world to be so generous and expansive that I actually swooned for a moment.

David saw me swoon and said, "Are you having a dizzy spell?"

"No, I'm fine," I said, and took a deep breath. "Come in, David. I'll put the kettle on for tea. Or would you prefer something else? Organic coffee? Juice?"

"Tea's fine," he said.

"I've got Jasmine Green Tea," I said.

"Excellent," he said, and took off his shoes. Then he went to say hello to the boys who were watching Mark's latest addition to his Star Trek collection, *The Undiscovered Country.* They thanked David for the sticky buns, and then David made himself comfortable on the sofa chair where he always sat.

When I returned with the tea and a plate with three brownies (I couldn't resist and ate one in the kitchen waiting for the kettle to whistle), I asked the children to give us some private time and closed the sliding French doors to the family room, sat down, and stared at him, unselfconsciously.

"I get the feeling you're reading me," he said.

"I am. I don't know what's happening to me, David, but I seem to have acquired some kind of spiritual sight this week. It started

Monday morning, I think."

"Oh. And what do you see now?" he asked.

"I see a very generous Soul," I replied.

"You don't need spiritual sight to see a person's character," David said, not questioning how I *saw* him with my new sight. "That comes naturally with experience."

"I know. But this is different. I can tell where a person is at on their journey through life. I just *know* where they are. People I talk to now can't hide who they are from me. I can't explain it, David; I just *know* them. Does that make any sense to you?"

"Perfect sense," he said, with that smile that was both charming and intimidating. "Do you remember the three qualities of the self-realized Soul? They're mentioned in the *Shariyatma*."

"Give me a moment," I said

"Knowing, being, and *seeing,"* David said, not wanting to lose his train of thought waiting for me to remember. "These are the three defining qualities of the spiritually self-realized Soul. First, you experienced the *being* quality of Soul. This is why you said to me, `Life *is,* and I *am.*' Remember?"

I knew where David was going with his thought. I sensed it; or, rather, I *saw* it in that spiritual way that I now saw, and I had to share this with him. "I have experienced just *being*, David. Ever since the night of the snowstorm when we made love I haven't been the same. I'm complete now. That's all I can say about myself. I don't feel like I have to try to be myself anymore. I just *am* myself. Does that make any sense to you?"

"Perfectly," he said, again with that same smile that for some strange reason seemed a little menacing now. "You've shifted your center of gravity and coincided with yourself. That's the *being* quality of Soul. And what you now sense a person to be, that's the *seeing* quality of Soul. And the third quality that you have realized now is the *knowing* quality of Soul. You've entered into the mesoteric middle circle of life, Cassie. This is the spiritually conscious stage of evolution. You're experiencing the first stage of spiritual self-realization consciousness when Soul wakes up to its own nature. Remember, you live life in the outer circle of life. This is the unconscious karmic stage of man's evolution. In the outer circle of life there are many levels of consciousness, because every person is at their own level of karmic resolution. This is why you sense where a person is at on their personal journey. You can tell just by what a person says and does what their level of consciousness is, and you're going to have difficulty adjusting to your spiritual sight. Everyone does. I know I did. It's a very strange place to be, knowing a person's inner life; but you'll get used to it."

Suddenly I got it! *"These circles of life are real, aren't they? They're not metaphors, are they? Humanity does evolve through these three stages, doesn't it?"*

David laughed at my epiphany. "Cassie, that's the joy of spiritual self-realization consciousness. Suddenly the obvious becomes the spiritual, and then the spiritual becomes the obvious again; but only now the obvious has become *your* truth. This is what waking up to life is all about. This is what Jesus tried to get his disciples to do when he told them to stay awake.

I didn't have the courage to ask him, but David read my mind. With that twinkle in his eye that looked a little mischievous but was really more of a cheeky spiritual certainty, he said, "I've journeyed to the inner circle of life, Cassie; and as conceited as this may sound, I am what everyone is striving to become."

"Which is?" I quickly asked, with a sudden rush of discomfort.

"One's true self. This acorn seed has become an oak tree, if you will. I'm in the realization stage of my own divine nature. Just as you are now in the throes of the middle circle of life, I'm in the throes of the inner circle of life. As you are waking up to Soul's qualities of *being, knowing,* and *seeing,* I'm waking up to the divine qualities of God-realization consciousness *love, goodness,* and *divine wisdom.* Do you see how bold this sounds? This is why this third stage of evolution is never talked about. It can only be experienced. One cannot talk about God-realization consciousness, Cassie. It's too much for people. This is why Atma Masters seldom talk about it. They just do what they do to serve God. They are God-realized beings that serve God by serving life. This is what all of life strives to become. This is the purpose of life. This is how God grows. This is every man's destiny."

"I understand, " I said, sensing a different sound to his voice. "But can I get used to this reality? I've never felt so out of place in my life as I have this past week. It's like I'm living in a completely different world from every person I know, except for you that is."

"It's not an easy place to be," David said, in the same voice that didn't quite sound like the David I knew. "When your spiritual senses awaken, you begin to feel out of place in life. You will always feel out of place until you adjust to the evolutionary process of life."

"What do you mean?" I asked.

"Life is in a constant state of evolution," he explained, and I *knew* by the sound of his voice now that his private world was opening up to me. "We're all evolving, whether we realize it or not. Karma is the spiritual dynamic of human evolution, and everyone creates karma. This is how people grow—by creating and resolving karma. What you see now with your spiritual eye is these karmic stages of a person's life. Don't interfere in a person's karma, though. If you do, you will only frustrate your own journey. This is the wisdom behind the Atma Master's blessing, *Baraka bashad.*"

"How did you adjust? Do you feel like a stranger in a strange land like I do now?"

"Yes, I do. What surprised me most though was the Atma community. I didn't expect to see the distinctions that I did."

My ears perked up. "What distinctions?"

David paused for a moment, giving me the impression that he wasn't supposed to share this information with me; but he smiled, and said, "Let's take Marlene Anderson's understanding of the Spiritual Law of Giving. She has a good grasp of this law, but she has not yet *become* this law. That's the distinction I'm talking about. She believes that the more we give to the Atma, the more the Atma will give to us, but it's still a belief with her. She has to make this belief a part of her being before she realizes what it means to give it all up for the Atma, and the only way to make this a part of her being is to give and give until she loses all fear of giving."

"Have you lost all fear of giving?" I had to ask.

"Yes," David replied, but much too quickly. In that fleeting moment I *saw* something that I had not seen before, a fear that David himself was unaware of; but I overrode my feeling and listened to what he had to say. "If I may, let me illustrate how the Satma takes care of those who give it all up for the Atma," he continued, with absolute certainty in his voice that masked the fear that I had just caught in his eyes. "The morning after I made my donation at the worship service in Peterborough, I got a call to build an addition to a Century home, just like the addition I put on here only twice as large. This included a complete renovation of the two floors of the house. This contract will keep me busy for four or five months. And the nice thing about it is that I'm not under pressure to complete the job. The new owner is from Toronto, and he would like it completed by the end of June; so I've got work for Tim and myself all winter and spring. The skeptic would say that it was pure coincidence that I picked up this contract so soon after I made the generous donation at the worship service in Peterborough, but this kind of thing has happened to me so often it's become a way of life for me. This is the distinction between believing in the Spiritual Law of Giving, and *being* the Spiritual Law of Giving. One has to do to *be*, Cassie."

"I'm puzzled," I said, frowning at my confusion. "Marlene is a Higher Initiate. Shouldn't she be past the belief stage? Shouldn't she also *be* what she believes?"

"One would think. Apparently it takes time to *become* these higher spiritual principals. Higher Initiates puzzled me also, Cassie. Their behavior was so contradictory at times that it almost turned me off Atma-Gare. I was ready to go back to Sufism. In fact, I went to see Binny about my feelings..."

"What? You thought of leaving Atma-Gare?"

"Yes, I did. I was so put off by some Higher Initiates that I was going to take my chances with Sufism, but Binny set me straight."

"Isn't Binny a Sufi teacher?"

"He's a Sufi Master. You won't find another teacher like Binny. His intimate understanding of the Path highlighted Idris Shaw's magnificent works for me, starting with his books on the exploits of the incomparable Mulla Nasrudin. Binny knows all about Atma-Gare, Cassie. He knows about the Satma, the Living Atma Master, and the HU. The Sufis have being doing the HU chant for centuries. Binny also knows the Atma Master Shams of Tabriz who initiated Rumi into the Sound and Light of God. Binny Soul travels too, Cassie; but his mission in life is to pass on the *subtlety* to an unsuspecting public, especially through his copper artwork that he has in galleries here and in Europe. And he does this so well that it changes people's lives. He's had many people take up the Path because of his Mulla Nasrudin etchings. When I told him about my dismay with some Higher Initiates, he just laughed and said, `Why would you let your life be ruled by another person's behavior? Don't be fooled. Higher initiations are not fixed states of spiritual consciousness. If you're happy with your relationship with the Atma, that's all that should matter to you.' I was happy, so I stayed in Atma-Gare. But I do rub some Higher Initiates the wrong way."

"I know you do," I said, with a bemused smile because I *knew* precisely why he rubbed them the wrong way. To my astonishment, I *saw* that David mirrored their spiritual conceit just as they mirrored his overweening spiritual confidence, and it was his own vanity that David found so hard to take because he refused to see his own *shadow.* "Grace has told me what some of them think of you, too," I added, with a snicker.

"Oh?" David said, but he didn't inquire further. "Speaking of Higher Initiates," he said, "the Atma Quartet is going to be in Orillia this Sunday. Are you up to attending the service?"

The Atma Quartet is a group of Atmans who travel across Ontario once a month to Atma Worship Services to give spiritual talks and sing.

I didn't respond right away. I was frozen in that moment of *knowing* something about David that I would never have fathomed. I didn't want to believe what I *saw* in David, but I could not deny his tragic flaw, and I *knew* in my heart that I was to be the instrument of his spiritual test. The defiant look of fear in David's eyes and thinly veiled smile of pride on his lips in Lance Henrikson's portrait of David had come alive, and I shuddered in fright.

Suddenly, I was transported to my childhood in my mother's boarding house when I met my teacher Paul Mathew. He was writing his book *Seeker By The Lake*, which became my favorite Atma Book. I heard Paul's teacher, the Atma Master Zak Tarzman, speaking to Paul as Paul recorded his words for his book, "The greatest freedom of Soul is in humility. Love for woman should give man a greater love for God, and in developing a greater love for God, man's ego will dissolve, and its limited, petty self will be overcome and he will find transcendentalism of the Lord," and as I listened I *knew* that Zak Tarzman was speaking to me. I couldn't take my eyes off David, but he didn't seem to notice that I was transfixed. "For the woman," said Paul's teacher, "can lead man to God. This is her duty and responsibility in this world," and in a flash I *saw* that my spiritual test was to help David surrender his fear to love just like the seeker had to surrender to the woman's love in *Seeker By The Lake.*

"I'd love to go to the worship service," I replied, as though nothing had happened. Mark and Cindy might like to come. They like the Orillia service. I'll ask them," I said.

"No charbroiled burgers though. Webers is closed for the winter. Maybe we can go for pizza or KFC after the service," David said.

"I'm sure they'll go for that," I said, my head reeling with my new spiritual insight into David's profound character flaw. "David, can you explain something for me, please?" I asked, to clear up a mystery about the three circles of life. "This outer circle of life puzzles me. You call it the Exoteric Circle of Life, don't you?"

"Yes."

"This is the circle of life where most people live, right?"

"Yes. The vast majority of mankind is evolving through the outer circle of life, from the least evolved human being to the highest."

"That's what puzzles me," I said, trying not to betray my new feelings about David now that I *saw* that he was less perfect than I believed him to be. "Who are the highest evolved people in the outer circle of life? The intellectuals? The scientists? Who?"

"The artists," David said, and crossed his legs for conversational ease; but even in this simple physical gesture I *saw* the conceit of his overweening confidence, which gave me a fleeting feeling of disgust. "Evolution in the outer circle of life is twofold: the evolution of human consciousness, and the evolution of spiritual consciousness," he explained, in that new voice that I had not heard before that night. I could *hear* shades of David's conceited ego, and I listened intently with the heightened awareness of my mixed emotions. "The most spiritually evolved people in the exoteric world are those whom Jesus said were ready for the kingdom of heaven," he continued, with all the authority of his spiritual conceit. "This can include anyone, from the illiterate peasant crop farmer to the Nobel laureate. Everyone else who's not ready to be harvested for conscious spiritual evolution continues to evolve karmically in their lower human consciousness. It doesn't matter who they are. Priests, lawyers, scientists, artists, whoever; they will evolve to the edge of the outer circle of life. But they cannot penetrate the mysteries of the middle circle with their mind or faith, however brilliant their mind or strong their faith may be; and in their despair they shout things like—God is dead, life is a tale told by an idiot full of sound and fury signifying nothing, man is a useless passion, hell is other people, life is absurd, and on and on *ad nauseam.*"

"That's why I'm asking," I said, genuinely excited by David's explanation despite his overweening ego that I could *see* in his personality now and which Lance had so brilliantly captured in David's thin smile. "Wednesday night I couldn't sleep, so I stayed up later than usual and watched television. I happened to catch a program called *The Question of God.* A diverse panel of intellectuals discussed the life and works of the atheist writer Lewis Carol, who converted to Christianity, and the psychiatrist Sigmund Freud, who was a lifelong atheist. The panel was made up of a medical doctor, a Jungian analyst, an atheist psychologist, a Christian minister, a journalist, a social philosopher, and an agnostic lawyer, plus the moderator of the program; but not once during the course of the show did they mention karma and reincarnation. This puzzled me. Why did they limit their inquiry of God to the atheist and Christian perspective?"

"I'm familiar with the program. I saw it last year on Christmas day. Why, you ask? The premise of their inquiry was the question of Christian faith versus scientific inquiry. Talk about storming the gates of heaven! They were fishing in a lake with no fish, Cassie. It's not blind faith or brilliant logic that will answer the question of God; it's experience. One has to experience his own divine essence to know

God. There's no other way. And that's what conscious spiritual evolution in the middle circle of life is all about."

"David," I said, smiling at the coincidence of having seen the same program, "I saw something in those panelists that bothered me. I felt their pain of not knowing God. But I also saw their vanity. It came out differently in each person, with its own recognizable face; but it was the same face of vanity in all of them. You say they were fishing in a lake with no fish, but how could they catch God in the lake they were fishing in? They couldn't, could they?"

David drank his tea before replying. In a very personal tone of voice, which changed the tenor of our conversation, he said, "Vanity has many faces, Cassie; but I had no idea that the layers of vanity could be so deep. It wasn't until I did a job for a man whose life was so ego centered that he forced me to come face to face with my own vanity. Shortly after I moved to Georgian Bay and started my own business, I got a job to paint this man's house. I thought I had mastered house painting when I worked for Sam the Man, but this little Sicilian proved me wrong. He was a body-man who owned three body shops in the Greater Toronto Area before he sold out and built his retirement home here. He spotted so many flaws in my paint job that it crushed my spirits. I was too much of a Sufi to justify myself, so I had to take it in the chin. It was such a blow to my ego that I never slept for weeks. I had to go in every day to this man's house and suffer his brutal indignities while I corrected every single flaw he spotted and by the time I left his house I felt like a used dishrag. There was no more vanity left in me to wring out. Two weeks later I got my pink slip in the mail for my Fifth Initiation. I had finally broken through the Mental Plane of Consciousness with the most humiliating experience of my entire life. What did I conclude from this? The only way to enter the middle circle of life is by resolving enough ego consciousness to shift our center of gravity from the outer circle of life to the middle circle of life. If we can't do that on our own, life will burn off our vanity for us."

I was on the edge of my seat, as I always was whenever David revealed his personal life to me, but this time I *saw* that David's wisdom came through *him*, and not to him as I first thought. David *was* his own truth because he *lived* his truth, and he had become a spiritually self-realized Soul; but what he didn't know was that this was also the source of his spiritual conceit. As he was telling me his story, I *saw* the proud, boastful face of his vanity that he could not see, and it made me shudder.

He hadn't finished yet. He poured another cup of tea and took a sip. "My experience painting this man's house was a waking dream," he continued, in a pensive, almost confessional tone. "This little man with an enormous ego was my father growing up. He was me, had I not become a Sufi. This little man with the most critical eye of any human being I have ever met is the natural product of human evolution. His ego has taken him as far as he can go in this lifetime. He cannot evolve any further. He is so fixed in his own ego that he cannot be deconstructed in this lifetime. He will have to burn his vanity off in a future life..."

"May I?" I interrupted.

"Of course," David said.

"I'm assuming that he was critical of your paint job because he painted cars for a living. Am I right?"

"Exactly. That's what made it impossible to satisfy him. He expected the same impossible standards of excellence and wouldn't accept anything less. He was so inflexible that he made my life hell. That's why this whole experience became a waking dream for me. His critical eye didn't stop with my paint job, though. He was no less critical with every other tradesman who worked on his house. I wanted to curse him at first, but being who I am I knew the Atma was teaching me the lesson of my life, so I went with it. I suffered his abuse because I wanted to see how far he would go, but he had no limits. He was shameless in his criticism of my work and the work of every other tradesman. I learned later that when he got married his criticism destroyed his young wife's confidence, and over the years it cost him over five hundred thousand dollars for her therapy. She finally learned to live with him by deflecting his criticism with humorous retorts; but I couldn't do that because he was right about my work. My paint job was not as good as it should have been because I had squeezed him in between my other jobs and didn't give it my full attention, so I had to take his criticism. But all of that conscious suffering burnt off layers of vanity. That's how I earned the stripes for my Fifth Initiation. So as much as I wanted to grab that little peacock by his scrawny neck and choke the life out of him, I thank him privately for being such a miserable bastard. He did me the favor of my life by being so critical about my work..."

"Do you mean to tell me that you actually thought those things about this man?" I asked, *knowing* that until David forgave him he would never be free of him.

"Oh yes," David said. "And much more. I wanted to do the same with my father a thousand times over, but I'm glad I didn't."

"Your father criticized you growing up?"

"Non-stop. I don't know if he was compensating for the loss of his leg in the war, or if he was just an angry man, but however he got to be wired that way my father was never satisfied. I don't know how my mother put up with him all those years."

"What do you think of your father now?"

"I neither hate him nor love him."

"And your mother?"

"My parents brought me into this world, and I thank them for that. They gave me a lot of karmic baggage to work off, Cassie. Without that baggage, I might not be an Atman today," David said, and fell silent.

In that moment of silence, I *saw* that David's hidden fear came from the deep layer of parental vanity that was much too close for him to see but which Lance had captured in that fleeting moment in David's obdurate, fearful eyes. "Yes, we do owe our parents a debt of gratitude," I said, with an ironic smile.

David broke into a gentle laugh, and I joined him; but my new spiritual sight weighed down my laughter, and suddenly I had a tear in my eye for him.

Sunday morning he joined us for an early Sunday breakfast, and then we drove to Orillia in the Odyssey. Mark and Cindy chose to stay home. Mark was going to work on his Karma Buster story, and Cindy was having a friend over to work on a school assignment; but before we left we did a nice HU song together.

I had time to reflect on David's private life all day Saturday as I did the week's laundry, changed the beds, and scrubbed the washrooms while Cindy vacuumed the house and watered the plants. I felt a twinge of disappointment at first, because David had stepped out of his enigmatic shell and proved to be very human; but upon reflection I had to respect him even more, because the more I thought about it the more convinced I was that he had told me what he did about himself to take the stars that I had for him out of my eyes. What he didn't know however was that the Atma had already done that by letting me see into that dark corner of his heart where he was afraid to go. Feeling as I did then, I wanted to draw David out on his relationship with his parents even more now, especially with his mother.

I felt I understood his father's personality. I had met many men like Aldous Oakly in my professional life, but not many women like his mother. I didn't know how to broach the subject, so I just came out with it. "David," I asked, on our drive to Orillia, "do you love your mother?"

"Yes," he readily answered. "My mother's a lost Soul, Cassie. She's lost in the darkness of her own mind. My mother rejected God when that drunk driver killed my sister, but God doesn't conform to us; we have to conform to God. That's why she gets depressed. Depression is nothing more than ego's rejection of life. That's all it is. Ego wants everything its own way, and when life doesn't conform to us we get depressed. But life is all about waking up to the divine within, and we can't do that if we reject life; can we? In her own way, my mother taught me to embrace life. I tried many times to shed some light into her life, but she's adamant. It takes courage to believe in God, Cassie. More courage than to not believe, because with belief comes the responsibility to awaken to the divine within. Between my father's smothering personality and my sister's tragic death, I think my mother used up all of her courage and has resigned herself to a life of quiet desperation. I feel sorry for her, but I can't help her. She won't let me in. She won't let anyone in. She's much too proud."

"And lonely and scared," I volunteered. I didn't expect to understand so quickly, but the way David explained his mother's situation resolved whatever conflicting feelings I had about her, and I decided to not pursue the subject. I focused on David instead. "I gather the baggage that you got from your father was his critical eye. Was that what you had to work on when you became a Sufi?"

"That was my mother lode. I'm not sure if it was Sam or Binny, but one of them told me that our biggest vice could be the source of our greatest virtue if we know how to mine it. My vice was my critical eye, which I definitely got from my father. He has an unerring ability to zero in on a person's faults, and so do I. I couldn't help myself, Cassie. I believed it was good to point out faults in people because it could only make them better, but Sufism taught me that there's a world of difference between negative criticism and positive criticism. One destroys and the other inspires. Sufism taught me how to inspire people by pointing out their virtues, not to destroy them by pointing out their faults like my father takes pleasure in doing. As Rumi said, *`you cannot teach by disagreement.*'"

"Sufism has been good to you, hasn't it?" I said, with an ironic smile at David's candor, because as he was talking the veil of his enigmatic personality was magically lifted and I *saw* that to overcome his hidden fear he had to forgive his parents, just as he had to forgive Higher Initiates for their spiritual conceit that he found so offensive; that was the only way he could surrender to love. He was much too proud to see it, but forgiveness was David's road to humility and the love he feared to embrace.

"You have no idea how good Sufism has been to me," David said, blissfully unaware of how I saw him now. "Without my Sufi training I wouldn't appreciate Atma-Gare as I do. I don't take Atma-Gare for granted, Cassie. Atmans are forever talking of giving love, but they have very little awareness of the dynamics of human evolution that led to this joyful insight. Giving love fulfills the desire in man to complete his destiny. Rumi spells this out in his poetry, and anyone who reads Rumi knows this. In my eight years with Sam the Man I learned something I wish I could get across to the Atma community, but I have trouble because they insist on putting the carriage in front of the horse."

"What did you learn from Sam?" I asked, with excited curiosity.

"Sufism, like the Atma, has secrets," David replied, with absolute confidence in his spiritual wisdom but strangely blind to the chameleon face of his own vanity. "But these secrets must develop within the student. Sufism, like the Atma, is something that happens to a person, not something that is given to him like so many Atmans believe. That's why I'm thankful for my Sufi training. By working on myself under Sam, I learned to put my horse in front of my carriage. This is why my chair stands apart from the rest of the Atma community."

David had not forgotten. I knew he wouldn't, but this was the first time that he made reference to the chair incident at the worship service in Newmarket, which I had made the symbol of our relationship, and by sharing it with me my chair seemed closer. But I also *knew* that I had to win David's love inch by inch without scaring him from making a commitment, because that was the only way we would ever realize our spiritual destiny together.

I silently called upon the Satma for help, because I decided right then and there to make the first move. I took a deep breath, and said, "David, do you love me?"

Keeping his eyes on the road, he thought long and hard before replying. His silence frightened me. He reached over with his right hand and grabbed mine and held it. He squeezed it very gently. "Yes," he said, and my heart fluttered.

I had to ask. I took a breath, and said, "Why?"

"You complete my life," he answered.

"How do I complete your life?" I asked, my heart pounding.

"How?" David asked, and fell into thoughtful silence again. After several minutes, speaking softly, as if from a distance, he said, "It's like writing a poem, Cassie. You just know when it's right. You just know when it's complete. I write poetry to connect with the Holy Current of God. I love this feeling, Cassie. It's the most satisfying feeling in the world. It's even better than the high of a marathon race. You do the same thing for me. When we're together, it feels like I have a direct line to the source of Love itself. I do love you, Cassie. My love for you keeps my line to God open. That's how you complete my life."

David had taken the first courageous step to commitment, and I was speechless. If ever I had any doubt about his love for me, it vanished in that moment.

I kissed him on the cheek. "Thank you," I said, with tears in my eyes.

At the worship service, the Atma Quartet was ready to start. We walked in just in time. Giving us a minute to get comfortable, Donna McDirmit, a smartly-dressed divorcee in her mid-fifties who was officiating the service, said, "We're going to sing the Love Song to God for a few minutes, and then Alex is going to talk on how we grow spiritually through service to the Atma, followed by Brandon's talk on the Satma's love for Soul. Then I'll give a talk on giving love to get love, and Jennifer will bring our service to a close with a beautiful Atma song that she wrote for her new CD. Please make yourselves comfortable and sing HU along with me..."

Our Atma Worship Service was held in the games room of the Leacock Care Center. The intercom system for staff announcements often interrupted us, but it was such a wonderful room that we dared not complain.

As we sang our beautiful Love Song to God I could not get David's declaration of love for me out of my mind. Did his love for me really keep his line to God open? Was that possible? I asked myself. Just then, as divine coincidence would have it, an announcement came over the intercom, "Ms. Patricia Love, please. *Love on line one....*"

Chapter 24

An Open Forum on Abortion

I didn't know what to expect. I didn't know if I had added fuel to the fire or thrown water onto it. I could not judge by the response to my open letter to Father McDuffy's public challenge, because I didn't get that much reaction to it, not personally, anyway; but I knew people were talking about it. Their silence told me.

My friend Grace Iverson told me that some of her friends in Barrie had read it, but didn't quite know what to make of it. I'm sure it was the same with people in Wyedale. That's why I was so nervous about going to the open forum. That's when I would find out one way or the other what the community really thought of me.

It was a long three weeks, and the silence was deafening. Father McDuffy did not call for an open forum debate on the abortion question until one week after my letter was published, and every day until the night of the open forum kept me on tenterhooks. What would Father McDuffy do? What would his devout little group of anti-abortionists say? Would they attack me personally? Would they label me strange, weird, off-balance? I didn't know.

And would I have any support at the forum? I knew that many of my nurses didn't care for Father McDuffy's little group of anti-abortionists. They didn't want the law re-legislated. Would they be there to support me? I didn't know. I knew David would be, but how was the general public going to respond?

Wyedale was a Christian community. What could I expect but a negative response? Would that affect my career? What would happen to me?

Father McDuffy's devoted little support group was made up of five female parishioners from the Catholic Woman's League who belonged to the Holy Rosary Prayer Society for Women. They described themselves as anti-abortionists who believed that it was an act of murder for a woman to terminate her pregnancy. This is why Father McDuffy issued his challenge for any scientist to prove that a fetus is not a little person. My letter challenged what they implicitly believed to be an irrefutable truth. That's why the open forum made me so nervous. I was vulnerable and I dreaded going, but I had to.

This movement was started shortly after I moved to Georgian Bay. These women spearheaded by Father McDuffy were trying to solicit local support to test the waters before they launched their crusade on the Internet where they hoped it would catch fire across the province and nationwide. If the local response was any indication it didn't seem like their crusade was catching fire. That's why I didn't know if I had thrown fuel onto their fire or cold water.

The open forum was to be held Saturday evening at seven o'clock at the Wyedale Community Center. By pure chance, Friday evening I happened to catch a program on television called *30 Days*. I had never seen this show before, but it caught my attention when I heard that an atheist was to spend thirty days with a devout Christian family. The premise of this show was to place people in situations where they would be challenged, like having a straight heterosexual Christian man live with a homosexual for thirty days—or having a pro-choice Atman who believed in reincarnation placed in an open forum debate on abortion in a room full of pro-life Christians who believe that we only live one life!

It wasn't a coincidence that I landed on this channel when I was searching for something to watch. The Holy Spirit of Atma wanted me to see this program to prepare me for the open forum. I knew that there was a message in it for me, so I sat with rapt attention waiting for the Golden-tongued Wisdom of Atma to speak to me.

The atheist who was to live with a Christian family was a wife and mother who had lost her Christian faith. She no longer believed there was a God who played a part in man's life. She believed in rational thought and the natural laws of life. Her husband, who was raised a Roman Catholic, shared her beliefs also, and they brought up their three children to believe that they were responsible for their own life and that natural laws governed human behavior.

I empathized with the woman. Being an Atman, I was no less of an alien to the Christian community than she was. Ironically, however, I had experiences throughout my life that defied rational thought and natural laws, especially the experience with my unborn child. My experience not only defied rational thought and natural laws, it also threatened the very foundations of Christian dogma that we only live one life which Jesus died upon the cross to save for us. I was neither on the side of the atheists nor Christians. As an Atman, I stood alone.

All the same, I was very anxious to see how the Christian family was going to receive this former Christian who had become an atheist. This was a waking dream, and I knew that the Atma was going to tell me how I was going to be received by the Christian community of Wyedale at the open forum debate on abortion.

When the atheist mother entered the Christian family's home, the look on her ashen face told me that she had just walked into the lion's den. This look did not go away for the first two weeks of her stay, but as intimidated as she was by the overwhelming spiritual culture of her Christian host family she did not give an inch on her beliefs.

She listened, she went to Church with the Christian family, and she sat in on their weekly Bible study classes. They talked, respectfully exchanged views, and tried to understand each other, but the Christian host husband simply could not fathom how a person could not believe in God. This was too much for him, and it showed on his incredulous face. The thought of not having God guide his life horrified him.

Conversely, the thought of being responsible for your own life gave the atheist something that the Christian family did not seem to have. By turning their life over to their savior Jesus, I felt the Christian family lacked something that the atheist had. This "something" was the chasm that separated them and could never be bridged by blind Christian faith. The most that they could hope for was mutual respect and tolerance of each other's beliefs.

I could not help but feel that this "something" that I sensed the atheist to have and not the Christians was what David called the *subtlety*. It wasn't that the Christians did not have it; they just did not have enough of the *subtlety* to define them. Which, ironically, told me they were not yet ready to be harvested for the kingdom of heaven! This brought to mind my uncle Timothy's favorite saying, "*Many are called, but few are chosen.*"

When the program ended I got my journal, made a pot of green tea, and sat at my kitchen table. I had to thoughtfully reason out what to expect at the forum the following evening. I missed my children, but I was happy that they were with their father.

"I honestly don't know what to expect tomorrow night," I wrote in my journal, "but I think the Atma has given me a glimpse with the waking dream of the show *30 Days* that I just watched on television. Like the atheist, I feel I will be walking into the lion's den tomorrow night; I know I'm going to be intimidated, but I won't let them get to me.

"Given the outcome of this show, what can I expect from the open forum tomorrow night? What would the atheist mother think of abortion? Would she stand up for the rights of the fetus or the legal rights of the mother? Does the fetus have the same legal rights?"

I took a drink of tea and sat back to reflect. Anti-abortionists believe the fetus has the same rights as the mother, but the government chose to respect the mother's right of choice over the rights of the fetus to life. What would the atheist think?

An atheist by definition believes that we only live one lifetime that ends when we die, and the fetus has to be a little person, if not complete, definitely in the making. At what point then would the fetus be a little person for the atheist? At conception? When it has developed some of its vital organs, or all of its vital organs? After birth? When?

The atheists can't help me. They don't know when a fetus becomes a little person. Even if they maintain that a fetus is a little person from the moment of conception, they're still stuck on the horns of the abortion dilemma: is it right or wrong to abort?

I had made it clear in my open letter to Father McDuffy that I did not believe a fetus is a little person until it is animated by a pre-existent Soul. The logical consequence of this belief is that it would not be an act of murder for a mother to terminate her pregnancy, because the fetus has not yet become a little person. It is a biological host for Soul. I went on to explain that the belief in reincarnation is held by as many if not more people than there are Christians who believe that we only live one lifetime, so why do Christians believe themselves to be right and everyone who believes in reincarnation wrong? How did Christians come to assume the moral high road on the issue of abortion?

I appealed to reason in my open letter to Father McDuffy. Perhaps I struck a chord, because I did not get that much response to my view; more likely I had shocked everyone into silence with the experience of my unborn child. Given the way the program *30 Days* concluded, I felt that the most I could hope for at the open forum was the same sense of grudging mutual respect for each other's beliefs.

But still, the Christian father of the family in the documentary could not wrap his head around a world without God. That horrified him. Maybe Father McDuffy and his camp couldn't wrap their heads around the pre-existence of Soul that millions of people believed in and which my personal experience with my unborn child proved.

I was back to the basic question: whose rights do we respect more, the mother's or the unborn child's? Society has chosen the mother's rights. Why, then, does this Christian anti-abortion movement want to re-legislate the law on abortion? On their website they argue that abortion is morally wrong. The fetus has no one to defend its right to life, and they have chosen to "take a stand for the unborn little person's right to life."

"Given their premise, they can't help but come to this conclusion," I wrote in my journal. "But given my experience with my unborn child, I cannot help but come to a different moral conclusion. They believe on blind Christian faith alone that a fetus is a little person, but I experienced the pre-existence of Soul with my aborted daughter!

"I have to stand up for the existing legal position because Christianity is trying to impose its moral sense of right and wrong upon the rest of us. I believe that we live more than one lifetime. I believe that we are responsible for our own karma. I do not believe that Jesus died for our sins. And I believe that a fetus is a carrier host for Soul and does not become a little person until it is animated by Soul, which I believe takes place the moment the child takes its first breath of life out of its mother's womb!"

That was my argument for the open forum debate, and I made crib notes just in case I got flustered. I knew I would, because the docudrama *30 Days* told me that I would. The atheist mother of three children got flustered a few times defending her belief in rational thought and the natural laws of life over blind Christian faith, and I had to be prepared.

At the end of the program, the Christians believed in the Word of God as they understood it, and the atheist did not; and they respectfully parted company.

Nothing was resolved, so I did not expect anything to be resolved at the open forum debate either. We would walk away with the realization that we no longer live in a Christian dominated society, and that there are other ways of looking at the world, and that was the best that I could hope for. Saturday evening finally came.

"Here I go, Satma," I said, as I left the house. "Please protect me."

I sang HU as I drove to the Community Center. I needed all the spiritual help that I could get. I even called upon Paul Mathew to be there for me. "Please, Paul," I pleaded with my childhood teacher, "help me get through this in one piece." I parked the Odyssey and waited four or five minutes. My heart was racing madly. Three cars pulled up before I decided to get out of my van and walk into the lion's den. I couldn't back out now. I wanted to die.

I expected more people in the all-purpose room that they used for the weekly charity bingo, but there weren't more than forty people scattered here and there. The woman at the door gave me a piercing look as she handed me a leaflet. It outlined the purpose of their cause to re-legislate the abortion law and how to get involved in their movement. "Thank you," I said, and gave her a pleasant smile. She didn't respond.

Father McDuffy was sitting at the front, behind a table. He had a Bible on the table, as well as a yellow pad of paper and pen, and a gavel. My heart was pounding. I scanned the room for David. But he wasn't there. My heart stopped. Was I going to be all alone in what suddenly felt like a cavernous den of hungry lions? A cold chill ran up my spine.

I scanned the room again. A strained silence filled the air. Father McDuffy acknowledged me with a nod when our eyes met. His long face was stern, serious, his eyes cold. This was not going to be an easy night, I thought. My heart was thumping madly.

I heard the door open. I turned to see who had come in. It was my nurse Pauline. She saw me, smiled, and waved. I waved back, hoping she would sit beside me, but she didn't. More people trickled in. By seven o'clock there were close to fifty people present. No one spoke. The silence was terrifying. My legs were shaking.

Father McDuffy pounded three times with his gavel and called the forum to order. He startled me. He waited a moment, and then stated that the purpose of the Christian Committee for the Rights of the Unborn Child was to launch a province-wide campaign to re-legislate the law on abortion, and that this public forum was to let everyone know where they stood and how people could get involved. "Ultimately," he concluded, "unless it can be proven in the cold light of pure science that a fetus is not a little person, we consider it to be an act of willful murder to terminate a pregnancy. This is why we want the law re-legislated."

"So what if science can't prove that a fetus is not a little person," said a loud, very confident voice, which belonged to Ethel Copeland, a middle-aged strident eighties feminist and mother of three grown daughters and one younger son who had been on AIDS medication for the past seven years. Ethel owned and operated Ethel's Hair Salon and was the secretary of our Hospice House Committee. Everyone in Wyedale knew Ethel. "That still does not give you the right to tell us what to do with our body. What gives you the right to tell me what to do with my body? That's what I want to know!"

The debate was launched. The room instantly loosened up. Ethel was used to this kind of personal confrontation, and by the way she felt about women's rights she wasn't going to stand for anyone taking away her right to choose what to do with her own body. As shrill as she could get on abortion and other feminist issues and gay rights, I admired her courage to speak up for herself and was very thankful that she was there.

"Someone has to protect the rights of the unborn," replied Father McDuffy, in a haughty, overbearing tone of voice.

"You can protect the rights of the unborn all you want," rebutted Ethel, "but you can't tell me what to do with my body. Who do you think you are, anyway?"

"Defender of the unborn," snapped Father McDuffy, which inspired a loud round of applause from the pro-life camp, started by his five staunch supporters sitting in the front row and followed loudly by one short, fat woman sitting just behind them.

"And who's going to defend my rights and the rights of all women who choose to have an abortion?" Ethel shot back, above the applause.

A few others and I applauded Ethel's response, but it didn't sound like we had a large following. I knew that pro-choicers were not as loud and vociferous as pro-lifers, so this did not discourage me. I very nervously bided my time to speak.

The clergy of the community sat together at the front and to the side facing both Father McDuffy and the public, but not all clergy were in the pro-life camp. Reverend Samuel Rutherford, the Anglican Church minister, let everyone know in no uncertain terms that as much as he believed it was a sin to take the life of an unborn child, he personally believed that a woman's right to her own body superseded the rights of the fetus, and for this he was jeered, with one woman saying, *"Shame on you!"*

The rest of the clergy were pro-life, but the most vociferous was not Father McDuffy, as I expected; it was Reverend Gordon Harvey of the Baptist Church, a red-haired young man with a freckled Howdy Doody face and large eyes who had the zeal of a fundamentalist preacher in his first parish. The other two ministers were Gale Anderson-Wilson, pastor of the United Church, a quiet, scholarly-looking woman with her reading glasses hanging around her neck; and

Ken Stevenson of the Presbyterian Church, an older man who looked nervous and out of place. Both ministers defended the rights of the fetus, but they were reserved in their comments and sat like silent sentinels throughout the whole debate.

The debate quickly became an emotional seesaw between those who wanted the law re-legislated and those who didn't, but I could not get over how no one mentioned my letter in the *Gazette.* It was as though everyone was afraid to open up that door, and the suspense was unbearable. I could feel an explosive expectancy in the room, and the glances I got dared me to speak. I had to. That's why I was there.

I took a deep breath, then another. I implored the Satma to give me courage, but just as I was about to speak I heard a familiar voice say, "If I may, I would like to shift the focus of this debate." I turned around to look. It was David Oakly. He was standing at the back of the room. He still had his work clothes on; his brown Carharrt carpenter's jeans and matching canvas work jacket. He had his arms crossed, and he looked like he meant business. My heart skipped a beat. "I would like to focus on what I consider to be the central issue of this whole abortion debate," he continued, speaking very clearly. His voice was challenging, but not confrontational. "I would like to address my question to all defenders of the unborn child, and I welcome anyone to respond. But please, it would be appreciated if you would put some thought into your answers before responding. I appeal to your good reason, not to your emotion. I would like to know how defenders of the unborn can be so certain that a fetus is a little person and not a biological organism which grows to become a little person. The Christian camp says that a fetus is a little person from the moment of its conception, but Christianity does not believe in the prior existence of the individual self. Christianity believes that the self is created at the moment of human conception, but there is a tradition in the world much older than Christianity that believes in the prior existence of the individual self. This tradition is called reincarnation, and it holds the view that the individual self is not created at the moment of human conception. This ancient tradition holds the view that the self pre-exists the conception of the human fetus, so the question that I would like to ask all defenders of the unborn child is this: if there exists in the world a tradition older than Christianity which believes that the self pre-exists the physical body, then how can you be so certain that a fetus is a little person and not a biological organism which will host the pre-existent self? I'm sure everyone here has read the letter that nurse Cassie O'Shaunnesy published in the local *Gazette*. She has courageously bared her Soul by sharing her experience with her unborn child. Her experience, however subjective it may be, attests to the view that the self pre-exists its carrier host. But Cassie O'Shaunnesy is not alone in this experience. I've done some research on the Internet, and there are many women who have had experiences with the Soul of their unborn child before it is incarnated. These Souls appear to the mother of the unborn child in what are called 'announcing dreams.' They come to the mother in her dreams before the child is born to let the mother know that they are going to become their new family member. Some Souls even tell the mother what name they wish to be called. If I may then, let me repeat my question. Which tradition do we believe? The Christian tradition, which believes that the immortal Soul is created at the moment of human conception, or a much older tradition of reincarnation that believes the individual Soul pre-exists its physical body? I invite anyone to answer this question."

An ominous pall fell over the audience. You could hear gasps of astonishment. David had thrown down the gauntlet, and a very nervous tension filled the room again. They had no choice now. David had opened the door that everyone was afraid to open. I was no longer alone in the lion's den, and I breathed a huge sigh of relief. Once again, I took a deep breath and was just about to speak when I heard another familiar voice. It was Doctor Hillory Jordon, a longtime family physician in the Wyedale community.

"That's a wonderful question, David," he began, as he stood up, "and I appreciate it very much. I was wondering if this question would come up at all, and I would like to thank you for the opportunity of responding to it. I've been a student of world religions for many years now, as many of you know from our conversations in my office, and for which I was handsomely paid, I might add. But in all seriousness, folks, I have had to grapple with this abortion issue not only to appease my professional conscience but my personal conscience as well. I personally don't believe that a fetus can strictly be called a little person, which is the phrase that has been adopted here, until it has developed all of its vital organs. I cannot in all good conscience, both professionally and personally, call a fetus a person until then. Now, with respect to your incisive question, David, which I also believe to be central to this whole contentious issue, given that the ancient tradition that you refer to is correct, I don't believe anyone can prove conclusively at what point the fetus is animated by the pre-existent Soul, as you put it. I believe the word most commonly used is incarnate. If you are familiar with past-life regression therapy, which I know some of you are from our conversations in my office, you might perhaps know that some people have been regressed prenatally under hypnosis. This suggests that the Soul incarnates the fetus prior to the birth of the child. Some even believe that Soul enters the new life at the moment of human conception. But I should add, to be completely fair to all sides, there is also a belief held by another camp that regressees, if I may call them that, can identify so strongly with what is referred to as the cellular memory of the unborn child that they believe themselves to be the fetus even prior to their incarnation of the fetus. They believe that the Soul takes on the cellular memories of the fetal body. If one is to believe this, it suggests that the Soul may or may not incarnate the new life until after the child is born into the world. But I confess, I have no idea how any of this can be proven scientifically. From a personal point of view, I find it fascinating that this question of other spiritual traditions has been kept so hush all this time, and I would like to thank nurse Cassie O'Shaunnesy for bringing it out into the open with her own post-abortion experience. We can call it a paranormal experience, a hallucination, or a miracle even, but I'm sure it was not an easy decision for her to go public with it, and I admire her courage. I personally believe that all spiritual traditions should be respected, seeing that there are as many people in the world who believe in multiple lives as those who believe that we live only one lifetime. This means that in the final analysis I have to come down on the side of the pro-choice camp. Until we can prove conclusively which spiritual tradition is right, we have to respect the rights of a woman to decide what to do with her own body. I think we owe them at least that much. After all, they are the fairer sex..."

"Right on!" shouted Ethel Copeland, springing to her feet. "A woman's right to choose is the real issue here! I agree with Doctor Jordon! A fetus is just a baby in the making! I can respect that! Until someone can prove that a fetus is a person before it is born I think a woman's rights have to be given first consideration. Good for you, Doctor Jordon! I'm glad you have the guts to speak up for the fairer sex! *We need more men like you!"*

I never thought it would happen, but David Oakly's question and Doctor Hillory Jordon's response turned the tables on the anti-abortionists, and for the remainder of the evening the clamorous Christians were on the defensive.

I summoned my courage. "I'd like to hear what Father McDuffy has to say to Doctor Jordon. I would like to know how you can prove that a fetus is a little person before it has developed all of its vital organs."

Father McDuffy coughed nervously. In a strained, hollow voice, he replied, "Just because a fetus is not fully developed does not make it any less of a person than a fetus that is fully developed. After all, everybody has to come from somewhere. The fetus is where we come from, beginning at the moment of conception. The Catholic Church believes that a fetus is a little person even if it does not have all of its vital organs developed, and we have to defend the rights of the fetus to become a fully-grown person. We have rights, and so must the fetus be given the same rights because the fetus is what you and I become. I don't think that I have to prove that a fetus is not a little person because a fetus is where people come from. This is so obvious to the Catholic Church that it does not need to be proven."

"Just as it was obvious to the Catholic Church that the astronomer Galileo was wrong to believe that the earth revolved around the sun," David spoke up. "It took your Church three hundred and fifty years to admit that it was wrong to condemn Galileo as a heretic. How can we be certain that Christianity is not wrong about this? Of course, in the strictest biological sense, a fetus is a person *in potentia.* No one will deny that. But that's not the question here. The question is this: why do you believe your Christian tradition should take precedence over other traditions that are as much a part of the social fabric of our global society as Christianity?"

"Yes," Ethel said, and stood up again. "Tell us why you think Christianity should have more say than other traditions. I don't believe in reincarnation myself because I don't know that much about it, but I have to respect that tradition, don't I? Look at all the Buddhists in the world today. They believe in reincarnation, don't they? The Dalai Lama was just here in Toronto last week. He believes in reincarnation, and thousands of people in Canada follow his teaching. We live in a democratic society in Canada. We don't persecute people because of what they believe. Buddhists don't tell us how to live our life, do they? So why should Christianity have the right to tell other religions that they're wrong? I don't think it's right for one religion to impose its will on other traditions, and I certainly don't think it's right for anyone to impose their will on me—*and no one is going to if I can help it!*"

"Actually, Ethel," Doctor Jordon very calmly said, standing up, "the Christian tradition did at one time believe in the theory of multiple lives. The Gnostics were an early Christian sect that believed in reincarnation. I realize that this is a theological question, but I happen to be partial to the Gnostic belief system, and I personally favor the early Gnostic tradition over Christianity in its present form. So not all Christians believe that we only live one lifetime. The ball is back in your court, Terrence?"

"You're not a Christian if you believe in reincarnation, Hillory," Father McDuffy replied, in a haughty, but very nervous voice.

"Not in your restricted sense of the word," Doctor Jordon replied, and stood up again. "Like I said, this is a theological question. I only wanted to make the point that Christianity has gone through many changes over the centuries, and not all changes were necessarily for the better, starting with that disastrous decision made by the Christian bishops assembled by the Roman Emperor Constantine at the First Council of Nicaea in 325 AD. These bishops arbitrarily decreed Jesus Christ to be the only begotten Son of God so they could assemble all of Christendom under one universal Church. In my humble opinion, that's where Christianity departed from its Gnostic roots and took a left turn."

Doctor Hillory Jordon was a charming eccentric, and a very kind, compassionate man who loved to share his philosophy with everyone; but as I learned from one of my senior nurses he was not always so charming and kind.

Shortly after he moved to Wyedale with his young family from Nova Scotia, Doctor Jordon treated a twelve-year-old girl whose unexpected death led the girl's mother to believe that Doctor Jordon was responsible because he refused to send her to a specialist at her request. So grief-stricken was she that she became psychotic and avenged herself by throwing caustic acid in Doctor Jordon's face late one night after a town counsel meeting. Doctor Jordon was a town counselor and deputy mayor. She waited for him in the back seat of his station wagon. The acid scarred his handsome face for life and did irreparable damage to his eyesight. Despite extensive facial surgery, his face was permanently disfigured. For the next ten years Doctor Jordon withdrew into himself. This was a very difficult period for him and his family. Darlene told me that he was hard, bitter, and very difficult to work with. The hospital lost a number of nurses and one doctor because of his bad temper. But then something happened to him. She didn't know what, but she said Doctor Jordon changed from the day he returned from a trip to India. He began studying world religions, eastern philosophies, esoteric teachings, and the occult; and out of his many years of Soul searching he created his own eclectic philosophy, which he shared with most of his patients in one form or another.

I had to speak up. Doctor Jordon gave me the courage to say what I felt in my heart. I stood up and looked directly at Father McDuffy and focused all of my attention on him, the wielder of Christian power...

"I would like to hear from you why Christianity has elected itself to be the moral arbiter of society," I heard myself say. "Every time you point a finger at a woman who has an abortion and call her a murderer, you pass judgment on her. By what authority do you feel you have the right to impose your morality upon the rest of society?"

"By the authority of Jesus Christ!" Gordon Harvey, the freckled-faced young Baptist minister blurted out. "The Bible tells us that it's

wrong to take the life of another person, and Jesus came into this world to show us how to live so that we might be saved! That's why we're right—because the Bible tells us so!"

"Yeah!" the short fat woman shouted. "By what authority do you have the right to take the life of an innocent baby? Tell me that, why don't you?"

"That's the point I want to make," I replied, and stood up again. "You believe you have the right to condemn women for having an abortion because your Christian conscience tells you it's wrong, but my conscience tells me otherwise. My spiritual values do not condemn abortion, so why should society bow to your moral standards?"

"Because we're right, that's why!" the same fat lady shouted.

And back and forth it went, until Doctor Jordon stood up again and addressed the audience. He turned and gave everyone a long, sobering stare.

"I have performed many abortions since the government made it legal," he said, speaking softly so we were forced to pay close attention, "and I have to tell you that in my experience women who have abortions are no less conscionable than women who do not have abortions, if not more conscionable. As nurse Cassie O'Shaunnesy said, by what authority do you believe yourselves to be right and her wrong? Is your God a better God than her God? Is your God better than my God? And if your God is a better God, I want to know why so many people have been murdered in the name of your God, like the thousands of Gnostic Christian Cathars in the Languedoc region of northern France in the 12th and 13th Centuries because they threatened Church doctrine, and during the Spanish inquisition that started in the 15th Century and wasn't abolished until the eighteen hundreds. Not to mention the atrocities committed to the indigenous people of many foreign lands, including our own country. Can you tell me that, please?"

No one spoke. Doctor Jordon commanded a great deal of respect in Wyedale. He was seventy-eight years old and had served the community for almost fifty years, long before they had built the new wing to the community hospital, and he had probably delivered some of the people sitting in that room, so when he spoke he was given the respect he deserved. But the brash young Baptist minister could not help himself. In a falsetto voice he said, "I'm not going to justify the blood shed in the name of Jesus Christ, but I don't think you can compare the two. We're talking about taking the life of innocent babies here, not the shedding of blood to convert native people. And as for the difference between my God and yours, I believe there is only one God, and I believe it's a matter of personal faith whether we do the will of God or not. I believe it's not God's will to shed the blood of innocent babies. This is why abortion is wrong. It's murder. It's not the Christian thing to do, and we have to put a stop to it. *That's what I believe!"*

"Me too!" shouted the short fat woman, and people applauded.

David spoke up. "With all due respect, do you honestly believe that a woman would willingly take the life of her own child?"

"Not if she doesn't know any better," the Baptist minister replied. "And I don't think a woman who has an abortion knows better. This is why we have to educate them. God's law is no different than civil law. Ignorance of the law is no excuse to break it. That's why they have to be told it's wrong to break God's commandment. Thou shalt not kill. That's one of the laws God gave to Moses for man to live by. We have to re-educate society about the Ten Commandments of God. It's our moral duty to do this or God will destroy the world just like he did Sodom and Gomorra!"

Another round of applause for Christianity.

"You're crazy!" shouted Ethel Copeland above the applause. "No one has to educate me about the Ten Commandments! What do you think we are, stupid? You're the one who needs to be educated about human rights! I have the right to control my own body and no one is going to take that right away from me! You're the one who needs to be educated, reverend!"

"I think you're wrong, Ethel," he replied.

"And I know you're wrong, Gordy boy!" Ethel shouted.

David spoke up again, "You're free to worship your God and live your own faith, are you not, Gordon?"

"Yes," he replied.

"Then why can't you let us worship our God and live our faith?"

"What about the baby who doesn't have anyone to defend it?" someone shouted.

"Yeah?" shouted the short fat woman.

"This baby in question is the central issue here, isn't it?" David replied. "I see the baby as a biological entity that will become the carrier host for the new Soul that is going to inhabit its new physical body. But until Soul takes over its new physical body, I cannot in good conscience call the baby a little person. This brings us back to the question raised by Gordon: why should my God of freedom of choice bow down to your God of no freedom of choice?"

"Your God is Satan!" the short fat lady yelled out.

Father McDuffy pounded his gavel. "Let's have none of that. This is an open debate, not a free-for-all."

"Thank you," David said. "I would like to say something else, if I may. Judging from the events in the world today, a wave of freedom seems to be washing over the planet. Dictators are falling like dominos. Ever since the fall of the Twin Towers in New York city, the world has been startled by the tenacity with which old world values want to hold onto social conscience, as witnessed by all the new political turmoil in the Middle East and in this very room tonight. But the spirit of freedom has possessed the soul of man, and no amount of rhetoric or brute force is going to keep man from realizing his personal destiny of spiritual freedom. It is becoming impossible to maintain this tyrannical hold upon the psyche of man, as you vainly attempt to do by telling women they have no right to their own body. You do not have the right to our body, nor to our mind or Soul. Ethel Copeland is right to fight for her freedom of choice. I'm at a loss to see why Christianity cannot see this new wave of spiritual freedom that is sweeping across the world. Everywhere we turn we're witnessing the death throes of this old world God of no choice and the birth pains of a new God of freedom of choice and personal responsibility. Just look at how conscious we're becoming of our environment. The zeitgeist today is all about becoming accountable for what we're doing to the planet and to ourselves. This bold new spirit sweeping across the world from one country to the next is about responsible personal freedom, and Cassie's spiritual experience with her unborn child speaks to the awakening spiritual consciousness that is going to shape the moral character of the 21st Century. You cannot turn the clock back with your desire to re-legislate the abortion law. It won't happen. The new spirit of our times won't let you. At the risk of offending you, Terrence, I think you're tilting at windmills."

After a startling moment of stunned silence, Doctor Jordon stood up. "I agree with everything that David said," he said, gently breaking the spell of silence, and then sat back down. Then he stood back up again. "Give it up, Terrence. Like David said, you're not going to turn back the clock. Let's step into the 21st Century, why don't we?"

Doctor Jordon got a modest round of respectful applause and Father McDuffy had the most startled look on his ashen face that I have ever seen. He was rendered dumb. By agreeing with David's commentary, Doctor Jordon had brought the debate to a dead stop. There was nothing more to be said. The silence was so loud that people became anxious and nervously got up to leave. Father McDuffy made a feeble attempt to thank everyone for coming and asked anyone who was interested in their cause to contact him or one of the ladies in his committee, but people were very anxious to make their escape. Some gravitated into little groups, but they all made their way to the exit for fear of getting caught up in a bigger discussion. The open forum debate on abortion was over.

I walked over to Doctor Jordon. "Thank you, Hillory," I said, choking back tears. "I appreciate everything you said. Thank you..."

He stood up, grabbed my hand with both of his, and held it tenderly before speaking. His eyes, full of love, warmed my heart. "They came to crucify you, Cassie," he said, in a loud whisper. "I couldn't let them do that to you."

I was shocked. "What do you mean?"

"Trust me, Cassie. They came for blood."

I couldn't believe it. "You're serious, aren't you?"

"Yes. But they can't touch you now," Doctor Jordon replied, with the sweetest smile on his disfigured, adorable face. "They would look foolish if they tried."

"You must know this community very well, Hillory. I would never have thought that these good people would be out for my blood."

"You have no idea what these people are capable of," Doctor Jordon said, and squeezed my hand again with both of his. "We have to get together sometime. I'm very interested in your experience. I understand you're an Atman."

"Yes, I am. How did you know?"

"David told me. He certainly championed your cause, didn't he?"

"Yes, he did," I said, and smiled. Just then I felt a tap on my shoulder. It was David. I turned. "Oh, David. *Thank you so much!*"

"You're welcome," David said, with a triumphant smile. Then, turning to Doctor Jordon, he said, "You sure gave them a lot to think about, Doc."

"You know, David," Doctor Jordon sighed, "I'm beginning to think that Binny's right. You just can't teach donkeys to read no matter how many books they carry..."

David burst into laughter. He turned to me and said, "That's an inside Sufi joke. Doc's playing the role of the incomparable Mullah Nasrudin. He loves to do that, especially when he has you cornered in his examining room. So, Cassie; it's out in the open now. How do you feel?"

"I don't know what I would have done without you two. Thank you both so much. I'll never forget this. Never," I said, with tears in my eyes.

Doctor Jordon patted me on the shoulder. "Just doing what we're here to do, Cassie. So, David, have you seen Binny lately?"

"I had lunch with him at his diner two weeks ago."

"He's still slinging hash, is he?"

"You know Binny. He can't stop passing it on."

By the way Doctor Jordon laughed I got the feeling that they shared a secret. I had to find out who Binny was, and I had to find out what David's relationship with Doctor Jordon was also. I got the feeling that they had a special relationship that spoke to David's mystifying personality, and I was dying to find out what that was.

As we walked to our cars Doctor Jordon said, "I'm sure you two have plenty to talk about. I'll see you Monday, Cassie. Have a good night."

I had to give Doctor Jordon another hug. "Thank you again, Hillory. I can sleep peacefully now. I'll never forget what you did for me tonight."

Doctor Jordon smiled and gave me a parting wave.

I turned to David. "Would you like to drop over to the house, David? I could sure use your company tonight."

"Let's pick up a pizza first," David said. "I've been installing the hardwood floors in my house all day and I'm famished."

"That's a wonderful idea. I haven't eaten all day either. I was much too nervous to eat. Let me treat pizza. That's the least I can do after what you did for me tonight."

"I had no choice. I had to stand by you, Cassie."

"Why?" I asked, intrigued by his comment.

" 'Tell it unveiled, the naked truth! The declaration's better than the secret,' " he replied, quoting Rumi once more, but I understood what he meant this time.

"That's why I had to do what I did, David," I said, as fresh tears came gushing to my eyes. I could not hold them back. I felt such relief.

David put his arms around me. He held my trembling body in his powerful arms for the longest time. I couldn't stop crying.

Chapter 25

The Miracle of My Unborn Child

We ate pizza, sipped on a glass of chilled white wine, and talked over the events of the evening, and then I curled up into his strong, muscular arms on the sofa.

"I can't believe it," I sighed into his chest.

"What?" he asked.

"Tonight. I was prepared for the worst, David."

"This has been a long day for you, hasn't it?"

"You have no idea."

"Well, it's over now. Just relax and let go."

"David?"

"What?"

"Can you please stay? I don't want to be alone tonight."

"Of course," he said, caressing my cheek.

"Thank you," I said, and snuggled closer.

Years of emotion washed through my tears onto David's chest. I could not believe what I had done. It was as though the last six years of my life were all a dream and I was just now waking up. "David?" I said, looking up at him. "What happened tonight? Doctor Jordon told me that they were out to get me. What happened?"

"To be honest with you, Cassie, I feared the worst too," he said, again caressing my cheek. "The Satma must have been there for you, that's all I can say."

"I did ask for his protection when I left the house this evening.

365

And Paul Mathew's. Do you think they were there, David?"

"How else can you explain the outcome?"

"I had no idea it would end this way," I said, with a grateful sigh.

"We can thank the Mullah Doctor Jordon for that," David said, and laughed.

"And you," I said, and reached up and kissed him tenderly on the cheek. "Thank you, David. You're my Lancelot!"

David laughed again. "Every man should have a fair maiden, Cassie. Without love, what are we really?"

"Incomplete!" I exclaimed, letting out my emotions.

"You're absolutely right. We're incomplete without love."

"I believe it, David. That's why my mentor said that our final lesson in life is to learn how to love and be loved unconditionally. What an incredible woman she was. I wish I had one tenth of her courage," I said, as I slid back into David's body.

"Who, Elisabeth Kubler-Ross?"

"Yes. She has given me so much inspiration in my life, David. I would never have had the courage to go public with my experience had she not been my role model. Doctor Kubler-Ross went against the establishment her whole life. Did you know that she was called the "Vulture" when she started her research on death and dying? Now her work has become the standard model for the grieving process. Isn't that ironic?"

"Yes. But life always resists the living *Shariyatma,* Cassie."

"What do you mean by that?"

"Oh, that's just my way of saying that anyone who has new ground-breaking insights is going to encounter resistance," David replied, in a melancholy tone of voice that seemed to speak from deep personal experience. "The status quo is always afraid of anyone who steps outside the box of conventional thought. That's why I'm surprised by tonight's debate. I had no idea what was going to happen. I just put my trust in the Atma and went with it."

I sat up again and looked at David. "You did?"

"Yes. I feared for you tonight, Cassie. I had no choice but to give it to the Atma," David said, completely surprising me.

"Why did you fear for me?" I asked.

"Your open letter threatened the status quo, that's why. It's not easy for people to let go of what they believe. Had it not been for Doctor Jordon, I'm sure it would have ended differently tonight. People may call him eccentric, but they don't dismiss him. They take what he has to say very seriously. Like Sam the Man once told me, 'It's not what people say about you that matters, it's what they think about you.' And the people of Wyedale think very highly of the Mullah Doctor Hillory Jordon."

"Why do you call him Mullah?"

"Hillory is a practicing Sufi. His teacher is my friend Binny."

"Really?" I said, tingling with curiosity. "Did you know that he would be there tonight?" I asked, wondering if David and Doctor Jordon had planned their rebuttal.

"No, I had no idea. But I'm sure glad he was. He lent so much credibility to what we had to say that everyone was forced to listen. And Ethel Copeland made sure they heard. She's quite the woman, isn't she? I certainly admire her convictions..."

"Me too!" I interjected. "I'm going to drop by her shop tomorrow to thank her in person for her support. She's on our Hospice House Committee, David. She's very dedicated to our project. I didn't expect her to be so vocal tonight, but I sure appreciate it."

"She came through for you, didn't she?" David said, with a private chuckle at Ethel's fearless personality. "But then, she's earned it. She's been put through a lot with her son. I know her husband Brian pretty well. He's an electrician. I've used him on two or three jobs. Rumor has it that one of their daughters had an abortion. Guess who did the procedure?"

"Doctor Jordon?"

"Yes."

"So that's why she was so vocal!"

"Now you know. I honestly don't know how far this anti-abortion movement will go, Cassie; but I doubt it will go anywhere now."

"Why do you say that?" I asked, excited by all the information.

"I think Ethel said it best. She not only speaks for the modern woman, but the coming age of spiritual enlightenment. The door to more personal freedom has been opened, and it can't be shut again. Ethel Copeland refuses to give up her new freedom, and with the door that you opened I think you've made it easier for women to hold onto this new freedom."

"What door? My belief in reincarnation?"

"Yes, of course. Your experience with your unborn child opened that door. You publicly linked abortion with reincarnation, Cassie. No one has ever done that before. I checked the Internet, and as far as I know you're the first person to look at abortion from the perspective of reincarnation. That's an incredible contribution you've made to the living *Shariyatma.* That's why I had doubts about tonight's debate. I thought it was going to get really nasty."

"Did you really?"

"Yes, I did."

"Why, David?"

"Why?" David repeated, and thought for a moment. "Because I know that the amount of resistance to the living *Shariyatma* is directly proportional to the truth revealed. The greater the truth revealed, the greater the resistance will be. That's Sam's Law."

"Sam the Man?"

"Yes."

"I think I understand Sam's Law, but I'm not sure I understand what you mean by my contribution to the living *Shariyatma.* Can you explain that for me, please?"

"The living *Shariyatma* is the natural way of evolution in the outer circle of life. Your experience with your unborn daughter proves that a fetus is a carrier host for Soul, the pre-existent self. This is way outside the box of conventional thinking, but this perspective will wake society up to the true spiritual nature of man. This is your contribution to the living *Shariyatma.* You helped to raise the consciousness of society tonight, Cassie," David said, as he softly caressed my cheek.

I loved being in David's arms. I felt so safe that I did not want him to stop. "All I did was tell my story. I had to respond to Father McDuffy's challenge. I had to, David. I couldn't let him get away with it. I only wish I could have told the whole story!"

"You mean there's more?" David said, with some surprise.

"Would you like to hear the whole story?" I said, excited by the opportunity to finally share my miracle story with David.

"I can't wait!" he said, excitedly.

"Are you sure you're not too tired?"

"I'm never too tired to hear a good Atma story."

"But there's so much to tell, David. Where do I start?"

"At the beginning. Go ahead, Cassie. I want to hear it all."

"Alright," I said, excited by David's unexpected show of emotion. I finished my glass of wine and silently asked the Inner Master for guidance. Then I felt nudged to do a HU. "David, can we do a short HU first? I feel I need it to give me courage."

"Of course," he said, and we did a soft, loving HU for about five minutes before I felt ready to tell the incredible story of my unborn child.

"Baraka Bashad," I said, and brought our HU to a close. With all the confidence in the world, I began. "It started before I had my abortion, David," I said, letting my mind drift back to the beginning. "For about two weeks before I went ahead with my abortion, I began to get the strangest feeling that someone was in my bedroom just before I drifted off to sleep. I dismissed this feeling the first two or three nights, but I had to sit up in bed every night after that for an hour or two before sleep forced me to lay down. I just sat and stared into the darkness. I knew someone was in the room with me, but I wasn't afraid. In fact, I felt good. Really good. I felt just the same as I felt after I gave birth to my children. It was the strangest feeling.

"I was wide awake. I knew I was going to abort my child because I had made up my mind, but I still had nagging doubts in the back of my mind. Should I carry the baby to term and put it up for adoption? I could never put my baby up for adoption. How could I? But could I live with myself if I took my own baby's life? What would Kevin say? Could I be sure he would come back to me if I aborted? What would my mother say? What would my uncles say? It was a mortal sin. What right did I have to take the life of an innocent child? But whose life was more important, my unborn child's or mine? What if my husband didn't come back to me? If I went to term, I would have to take another maternity leave. Could I do that? What about me? I had a right to choose, didn't I? These questions haunted me. But I had gone over all these questions on my walk in Stanley Park, and I came to the conclusion that my life was more important to me than the life of my unborn child, so I decided to abort my fourth child.

"It was the most selfish decision of my life. It went against everything that I had been brought up to believe, but I had to put my life above the life of my unborn child. I had to! I was the mother of my child. Kevin and I created our baby, but my husband didn't want another child. He wanted his freedom. He left me for another woman, not another child. If he could make a decision like that, so could I. I was very much the feminist, David. I didn't want my freedom to be any less meaningful than my husband's, or any man's freedom for that matter. I wanted my freedom to be equal to a man's freedom. That's what I believed.

"I tried to tell Kevin, but he wouldn't talk to me. He said he had to stay away from me because he would not have the strength to leave me again if he came back. I tried to tell him about our new baby, but he told Belinda, his new lady friend, to tell me he had made up his mind. He said he felt caged in with me. He said all he did was work and take care of the children. He wanted more out of his life, so he left me.

"Kevin loves our children, David. He really does. He'll do anything for them. That's why I felt another child would keep him from leaving me. But I was wrong. Another child meant less love for him, so I decided to abort our child to prove to Kevin how much I loved him. I tricked him into my pregnancy, and I wanted to untrick him back. I told Belinda to tell Kevin that I had to talk to him. It was a matter of life or death. He never got back to me and I decided to have my abortion anyway. I didn't care about the consequences now. I had to undo what I had done. I knew in my heart that what I had done wasn't fair to Kevin. I seduced Kevin. Oh God, how I loved that man! And he loved me so much I felt it was impossible for him not to come back to me. But he wanted out of our marriage. His freedom was more important to him than his love for our children and me, and I could not take that. I could not..."

I started to sob. I could not stop myself. I was back there again, in the moment, and I could not stop the emotions. David waited patiently.

Through sniffles, I continued. "I decided to abort because I had tricked Kevin and I had to undo what I had done. Can you appreciate my dilemma, David?"

David did not reply. He just nodded, and smiled.

"You do, don't you?" I asked, for reassurance.

"Yes," he said.

"Well, it proved to be much more difficult to abort than I thought. The presence that I sensed in my bedroom was my unborn child. I didn't know that immediately, but after the first three or four visits I was certain it was my unborn child. And then I saw it. My lights were out, but I saw the outline of my baby girl on my bed just by my feet, a glowing baby girl playing with her toes. I saw her, David. There was a blue light all around her. She just lay there naked and so beautiful, playing with herself. She had her knees bent and she was playing with her little toes. It only lasted for a minute or two, but I saw her three separate times. My children saw her, too. They don't remember seeing her now, but they all saw her.

"Seana. That's the name I had chosen for my baby girl. Seana visited my children in their bedroom like she visited me. Patrick doesn't want to talk about it, and Mark has a faint memory of her; but it doesn't mean as much to him, so he's pushed it to the back of his mind. And Cindy was too small to remember. Anyway, I had to make up my mind. But it was torture now. I thought nothing could keep me from aborting, but after I saw my baby Seana I began to feel so much guilt for even thinking of aborting her that I nearly went out of my mind.

"How could I take the life of my precious baby? What right did I have to deprive Seana of her life? You cannot believe the agony that I went through, David. I thought about this for years after I had my abortion, and it all came down to one thing—my freedom.

"I chose to abort because I valued my freedom more than anything in the world, even the life of my unborn child. God knows I wanted Kevin back. But I had tricked him. I didn't want him back on those terms, David. I had to abort to start fresh. I had to let go of my feelings for Seana. I don't know how to say this, but it was as though my unborn child now symbolized everything that kept me from being free. In that tiny little body I saw my bondage and the bondage of all women to life, and I had to abort my child. I did not want to let my feelings keep me from the freedom that I felt I deserved and every woman should have. I had to do it. I had no choice. My freedom was as important to me as it was to Kevin, and my very life depended on it. I just knew that if I didn't have this freedom I would never be whole. I would never be satisfied. I would always be wanting. I can't explain it. That's just how I felt.

"I wanted Kevin back, David; and I believed he would come back to me if I had my abortion. I couldn't see that he was using the excuse of not wanting another child to get out of our marriage, but that's how I felt. I wanted my freedom, but I wanted Kevin back too, and I thought I would get him back with my abortion. The honest truth is, I wanted Kevin back more than I wanted another baby, so I decided to have my abortion, clinging to the hope that my husband would come back to me. It was wrong of me, but that's how I felt.

"I did not want a baby that Kevin did not want, but when I saw her lying on my bed playing with her little toes I had to think again. I cried, David. You have no idea how I cried before I decided to have my abortion, but I did it and that was that. I promised myself I would have no regrets, but I did not count on the reaction that I got from my family. That's when I tried to take my own life. I blame my uncle Clancy for that. He pushed me over the edge. I don't know if I can ever forgive him for what he did to me. I've tried, but there's a part of me that can't forgive him. I try not to think about it, but I know I will have to deal with it someday. Would you like some tea, David? I have to collect myself..."

"By all means," he said.

As the kettle boiled I composed myself in the kitchen with a quiet HU. I couldn't stop now. I had to tell the whole story. I poured the hot water into the teapot and brought the tray into the living room and sat in silence.

David poured the tea. "Take your time, Cassie. We've got all night."

"Thank you," I said, and took a sip of tea. "I made Chamomile to relax my nerves," I said, with a nervous smile.

"That's fine," he said, and took a sip.

"It didn't hit me right away," I continued, with a lump in my throat, "but after my mother came at me like a wild banshee I began to feel the guilt of what I had done. I tried to explain why I had done it, but she would have nothing to do with it. I had taken the life of her grandchild and I had to ask God for forgiveness. I had broken the Sixth Commandment, and if I didn't go to confession I would be a heathen like my father and go straight to hell when I died. My mother would not let up. I finally did go to confession, but..."

I stopped talking. I had to fight back the rush of emotions of my last confession. I took a drink of tea, sighed, and continued. "I don't know if it's just me, but I couldn't live with myself without my mother's forgiveness. I know that everyone will always be their mother's child, and we all want our parent's approval, but with me it was almost a pathological need to have my mother's forgiveness, so I pressed her. But the harder I pressed her, the more she resisted. Maybe this was Sam's Law; I don't know. But I tried, David. I really tried to get my mother to understand why I had to abort my child.

"This was the most critical period of my entire life, but I knew that if I continued to press my mother for forgiveness I would never be my own person; so I decided to cut the chord once and for all. I had to tell my mother that I no longer cared whether she forgave me or not. I had done what I did because it was my life, not hers. I had made my decision, and I would suffer the consequences. I didn't care anymore. If I had to go to hell for what I did, then so be it; but I was not going to beg my mother's forgiveness anymore.

"Finally, after all those years I cut the chord with my mother and became my own person at last. But I still had ties to sever with uncle Clancy and uncle Tim. I went to them both and asked them to talk with Mother, but they sided with Mother; so I had no choice but to go it alone. My husband had abandoned me, my family had stranded me, and so it was no wonder that I tried to take my own life. Not my brother, though. Michael stood by me. I wanted so much to be forgiven

by someone in my family, and I'll be forever grateful that Michael did;
but when I went to see my uncle Clancy right after Michael forgave
me, my uncle pulled me down so low that I fell into suicidal despair
and I went home and tried to take my own life. I thought about this for
years, David, and I've come to believe now that my uncle hates
women. There's no other explanation for his behavior that day. My
uncle Clancy, the good homosexual priest that he believes himself to
be, is a misogynist. I'm convinced of that now."

I paused and waited for David's reaction, but still he said
nothing. He smiled and waited for me to continue.

"Do you think a man can hate women that much, David?" I
asked.

"Yes," he replied, without further explanation.

"My uncle used to cringe at the sight of me sometimes.
Especially when I was all made up. He never touched me, David. He
never hugged me, or kissed me. Never. He always patted me on the
head until I was too tall for him to do that. But I never made sense of
that until my brother told me that he was a homosexual. I would never
have guessed, given his sermons on the sins of the flesh. I was too
naïve to see that my uncle could commit such an abominable sin like
homosexuality. He was so fire and brimstone in his sermons on the
sins of the flesh that I just couldn't imagine him involved in a
homosexual relationship. I couldn't, David."

I paused again. I took another sip of tea. David refilled my cup
and said, "How did your uncle push you over the edge, Cassie?"

"I was feeling so high from my visit with my brother that I didn't
think anything could ruin how I felt, but my uncle did. I thought I
could go over there and trade forgiveness with him. My brother told
me that my uncle was a homosexual, so I thought I would work that
into the conversation and forgive him, and then he could forgive me
for my abortion. But it didn't go that way at all. Uncle Clancy sensed
that I knew he was a homosexual, but he wasn't going to let me have
the satisfaction.

"My uncle wanted to preserve the image that he had cultivated
with me over the years of being an obedient servant of the Lord. He
picked up on my feelings. He knew why I was there, and he attacked

me with the ferocity of a wild beast. I never saw my uncle get so worked up about anything in my life until that day. I had become the symbol of his own foul wickedness, and he turned on me until he broke my spirit. I would never have dreamed my uncle could be so cruel. If I hadn't experienced it I wouldn't have believed it. Not in a million years.

"I went straight home and took half a bottle of sleeping pills, and all because I thought I could trade forgiveness with my uncle. My sin for his sin. Can you imagine that? But he didn't want his sin to be forgiven. That's why he turned on me with such ferocity. I wanted my uncle to forgive me, but he didn't want me to forgive him his homosexuality. He wanted to protect his dark sin with the sanctity of his collar. *What a hypocrite!"*

"Take your time, Cassie," David said, with a reassuring pat on my thigh.

"He raped me of my will to live, David. I was a godless sinner just like my father, he said. I had no conscience. I had murdered my own child. 'SINNER!' he kept screaming at me until I broke into hysterical tears. God Almighty, I don't think there's anything in my life I feel more ashamed of than that moment, and I promised myself that I would never let anyone make me cry like that again. *Never!"*

David patted my thigh again. "Have some tea, Cassie."

"No. I have to get this out. My uncle made me feel like I was the most wicked sinner in the world. I had taken the life of my own child and I wasn't worthy of God's love. I could not be forgiven because I was born with the sin of Lucifer like my father. I cried my heart out in front of him, but he kept screaming at me until my spirit broke and I felt I didn't deserve to live. And he calls himself a servant of Jesus Christ? My God, David. My sweet God..."

I had to stop talking. David said nothing. I looked into his warm, loving eyes, begging for solace. He said, "Go on, Cassie. I'm listening. I want to hear the whole story."

I paused for a minute, and then continued. "After I tried to take my own life I had to get my life back in order, but I could not. I was a basket case, David; and I don't think I could have come around without the Inner Master's help. I had no idea what was happening to me at the time, but when I joined Atma-Gare later I learned that the dreams I had after my suicide attempt were the Satma's way of healing my psychic wounds. My uncle took my spirit away from me, David. He raped me of my will to live, and even though my life was spared..."

"How were you spared?" David interjected.

"My son Patrick found me and called his father at work. He called an ambulance and they rushed me to the hospital just in time. It was fate, David. I wasn't meant to die that way. But because my life was spared it only made me feel more guilty. I couldn't do it again. Not after I saw what it would do to my children. I just couldn't do that to them. And that made me feel even more remorseful.

"I was trapped by my own guilt, and I didn't know how to get out. That's when I began to have these strange dreams. I was so distraught that I did not get out of bed for days at a time. I drifted in and out of my dreams. I was in a healing temple. I was treated with light and music therapy, and I was taken to a garden where I talked with other people who were being treated like me. Then I would wake up.

"I don't know what I would have done if I hadn't been healed in my dreams. But after I found Atma-Gare you wouldn't believe the relief I felt when I found out that this is all part of the secret teachings of Atma. My God, I said to myself, to think that for years I was praying to a God whose only love for me was to be worshipped on bended knee! What kind of God was my Christian God, anyway?"

"The question of God is much too complicated for Christians, Cassie," David offered, by way of comfort. "It's best to leave it alone and let them find out for themselves that God has many faces."

"I think you're right. But I had a lot of issues then, and I reacted to God with anger. Anyway, I remember my healing dreams vividly. Not only was I taken to an inner temple to be healed, but I was also given spiritual therapy. After every light and music healing session, I was taken to this beautiful garden where I talked with other people, and then a bald-headed man with penetrating eyes whom I learned later was the Atma Master Shabda Das would talk with us.

"It was like group therapy. I remember talking about my abortion and why I tried to take my life, and the man told me that suicide didn't solve anything. It only put things off that had to be dealt with eventually, and he told me how to deal with those issues. He also told me abortion was not a sin, because life begins when the child takes its first breath of life. He said it would be hard for me to get over my guilt because I still had a lot of karma to burn off. But he said I would one day be free of all my guilt and my life would be my own to live as I chose. Finally my healing dreams stopped. I went back to work and started to get my life back in order. But I was still plagued by nagging doubts about my abortion. I didn't want to admit it, but I still felt guilty for taking the life of my unborn child, and depression began to set in again. I feared the worst, and then the miracle happened."

This was the part of the story I couldn't wait to tell, and my heart started racing again. The memories came flooding back, filling me with the same miraculous, heart-stopping excitement. David reached over and grabbed my hand and held it. "Take your time, Cassie," he said. "Just take your time …"

A few minutes later, I continued. "About three weeks after my healing dreams, I fell into deep depression. I wanted to die. That's when I was blessed with the miracle of my unborn child. I went to bed one night and tried to read myself to sleep. But once again, I felt that I was not alone in my room. I felt the presence of my unborn child. I knew it was her. 'Seana,' I called out. 'Is that you?' Then I began to feel warm all over, and the whole room filled with a bright light. I felt so much love that I could hardly believe it. I just sat there for the longest time and smiled at the light. It was the most beautiful feeling, David. But I knew that something was going to happen. I could feel it. And then I saw the same outline of a child at the foot of my bed that I had seen before I had my abortion, and I just stared as the little baby began to grow before my eyes. I rubbed my eyes two or three times, thinking this was just another dream, but it wasn't. I know this may be hard to believe, but something else was happening as my little girl was growing up in front of my eyes. I was experiencing my life with her as she was growing up. And you would not believe the emotions that I experienced. I went through every emotion that I had for Seana as I watched her, like time had been sped up and stopped at one and the same time. It was strange, and I don't expect you to believe me, but every moment that I had with Seana was as much a part of me as every moment that I have had with my other children, and I wept and laughed and giggled and smiled as Seana grew up into a beautiful young teenager who stood before me at the foot of my bed. Every word that I had spoken to her and about her, every thought that I had about her, and every feeling that I experienced for her were as real to me as my own life, and I stared at my unborn daughter with more love than I have ever had for any of my children, and I started to weep with joy. I wept with boundless joy, David. I wept an ocean of emotion before Seana came over and put her arms around me and said, 'Please don't cry, Mother.' I held my aborted daughter in my arms and just sobbed my heart out..."

Tears were streaming down my face. David slid over and held me in his arms. I wept into David's chest as he held me. I wept, and wept, and wept...

"Thank you, David," I sniffled. "I'm fine now. Seana was my little girl. She was as real to me as my other three children, but she wasn't born into life. She was the child who would have been had I not aborted her body. She had strawberry blonde hair, like me. She had Kevin's eyes, but my nose and my body. 'Thunder thighs,' I teased her. I could not believe what I was experiencing, but it wouldn't stop. Time stood still, and we talked about everything as though we had to refresh our memories of our life together, and then I had to ask her what happened after I aborted her body.

"I don't know why I asked her. It just came out. 'Seana,' I said, 'what happened to you after I aborted your body?' 'Nothing. I stayed over there,' she said. 'Where?' I asked. 'Over there, on the other side,' she said. 'And now?' I asked. 'Where are you now?' 'I have another body,' she said. 'Where?' I asked. 'Philadelphia,' she said. 'You mean you're an American now?' I asked. 'Yes,' she said. 'How come?' I asked. 'This family was right for me,' she said. 'Seana,' I said, with my heart in my throat and more tears in my eyes, 'are you angry with me for aborting your body?' 'No, Mother. It was your choice,' she said. 'I have another body which will serve me for what I have to learn in this lifetime. My name is Patricia. And you know what, Mother? We're going to meet one day at a spiritual seminar. We have the same

Master. You will like me, Mother. I will be a little bit like I am now, only I won't look like I do now. I have brown hair in my new body. I wish I could have the hair I have now, but I can't. I love you, Mother, but I have to go back now. Please don't cry for me anymore. I love you,' she said, and faded before my eyes. I could not move. I sat in my bed and stared into the darkness for hours just savoring the memories of the daughter that I could have had had I not aborted her body."

David stroked my hair, kissed me softly on the cheek, and pulled me close to him and held me in his arms. "What a beautiful experience, Cassie," he sighed. "What a fortunate woman you are!"

"I wish I could tell the whole world, David," I said, and sniffled into his chest.

"You will one day. I can't believe the Atma let you have this experience not to share with the world. It's much too precious to keep to yourself. I'm sure the time will come when you will be called upon to tell your whole story, and when it does come promise me one thing. Look at me and promise."

"What?" I asked, looking into David's eyes.

"That you will tell it unveiled," he said.

"Why?" I asked.

"Because the declaration's better than the secret, that's why. Too much has been kept hidden from the world for far too long. The floodgates of heaven have been opened, and a wave of spiritual truth has begun to wash over the world like no other time in the history of this planet, and your story will be one of these truths."

"I'm falling madly in love with you, David Oakly."

"Fall, fair maiden," David said, and held my head in his strong hands and gently pressed his mouth to mine and kissed new love into my aching heart.

My Unborn Child

Chapter 26

The Guilt of Agnes Mactavish

The call to tell my story came sooner than I expected. Just before Christmas. It came by way of Agnes Mactavish, a ninety-two year old geriatric patient who had lived through the dirty thirties in the dust bowl province of Saskatchewan.

Agnes had four children, but the depression was so hard on her family that they could not afford to bring another child into the world, so she had an abortion the next two times she got pregnant. This was her dark secret.

"I'm going to meet my Maker," she said quietly, with a tragic look in her tired, teary eyes. "I'm going to meet my Maker..."

I pulled up a chair and sat beside her bed and held her hand. I felt the end was near, and I wanted to comfort her as much as I possibly could. My mentor came to mind, as she always did at such moments. I admonished myself: *"Listen to her every word."*

I liked Agnes. I learned to like all of my patients, but something about Agnes Mactavish reminded me of my mother, and I felt sorry for her. She had suffered to raise her children during the depression, but not one of her four children or grandchildren had come to visit her. It was sad. I didn't know what the back-story was, but it had to do with the children's father. They blamed her for how he mistreated them.

Her abusive husband was long dead, and her children were scattered all over the country, but distance and family troubles were no excuse to keep her three sons and daughter from their dying mother.

There were no excuses at all.

"God is punishing me," Agnes confessed, her feeble voice cracking. "He's keeping my children from me because I refused to accept two of his children into my family. Oh God, please forgive me; please forgive me..."

"Agnes, your children will come," I said, trying to comfort her.

"It's too late," she sighed, the tears forming in her tired old eyes. "I didn't watch out for them. I couldn't stop him. It's too late now. God is punishing me..."

"No, it's not too late. They'll come, Agnes."

"It's too late. Oh God, I'm sorry. I'm so sorry..."

"Agnes, don't cry. Your children will come to see you."

"God is punishing me. God is punishing me for my sins. He made me take the life of my two unborn children. Oh my God, please forgive me..."

"No," I said, squeezing her hand firmly. "God is merciful, Agnes. God is not punishing you. God does not punish us. God loves you, Agnes. Try to get some rest, please."

Agnes turned her head slowly to look at me. She stared at me for the longest time. She had a vacant look in her eyes. She was back on the farm. She did not recognize me.

"We could have managed," she said, in a far-away voice. "We could have managed. May God have mercy on my Soul," she said with tears streaming down her face.

Agnes drifted off, in and out of consciousness for a few minutes, and then she said in a remorseful, plaintive voice, "We had too many mouths to feed. We could not bring any more children into this world. May God have mercy on my Soul..."

"Agnes, God is not judging you," I said, stroking her hand. "You did the right thing. You had to take care of your family. Please don't punish yourself. You did what you had to do. God loves you, Agnes. God has forgiven you."

"We could have managed," Agnes said, with a new flood of tears.

"Please don't blame yourself, Agnes," I pleaded, gently gripping her hand. "God has forgiven you. Please don't punish yourself..."

"May God have mercy on my Soul," Agnes gasped, and her head

fell gently onto its side and her spirit left her body with the stamp of guilt on her wrinkled face.

"Oh my sweet God, no. Not like this. Not like this..."

I sat holding her hand in both of mine. Then the tears came. For the longest time I sobbed quietly, crying for her children and grandchildren. Then I thought of my mother, and my father, and suicide, and life after death, and God and sin and punishment, my children, St. Paul's Hospital, Kevin, his wife and new baby girl, my abortion and attempted suicide, my unborn daughter Seana, my uncle Clancy, homosexuality, forgiveness, salvation, Jesus, reincarnation, David, starting over, poor lonely Agnes, fear, Ethel Copeland, Father McDuffy and the anti-abortionists, shame, spiritual ignorance, my mentor and role model, courage, AIDS, dying with dignity, Elba, Stumpy's secret, blind, stupid selfishness, sin, repentance, anger, confession, guilt, more shame, remorse, lies, lies, and more lies, the undeclared truth, and I broke down and sobbed with Agnes's frail, dead hand in mine.

"Satma," I pleaded, through fresh tears, "I commend this Soul to you. Please, let this dear Soul find peace. She did not deserve to die this way. I love you, Satma. I love this dear Soul. She did not have to die with so much guilt. Please, Huzee; give me the courage to tell my story. I don't want to see another woman die with this guilt on her conscience. It's not fair. I have to tell my story for every Agnes in the world. I have to, Satma. I have to..."

Doctor Jordon walked into the room.

I could not let go of Agnes's hand. I wept like a child. Doctor Jordon very gently but firmly unclasped my hand, and then put his hand on my shoulder.

"I'm sorry, Cassie. It was her time."

"I know," I sniffled.

"Are you okay?"

"I'm fine. I'm just feeling sad. I'll be okay."

Doctor Jordon looked at his watch and made a note of the time of death. "Come with me, Cassie," he said. "Let's let the girls take care of her."

"Oh God," I sighed, and put my arms around Doctor Jordon and hugged him close to me. "I'm so terribly frightened, Hillory."

"There, there," he said, patting me gently on the back like the frightened little child that I was. "Come, dear, let's go to my office."

Doctor Jordon walked me to his office in the old part of the hospital and then he sat me down in the chair in front of his desk. He went behind his desk and sat down and looked at me. I had never been to his office, and my eyes were immediately drawn to the spectacular copper artwork on the wall directly behind Doctor Jordon. It had to be three feet square. "Why are you taking this so hard, Cassie?" he asked me.

I took my eyes off the imposing copper art. "Agnes told me something before she died," I said, and sniffled. "I apologize for my behavior, Hillory. It's so unprofessional."

"Apologize? What in heaven's name for? For being human? For having a heart? This is what life is all about. You have nothing to apologize for, Cassie. Are you up to talking about this? I can be a good listener."

"I know," I said, and sniffled again.

"Are you afraid of dying, Cassie?"

"No, I'm not," I said, glancing up at the copper etching just above his partially bald head where he had to have skin grafted after his caustic acid attack.

The copper art piece was of a spectacular peacock, with its proud chest puffed up and all of its exquisitely detailed feathers fanned out into a rainbow of magnificent splendor. It was the same kind of copper art that Binny had on his diner walls, but eminently more beautiful in its baked colored patterns. And scribed on the bottom were the words, again in florid lettering, *"My Name is Iblis."* I had no idea what that meant, and I made a mental note to ask David.

"What is it, then?" Doctor Jordon asked. "Was Agnes special to you?"

"Yes, very," I said, taking my eyes off the peacock and fixing my gaze on Doctor Jordon's warm, loving eyes. "Agnes crossed over with so much guilt on her conscience, Hillory. That's what made me cry. It wasn't fair. She didn't have to die with that guilt."

"Oh? Would you like to talk about it?"

I glanced up at the peacock and fixed my gaze for a long moment or two, and then I gave Doctor Jordon a warm, loving smile. "Agnes Mactavish died with the crushing guilt of two abortions that she had over fifty years ago when she lived on a farm in Saskatchewan," I said, and sniffled. "That's why I feel so sad, Hillory. It was not necessary. She did not have to carry that guilt her whole life. She did not..."

"So that's it. This is very close to your heart, isn't it?"

"Yes. It wasn't necessary, Hillory. It wasn't. I felt so helpless."

"You've gone public with your own abortion, Cassie. What more can you do to help women overcome their guilt for having an abortion?"

"I can write a book, Hillory; that's what I can do. I can reach a lot of women with my story, but the thought terrifies me."

"Why? You've tested the waters already. I think you should tell your story, Cassie. That's a great idea. You should do it for your own peace of mind."

"I should, shouldn't I? If it would spare one woman from dying with the kind of guilt that Agnes died with, it would be worth it, wouldn't it?"

"Just do it," Hillory said. "Make your story your legacy to the world. You've lived it, Cassie. It's your truth. Don't deny yourself. You can do it."

"It's not right for a woman to die with this kind of guilt, Hillory. It's just not right," I said, and broke into fresh tears.

"Guilt is a fiendish monster, Cassie," Doctor Jordon said, with a look in his eyes that went from loving kindness to fierce defiance. "It took the better part of ten years before I could admit to myself that I had made a mistake that took the life of a young girl. I was a proud young peacock then. I was all head and no heart. I could not admit my mistake. But I'm reminded every time I look in the mirror now. I know guilt intimately, Cassie, and I don't think women should feel guilty for having an abortion. Guilt doesn't have to be a curse for the rest of a person's life. Tell your story. Let the whole world know about your abortion. It's an incredible story, and it's worth sharing with every woman who has had an abortion. Tell it, Cassie. You have my heartfelt blessing."

I looked at Doctor Jordon, at the scarred right side of his face and shiny temple, and I glanced up at the peacock above his head. I thought of the scar on Agnes's Soul and felt her agonizing guilt. I lowered my gaze back to Doctor Jordon's disfigured face, and his eyes pulled me deep into his Soul and I felt such incredible love that all my grief just lifted.

"You're a kind man, Doctor Hillory Jordon," I said, with a lump in my throat. "A very kind, considerate, honorable man. I'm fine now. I really am. I want to thank you for listening to me. I really needed this, but I have to get back to work now."

"My door's open anytime, Cassie. Anytime," Doctor Jordon said, standing up.

"I know," I said, and gave Doctor Jordon a warm hug.

His face glowed with love. "You'll be fine, dear. Write your story. The world's waiting for it. Who knows, Cassie; your story could be the hundredth monkey."

I knew the concept, but I didn't understand. "Hundredth monkey?"

"It has to happen. One day there will be a shift in the center of man's spiritual gravity from unconscious karmic evolution to conscious spiritual growth. If your story ever catches fire, it could help to bring about the tipping point. It could be the hundredth monkey."

With that, Doctor Jordon gave me the sweetest smile.

"Wouldn't that be something?" I said, returning the smile. "Thank you, Hillory. I'm fine now. I really am," I said, and walked back to my workstation in deep thought.

After work I went straight to the curling club. I was skipping our hospital women's team. When I got home, I was emotionally exhausted. I went into the kitchen. The dishes were all done. I went upstairs to check on the children. They were still doing their homework. I went back down to the kitchen, made a cup of hot chocolate and slumped down on the sofa, putting my feet on the ottoman and turning on the TV. By chance, I landed on a re-run of an old LA Law episode.

I sipped my hot chocolate, savoring every drop, but the more I got into the show the more excited I became by the story.

A pregnant mother was dying of leukemia. She refused chemotherapy because she did not want to endanger the life of her child. Because her life span was so limited, her doctor wanted her to have a cesarean to give her child a better chance of survival, but she insisted on a vaginal delivery. Her husband supported her decision. Her doctor felt that the life of the child was threatened, so he sought a court order to protect the rights of the fetus. I was sitting up now, my eyes glued to the TV. I knew the story was fiction, but my heart began to race.

The mother was so weak she could die on the operating table. The doctor reasoned that because she was going to die anyway, he had a moral duty to protect the life of the fetus. He hired a female lawyer and they won the court case. The fetus was made a ward of the court, and the woman was ordered to have a c-section to save the life of her unborn child. The woman died, the child lived. *"You bastard!"* I shouted. *"We can't win, can we? You always have to have your way with us!"*

I thought of Agnes suffering her whole life for something that her husband made her do, and this arrogant doctor was no different. He made my blood boil, and my whole body trembled with rage. I never felt so much anger for a man in my entire life as I did for that doctor who took away the dying woman's rights to her own body, and I knew in that instant that I had to write the story of my unborn child. I had to speak up for every helpless woman in the world.

"Boys!" I shouted. *"Come down here! You too, Cindy!"*

The children dropped their homework and came downstairs. Mark poked his head into the family room. "Mom's got her Irish up," he said to his brother and sister.

Cindy stood back, waiting for the boys to clear the way. "What, Mom?" Mark asked. "We didn't do anything."

"Come over here, boys. You too, Puppy Face. I have something very important to share with you. I need your approval. Come in here, please; it's family time..."

The children gathered around me. "What, Mom?" Cindy asked.

"I'm going to write a book. I'm going to tell the whole story about your aborted sister Seana. You know I love you, and I won't do this if you don't want me to, but it's very, very important to me..."

"Did somebody die today, Mom?" Mark asked.

"Yes. A nice old lady died this morning. I have to do it for her and all the women in the world like her. But more important, I have to do it for me. I have to tell the story of your unborn sister Seana. It's crazy, I know; but if I don't tell my story women will always feel guilty for having an abortion, just like poor old Agnes Mactavish who passed away this morning. That's not right, and it's not fair. Soul is Soul, and we're all equals. Seana came into our family for a reason. She came to tell the truth about Soul. We are Soul, and our body is just a body for Soul; and it's time for this truth to be made public knowledge. I know this could be hard on you because this truth will cause a lot of resistance, but I have to tell my story. I have to let women know that a fetus is not a person until it is born into life. I don't have a choice anymore; I've been called. What do you say, guys? Do you think you can take the heat?"

"We're the O'Shaunnesys, aren't we?" Patrick exclaimed, puffing his chest.

"Yeah, we're the O'Shaunnesys, Mom!" Mark repeated.

"Go for it, Mom!" Cindy added, all excited.

"Don't worry about it, Mom," Mark said, standing like a proud little soldier beside his husky big brother. "You've got the Light, Mom. No one can harm an Atma Warrior!"

"Go ahead Mom, write your book. We've got your back," Patrick said, with that Irish look in his eyes that spoke for generations of people struggling for independence.

My eyes filled with tears. "Come here," I said, and held them all in my arms. "I love you all so much! *Thank you thank you thank you!"*

"When are you going to start your book, Mom?" Cindy asked, as she wiped tears from my cheek with her soft little hand.

"The sooner the better," I said, sniffling.

"Go for it, Mom!" Mark said, giving me a high five.

"Yeah! Go for it, Mom!" Cindy exclaimed, following suit.

"Just do it, Mom," Patrick said. "Seana would like that. I saw her, Mom. I remember. She comes to me in my dreams, you know. Go ahead, Mom. Tell your story for Seana. Who cares if nobody believes it? We know its true."

I could not believe what I had just heard. I pulled Patrick into my arms and looked into his deep, clear, blue eyes. "You're an old Soul, son. A very wise old Soul. Come here, you two," I said, and as I held my children in my arms I knew that I was protected by their love.

I thanked my children, put on a pot of tea, and went straight to my computer.

I stared at the blank monitor for a few minutes, when I got a strong nudge to do a spiritual contemplation. I sat back, closed my eyes, and began quietly singing the magical Love Song to God. As I sang HU, I felt my whole world stirring up inside me like an emotional smoothie, and I said, "Satma, please help me get my story started…"

My room was silent except for the soft humming sound of my computer. The word "gratitude" popped into my mind. I reflected for the next few minutes on all the wonderful gifts of my life, and then I began my gratitude contemplation…

"Thank you, Satma, for letting me be with Agnes when she crossed over this morning. Thank you for Doctor Jordon's understanding. Thank you for the program on television tonight. Thank you for my beautiful children. Thank you for my exciting new life here in Georgian Bay. Thank you for bringing David into my life. I do so love that man, Satma. He doesn't know it yet, but he's going to be— well, may the blessings be."

I opened my eyes. My fingers began typing: *My name is Cassie Patty O'Shaunnesy. I am a registered nurse, and have been for over twenty years. I am a single mother of three wonderful children. Six years ago, I had an abortion, but I am not guilty of murder…*

My Unborn Child

About the Author

Orest Stocco, author of the provocative novel, "What Would I Say Today If I Were To Die Tomorrow?" was born in Panettieri, Calabria, Italy. He immigrated to Canada and studied philosophy at university. He Lived in Annecy, France before taking up residence in Georgian Bay, Ontario, Canada, where he continues to write novels, short stories and poetry. Visit him at http://www.oreststocco.com

My Unborn Child

If you enjoyed *My Unborn Child* consider
these other fine Books from
Savant Books and Publications:

A Whale's Tale by Daniel S. Janik
Tropic of California by R. Page Kaufman
The Village Curtain by Tony Tame
Dare to Love in Oz by William Maltese
The Bahrain Conspiracy by Bentley Gates
Called Home by Gloria Schumann
Poor Rich by Jean Blasiar
First Breath - 2010 Savant Anthology of Poems, Z. Oliver (editor)
The Jumper Chronicles: The Quest for Merlin's Map by W. C. Peever
William Maltese's Flicker by William Maltese

Scheduled for Release in 2010:
Mythical Voyage by Robin Ymer
Ammon's Horn by Guerrino Amati
Perilous Panacea by Ronald Klueh
Last Song of the Whales by Four Arrows (D. T. Jacobs)

If you are an author or prospective author who would like to be
published contact Savant Books and Publications at

http://www.savantbooksandpublications.com